Elizabeth Moon joined the US Marine Corps in 1968, reaching the rank of 1st Lieutenant during active duty. She has also earned degrees in history and biology, run for public office and been a columnist on her local newspaper. She lives near Austin, Texas, with her husband and their son.

To find out more about Elizabeth and our other Orbit authors, register for the free monthly newsletter at www.orbitbooks.net

REMNANT POPULATION

ELIZABETH MOON

www.orbitbooks.net

ORBIT

First published in Great Britain by Orbit 2002
Reprinted 2007, 2009 (twice), 2012

A CIP catalogue record for this book
is available from the British Library.

ISBN 978-1-84149-136-3

Printed and bound by CPI Group (UK) Ltd, Croydon, CR0 4YY

Papers used by Orbit are from well-managed forests
and other responsible sources.

MIX
Paper from
responsible sources
FSC   FSC® C104740
www.fsc.org

Orbit
An imprint of
Little, Brown Book Group
100 Victoria Embankment
London EC4Y 0DY

An Hachette UK Company
www.hachette.co.uk

www.orbitbooks.net

Dedication

To Betsy, who provided the spark,
And Mary, Ellen, and Carrie
who responded with warmth and light.

Acknowledgements

This book had a number of godmothers, both old and new. Its literary antecedents include an essay by LeGuin, *The Wall*, by Marlen Haushofer, and a book I had not yet read (but heard about) when I began it, *Two Old Women*, by Velma Wallis, and those folktales in which wise old women know something worth learning. But it could not have been written without the living experience of women much like Ofelia, from whom I learned much less than I should have. They are too many to name, but they should not be forgotten. Lois Parker helped in revision, especially her willingness to share her own experience of a long life.

ONE

Between her toes the damp earth felt cool, but already
sweat crept between the roots of her hair. It would be
hotter today than yesterday, and by noon the lovely spice-
scented red flowers of the dayvine would have furled their
fragile cups, and drooped on the vine. Ofelia pushed the
mulch deeper against the stems of the tomatoes with her
foot. She liked the heat. If her daughter-in-law Rosara
weren't within sight, she would take off her hat and let
the sweat evaporate. But Rosara worried about cancer from
the sun, and Rosara was sure it wasn't decent for an old
woman to be outside with nothing on her head but thin-
ning gray hair.

Not that it was so thin. Ofelia touched her temples, as
if to tuck an errant strand in place, but really to confirm
the thick strands of the braid she wore. Still thick, and
her legs still strong, and her hands, though knotted with
age and work, still capable. She eyed her daughter-in-law,
at the far end of the garden. Scrawny, hair the color of
scorched paper, eyes of mud. Thought she was beautiful,
with her narrow waist and her pale hands, but Ofelia knew

better. She had always known better, but Barto would not listen to a mother's wisdom, and now he had Rosara of the narrow body – like a snake, Ofelia had said once only – and no children.

She minded that less than the others thought. She could have welcomed a daughter-in-law independent enough to refuse children. No, it was Rosara's determination to enforce on her mother-in-law all the petty rules intended to preserve the virtue of virgins . . . *that* she could not tolerate.

'We should have planted more beans,' Rosara called. She had said that at planting, knowing that Ofelia could not use all the beans she normally grew. She wanted Ofelia to grow beans to sell, as well as beans to eat.

'We have enough,' Ofelia said.

'If the crop does not fail,' Rosara said.

'If the crop fails, a bigger crop would be a bigger failure,' Ofelia said. Rosara snorted, but did not contradict. Perhaps she was finally learning that it did no good to argue. Ofelia hoped so. Ofelia went on working on the tomatoes, pushing the mulch here and there, tying up straggling ends of the vines. Rosara claimed the tomato vines made her skin itch; she stayed away from them. Ofelia hunkered down to hide a smile as she thought of this, enjoying the strong green tomato smell.

She dozed off, there among the tomatoes, rousing only when the slanting afternoon light probed between the rows. Light in her eyes had always waked her; she was still sure she had not slept at all in the cryo tanks because the lights stayed on all the time. Humberto had said that was ridiculous, that no one was awake in cryo, that was the point. Ofelia had not argued, but she was sure she remembered the light, always stabbing through her eyelids.

Now, lying drowsy on the crumbly mulch between the rows of tomatoes, she thought how peaceful it looked, that little green jungle. Silent, too, for once; Rosara must have gone back inside without noticing she was asleep. Or perhaps the bitch didn't care. Ofelia rolled the insult on her tongue, silently, savoring it. Bitch. Slut. She didn't know many such words, which gave the few in her vocabulary extra richness, all the anger that some people spread over many words on many occasions.

Bartolomeo's voice in the street cut across her reverie, and she sat up as fast as she could, hissing at the pain in her hip and knees.

'Rosara! Rosara, come out!' He sounded excited or angry or both. He often did. Most of the time it was nothing, but he would never admit it, even afterwards. Of all her children, Barto was the one Ofelia had liked least, even in infancy; he had been a greedy nurser, yanking on her nipples as if she could never be enough for him. He had grown from greedy infancy to demanding childhood, the son whom nothing satisfied; he had quarreled incessantly with the other children, demanding fairness which always meant his benefit. In manhood he was the same, the traits she had liked least in Humberto magnified ten times. But he was her only living child, and she understood him.

'What?' Rosara sounded snappish; either she had been napping (something Barto and Ofelia both disapproved of) or working on her computer.

'It's the Company – they've lost the franchise.'

A shriek from Rosara. It might mean that for once Barto was upset about something worth the trouble, or it might mean that she had just found a pimple on her chin. With Rosara, it might be either, or anything in between. Ofelia struggled to her knees, then, with a hand on a tomato stake, to her feet. Her vision grayed slightly and she waited for it to come back. Age. Everyone said it was age, and it would get worse. She didn't think it was that bad, except when people wanted her to hurry, and she couldn't. 'Mama!' Barto, bursting out the kitchen door into the garden. Ofelia was glad to be upright and obviously working; it gave her a tiny bit of moral leverage.

'Yes?' She had spotted a fat caterpillar, and when he loomed over her she had it fast in the loop. 'See?'

'Yes, mama. That's nice. Listen, it's important—'

'A good crop this year,' Ofelia said.

'Mama!' He leaned over, pushing his face into hers. He looked more like Humberto than anyone else, yet Humberto had had gentle eyes.

'I'm listening,' she said, putting out her hand to the tomato stake again.

'The Company's lost the franchise,' he said, as if that meant something.

'The Company's lost the franchise,' Ofelia repeated, to prove she'd been listening. He often accused her of not listening.

'You know what that means,' he said impatiently, but then went on to tell her. 'It means we have to leave. They're yanking the colony.' Rosara had come out of the house behind him; Ofelia could see the patches of red on her cheeks.

'They can't do that! It's our home—!'

'Don't be stupid, Rosara!' Barto spat onto the tomato plants, as if they were her body; Ofelia flinched, and he glared at her. 'Or you, mama. Of course they can make us leave; we're their employees.'

Employees who never got paid, Ofelia said to herself. Employees with no retirement, no medical benefits except what they produced for each other. Employees who were supposed to support themselves and produce a surplus. Not that they had produced the regular shipments of tropical woods that they'd been assigned . . . it had been years since they'd had enough adults to continue logging.

'But I worked so hard!' Rosara wailed. For once Ofelia agreed with her; she felt the same way. She looked sideways at the tomato plants, avoiding Barto's glare, focussing on the fringed margin of the leaves, the tiny hairs bristling from the stems. The first flower buds hung like little chandeliers, still folded tight, ready to open in the light, take fire, and—

'Listen to me,' Barto insisted. His hand came between Ofelia and the tomatoes, caught her chin and forced her face around. 'You still have a vote in the council, mama. You have to come to the meeting. You have to vote with us. We have a chance to choose where we're sent.'

A meeting. She hated meetings. She noticed he didn't tell Rosara, but then he knew Rosara would come anyway, and vote however he told her.

'A vote is a vote,' he told her now, louder, as if she were deaf. 'Even yours.' He released her chin. 'Go inside now; get ready.' Ofelia edged past him, her bare toes safely distant from his hard-soled boots. 'And wear shoes!' he yelled after her. Behind her, his voice and Rosara's were lower without being softer, harsh mutterings she could not quite hear.

She had bathed, washed her hair, and put on the best clothes she had left. The dress hung loosely now, the waist dipping where she had nothing left above to fill the bodice, the hem lifting behind to accommodate the stoop in her back. On her feet, the shoes she had not worn for months cramped her toes and rubbed her heels. She would have blisters from this meeting, and what good would that do? She had leaned her head on the kitchen door and heard Barto tell Rosara that on another world his mother would surely be forced to dress decently again. He meant wear shoes, and a dark dress like this, all the time.

She sat quietly on the bench beside Rosara, and listened to the sounds of grief and anger that filled the room. Only a few saw this as opportunity – a few men, a few women, about half the younglings. The rest saw only wasted years, loss, misery. They had worked so hard, and for what? How could they start over, face the same hard work again? Here at least they had houses already built, gardens already planted.

Carl and Gervaise interrupted the complaints and presented the alternatives to vote on, though they never said how they'd learned about them. Ofelia did not believe the Company would give them a choice; she was sure the vote would come to nothing. Still, when Barto reached across Rosara to prod her ribs and hiss at her, she stood when he did, voting for Neubreit rather than Olcrano. The others voted for Neubreit, almost two thirds of them, and only the most stubborn, like Walter and Sara, insisted they would not go there.

Only at the end of the meeting, when she stood up and turned around, did she notice the Company rep, standing at the door. He had the sleek, youthful look of a shipman, someone whose skin never saw starlight but through a hatch. No sun had baked him; no winter had frozen him; no rains had washed, or winds dried, him. In his crisp, clean clothes, his polished shoes, he looked like an alien. He said nothing. Before anyone could speak to him, he had turned and walked away, into the darkness.

Ofelia wondered if he knew about the slimetrails, but of course he would have shipeyes; he would be able to see where colonists could not.

The next morning, Ofelia rose at dawn and went out into the garden, barefooted as always and wearing her oldest workshirt. Until the sun rose, she refused to wear her hat, and so she saw the movement along the lane beyond the garden, the Company reps in their crisp shipclothes. Many of them. All wearing the same blue-gray uniforms the color of morning fog, with the Sims Bancorp logo.

One of them stopped to stare back at her. 'Ma'am,' he said, unsmiling but polite.

The thing she loved most about dawn was the silence, the emptiness of it. He stood there, as if he had a right to ruin her morning solitude. He was going to ask questions, and in courtesy she must answer them. She sighed, and looked away, hoping he would think her too old and fuddled to be worth his time.

'Ma'am, did you vote last night?'

He wasn't going away. She looked at him, seeing the youth, the differentness . . . the skin untouched by weather, the eyes that stared right at her as if he had the right . . .

'Yes,' she said shortly. Then, because courtesy would not allow her to be so abrupt, she found herself saying, 'I don't know what to call you . . . I don't mean to be rude.'

He smiled, genuinely amused. Was courtesy so rare among the shipfolk still? 'I wasn't offended,' he said. He came nearer. 'Are those *real* tomatoes?'

He had not answered her question. She would have to be more direct. 'I cannot talk to someone when I have no way to address them,' she said. 'My name is Sera Ofelia.'

'Oh – I'm Jorge. Sorry. You reminded me of my grand-mother; she calls me Ajo. But – do they really grow like this, in the open . . . contaminated?'

Ofelia stroked the leaves with her hand, releasing the heavy scent. 'Yes, these are tomatoes, and yes, they grow in the open air. They have no tomatoes now, of course; they are just blooming.' She turned up several leaves to show him the clusters of flower-buds.

'It's too bad,' he said, in the tone of one who is politely regretting some inconvenience he will not himself endure. 'You have such a garden, and it's wasted—'

'Nothing is wasted,' Ofelia said.

'But you're leaving in thirty days,' the young man said. She reminded herself that his name was Jorge and he had a grandmother who loved him. That seemed impossible; he could have popped from a gliss-wrapped package like the holiday gifts of her childhood, brightly colored and smooth all over. Surely he had not been born in blood and mess like real children. 'You don't have to work in the garden any more. You should be packing.'

'I like working in the garden,' Ofelia said. She wanted him to go away. She wanted to find out what had just changed in her, somewhere inside, when he said 'But you're leaving.' She looked down. On the ground, on top of the mulch, a slimerod oozed along looking for some-thing to puncture with its one hard part, its little hollow cylinder of shell. Ofelia picked it up by its soft hinder end and watched it lengthen until it was at least ten centimeters long and thin as yarn. Then she flicked it around with a practiced snap of the wrist, and cracked its shell on her other thumb. It made her thumb sting a moment, but it was worth the sting for the look of shocked horror on the young man's face.

'What was *that*?' he asked. From his expression, he expected to hear something terrible. Ofelia obliged. 'We call it a slimerod,' she said. 'And the piercing part is like a medical needle, hollow, so it can suck—' She didn't have to say more; the young man was backing away already.

'Can it go through . . . shoes?' He was staring now at her bare feet. Ofelia grinned to herself, and made a show of scratching the back of one leg with her other foot.

'It depends on the shoes,' she said. She supposed it might go through a pair of thin cloth shoes with holes in them already. And it didn't go through human skin (she didn't know why) but she didn't say that. Mostly it went through the stems of her plants, not finding what it wanted and leaving wounds the plants spent precious calories mending. But if it made the young man sick enough to go away, she would imply horrors.

'I guess you'll be glad to leave,' the young man said.

'Excuse me,' Ofelia said. 'I have to use the . . .' she gestured at the shed at the end of the garden. That did it; he flushed an uncomely color and turned away abruptly. She almost giggled. He should have known they had inside conveniences; the first thing the colonists had done was install their waste recycler. But she was glad to see him go. In case he turned back, she walked the rest of the way to the toolshed and went in.

Ofelia had moved before. She knew that it took longer than thirty days to move, if you tried to take things with you. The Company reps had told people they need take nothing; it would all be provided. But forty years is forty years, a lifetime for some, more than that for others. Few of the originals were left; Ofelia was the oldest of these.

She had the clearest memory of other places, and she sometimes woke with vivid flashes of that memory. The smell of corn porridge spiced with *mezul* . . . a spice that could not be grown here. She remembered the day she had used the last of it, after Humberto died. The way the street looked outside their apartment in Visiazh, with the vendors' bright awnings over piles of ripe fruits and vegetables, mounds of colorful clothes, racks of pots and pans. She had thought once she could not live without that much color, that much noise and that many people; she had moped a whole year here, miserable until she found the one kind of bright flower that would grow along the edge of the garden.

She had little to pack. She had not drawn many clothes from the community store in the past decade. Her old keepsakes had vanished over the years, one after another – most left behind when they became colonists, the rest broken by children, gnawed by insects, dissolved in one or the other of the two big floods or rotted afterwards by fungus. She still had a chipic of Humberto and herself at their wedding, and one of the first two children, and a ribbon she had won in primary school for spelling, now faded a pale pearly gray. That and the fruit dish her mother-in-law had given her, an ugly thing which had survived her intentional carelessness when more beautiful things perished. She could easily be ready in less than thirty days. Except – she leaned her head against the handle of the hoe hanging on the toolshed wall. Somewhere inside, at the moment the young man had said she was leaving, things changed. She felt for that change, as she would have fumbled in the shadowy house for her crochet hook in its bag of yarn.

She wasn't going. Ofelia blinked, suddenly wider awake

than she remembered being for a long time. A memory welled up, clear as morning dew that reflected tiny curved pictures of the world around it. Before she married Humberto, before she got involved with that fool Caitano, back when she had just finished primary, she had flourished that spelling ribbon in her father's face and insisted she was not – absolutely was *not* – going to quit school and go to work in the local branch of Sims Bancorp cleaning the floors at night.

Her mind recoiled from the memory of what had followed that defiance; the facts were enough without the emotion. In the misery of being only a janitor – she, who had won a scholarship to secondary, a scholarship Lucia had taken instead – she had fooled herself into a relationship with Caitano.

But – she retreated from all that to the cool dawn shadow of the toolshed. But she was here, and she was not going. She felt light, suddenly, as if she were falling, as if the ground had disappeared from under her feet and she would fall until she found the middle of the planet. Was this joy, or fear? She could not tell. She knew only that with every heartbeat her blood carried the same message to bone and muscle: she was not going.

'Mama!' Barto, at the kitchen door. Ofelia grabbed the first tool her hand fell on, and she backed out of the toolshed. Pruning shears. Why pruning shears? Nothing needed pruning. She turned around, and found the words to say.

'I can't find the little nippers, the ones for the tomatoes.'

'Mama, forget the tomatoes. We won't be here to harvest them. Listen – we're having another meeting. The Company says it doesn't care about the vote.'

Of course the Company didn't care. That's what it

meant to be on contract. She understood that, if she understood nothing else, what it meant to be signed, sealed, delivered to the masters. They would not listen to the colonists any more than Humberto had listened to her. She did not say this to Barto. It would only provoke another argument, and she disliked arguments, especially in her special time, the early morning.

'Barto, I am too old for these meetings,' she said.

'I know that.' He sounded impatient, as always. 'Rosara and I are going; we want you to begin the inventory.'

'Yes, Barto.' Easier that way. He and Rosara would go, and she could come back out and smell the garden in the morning, its best time. 'And we need breakfast,' he said. Ofelia sighed, and hung the pruning shears back on their hook. Already the sun was burning away the morning mist, and she could feel heat on her head. Already she could hear voices from other houses, other gardens. Rosara could cook breakfast; she usually did. She didn't like the way Ofelia cooked.

Inside, Ofelia mixed flour and oil and water to make the dough, patted it out, and flipped the thin rounds on the griddle. While they browned, she chopped onions and herbs, leftover sausage, cold boiled potatoes. When the flatcakes were done, she rolled them deftly around the cold filling, adding a dash of vinegar and oil. Barto liked these; Rosara wanted a hot filling. Ofelia didn't care. This morning she could have eaten metal shavings, or nothing. She paid no attention to Rosara's ritual complaint, or Barto's ritual compliment. As they finished dressing, she scraped the cutting board into the garden pail.

After they left, Ofelia carried the garden pail out and dumped it into the trench, kicking dirt over the curls of potato peels, the limp ends of carrots and turnip greens, the bits of onion and herbs. The sun laid a warm hand on the back of her neck, and she realized she'd come out without her hat again.

That would be one benefit of staying behind. No one would nag her to wear a hat.

TWO

TWO

Barto and Rosara returned from the meeting in exactly the mood Ofelia expected: angry and depressed and ready to take it out on her. Luckily, the meeting had taken longer than she'd thought – they must have argued strongly – so she had the inventory well under way.

'We don't need those things,' Barto said, of the first category. 'I told you – all these things made here – they're worthless.' He went into their bedroom, and from the sounds he made was throwing all the clothes on the floor.

'They say we have no right to choose where we go,' Rosara said. She moved around the kitchen restlessly, picking up and putting down one utensil after another. 'They say we have to be ready to leave in twenty-nine days, and all we can take is twenty kilos per person. We'll have to go in cryo, and we won't know where we're going until we arrive—'

'Barbarians!' Barto stood in the doorway, arms full of clothes. All, Ofelia noticed, were his clothes. 'Everything we've done – all these years—' Ofelia did not remind him that he had been a baby at first; most of the time he had enjoyed the work of others.

'What will they do with the colony itself?' she asked.

'What do I care? Destroy it, leave it to rot, it doesn't matter.' He retreated to the bedroom again; Ofelia heard the clothes hit the bed in a soft *whumph*. 'Mama! Where's the luggage?'

Ofelia bit back a laugh and tried to answer calmly. 'There's no luggage, Barto.' Why would he think they had luggage? They had never needed it.

'You and papa had to carry things here in something.'

'The Company gave us a box.' The box had gone into the structure of the recycler; everyone's boxes had. Everything that came down had been put to use.

'They won't give us anything, they said. They said we have to pack it ourselves, in something that will stack in the hold.' He glared at her as if that were her fault, as if she were supposed to solve this problem.

'We can sew something,' she said. 'There's all that cloth in the supply room. If we're not going to need it for clothes for everyone, we can make something to hold the allotments.' She wasn't going, she reminded herself, but it was an interesting problem. She had always liked solving problems. Already her mind ran over what she could remember about luggage seen all those years ago, before they emigrated. Other peoples' luggage – she and Humberto had never traveled – some of it made of fabric shaped into boxes or tubes, some of it molded from plastics. In thirty days, it would be easier to sew it. She thought of the others who used the machines, the ones who were quickest, the ones who could make patterns.

'You take care of it,' Barto said. 'And while you're at it, mend all these things—' He gestured broadly at the piles of clothes on the bed and floor.

It would be easier to take the clothes and go to the center's sewing rooms than argue that most of the clothes needed no mending. Or that they might not be appropriate to wherever they were being sent. Ofelia picked up an armload, and turned to leave.

'Wait! What about these others?'

'I can't carry more than this, Barto,' Ofelia said. She didn't meet his eyes. After a moment, he let his breath out in a huff, and she knew the worst of it was over. She carried the clothes to the center, where she found a small group of women chattering in the hall outside the sewing rooms. They fell silent when they saw her. Ariane finally spoke.

'Sera Ofelia . . . may I help you with that?'

Ofelia had always liked Ariane, who had been a friend of Adelia's. The two little girls – for a moment memory overcame her, a vision of the two leaning head-to-head whispering, under the first orange tree. When Adelia died, Ariane had come every day to sit with her; she had asked Ofelia to be the name-mother for her own first baby. Now Ofelia smiled at the younger woman.

'It's only Barto wanting to be sure all his clothes are mended – and I don't expect to find much to do.' Should she tell Ariane about her idea, to sew luggage from the fabric in stores? Surely someone else would think of it.

'We haven't any boxes, Sera Ofelia,' said Linda. Trust Linda to blurt out a problem. 'I know our parents came with boxes from the Company, but something happened to them – and now they won't give us boxes.'

'The boxes went into the walls of the recycler,' Ofelia said. The children had been taught that in school, at least when she was helping there. Linda should have known.

'But what will we do, Sera Ofelia?' Several of the other women looked as annoyed as Ofelia felt. They knew Ofelia wasn't the right person to ask; they didn't expect her to have any answers.

Mischief bubbled; impossible answers raced through her mind like noisy children, making her mind trip and struggle to regain its balance. It is not my problem, she imagined herself saying. I am not going. 'It is simple enough,' she heard herself say aloud. 'We will sew containers – luggage – from the fabric that will not be needed to make new clothes this year.'

'You know how to do this?' Linda asked. Her expression showed indecent surprise. Ofelia smiled at the other women, one face after another, forcing their attention.

'I know how well the best of our sewers can plan new things and make them,' she said. 'I myself could not do it alone—' The ritual disclaimer; it was not polite to claim expertise, especially exclusive knowledge.

'Like a carry-sack,' Kata said. Her voice sounded happier.

'More like a box, but of cloth,' Ariane said.

'Is there enough cloth?' Linda asked.

'Go and see,' Ariane said. 'Come back and tell us how many rolls.'

'If we have to ask the machines for more, we should do that today,' said Kata. 'And it must be allotted fairly.'

Ofelia said nothing more, but entered the first sewing room. She laid Barto's clothes on one of the long tables and began looking over them. One by one, the other women came in after her, now talking about how they would make fabric boxes to hold their belongings. Ofelia found a frayed collar on one shirt and a small triangular tear in the leg of one pair of pants. She turned on one of the bright work-lamps, shifted the magnifier around, and set to work mending the rip. She hardly needed to see it; her fingers could feel the edges of torn cloth as easily as her eyes could see. But she liked the way the magnifier made the threads look like fat yarn.

When she returned home, the clothes neatly folded in her arms, Rosara was standing amid piles of their belongings in the living room. Her eyes were red; she looked as if she were about to be sick. Ofelia nodded at her, and went to put away the clothes she carried. The bedroom was tidy again; Rosara must have put away the clothes Barto had thrown around. A pile of mending lay on the bed. Ofelia picked it up and headed back to the center, hoping to avoid any conversations with Rosara.

Now the center was full of busy women. She could hear the fabricator humming and clicking; someone must have decided they needed more fabric. In both sewing rooms, the long tables were covered with strips of cloth. Two women – Dorotea and Ariane – huddled over patterns cut from the thinnest cloth, pinning together the first fabric box. A few children wandered in and out, looking worried.

'This is too thin,' someone said, yanking a length of green from the table. 'We must have the strongest material.'

'But not too heavy,' said someone else. Ariane looked up from her pattern-pinning and saw Ofelia.

'Ofelia – here – look at this. Will this work?' Ofelia made her way past chattering women to that end of the table. 'We want it to be easy to make,' Dorotea said. 'As little sewing as possible, because we must be very quick. Yet strong. Safely fastened. Some way to mark it for each family—'

Ofelia looked at the limp pink fabric glinting with pins, and set down her pile of mending. 'Will this go inside?' she asked. The two younger women arranged their bits of flimsy pink fabric around the bundle. Now it looked more like the shapes Ofelia remembered – flat boxlike shapes – but the limp fabric drooped against the contents.

'That will work,' Ariane said. 'But we need a way to fasten it.'

'Stickystrips,' Dorotea said. 'The machine can make them fast; we can sew them on the long piece that wraps around – make it wider, so it overlaps.'

Ofelia wandered away, into the other sewing room. Here Josepha and Aurelia headed the design team; their solution had the basic boxlike shape, but closed with a clever fold that required only one short length of stickystrip. It did use more fabric, and it required precision sewing of the folding angles.

Ariane came after her, with the stack of mending. 'I did it for you,' she said. 'You don't need to be straining your eyes with little things like that, Sera Ofelia. Your idea of making fabric boxes—'

'It was nothing,' Ofelia said automatically. 'Thank you for the mending, Ariane.'

'It is my pleasure, Sera Ofelia. And if you need help with anything—'

'No, thank you. Rosara and I can do it.' Ariane, after all, had children and grandchildren. Besides, to admit she needed help would be to admit that she and Rosara did not cooperate – something everyone knew, but no one acknowledged. 'I would like to help with the boxes,' Ofelia said. 'Although I am not as fast as I used to be, we have so little to pack—'

'If you have time, of course we would be glad of your help,' Ariane said.

'Barto suggested it,' Ofelia said. Ariane's mouth thinned; she understood exactly what that meant.

'Perhaps you could do the first one,' Ariane said. 'We need a model for others to follow.'

Ofelia eased the fabric through the machine, careful to

keep the tension even. She had once been very good at sewing, but lately had trouble keeping her mind on the task once she had the fabric lined up. Barto had complained about the uneven topstitching in the last shirt she'd made him. She had made so many shirts, over the years; she was tired of straight seams. But this box was something new, something she'd never made. She had to think how to turn such sharp corners – she stopped and called to Ariane.

'Do the corners need to be so square? If we rounded them, then we could put that cord here, and make it stronger.' Ariane carried away the sample, to talk to Dorotea.

Ofelia sat where she was and closed her eyes. She felt divided inside. One little voice kept saying I'm not going, I'm not going. But the voice she was used to hearing continued to talk about the problem of the fabric boxes. She knew how to plan work with others; she knew how to listen to the voice that spoke for her when she did. That other voice felt strange.

Ariane came back, with Dorotea. 'We'll round the corners, add the cord – anything else?'

'No . . . I was just thinking.' Ofelia went back to work, stitching around the curves, her fingers automatically shifting the material through the machine. She had the box almost complete when she realized how hard it was going to be to sew stickystrips on the rim now that it had been sewn to the sides.

'We'll tell the others to sew the stickystrips on first,' Ariane said. 'You should rest now – it's past lunchtime.'

She had not noticed. She had always enjoyed figuring out ways to do things, though usually someone just gave her directions. She had followed the directions; now she followed Ariane, slowly, aware of the kink in her shoulders from hunching over the machine.

'Will you eat with us?' Ariane asked. Ofelia shook her head.

'I should go home; Barto will want me. But I'll come back later.' Ariane gave her a little hug; for the first time Ofelia could feel the bones through Ariane's flesh. She looked at her daughter's friend. Ariane was aging; she had hardly noticed before, but there were gray streaks in Ariane's hair. In Ofelia's mind, she had stayed the same age as Adelia – who had never aged past twenty, when she died.

At home, Barto and Rosara were out somewhere; the house felt peaceful and cool without them. Ofelia laid the stack of completed mending on their bed, and went into her own room. Someone had dumped all her clothes onto her bed, pushing them into messy piles. Underwear, shirts, skirts, the one dress. She hated seeing her clothes like that. Underwear always looked vaguely indecent, even if it was plain and old, like hers. Limp unattractive shapes of beige and white, designed only to cover twice what her baggy clothes would have covered anyway.

She was not going. She would not have to wear underwear once there was no one to be scandalized because she did not. She felt her heart pounding, and a delicious sense of wickedness rose from between her toes to the top of her scalp, bathing her in heat. She went back to the living room and looked down the lane. Nothing. They would be eating in the center, more than likely.

Ofelia went back to her room and shut the door. She had no window in her room. Stealthily, she took off her clothes. In broad daylight, her public voice scolded. For no reason. Her new voice, the one that said she wasn't going, said nothing. For an instant, breathing hard, she stood naked in her room, and then she slipped her outer clothes back on, leaving a pile of underclothes on the floor. Indecent! shrieked her public voice. Shameless! Disgusting!

She could feel the skin on her belly, on her hips, on her thighs, touching the cloth of her skirt. She took a tentative step, then another. A little draft between her legs, coolness where she was used to heat.

No! her public voice told her. You can't do that.

The private new voice said nothing. It didn't have to say anything. She could not do it now, not while other people were there to condemn. But later . . . later she would wear only what felt good on her body. Whatever that was.

Quickly, without paying attention to herself or her feelings of distaste, she undressed and dressed again, properly. The underclothes, all of them. The outer clothes, all of them. For now. For twenty-nine more days.

She had just dressed, and refolded her clothes into neater stacks, when Barto and Rosara came back. They had a new grievance.

'They say you are too old,' Barto said, glowering at her as if she had chosen that age on that day.

'Retired,' Rosara said. 'Too old to work.'

Ridiculous. She had always worked; she would work until she died; that's what people did. 'Seventy,' Barto said. 'You're no longer on contract, and they say it will cost them to send you somewhere else, and you won't be of use to the colony anyway.'

It did not surprise her, but it angered her. Useless? Did they think she was of no use now, because she had no formal job, and only kept the garden and the house, and did most of the cooking?

'They are going to charge our account,' Rosara said.

'We will have to pay back the cost of shipping you.'

'There was a retirement guarantee in the contract,' Barto said, 'but when you didn't remarry, didn't have more children, you lost a portion of it.'

They had not told her that. They had said she would lose her productivity bonus, even though she kept working full time. They had said nothing about retirement. But of course, they made the rules. And with this rule, perhaps they had made it easy for her to stay behind.

'I could just stay here,' Ofelia said. 'Then they wouldn't charge you—'

'Of course you can't stay here!' Barto slammed his fist on the table, and the dishes rattled. 'An old woman, alone – you would die.'

'I will die anyway,' Ofelia said. 'That's what they mean. And if I stayed, it wouldn't cost you anything.'

'But, mama! You can't think I'd leave you here to die alone. You know I love you.' Barto looked as if he might cry, his great red face crumpling with the effort to project filial devotion.

'I might die alone anyway, in the cryo. Isn't it supposed to be more dangerous for old people?' She could see by the look on his face that he knew that already, had probably just been told that.

'That would be better than dying here, the only person on the whole planet,' Barto said.

'I would be with your father,' Ofelia said. It was an argument that might work with Barto, who remembered his father as a godlike person who could do no wrong. But she hated herself for the lie, even as she said it.

'Mama, don't be sentimental! Papa's dead. He's been dead for—' Barto had to stop and work it out; Ofelia knew. Thirty-six years.

'I don't want to leave his grave,' Ofelia said. Having begun, she could not stop. 'And the others—' The other two boys, the girl who had died in infancy, Adelia. Over those graves she had cried real tears, and she could cry over them now.

'Mama!' Barto stepped toward her, but Rosara came between them.

'Barto. Let her alone. Of course it matters to her, her own children, your father—' At least Rosara had it in the right order. 'And besides—' But trust Rosara to ruin the effect; she was going to explain that it would, after all, be a solution, even though they could not allow it. 'If she *did* stay,' Rosara said, fulfilling Ofelia's expectation, 'then we would not have to pay—'

'No!' Barto slapped Rosara; Ofelia had prudently backed away, and Rosara's backward stagger didn't hurt her. 'She is my mother; I'm not leaving her here.'

Ofelia said, 'I'm going to the center to sew the fabric boxes.' Barto would not follow her into the open; he never did. He might think her remark was capitulation, too.

That evening, neither Barto nor Rosara mentioned the incident. Ofelia said she had completed a fabric box, and would do more tomorrow. 'If the machines produce enough fabric, we can make a box for each person in the colony. It will be difficult, in the short time, but—'

'Rosara will help tomorrow,' Barto said.

Rosara sewed slowly and clumsily. 'The machines are all busy,' Ofelia said. 'I can make the other boxes for our family.'

'And I am supposed to report for vocational testing tomorrow,' Rosara said.

'It is ridiculous to test you before me,' Barto said. That began a tirade against the Company. Ofelia didn't listen.

After eating, she scraped the dishes and carried out the scraps to the garden. She had not been in the garden since dawn; she drew a deep breath of the evening scents. There was just enough light to see the slidebug's web between the rows, and avoid it. When she came back to the kitchen door, she peeked. Empty. The door to Rosara and Barto's room was shut. That suited her. She cleaned the dishes and set them to dry.

In the morning, her first thought was *Twenty-eight days*. Her second thought was *I'm not going. I will be free in twenty-eight days*.

She had wakened early, as always, and when she came into the garden the dawn mists still blurred her view down the lane. Plant by plant she examined the garden: the beans, with their tiny fragrant flowers, the tomatoes, the young spears of corn, the exuberant vines of gourds. Some of the tomato flowers had opened, curling back their petals like tiny lilies.

She heard brisk steps coming down the lane, and crouched. A Company rep went by, hardly glancing over the garden fence. After that, she hurried her garden work, plucking off the leaf-eaters and stemsuckers. She knew Barto would scold if he found her working in the garden now, when the work was useless. He might even be angry, and destroy the plants. When Barto and Rosara came out of their bedroom, she had breakfast on the table. She smiled at them.

'I'm just leaving for the center. I'll be there all day, I expect, sewing.'

All day, sewing with the other women, in the rooms full of machines and women and children, shaping the bright cloth into fabric boxes. When her shoulders tired, someone always noticed and came to knead them and take a turn at the machine. Ofelia sat for awhile in a padded rocker in the passage, telling stories to small children. They were not her grandchildren, but she had been telling stories to small children for so long it didn't matter. Here, with everyone talking as they worked, speculating on where they might be sent, and what it would be like, she could hardly remember she wasn't going. The women all called her Sera Ofelia, and asked her advice. She began to think she would be with them always, always have these toddlers crawling into her lap, always have some younger woman confiding a problem with her husband or a quarrel with a neighbor.

Only that night, in her bed, her skin remembered the feel of clothes without underclothes. Her hands swept across her belly, her sides. She was old . . . her public voice said that, the voice that knew what to say in the center to the other women. She was old and wrinkled and beyond any of the feelings that she had felt in her youth, when she had been in love with Caitano and then Humberto. That was what the public voice said. But the private voice, the new voice, said *I'm not going. They'll be gone, and I'll be here. Alone. Free.*

The next morning she woke remembering that it was now twenty-seven days. And that day, and the next, and the next, fit the same pattern. She spent the days at the center, helping everyone else make the fabric boxes, helping them decide what to take and what to leave, holding the little children when they were frightened, telling stories to the older children. In the days she was one of them, one of the group being torn away from everything they had built in forty years, helpless and hopeless but still enduring. In the nights, she was herself, a strange person she did not know, a person she might just remember, from childhood.

Then it was five days. Only, the Company had lied again, and already the shuttle was on its way back to orbit with the first passengers: thirty days to clear the planet, not until the first ones left. Each colonist had a number, in order of evacuation. Mothers and children first, because children were troublesome until out of the way. Single adults last. Ofelia gave a last hug to the children who thought of her as grandmother, and waved as they were led into the shuttle.

Another shuttle landed within the hour. The Company reps had explained how it would be, how perfect the schedule. By the time each new shuttle-load arrived at the ship, the previous load would have had its possessions marked and stored, and be already in the cryo tanks. Ten shuttle loads a day for five days, and the last shuttle would lift in time to make the legal deadline.

Ofelia had not thought how quickly the colony would seem empty. By the end of the first day, it reminded her of the terror after the first great flood, when so many had died. By the end of the second, she and the others looked at each other wide-eyed. The Company reps moved among them, keeping them busy, preventing panic. Ofelia still had meals to cook and clean up after – she would go up with the last shuttle, the reps reminded her. Rosara and Barto, protesting this separation, were scheduled for the first shuttle on the last day. She heard them try to explain that she could not be trusted, that she was old, that she forgot things. The Company reps glanced her way, and she looked down, as if she had not heard. She knew they would not care.

On that last day, the alarm woke them all much earlier

than usual. It was still dark; the morning fog lay cool and damp against her skin as she walked with Barto and Rosara to the landing field. They joined the end of the line. A shuttle landed, its lights blurry glows in the darkness. The line stirred into motion. The moment came. Rosara hugged her, fiercely. Barto said 'Mama . . .' in an uncertain voice, a boy's voice.

'I love you,' Ofelia said, and pushed them away. 'Don't be late. They will be angry if you're late.'

'Don't you be late,' Barto said. He stared at her as if trying to see inside her head, hear the new little voice which sang of freedom.

'It's all right, Barto,' she said. By the time he found out it wasn't, it would be too late. When that shuttle took off, she had the whole day until her own . . . the one she would not take. She walked back, past the line forming for the next shuttle, and went into the house. Her house, now. The new voice was louder, more insistent. She would have to find a place to hide – the Company reps would make at least a token search for her. They would not leave her behind easily; if they found her, they would force her onto the shuttle.

Behind the house, beyond the garden, lay a strip of pasture. Beyond that, the lanky plants that ventured out from the native scrub to dare a bout with terraforming soil bacteria. Behind, the wall of native plants . . . first head-high scrub, then the high ramparts of the forest. If she could get across the pasture unseen, she would be invisible. They would not search long. They would curse and call . . . and then they would leave.

In the first gray light of dawn, in the morning fog, Ofelia set off with several days' supply of food in a pillow-case, and a small sack of seeds. If they destroyed her garden, she could replant . . . she did not think further than that.

The pasture felt springy beneath her feet, the wet grass brushed her legs, wetting her skirt. She realized she might leave a trail, dark against the dew-silvered grass, if anyone looked too early this morning. Perhaps they would think it was an animal. In the distance, she heard one of the sheep bleat, and wondered if they would leave the sheep alive. She hoped so. She liked knitting and crocheting. The tall weedy growths beyond the pasture swiped at her with rough wet leaves, soaking her skirt to the hip. Behind her, she heard voices calling – not her, but a warning to those who should catch the next shuttle. Then darkness loomed out of the fog, and she passed between the first tall shrubs.

She sat down to rest once she was well into the trees; it was too dark here to walk anyway, and she had already stumbled over enough roots and knobs. Light filtered through the canopy, revealing more shapes and colors as the sun rose higher. Something very high up moved along the branches, rattling and squeaking. Ofelia stirred, but did not move.

Soon the sun began to burn away the fog. When she could see well enough, she got up and walked on, slowly, picking her way to save her feet any more bruises. She had been to the forest before, after Humberto died; she had discovered then that she could always find her way back. No one else had believed her; they had worried and nagged so that she finally quit making those trips. But she had no fear now that she would get lost.

When she felt hungry, she sat down and ate from her sack of food. She dug a little hole to use, and piled leaves back over it when she was done. As the light waned, in

the afternoon, she piled sticks and leaves to make herself
a nest for the night. Her shuttle had been supposed to
leave just after sundown. She expected another shuttle
would come for the Company reps. She would not go
home for two days.

THREE

If they called, she did not hear them. If they searched, they did not come her way. She lay awake long after dark, waiting, and heard nothing of humans but the departing roar of the shuttle. Closer, she heard rustlings in the leaves, something falling through the limbs above her, hitting one after another until it smacked into the ground an unknown distance away. A soft whirr, like a muffled alarm. A resonant sound like a stone dropped on another, repeating at intervals. Her heart raced and slowed, as exhaustion burned her eyes and wore out her fear. When she fell asleep at last, she had no idea how long the night would last.

Before dawn, she woke cold and damp at the sound of another shuttle landing; she could not go back to sleep, even though she forced herself to close her eyes. When the first light came, she wasn't sure if it was real; she half-believed her eyes were making it up, tired of the dark. Slowly the nearby trees took form, dim shapes lifting overhead, dark against colorless light. When the morning light was strong enough that she could see the rust-orange and pale green of the patchy growths on the tree nearest her, she heard the shuttle taking off, its roar vanishing into the sky above the trees.

It should be the last one. She could not be sure, though. If they had lied to the people; if they had wanted to take back more things from the buildings – equipment, machines, she couldn't guess – then they would have to send more shuttles. She had no idea how long it would take them to set the spaceship itself in motion. She should hide at least another day.

She wished she had brought dry clothes; she had not thought how wet she might be, or how stiff. She did not feel free, from having slept on the ground in the open; she felt sticky and miserable, her joints aching sharply. When it finally occurred to her that she could take off the damp garments sticking to her skin, she laughed aloud, then stopped abruptly, a hand to her mouth. Barto had not liked it when she laughed for no reason. She waited, listening; when no voice scolded, she felt her body relax, her hand drop from her mouth. She was safe, at least from that. She peeled the clothes off, peering around to be sure no one watched.

In the dim light, her skin gleamed, paler than anything around it. If someone had stayed behind – if someone were looking – he would know at once she was naked. She did not look at herself; she looked at her clothes as she shook them out. Perhaps she could hang them somewhere. She flinched as a drop of water fell onto her bare shoulder, whirling around at the touch. Then it struck her as funny, and she giggled soundlessly at herself, unable to stop until her sides ached.

That had warmed her. She felt odd, more aware of the air touching her than anything else, but neither hot nor cold. When another drop of water struck her between the shoulders, and trickled down her spine, she shivered. It felt good. She hung her shirt and underclothes over a

drooping length of vine, then folded her skirt into a pad
to sit on. It was still unpleasantly damp, but it touched
her only where she sat, and the heat of her body warmed
it. She took out yesterday's flatbread, the chunk of sausage,
and ate it hungrily. Today it tasted different, as if it were
a strange food, something new. The water in her flask
tasted different too, in a way she could not define.

After eating, she dug another little hole and used it.
Perhaps she need not – if she was the only person in the
world now, who could be offended by her waste? – but
lifelong habit insisted that people did something with their
output. When she was sure the others had gone – truly
gone, forever – she would see if the recycler would work
for her. For now she pushed the reddish dirt, the odd-
colored leaves, back over the hole.

As the day warmed, Ofelia tired of sitting still; she missed
the familiar routine of her days, the gardening and cooking,
the chores she had performed so long. It would have been
nice to have a fire, to be able to cook, but she had no way
to make a fire, and would not risk detection from the smoke.
Lacking that possibility, she began picking up sticks,
arranging them, almost without thinking. A little platform
of crossed sticks, to keep her pack off the damp forest floor.
There, a larger fallen limb, its bark already rotted away . . .
it would make a comfortable brace at the back of the next
hole she dug. She tidied the little space in which she had
settled, arranging it to suit her. It took on more and more
the shape and feel of a room, a safe place.

At noon, when the few rays of direct sun fell straight
onto her head, she paused to eat again, and look around.
Her water flask nestled into the hollow between two roots;
she had picked large flat leaves to shade it. Another flat
leaf served as a platter for her meal. She had contrived a

comfortable seat, after several tries, from limbs propped against each other and a tree trunk, padded with her folded skirt. Her nakedness still bothered her; she felt every movement of the air, even the movements she made. Finally she had pulled on her underclothes, grimacing, a little ashamed to need privacy from nothing but her own awareness, and her shirt over them. She left off the long skirt that now served as a pillow. But her bare feet felt right.

Sometimes in the afternoon, a rainstorm came up. In the colony, it had been possible to see storms coming. But under the forest canopy, Ofelia had no warning except the shadow and rush of wind that preceded a downpour. She had been out in rain before; she was not afraid of getting wet. When it was over, she would dry out again.

But she had not been in the forest in a storm before. At first, she heard only the wind, and assumed the water, as the canopy absorbed the first rain. Then the saturated canopy leaked. Just when she thought the rain might be over (light returned, the thunder rumbled in the distance only), this lower rain found her. Drop by drop, drizzling trickle by trickling stream, until she was soaked, as evening came on. Because she had hunched in her improvised seat, the skirt under her was no wetter than before, but also no drier. Her sack of food, covered with large leaves, still seemed damp; the flatcake tasted stale and soggy. She did not want to lie down on the wet forest floor to sleep; she did not want to sit there awake all night either. Finally she rested her head against the tree trunk, and slept fitfully, waking at every unfamiliar sound.

By first light, she had decided that she could not stand another wet night in the forest. Not without supplies she had not brought. She wanted to complain to someone, insist that it wasn't her fault. She had never run away before; she couldn't be expected to get it all right the first time.

Until then, the lack of voices had not bothered her. She had been told her hearing was going . . . or her mind; Barto couldn't decide which. She had been able to hear what she wanted to hear, usually; she had often wished for silence. On the rare nights that Barto did not snore, and Rosara did not wake three or four times to stumble noisily to the toilet, she had lain awake reveling in the silence.

And the silence of that first day had not bothered her, because she did not hear it as silence. Inside, she had the bickering voices, the public voice that said predictable things, and the new private voice that said unimaginable things. Outside had been the progression of shuttle flight noises, one after another. On the second day, the sound of her own actions – the noises she had made dragging limbs, picking up sticks, breathing and eating and drinking – comforted her without her noticing, mixed as they were with the voices inside.

Not until she wanted an answer did she notice the silence.

It was a wall. It was a presence, not an absence . . . a pressure on her ears that made her swallow nervously, as if that could clear them. Silence wrapped its hands around her head, muffling and smothering.

When the panic subsided, she was standing rigid, mouth open, gasping for air . . . she could not remember what question she had thought to ask, that needed another's answer. Her ears reported that they had sound enough: rustling in the leaves, the drip of water, that stonelike resonant plonk. But those sounds carried no meaning, and the voices in her head, both the familiar and the new, held silence in her fear. Finally one of them – which, she did not notice – said *Go home now*. Said it firmly, with no doubts.

Ofelia looked around her room, and picked up her folded skirt. She shook it out, and stepped into it without thinking. She picked up the sack of supplies. Time to go home, even before full daylight. Her feet knew the way, through the strands of fog that obscured her vision, over the knotted roots, around the trees and stones. Light grew around her as she came to the edge of the forest, where the lower brush grew, and by the time she came to the edge of the cleared ground, soaked once more with morning dew, she could just see the dark shapes of the town's buildings through the fading mist.

She paused at the edge of that open grassy stretch, calmer now and remembering why she should not simply walk home. Here it was much quieter than in the forest. A breath of air flowed past her, carrying the smell of sheep somewhere to her right. No human sound. No voices. No machines. Would they be waiting for her to return? Was someone in the houses, in the center, holding his breath, watching her through some special machine and waiting for her to come within range?

She felt warmth on her right cheek and neck, the sun burning the mist away. Cool damp and warmth alternated, and then the sun won, and bright light shone on the town. Her house lay ahead – she had retraced her path so exactly that if her marks on the dew two mornings before had remained, she might have stepped into them as into familiar socks. But nothing marred the sweep of dull silver.

She stepped into the wet grass. She wanted to get home, and out of her wet clothes.

She changed from her wet clothes first, and used the bathroom for a hot shower. After that, she considered her clothes. What did she feel like wearing? Indoors . . . nothing.

But she wanted to go into her garden, and she was not yet ready to stay outside naked. She pulled on a shirt. What she wanted to wear with it was short pants, like those she had worn as a child, those she had made for Barto. In his room – *not his room, my room* she told herself – she found a pair of long pants he had not taken. She found her scissors and cut the legs short, but did not stop to hem them. When she tried them on, they were too big in the waist, but she did not mind the feeling as they rode low on her hips. Better than her underclothes or her skirt.

Leaf-nibblers had been at work on the garden in those two days, but all the tomato flowers had opened. Ofelia worked her way from plant to plant, capturing the caterpillars to feed later, breaking the three slimerods she found among the squash, squashing the aphids on the beans. She paid little attention to the time, until her stomach growled and she realized she was hungry.

She ate a cold snack from the cooler. In only two days, nothing had spoiled even though the light didn't come on. She flicked the kitchen light switch: again nothing. But the water had been hot . . . she puzzled over that until she remembered that the water tanks used the same insulation as the coolers. If the cooler could stay cold, the hot water could stay hot. Then she set out to find what had happened in the rest of the colony.

It felt strange – almost indecent – to be looking into windows and opening doors when the people who lived in those houses were not home to say *Welcome, Sera Ofelia* or *Our house is your house, Sera Ofelia*. No one had locked a door – the doors had no locks, anyway, only latches to keep small children in or out – and the first two or three times she pushed one open, she felt shy. Later it became a game; she felt deliciously wicked, the way she'd felt when she first took off her clothes and considered not wearing them. Now she could look under the Senyagins' bed. Now she could open Linda's closets and see if her housekeeping was as muddled as her mind. (It was – she found items that Linda would be sorry not to have when she woke up in another world, shoved in behind dirty laundry.) In the bright day, she hurried from house to house, flinging open doors that were shut, letting the light in, letting herself in. All the gardens looked the same as they had two days before. Dayvine's scarlet trumpets open . . . tomatoes and beans and squash and peas and chard . . . all the plants she could want, more than she could ever eat, producing more seed than she would ever need. She made note of certain ones: the special blue bean that the Senyagins had brought on their own, not part of colony seedstock, and traded at a high price. She would have that in her own garden at last. Melons here . . . the giant gourd there; she had never grown either giant gourds or melons, but she had traded for them. Lemongrass . . . herbs . . . she had always grown some cilantro and peppers for herself, but not tarragon and basil and parsley and dill. She would have to keep a close eye on the herb garden; the colony had had only one.

The center too stood open. The long sewing tables were littered with scraps and lengths of fabric. All the machines had been turned off, and did not come on when she pushed the buttons. She went to the door of the powerplant control room. It was closed but not locked; she pushed it open. A skylight let in ample light; she went to the big switches, all set at OFF, and pushed them ON. More light sprang out around her. The control panel was alight now, and all the markers were in green segments. She knew what that meant; they all did. Every adult had learned to run the powerplant; it was too important to leave to a few specialists.

Now the center's machines would work, and the cooler and lights at home. While she was there, Ofelia checked the levels in the waste recycler. She might need to replenish the tanks sometime; one person might not make enough waste to keep the powerplant running. But so far the levels had not dropped enough to measure.

From the center, Ofelia went cautiously toward the shuttle field. If the Company still waited to trap her, this might be where they waited. She kept to the edge of the lane as far as the last buildings. From here she could see down to the shuttle field, its surface scuffed and bruised by the heavy traffic of the past week, but otherwise empty. No vehicles moved; she saw and heard no one. The breeze blew across it toward her; she smelled nothing fresh in the faint scent of oils and fuels. A nearer stench of decay drew her. She followed it to a firepit where she supposed the Company reps had feasted on the colony's sheep, or some of them. Eight or nine badly butchered corpses lay rotting, the fleeces in a separate pile, stiff and bloody. Ofelia scowled. It was a waste of good wool and leather, leaving them like that.

Still, it gave her a load for the waste recycler, and it would be no easier if she waited. The smell kept her appetite at bay, though it was noon. First she went back to the waste recycler for the long protective gloves she had been taught to use when handling animal waste. Slowly, laboriously, she dragged the sheep carcasses and refuse into one pile. Then she looked again at the few vehicles, the old logging trucks and utility wagons near the shuttle field. Would they work? She had not driven any machine for years, but she knew how.

They might still be in orbit. They might notice if she started an engine; they might have noticed when she started the powerplant again. Would they come back? She could always hide in the forest again, this time taking her rain cape and dry clothes – but why would they?

Still – she walked back to the third house on this side of the village and found the Arramandys' garden cart in their shed. Moving the sheep carcasses to the waste recycler took her the rest of the afternoon. The cart would hold two at a time, and she found buckets for the slimy, bloated guts and organs. With all her care, some of the stinking mess got onto her clothes. When she had finished, she washed the gloves, dipped them in disinfectant, and then stripped off her clothes, not touching the wet places. She would have to disinfect them, too.

She could do better than that. Grinning, she picked up the clothes with a stick, and shoved them, too, into the intake hopper. Then she showered in the convenient shower, and dried herself on the big gray towels that hung there for anyone who needed them. She considered wrapping one around herself for the walk home ... or she could duck into someone's house and find real clothes.

Or. Or she could walk naked down the street where she had lived, where no one lived now to tell the tale. She padded to the open door and looked out. Twilight: the sun had sunk behind the distant forest. No one in the street, no one in the houses. Her belly tightened with excitement, with daring. Could she? She would someday, she knew that, had known it since that new voice first spoke inside her. And if she could do it someday, why not now, tonight, when it would still be a thrill?

She dropped the towel in a heap, and took one step. No. She turned, picked up the towel, and went back inside to hang it up. If she was going to walk down the street with no clothes on, she would start here, at the shower.

In the building, already dim with evening, she felt safe enough. At the door she paused again. No? Yes? She did not have to hurry. She could stand there a long time, until it was dark if she wanted. Until no one could see, even if everyone had been there.

But she would know. And she wanted to know. One step, out from under the doorframe. Another step, out from under the shadow of the eaves. Another and another, away from that building, and into the lane, along the lane . . . and no eyes peered from the dark windows, no voices rose to shame her. The cool twilight air touched her everywhere, on her back and sides and breasts and belly, all along her arms and legs, between her legs. It felt – when she calmed enough to notice – very pleasant.

Then she saw the lights of the center warm against the blue dusk. Fear chilled her; she could scarcely breathe. *Idiot!* How could she have been so stupid? If anyone was up there in orbit, if they were watching, they would surely see it. They would know; they might come back.

She hurried now, no longer aware of her bare skin, rushing in to find the light switches and turn them off. Then home, where she put out her hand and had the switch in her fingers before she remembered. She stood there a moment, her muscles cramping with the effort of stopping a familiar movement, before she could take her hand away without moving the switch. Her heart pounded; she could feel the pulse of her fear throughout her body. As her heart slowed, as she calmed, she scolded herself. Foolish, foolish. She could not afford to forget things; there was no one to remind her any more.

She ate a cold supper in the darkness inside the house. At least she was inside now, and if it rained she would not get wet. She closed the shutters, making the inside

even darker, and felt her way to her bed. Her room felt
tiny, airless. Tomorrow she would move to Barto and
Rosara's room, the room she had shared with her husband
until he died. But tonight – tonight she would not blunder
around in the dark. She pulled down the covers by feel,
and was almost asleep when she remembered.

She had not been alone like this . . . in her whole life.
She wondered for a long moment that she was not frightened, alone in the dark, the only person on the whole
planet. Not frightened at all . . . she felt safe, safer than
she could remember being. She fell asleep as her body
found the familiar hollows of her bed.

In the morning, as she woke in her own bed in her own
house, the familiar smells around her, she did not
remember what had happened. She rose as usual, fumbled
her way to the light switch in her room, and only when
it came on realized that she was naked, and why. The past
few days felt dreamlike, unreal. She caught up the robe
hanging on its hook, and slipped into it before opening
the door, half-expecting to hear snores from Barto and
Rosara's room.

Silence greeted her, the absolute silence of a house in
which no one dwells. She looked anyway. Already their
bedroom looked different, a room in which no one had
lived for some time. Barto had not wanted to waste their
packing allotment on linens, so the bed still had the cream
bedspread with the broad red stripe, and the pillows in
red cases. The open closet gaped, a blind mouth with a
rumpled sock for a tongue; Ofelia grinned, thinking how
Barto would complain when he unpacked and found a
sock missing. She picked it up, shut the closet door, and
latched it. It never had stayed shut on its own. The room

still looked strange, and she could not say why. A film of dew slicked the windowsill; as she looked, a slidebug dropped from the ceiling, trailing its tether.

In the kitchen, the cooler hummed blandly. Ofelia ignored it and went out into the garden. Here all felt the same, the plants responding to light and warmth with another day's growth. She worked her way down the rows, enjoying the silence. Somewhere a sheep bleated, and others answered. Far off, on the far side of the settlement, one of the cattle mooed. These sounds had never bothered her; they did not shatter her peace. She did think she ought to find the cattle and the sheep, and see if any of them needed anything. But in the meantime, there was the warm sun on her head, and the smell of bean blossoms, tomato plants, and the dayvine flowers. When she felt too hot, she let the robe fall open, and finally discarded it, hanging it on a hook in the toolshed. The sun felt like a great warm hand cradling her body; old aches seemed to vanish. When she went back inside, she felt a little feverish. Sunburn, she warned herself, as she opened the cooler. She would have to be careful, at least at first.

After breakfast, she cleaned out the cooler, throwing the stale food into the compost trench. She should check the other coolers. Most of them could be unplugged, kept as spares should she need them. It would be convenient to have a cooler in the center, and perhaps on the far side of the town, for when she went to tend to the cattle.

Most of the coolers had some kind of food in them. Ofelia cleaned them methodically, collecting anything stale or spoiled for compost. She carried the good food – the hard sausages, the smoked meats, the cheeses and pickled vegetables – back to her own house. She was already thinking which gardens to maintain, which to abandon, which to replant for grain for the sheep and cattle. She spent the entire day at this, uncomfortably aware of food spoiling somewhere . . . something she might not find in time. Not until late afternoon did she realize that even if she found no more, she would still have plenty. It would be a nuisance to clean out smelly coolers later, but she did not have to push herself.

At that thought, she quit work at once, and left the Falares' cooler standing open, half-cleaned. She had already unplugged it. She went into the bathroom she still thought of as 'theirs' and took a shower. It still felt daring, defiant, to use the facilities in someone else's home, even though the Falareses would never know. Still in that defiant mood, she left wet footprints across their tile floor and strolled back down the lane, making herself go slowly.

In the east, a storm was building, a tower of cloud snowy white at its peak, and dark blue-gray below. It would rain this evening; such storms moved inland from the coast every day or so in early summer. In the west, the highlands rose, step by step to distant mountains, but she could not see beyond the forest wall. She had heard about it – the map on the center wall showed the photomosaic made by the survey satellites before the colony was planted.

When she came into her house, the first puffs of wind before the storm tickled the back of her legs. She glanced back outside. Clouds obscured more than half the sky. Surely the ship, if it was still there, couldn't see her lights. She didn't want to spend another evening in the dark; she wanted to cook herself a good supper. She turned the lights on with the same feeling of defiance that had driven her to use the Falares' shower.

The storm rumbled, drifting nearer. Ofelia closed the shutters in the bedroom, leaving those in the kitchen open.

She cooked with one eye on the outside, waiting for the wind and rain. When it came, her sausages were sizzling with onions and peppers and sliced potatoes; she scooped the hot mix into a fresh round of flatbread, and sat near the kitchen door, listening to the rain in the garden.

Soon the darkening evening filled with the sounds of water: the rush of the rain itself, the drumming on the roof, the melodious drip from eaves onto the doorstones, the gurgle of water moving in the house ditches to the drain beyond. Much better than in the forest. Ofelia finished the last of her supper, and rested her back against the doorpost. A fine spray of water brushed her face and arms as the water rebounded from the ground outside. She licked it off her lips: more refreshing than any shower.

The rain continued until after dark. Ofelia finally got up, grunting at her stiff back and legs, and moved her pillow into the other bedroom. The slidebug had spent the day making a web in the corner; she smacked it with her shoe – the only good use of a shoe, she told herself happily – and tore down the web. Slidebugs were not venomous, but their clawed legs prickled, and she had no desire to be wakened by it in the dark.

When she lay down, the bed felt odd. She had slept in this bed when Humberto was alive, but had given it up to Barto and Stefan a year or two later. By the time Stefan died, Barto had considered the room his, and he had invited his first wife Elise to live there. Ofelia had not complained; she had liked Elise, who had died in the second big flood. But then, Barto had married Rosara . . . so it had been twenty years or more since she'd slept in the big bed. Her body had become used to the narrow one. It took some time tossing and turning and stretching to find her balance in the larger space.

Waking to the light filtering through shutters . . . she stretched luxuriously. Her skin itched slightly, and when she looked it had a faint flush. She would have to wear a shirt again today. But when she looked at her shirts, none of them pleased her. She thought of the houses she'd been in, the things left behind. At Linda's, there'd been a fringed shawl. Somewhere near there – her mind refused to come up with the name – someone had left a soft blue shirt behind. Or she could make herself a shirt with the left-over fabric in the center.

Not today. Today she would scavenge again, because she wanted to clear out more of the coolers and find what else useful had been left. She went out into the morning coolness and the fog left behind the rain, no longer worried that someone might see and criticize. The damp eased her sunburn; even when she found the blue shirt she remembered, embroidered with little pink flowers, she hesitated to put it on. Inside, she didn't need it. She wore it like a cape that day, throwing it over her shoulders when she went from house to house and leaving it off inside.

In the afternoon, she remembered again that she needed to look for the cattle on the other side of the settlement, near the river. She could check the pump intakes at the same time. She picked up a hat someone had discarded, and slung the shirt over her shoulders.

The cattle had been pastured between the settlement and the river, where terraforming grasses grew rank in the damp soil. She had had nothing to do with them for years, and had not realized that a stout calf-pen had been built to confine the calves. No one had thought to release them, but two cows had jumped the gate. A third grazed nearby. Inside the pen were two healthy calves, and one that looked thin and ribby. As she watched, it tried to sneak a feed from one of the cows, who butted it away. Ofelia looked at the cow outside the pen. She was not a herder but she thought its udder already looked tighter than those of the cows inside. Farther off, by the river, she saw the brown backs of the other cattle grazing. Perhaps it would be all right. Ofelia didn't want to worry about it. She opened the gate, standing behind it as the hungry cows surged forward, leading their calves out to grass. The other cow went to her calf, licked it all over. The calf grabbed a teat and started sucking, but Ofelia saw none of the milky foam on its muzzle that would mean it was getting milk.

Her conscience scolded her. *It's your fault, Ofelia. If only you had bothered to look, even yesterday. It's because you're selfish. Willful. Vain.* She walked over to check the water trough in the pen, even though she didn't intend to close any animals in it again. She noticed that the voice of her conscience sounded less like her own and more like . . . whose? Barto's? Humberto's? No, because it was older and not completely male. It had shadings of feminine ire, too. She was too tired to worry about it; she only noticed that it had been gone for several days, and now it was back.

That evening, in the cool twilight, she sat at the kitchen door sniffing the healthy smells from her garden. The new voice murmured, happily, much in the tone of the water that had run in the house-ditch. The old voice lay silent as a sleeping cat. The new voice talked to itself: *free, free, free . . . quiet . . . lovely, free, free.*

She dreamed. She had a yellow dress, with ruffles on the shoulders, and yellow socks that matched. She had two yellow bows in her hair. She had a plaid bookbag . . . it was her first day of school. Her mother had stayed up late finishing the dress and the bows. She felt excited, eager.

Last year Paulo had started school, and now it was her turn.

The room smelled of children and steam; it was in the basement of the crowded school, and by noon the ruffles on her yellow dress hung limply. She didn't care. They had computers here, real ones, and the children were allowed to touch them. Paulo had told her that, but she hadn't believed him. Now she stood in front of the computer, her fingers splayed on the touchpad, laughing at the colors on the screen. The teacher wanted them to touch the color squares in order, but Ofelia had discovered that you could make the colors drift and merge, and the screen before her was a riot of color.

Of course, it had been naughty. The teacher had said what to do, and she had done something else. That was wrong. She understood that now. But in her dream, the swirling colors escaped the screen and colored the room, making her memories more vivid than the reality had been. On the other screens, a square of color followed a square of color, pure and predictable, red, green, yellow, blue. On hers . . . a mess, the teacher had said, but she had already heard the other children exclaim over what she could see for herself. Magnificence, glory, all the things they weren't supposed to have.

She woke up with tears still wet on her cheeks, and blinked them out of her eyes. Something vividly red swung in and out of view at the window. Dayvine trumpets, in the breeze – the vine on that side of the house must have grown a foot overnight. Barto had insisted on keeping the house free of vines; she lay there and felt a deep happiness work out from her bones at the sight of those flowers dancing in the sunlight.

FOUR

Internal memo: Gaai Olaani, Sims Bancorp representative aboard sublight vessel Diang Zhi, to Division Head, Colonial Operations.

'In accordance with instructions, Colony 3245.12 was evacuated as per regulations. See enclosed appendices A for personnel list, B for equipment abandoned as uneconomic to recover, C for evidence of indigenous biological inhibition of standard terraforming biochemistry, perhaps explaining colony failure, including inadequate reproductive rate. Further research into the effect of local biologicals on the terraforming process should precede an attempt at recolonization. Whoever picks up the franchise might have a claim on us if we don't file this.'

Internal memo: Moussi Shar, Vice President for Xenexploration to Guillermo Ansad, Project Manager.

'I don't care how reliable your agent, this is something they concocted to worry us. We know Sims didn't give adequate support of material or personnel *and* they planted their people in a flood plain in the path of tropical storms. If the cows and sheep are still alive, the terraforming didn't fail. Stick to the schedule.'

*   *   *

Ofelia was not even sure which day it was that she lost track of time. She had been so busy those first few days – four? Five? And then, when she had all the coolers clean and disconnected, when she had checked each building for fire hazards, when she had established a routine that felt comfortable, she spent some days in a haze of pleasure.

Day after day, she was doing what she wanted. No interruptions. No angry voices. No demands that she quit this and start that. Day by day the tomatoes swelled from tiny green buttons to fat green globes. Beans pushed out of the wrinkled dry bean flowers, lengthened into fattening green strings. Early squash formed under the flamboyant flowers and puffed up, balloon-like. She worked in the gardens every morning, picking off suckers and leaf-eaters, snapping the slimerods, hardly having to think at all.

In the afternoons, she made a regular check of the machinery: the waste recycler, the powerplant, the pumps and filters. Though it had not been her duty for years, she had no trouble remembering what to do. So far all the gauges and readouts were in green zones. The power never flickered; the water never ran yellow or murky from the taps. After that daily check, she continued to gather what she wanted from the various buildings, storing things mostly in the center's sewing rooms. She felt comfortable there; she dozed off sometimes, toward late afternoon, waking when the sun sank behind the trees, alert and ready to look for the animals.

That bothered her a little; she did not want the animals to be like children, expecting her care. But she would need them, she supposed. She would want meat, more than lay frozen in the big center lockers. She would want new wool to spin. She did not look forward to washing and carding it. But the sheep had already been sheared; she would not have to worry about that until next spring.

Meantime, she made sure every day that she knew where the animals were. Neither sheep nor cattle strayed from the pastures; they could not eat the native plants. The sheep had been skittish for days after her return; she supposed the Company reps had been noisy and clumsy hunting the ones they killed for their feast. But they went back to their earlier blind trust in her; she had been familiar to them, and now their own shepherds were gone. The cattle, more standoffish to begin with, watched her with alert eyes and spread ears when she walked through the water meadows, but they did not run.

When she thought about it, she was angry all over again with the Company reps. If they had wanted fresh meat, they could have taken it from the community freezers; they hadn't had to spook the sheep and leave the mess for her to clean up. Even though they had not known she would be there to do the work, they should not have left such a mess.

In the evenings, before she was tired enough to sleep, she made herself comfortable clothes from the scraps and ends of others. With no one watching, she found her fingers straying to brighter colors than she had worn for years. The dayvine's red, the remembered yellow of that childhood dress, the fiery green of young tomato leaves, the cool pearly green of the swelling globes. Barto's hacked-off trousers went into the recycler; she had her own shorts now, fringed at the bottom.

The first tomatoes to change color startled her with a recognition of time passing. How long had it been? She tried to count back, but she had no events to prick her memory after the first few days. The machines could tell her, she realized after the first panic. They had an indelible calendar function. And she could enter things in the log, if she wished.

She didn't care, really. She would need to know when to plant, although in this climate some plants grew year round, and the machines could tell her. No one would read her report if she did log it, and she was sure she would not want to read her own words.

Finally she opened the log file and looked. It had been thirty-two days. That seemed too long. She tapped the screen suspiciously. The numbers didn't change. She scrolled back, to the last regular log report, counting the days on her fingers to be sure. Yes: the last entry had been thirty-two days back, a terse comment. 'Log copied onto cube for transport; colony abandoned; surviving personnel evacuated.' Back another thirty days, to the entries before the Company reps arrived. She had never been one to waste time reading the log, let alone writing it, but once she began the entries fascinated her. Someone had bothered to check the machines four times a day and enter all the gauge readings; someone had checked the river level, the temperature, the rainfall, the windspeed. There were brief mentions of the animals– 'Another stillborn calf today' – and plants – 'No bluemold on corn seedlings this season.'

Yet so much had been left out. She kept scrolling, looking for the events she remembered. Births were there, and deaths, family transfers, serious illnesses, trauma . . . but no mention of what lay behind them. From 'C. Herodis transferred from K. Botha to R. Stephanos' you would think someone had picked up a sack of personal belongings and moved across the street. Ofelia remembered the years of quarrels that had preceded Cara's departure from the Botha house. The stillborn children, the way Kostan accused her of witchcraft, the way she accused Kostan of withholding his seed for the benefit of 'that whore Linda' . . . and Linda's subsequent revenge on Cara, that had cost the colony their last remaining chickens. Reynaldo was the only man who would dare take Cara in after Kostan threw her out . . . and then she had died a half-year later, and no one had wanted to investigate too closely how someone could fall forward and hit the *back* of her head on the stone hard enough to kill.

It made no sense, to have a log that told nothing but numbers and dates. Ofelia hesitated. It had been impressed on all of them that this was the official log, that no one was to enter anything but those assigned the duty, those with training. No one would see what she did, but . . . but it could be *right*. She could know it was right.

She peered at the controls. The machine might not accept her changes. But she found the right combination; the display shifted to show only one day's entry, with an arrow pointing to a space where she could insert something.

It took most of that day to get the story of Cara and Kostan the way she wanted it. She knew how to tell stories; she knew the shape such a story should have. But to put the words down with her hands, to see them come up on the screen, that was much harder. She kept going back to explain: Kostan's mother had never liked Cara. His father had. His brother had been involved with Linda. Everything connected, everything had to be in the story, and things she could have conveyed with a wink, a tilt of the head, a shift in voice now looked clumsy and even unbelievable set down in bookwords.

When she quit, it was already dark. She had spent thirty-two days alone on the planet without noticing it, and today she had not done any of the maintenance. Her back ached; her hips hurt so much it took her a long time to stand. How did those people who worked at desks all day do it? She would not make that mistake again. She went home through a night that felt much darker, though when she looked up she could see the stars clearly. No storms tonight; the air felt mild and moist all around her body.

Her foot landed on a slimetrail, and she grunted. She hated slipping and sliding, and besides it would make her foot itch. In her own house, she showered, scrubbing at the foot, bracing herself on the wall so she wouldn't fall. She was aware that she had not worried about that before. All through supper, she could feel that she was holding something away, not letting herself think something. She scraped the plate, washed the dishes, and closed the shutters. Though it was almost too warm inside, she wanted to feel closed-in.

In bed, in the dark, she relaxed her hold on her thoughts, and let them wander. Thirty-two days. A great fear stood like a mountain on the edge of her mind. Was it coming nearer? No – the odd thing was she had already climbed over it, without even realizing the size or shape of it. This had happened before, with other fears. When she and Caitano first made love . . . when she and Humberto married . . . when the first baby forced its way out of her . . . each time, afterwards, she had been aware of a great fear not so much faced as ignored, passed without notice, without recognition. Here, too.

I was afraid. She remembered that one silent scream, forced back down her throat as if she had swallowed a child half-birthed. Now, in memory, she would have explored that mountain of her fear, but could not remember it. It stood there, vague and ominous, forever unknowable, at the end of her sight.

It was better so. Don't brood over things, her mother had always said. Don't waste time on the past; it's already gone, paper on the wind. She had meant the bad times; she also preached the value of remembering all the good.

Ofelia stretched wide on the bed in the darkness, and considered what she was feeling right now. Her left hip hurt more than the right, and her shoulders felt stiff – she would like to have had someone knead them for her. But was she afraid? No, not any more. The machines worked. The animals had not all died, and even if they did she would have food enough for years and years. She was not lonely either, not as most people meant it. She had not yet tired of the freedom from the demands others made on her. Yet the next morning, in the garden, she felt tears on her face. Why? She could not tell. The garden itself soothed her. The tomatoes, ripening day by day; one might be ready to eat this very afternoon. The green bean pods, the tall corn with its rich smell that always reminded her of Caitano's body. It was not that she wanted anyone to talk to her, but she would have liked someone to listen . . . and that thought brought her back to the machine at the center, with its log so full of data and so empty of stories.

It was too hard to put the stories down in full. It would take the rest of her life, and she would not have finished. She put clues to herself: Eva's bad headaches. Rosara's sister's birthday when the pitcher broke. How she had felt when the second flood destroyed the last of their boats, and no one could venture to the far side of the river, even in the dry season.

From these clues, she could fill in the whole story – the real story – later. She did not write every day; she wrote when she wanted to, when the memories itched worse than a slimerod trail, when she had to see them outside herself to be sure they had an end. Other days, she put only the official sort of entry, noting the readings from the machine gauges, the temperature, the rainfall, the harvest notes.

She sat on the doorstep, eating another ripe tomato. This year, she would have far more than she could eat. The noon sun lay hot on her feet; she did not move them into the shade, but slid them backwards and forwards until the sun felt exactly like hot shoes, covering just so much of her toes and insteps. Her feet were browner now that she spent longer hours in the open. So were her arms and legs. She put one hand out into the sun, admiring the bracelet she had twined, of the dayvine seed capsules. They rattled like tiny castanets. Something stung her back, and itched; she picked up the flyswitch she had made herself of a twig and fabric scraps and brushed her back with it.

These were the easy days, she knew. It would not be so easy, half a year from now. But she could not believe that. It would always be easy, thanks to the machines. If they kept running. She had checked them every day, and every day they were running, and all the gauges showed green. It must be easier for them, with only one person to maintain.

Away to the east, a bank of cloud rose to glaring turrets too bright to look at, but the bottoms had a dirty, smeared look. Sea-storms, the big storms of summer; it might rain for days. Some years they missed the colony entirely; some years they had suffered through two or three of them, losing most of a harvest. Though she usually slept in the heat of afternoon, she pushed herself to her feet, sighing, and picked up the basket. She would harvest anything ripe today, and check the machines yet again before the storm arrived.

That afternoon, fitful gusts turned the leaves of the garden plants over, showing the pale undersides. She picked steadily, moving from house to house. At each, she checked that shutters and doors were closed and barred, that toolsheds were properly secured. A skin of cloud moved across the sky, high up, changing the warm yellow of the sun to a milky glare. The air thickened; she felt breathless, stifled yet shivering from time to time with an odd chill. The house filled with baskets of ripe tomatoes, beans, peppers, squash, gourds, melons; their rich scent lay in drifts. When the first spatter of rain fell, she left off picking, and went to the center.

The barometer showed falling pressure, as she expected, and the weather warning buzzed. She shut it off, and called up the satellite display. She had not realized that it still worked, that the company had left a weather satellite aloft. Now the screen showed the cloudy spiral still offshore, the edge of the clouds just touching land. She looked at the numbers displayed on the margins of the screen, and wondered what they meant. Enough that it was a big storm, and about to engulf her. She should get the animals into the town, if she could . . . in such storms the river flooded, and the cattle could be swept away.

When she went back to the outside door, windblown rain scoured the lane, and a fine mist sprayed her when she looked out. It was almost dark; she could barely see the shapes of the buildings. She was not going out in the dark and rain to find stupid cattle who ought to have the sense to find high ground. She was going home, when the squall passed.

Between squalls, the air lay heavily around her, moist and intrusive as an unwanted lover. She splashed through the puddles, aware of odd noises from a distance. Was that oncoming wind rushing in the forest? Were those squeaks and grunts from wind-bent wood, or animals? In her own house, the scent of all those vegetables and fruits was overpowering in the damp warmth. She found a handlight, and went around the house checking the shutters, barring them with the heavy boards needed in storms. Then the kitchen door, the outside louvered door and the inside solid one. She came in through the door to the lane, and shut the louvered outer door, latching it firmly. She would leave the inner door open until later, when the wind came that way.

She had time to make more flatbread, fry onions and fresh vegetables to eat with it, and eat a peaceful supper, before the next squall came with a blast of wind that forced a draft through the kitchen door. Just try it, she thought to the storm. She and Humberto had built the house solidly, and kept it in repair. It had held in worse wind than this.

She went to bed in the squall, and fell asleep, hardly waking when one squall followed another with breathless pauses between. In the morning, no light filtered through the double shutters. She didn't need to look to know that the main storm pressed on the village now. She could hear the howl of the wind between the buildings, feel the drafts squeezed through every crevice by that immense force. She turned on the lights, glad that they still worked. They had worked in other storms, but she remembered from her childhood on another world that the power plants could fail in storms.

It was strange to feel so hot and breathless, with all

that wind outside, and those little drafts tickling her feet like mice. She made herself fix a breakfast she didn't really want, one of the golden melons from someone else's garden. She hoped she would smell it less once she had eaten it, but the cloying scent hung in the air. She could open a window on the downwind side. She went back in the bedroom, and opened the inside shutters. The smell of melon followed her, oozed past her out the window. She stepped into the corner of the room, then jumped as a bolt of lightning struck nearby, the white light spearing in through the louvers; the crack of thunder sounded as if someone had hit her head with a shovel.

She could stand the heavy smell of melon better than that. When her breath steadied, she closed the inner shutters and lay down on the bed. The bed did not feel safe enough. Reluctantly, she got up, and dragged off the bedspread and pillows. The closet would be airless, but safe from lightning. She made a nest there, and curled up.

The noise increased; the wind began to seem like a live thing, a demon determined to get to her and rip her apart. Ofelia cowered into the nest of bedclothes and pillows, trying to force herself into sleep. It didn't work; it had never worked. Every crash of thunder brought her alert, her breath short. Every new noise meant something wrong – something loose to blow against the doors and windows, something unmended that could break and let the storm in.

Phrases she had not said in years came to mind, prayers her grandmother had taught her, that she herself had said. In the storm it was easy to believe in powers and spirits. She had given all that up when she married Humberto; he had not so much forbidden it as ignored such concepts out of existence. Later, when they were trying to apply for a colony slot, he'd put 'none' in the blank for religion and Ofelia hadn't argued. Away from her family, here with others who expressed no superstitions, whatever they believed, with no structure to support her, the last of her childhood faith had frayed away to nothing.

She murmured the phrases now, stumbling over forgotten words, but comforted nonetheless. She dozed and woke in jerky alternation, miserable in the cramped stuffy closet, until she fell asleep at last, to waken in eerie silence.

Never go out in the middle of the storm. She had known that; she had always obeyed. She had made her children stay inside too, though she had heard, through the tight-shut doors, the wondering cries of other people and their children, and the scolding voices of those who sent them back inside.

Was it day or night? Was this the storm's center, or the storm's end? She peeked out of the closet and saw only the motionless rooms, lit by electricity as usual. Slowly, grumbling at the pain in her joints – always worse in these storms – she crawled out of the closet and clambered to her feet.

If it was the storm's middle, it would come back from the other way, which meant she should not open the bedroom shutters. The door to the lane, rather . . . She took one step and another across the chill, damp floor, listening for any returning threat. Far in the distance, thunder muttered. That meant nothing, either way.

She opened the inner door. It had been soaked by rain driven through the outer, louvered door. It dripped onto the floor, leaving a track of water. Now she could see that it was lighter outside. She slid the latch aside, and pushed the outer door. Rain-swollen, it did not budge until she hit it with her right hip. Even then, she had to shove hard to get it open; the little tree by the front door had blown down onto it.

Outside, a pale clear light filled the street, showing ditches abrim with moving water, and mud streaks down the lane. Ofelia looked up. Far overhead, a circle of clear blue . . . and all around, the wall of cloud, its tops brushed gold by the rising sun. Just as she'd been told, just like the pictures. But different, when she herself was out in it, her feet in the slick mud, and no one to tell it to.

She could go over to the center for the second half of the storm; she would be as safe there, or safer. But she wanted to see it come, wanted to see how fast it would come. *Dangerous.* The old voice said that, in the warning tones of her childhood. It could kill her, this storm, as easily as she swatted slidebugs or snapped slimerods. She should go back inside, hide in the closet again.

She stepped away from the house, eyeing the cloud to the east. It seemed no closer. Another few steps, and she stood in the lane, where she could look eastward down the length of it, and see that all the houses were standing. Her garden fence was down, and had taken with it all the tomatoes. Cornstalks lay flat, all pointing toward the forest. In the distance, she heard the animals.

The cloud wall looked closer, but it was hard to tell. She would like to wait until it reached the shuttle field, even the last houses at the end of the lane. Surely she could run back to the house in time. The wind would come from behind the house this time; the house itself would shield her.

She went eastward a few steps, feeling almost as naughty as when she first went naked. Then she backed up. It would be stupid to meet a sea-storm like this, in the open.

Lightning flickered, in the wall cloud; when she looked, she could see that the far side of the open space was definitely farther away, and the east side nearer.

It was so beautiful. She had always liked the pictures of such storms from space, the graceful spirals of white cloud on blue water, but she had not imagined how beautiful it could be from within. Every shade of blue and gray and purple in those walls of cloud, the gold tops now white as day brightened, the clear deep blue above. She had no words for what she felt, as the beauty contended with fear, and she took a few steps forward and then back again, in the cool mud that soothed her feet.

Then the wall of cloud loomed over her; the end of the lane vanished in a howl of water and wind, and she fled into her house, fighting through the writhing limbs of the fallen tree, as the first gust slammed against the other side of the house. That vision of silent gold and white and blue shifted in an instant to gray rain, wind, and intolerable noise.

She stood by the door, holding it open a crack, to watch. She could feel the house shudder with the wind's blows, but she had no desire now to retreat to her safe closet. Hour after hour she watched the rain stream by, watched it thrash the houses opposite. When her feet ached too much, she brought a chair near the door and sat. All day the wind and rain . . . but gradually it eased, the wind blowing less and less, the gusts more sharply separated from each other. By nightfall, squall succeeded squall again, with a steady, slower, wind between them.

The rain continued, a steady downpour. Ofelia slept that night on the bed, leaving a light on in the kitchen for no reason she could name, except it made her feel better. The room seemed breathless again, too full of the smells of the harvest, already musty from damp. She could not open the shutters in that rain, but she left the front door propped open. Her sleep was broken by dreams of water: waterfalls, rivers, tears streaming from stone faces, leaks in the roof, burst pipes. Each time she woke, certain that the dream was real, only to find herself safe in bed, and no damper than the air itself would make her.

In the morning, rain fell from high gray clouds, steadily as misery but without violence. Occasional squalls hustled past, a roil of lower, darker clouds and gusty winds, but in the east she could see a few patches of blue sky. Heat wrapped her, and moisture. She pushed her way past the fallen tree to the lane, and let the rain wash the sweat off her body. It felt warm, hardly cooler than her blood, and she put back her head and drank it in.

She could see no real damage to any of the buildings, though she did not check all of them that day. First to the center, where the essential machines had gone on as if the storm meant nothing. Perhaps it didn't mean anything to machines. The air smelled faintly of machine oil, and more strongly of damp and mold. Ofelia turned blowers on, to circulate the air in the sewing rooms. She remembered the last big sea-storm, when the needles had rusted and they had had to polish them again. In the last light, she carried across to the center the most strongly scented of the harvest. She would not have to smell melons again tonight.

That night, when a last squall shook the shutters, and bright light spiked through them, she lay in her bed and wondered why she had ever feared it. Her body felt heavy, but new, washed clean by the rain. When thunder rumbled, she felt it in her chest and belly; it shook her bones. It reminded her of Caitano.

She was a wicked old woman, and she deserved to die. The old voice scolded her, scolded her naked skin and her discoveries of herself. Beautiful, the new voice said. She had no more words than that, but the visions flashed, one after another: the dark rain, the winds, the tall clouds rising to the light.

She dreamed of castles and stars and the mountains she had never seen.

Tomatoes and corn were gone completely; most of the beans turned pale yellow and drooped: they had drowned. Along the edge of the garden, squash vines lifted ruffled fanlike leaves, unmarred by the assault of wind and water. Ofelia pushed the welter of tomato vines back off the paths, pulled the cornstalks for the compost, and went on to check other gardens. Anything tall had gone; anything low and leafy had survived. Some fruit trees still stood; others had been uprooted.

Checking the animals meant a muddy trek into the pastures. The sheep had drifted before the first onslaught of the storm into the brushy edge between grassland and forest; she found their muddy track. She followed it, and found most of them, fleeces water-logged, nibbling dispiritedly at the native vegetation. She drove them back to grass with a stick, wondering again why the gengineers had done nothing about sheep stupidity. Surely any animal so stupid that it would gnaw on brush it could not digest, rather than follow its own trail back to good pasture, needed some improvement.

The cattle grazed nearer to town than usual, since the river had begun to flood. She would have driven them nearer yet, but they could wade in water too deep for her, and when she tried to move them, a small group fled splashing into the water where two of them lost their footing, and were swirled away downstream, lowing miserably.

Ofelia glared at the cattle. They deserved to be drowned, to be eaten by monsters, to be marooned on a sandbar with no grass. She had only tried to help them. They were too much like people, that was their problem. Run from help, run to danger. She pulled her feet out of the muck with the determination not to risk herself again for beasts so ungrateful, and splashed back into the village.

The next day, more showers, mixed with hot, steamy sun. She thought of writing her feelings about the storm in the log, but she didn't want to struggle with the words. Yet she wanted to do something; she felt restless. In the center, the bright scraps in the sewing rooms drew her. No one had bothered to decorate the fabric boxes for travel; she found drawers full of decorative braid, beads, fringes, short runs on the fabricator which had, most likely, not been approved by the supervisors.

She couldn't find what she wanted. She looked in the manual for the fabricator. She wanted rain and wind and lightning, clouds and sunlight above them. Noise. Beauty. Destruction. She pushed buttons and set gauges. The fabricator squealed, as it always did on startup, and emitted a wrinkled strand of silvery-gray, followed by crinkly purple material. Ofelia took it out of the fabricator's bin, and laid it with the other scraps on the tables. Her fingers shifted this shape and that, this color and that, played texture against texture, and matte against glitter.

By dark she had . . . something. She wrapped herself in it, unsure. It felt right. Heavy here, light there. Long fringes rippling and tickling her legs. She had sewn metal shapes, rings and arcs, so they rang together. When she looked in the long mirrors, it was no garment she recognized, but it looked the way she had seen it in her mind. She wore it home, in the thick moist dark, and slept in it.

That was the only sea-storm of the summer. She added a check of the weather screen to her daily chores. Day by day she tracked two other sea-storms, that came to land hundreds of kilometers away. Her weather returned to the usual late-summer heat and sun, with one or two afternoon rainstorms a week. She cleared the gardens of storm debris, and planned which to use for winter gardens this year. She cut and dried the tomatoes she'd harvested, blanched and froze the beans. Some of the squash would store in the center's cool rooms; some she cut in strips to dry. The peppers, onions, and garlic went on strings, which she hung in the center's cooler, breezy rooms.

Then it was time to plant the late garden. For the first time, Ofelia really missed the others, when she struggled with the smallest of the tillers. She had never done the tilling herself; one of the strongest colonists had usually tilled for the whole community, trading that work for credits on the others. She got the little tiller out of the storage shed, but rolling it up the gently sloping lane to her house made her breathless and sweaty; her shoulders and hips hurt already.

When she turned the machine on, the loud raucous noise hurt her ears, and the machine dug itself a hole. She had to bounce all her weight on the handles to get the spinning tines up, and then she could not push it straight. She had made irregular grooves and holes in about a third of her garden when she quit in disgust. Her hands stung; she hurt all over. Her ears still rang from the noise. When she had rested, she rolled the tiller back down the lane. She would not leave it outside to rust; she had that much justice. But if she could have found the designers of such machines, she would have given them an earful. Why not make a machine that small people could use? A quiet machine? The next day, she took the fork and shovel from the toolshed, and began to turn the soil by hand. It wasn't so hard, if she went slowly. She would not try to prepare all the gardens; she needed much less space. Then she took the garden cart, and went out into the pastures to pick up dung. Even with all the rain, some of it had not melted into the soil; she found enough to mix with the soil, adding the terran bacteria and fungi the plants needed.

The winter crops included more roots and tubers: onions again, but also carrots, radishes, beets, potatoes, yams, leeks. Leafy vegetables, that could not stand the hot summer sun. And the heat-shunning legumes. With a choice of all the colony's seedstocks, Ofelia planted more of the ones she liked best: Tina peas and Barque lettuce, long white snowdrop radishes, yellow potatoes, Cardonnean parsnips. She planted the others as well, to freshen the seedstocks, but in less abundance.

With the planting done, she spent more time at the center, reading and revising the old logs again. She had almost forgotten Molly Suppert until she ran across the death notice: poor Molly, who had not been part of the original colony, but an assigned special technician. For five years, Molly had run the health clinic alone, as she trained her replacements from among the colonists. She was supposed to have been evacuated after five years, but when the ship came, Molly was dead.

Ofelia had never known what world Molly came from, but they had all known it was someplace strange, if its inhabitants had been anything like Molly, with her bone-white skin and yellow-green eyes, her orange frizzy hair.

And her attitudes. It had been Molly who suggested that
girls need not marry so young, that children need not be
slapped into obedience. If she had stuck to giving immu-
nizations and pregnancy tests, and teaching midwives how
to use the diagnostic machines, she would not have been
found with a knife in her neck out behind the center.

It had taken considerable work to make it appear that
she had fallen on a scythe while chasing cattle down by
the river, and Ofelia had wondered if the Company really
believed that. She had rather liked Molly, although she
had not been foolish enough to confide in her, like the
younger girls. It was all very well to say those things Molly
had said, but the world was the way it was, and had always
been, slapped children and all.

In the log, she added what she remembered about
Molly. She had never known for sure who killed her, and
she wasn't about to accuse without certainty. But the sun
in her frizzy hair, that she put down, the way it glowed
in a halo around her head as if she were a saint, but she
wasn't a saint because she cursed vividly in two languages.
At least, Ofelia supposed that from the tone and vigor
with which she spoke in her native tongue, whatever it
was. She remembered none of the words; she had never
really understood.

FIVE

It had been so long that when she heard the voices she did not know what they were. They sounded alien as the shrieks and squawks that came from the distant forest. She stood still in the street, her heart pounding. What? Where?

Her ears led her to the center, to the control rooms, where one of the gray boxes emitted a gabble that her brain finally sorted into words. She stared at the box for some time before realizing that it was not speaking to her, and it was not the machines speaking to the human caretakers they expected.

'Correct your course, eighteen-six-forty one—' The speaker had an accent different enough that she had to strain to follow it, but it was the language she knew. A male voice. A voice she could tell was used to command.

'Done,' said another voice. 'Shuttle One Sapphire, correcting. Get a six-oh-two and a thirty-twelve.' A hiss and crackle, then, '—Any sign of the other colony?'

'Sticks out on infrared like a blasted beacon,' said the first voice. 'The boundary between terraformed and indigenous vegetation looks stable. Shuttle field. Some buildings. Why? We aren't going near it.'

'Just wondered. They—' *Hiss, crackle.*

A longish pause, then: 'Well, we haven't made that mistake,' from the first voice. 'They were idiots to pick a tropical site anyway. I heard that they retrieved fewer colonists than they inserted.' A pause, as if someone had asked a question, though Ofelia couldn't hear anything but the open, soft hissing. 'No, not renegades – that many losses. Poor chills. Not like ours.'

Ofelia sat, hardly aware of the sudden cold sweat that ran down her ribs. Shuttle? Coming down? Chills? Colonists?

They would find her. They would find her and send her away, back to space, to some cryo tank . . . or, almost as bad, they would expect her to join them. They would expect her to fit her schedule to theirs, to do what she was told.

Her heart fluttered; she felt shaky and cold. She did not want that; she did not want to be caught, caged, ordered here and there. She tried to think what she could do. Move into the forest again? She might have the time to gather more things, but she could not live in the forest; she could not eat anything that grew there.

She went outside and looked up. Of course she could see nothing. The sky was a pale blue dome streaked with white clouds. If a ship hung up there in orbit, she could not see it. Could it see her? Unlikely, she thought, in daylight. But at night?

She could not turn on the lights. Although she had chosen to do without them many a summer evening, now she felt confined by the dark. She had things to do, if she was going to escape, and she needed the light. She sat in the dark that night, peering up at the stars. Could they see her even without light? Infrared . . . that was heat, she remembered; the colonists had once had goggles for seeing animals in the dark, but over the years these had failed.

So the spaceship up there might see her anyway, would certainly see the heat plume of the waste recycler. Would they believe it had been working by itself since the other colony left? That someone had merely forgotten to turn off the automatics?

After the months alone, it was hard to fit her thoughts to the shape someone else's mind might make. If it were Barto up there, what would he be thinking? How long until the shift is over . . . when is it my turn . . . is supper ready?

Dawn woke her; she had fallen asleep sitting against the wall, and her neck hurt. Her eyes felt gummy. She stretched slowly, painfully, and finally levered herself up beside the wall. Inside the center, it was just light enough to find her way from room to room. She went into the offices, and stared at the gray box, from which no voices came. Just as she began to wonder if she'd dreamed it, it crackled again and the voices resumed.

'Local sunrise,' said another male voice. Ofelia wondered where they were; the sun would not rise here for another hour. East of her? Only the sea lay to the east, unless you traveled far to the north. She flicked on the weather screen, which generated a map of the continent, showing the dawn-line. Somewhere along that line was the place they'd landed. It had to be over a thousand kilometers away.

Perhaps they would never find her. They would be too busy. In all the forty years of this colony, none of them had ventured more than a few kilometers from the base. They had planned to go farther, but things happened. She might be safe yet.

'Eight-eight will drop the heavies in two.'

'On it.'

Ofelia spent that day hunched over the receiver, following the invasion – she could not help thinking of it like that – in the half-understood comments. She remembered enough of her own landing to know the necessary sequence. The first shuttles could land without prepared ground; they carried the mechbots that scraped out a shuttle field. Then the main cargo shuttles could land, with the construction crews that quickly set up the temporary structures for storage and surfaced the strip. Finally, the passenger shuttles, with the newly-wakened colonists, in order of specialty. She imagined another woman like her young self, waking from the cryo tank, trying to comfort her children as they were revived, trying to keep them calm as they were herded into a shuttle . . . they had landed in the rain, she remembered, and Barto had screamed and butted his hard round head into her breast.

But that would be later. Today, somewhere east and north, the hard shuttles were unloading mechbots, and the big construction machines were gouging the native plants – she wondered if it was forest or brush up there – to make a longer landing strip.

That night, she went back to her house to sleep, trusting that she would hear any shuttle landing at the nearby field. She didn't turn any lights on – that would be stupid, as long as she knew a ship hung up there, watching. But it would leave, eventually, and the colonists would have hard work to do in their own place. Then she could turn the lights on. She began to be sure that they would not find her. She had heard them say that the tropical site had been a stupid choice; that should mean they wouldn't want to explore that way. And by the time they did – in ten or twenty years, in thirty years or forty – she would be safely dead.

They might read the colony logs – her additions to them, as well. It made her grin, lying there in the darkness, to think of them reading the truth, the stories of real people, instead of the official version, all dates and names.

'Pass six. On course.' Just like all the others, Ofelia thought. Five passenger shuttles had already landed; she had listened less tensely than before. Clearly no one was paying any attention to the site of an abandoned colony they had no use for. She had even left the center to tend the gardens, to cook and eat her meals, to sleep in her own comfortable bed. Although she had started to assemble a survival pack to take into the forest, she had not finished it. Now she relaxed in a chair in the sewing room, with the volume up high on the radio as she strung the beads she'd painted.

'Cleared to land.' A new voice, no doubt one of the colonists with special training, wakened first and put to work as soon as she landed. Ofelia tried to picture the woman in her mind. Young, of course. Did she have children? She sounded earnest, someone very serious about her work. If she had children, their clothes would always be neat. Ofelia looked at the pattern of beads she was making, and decided to put another blue one between the greens. That meant sliding off a yellow and a green; she squinted at the thread. 'We've got trouble,' she heard. The voice was trying to stay calm, and not succeeding. Ofelia looked up, half-expecting to see someone in the doorway talking to her. No. It was still in the gray box, happening somewhere else, whatever it was.

'What?' Bored, unworried response from the orbiting ship.

'There's some kind of – it's – there's not supposed to be any intelligent life, but that's—'

'Make sense, will you?'

'There's about a hundred or so big . . . brownish animals. Moving toward us. In formation. Bright patterns on them, and some kind of—' A noise Ofelia did not recognize, though it sounded dangerous, a noise her body understood before her brain could analyze it. '—They're trying to *kill*—' Incredulity from that voice. Ofelia felt the same way. Something – some animals – trying to kill them? Ridiculous! Storms, yes, floods and droughts and fevers, but not animals. Nothing capable of real damage had attacked the original colony in forty years; the planet had been surveyed; they were crazy up there.

She put down the beads and went into the control room. If these people were transmitting video as well as audio, she might be able to see them. She tried one channel after another, but found no images. She would have to listen.

Even her imagination could not make it clear. What the creatures were, no one seemed to know. More than one voice, in the next hours, said they were big. More than one exclaimed over their speed. How big was big? How fast was fast? Ofelia no more than those who actually saw them could guess if they were more like mammals or reptiles, how intelligent they were.

However intelligent, the creatures seemed determined to kill the colonists. Ofelia hunched over the speakers, listening to the now-familiar sounds: she had heard from the voices that this was an explosive, and that was the impact of stones hurled by some kind of machine. People were dead already, killed by the falling stones, the explosions. Only a few of the people had weapons. Some of them cowered in the shuttle presently on the ground; the pilot asked permission to return to space.

'You're overloaded for return – unload your cargo—'

'—Can't. They won't go out – we can make it—'

'Marginal. You've got to—'

'If they blow a hole in the strip, we won't have a chance; we have to go now—' No answer, but Ofelia heard the pilot mutter. 'Damned idiots – c'mon Tig, get that booster primed, we're going to need every bit of it—'

Then an explosion that hurt Ofelia's ears even attenuated by distance and the speakers' dampers. A few seconds of silence, then a call from the ship.

'—Come in – Carver, answer!'

'—Too late, you bastards – they got the shuttle and the strip!' That from one of the other local sources. Ofelia felt a pressure in her chest. The creatures had blown up a *shuttle*? 'Get us *out* of here!'

'Three hours until another shuttle can make it.' A new voice from the ship, older, with more authority. 'That will be after local sunset . . . they'll need lights for landing. We've put every trained person aboard—'

'In three hours, we won't be here to save!' the voice said. 'Lights – how can we – Dammit, do something *now*! These things are coming in – we can't—'

Ofelia felt wetness on her face and tasted it. Tears. She was crying for them, for the hopeless, helpless colonists, waked from cryo to be killed on a planet they had not even met. It was far worse than her own fate, far worse than working forty years for nothing. She knew, as they would learn, that Company ships hanging safe in space never risked themselves down in the dirty atmosphere for mere colonists. Cheaper to lose a few colonists than a deep-space carrier.

'We don't have any space-to-surface weapons,' the ship's voice said. 'Recommend you lay out a defensive perimeter—'

'With what?' The bitterness in that made Ofelia wince. 'I'll leave this on transmit, and you can get your precious record – tell whoever surveyed this place they were blind, deaf, and crazy—'

Ofelia hardly breathed as the distant sounds made clear what happened. The creatures overran the landing site; Ofelia could hear screaming, most of it incoherent, and sounds she supposed were made by the creatures themselves. The last sound transmitted was the thud, then crunch, of something knocking over and squashing the transmitter. Ofelia went outside; it was dusk, dusk of the same day. She heard a distant roar, then a crashing boom: a shuttle coming down fast, not on the course of the others.

She went back inside to listen. The shuttle crew was reporting to the orbiting ship. 'Visible light, yes. Thermal profile suggests burning debris, not any civilized source of light. Lots of infrared – thousands, tens of thousands of whatever-they-are. Recording in all frequencies. It's – Gods, look at that! Get us UP, Shin!'

And, over a gabble of returning questions from the ship, '—No doubt at all they're intelligent. Tool-users, absolutely. No way we can set down there in the dark. In the morning—'

'—Make a full report to the Ministry,' the calm voice from the ship said. 'A daylight survey, high-altitude. No use risking more lives. The Company can get a refund, I'm sure, on grounds of misrepresentation by the former franchise holder, and let the pols decide if they want to send a diplomatic expedition. Not our problem.'

'—consider old colony landing site?'

'No. If there's an indigenous intelligent species, the rules have changed. We won't touch it; we'll report. If your data are good enough, we won't even bother with the daylight survey. We've got the direct transmissions from the landing site, anyway.'

'I'd like to know how they missed this – these what-evers.'

'Not our problem.'

Ofelia had heard that tone before. Whoever it was up there in the safe, air-conditioned space ship, never considered it his problem when people were dying somewhere else. Her lip curled. She would like to tell him what she thought. The transmission switch suddenly caught her eye; she had not even considered it before. Now, though; if she could hear them, they could hear her. If she spoke.

It would do no good. It would only get her in trouble.

For a day or so, she could believe nothing had changed. The threat was gone; the new colony didn't exist. If the creatures had not found her in over forty years, why would they now? She could go on as before, living peacefully in the deserted village, stringing beads, playing with paints, gardening the small amount necessary to grow her own food.

Resolutely, she walked out among the animals, strolled the margin of the grassy pastures. In the sun, in the haze of pollen blown from the flowering grass, she could pretend nothing had happened. The sun warmed her shoulders; the sheep smelled like sheep, and the cattle . . . the cattle wagged their ears at her, snuffed with wet black noses, and edged away. The bull huffed, swinging his head back and forth. Not at her. At something across the river.

They were no more nervous than usual. She told herself that even as her breath came short and the back of her neck itched. She went back to the sheep, telling herself they were more restful, and then all of them jerked their heads up at once, staring at one point in the forest where she saw and heard nothing at all.

Sheep were stupid. Cattle were flighty. Ofelia glared at the forest, and went back to her garden. It was only accident that she kept ending up in the corner nearest the kitchen, hoeing the same bit of ground, staring across the tangle of dayvines on the fence she had never quite mended at the pasture and the brush beyond it.

Perhaps she had dreamed the whole thing. She had heard, in school, that no one could live long alone without going crazy, without thinking they heard and saw other people. She had never believed it, but she had been told. So if she had gone crazy, without noticing it, she could have imagined the whole thing. The other ship had never really come, and nothing had happened to it. Why she had imagined such a gruesome fate for its colonists she did not know; it must be some evil streak in her, probably the same one that made her decide to stay here alone.

That idea, once rooted, bore tempting fruit: it would be easy to find out the truth. The machines would have recorded the transmissions, if there had been transmissions. All she had to do was play them back. Or play back nothing, and know she had made it all up.

She knew what she knew; she didn't need any machine to tell her the truth. Day after day, she went into the center to check the gauges, the weather, to record the necessary items in the log. Day after day, she eyed the machine records and did not play them back.

It was, in the end, an accident. She had meant to check the date she'd planted carrots the year before. Something interrupted; her finger slipped off the control that reversed the calendar search.

'—With what?' asked a frightened, angry voice that was not her own.

It was real. It had happened. The machines did not lie,

could not lie, and that meant the voice on the tape had been a real person, real in fright and pain.

And now was dead. She began to shake without realizing it; her hands and then her arms, her feet and then her legs, her whole body, shaking with the same fear, with the same shock. They had been human – people she could have known, could have talked to – and now they were all dead.

With shaking hands, she fumbled over the controls until she turned the recording off. Silence rushed in on her, the silence she had grown used to, that she had thought of as peace. No voices. No voices anymore.

Slowly, slowly, her breath steadied. She felt tired; she wanted to go to sleep. When she looked at her hands, with their red, swollen knuckles and knotted veins and age spots, they looked more fragile than flowers. Her gaze slid downwards, caught on the fringed drape she had made for herself. It seemed more indecent than her body; she yanked it off as she stood, balled it in her hands and threw it on the floor.

'They're dead!' she said aloud, in a voice she hardly remembered using. Her mind divided like water running down a slope: she wondered why she was outraged, she wondered why she was afraid, why she was not more afraid. She would not have killed them, those strangers, though she had not wanted them here.

She went outside again, into another day that insisted on being like any other. Again it was hot, humid, the sky clotted with clouds moving slowly before a steady wind. Why did it matter if they were all dead? They had come; they had gone; she was alone again, and she had wanted to be alone.

It was not the same.

It would never be the same.

Something – no, some*one*, some creatures – lived on this world that wanted to kill her – that had killed humans – and she had not known any such danger existed. She could not unknow it, struggle though she might.

The air stank of strange smoke; a grassfire burned on in the distance, its smoke plume mourning the nests. Though the grass would return and cover the nakedness of the land with her shawl, the People would always know where the scars were. This smell would last.

Defeat, drummed the righthand. Not defeat, victory they are gone and we are here, drummed the lefthand. One by one, the righthand changed places, until the lefthand drumming carried all the power of the People.

Far above, a sinuous white streak where the monster had flown, scarring the very air. The righthand reminded that generations ago such streaks had been seen far off to the south. The lefthand continued drumming Victory, victory, safety, haven, return.

The scar in the sky blew away to nothing. No more monster noises from the air, no more bad smells. The People danced, winding around the burnt earth, sending out a long spiral coil of dancers to find live sprigs of grass, passed from one to another inward, until the site had been replanted. They danced on, drumming and dancing, until the wind drums answered, until the sky people gathered to dance in their own coils and spirals, weeping at the monster tracks, filling them with sweet tears that nourished the grass.

On the move again after the rain, following the wind drums across the grass, laden with the gourds of sky-light-maker, drum-beater, the youngest troop of the People called questions to each other. Why scars in the sky? Why monsters in gray and green? Why flat-faced? Why wingless, toeless—

Not toeless, one called back. Short-toed, foot-clothed in toeless garments.

Garments, not shells?

Not shells, garments.

None without them . . . shells.

No flesh-bond. Garments.

Then – the sky creatures also garments? A lively debate followed, whether the stinking corpses of great flyers had been shells or garments or separate creatures, allies of the monsters. One held out for machines, no more than complicated mechanisms like those of the stone-tossers. The others laughed scornfully. A city tale, something the shore-dwellers thought up when their brains were smoke-dimmed. Machines could not fly . . . who could draw the strings tightly enough to have the wings flap.

Those wings did not flap.

That we saw.

It could work. The same enthusiast; they knew that eager-ness for machines. The People had good machines; they were proud of this enthusiast. It could work, but it would need a new idea. They loped on, silent now. Never distract someone on the path of a new idea; it is like distracting a hunter on the trail of game, and means missing a feast.

The enthusiast fell behind; they knew what that meant. A time of sitting still, a time of seeking out other enthu-siasts, a time of playing with sticks and little stones and sinew, and eventually there would be a new machine, something no one had ever seen. It did not concern the rest of them until then.

If there are others, someone called, free now to call.

Others? Where?

The legends. The sky-scars. Somewhere south. Others. Allies of allies, allies of monsters.

All alert, they crowded around. More monsters? More nest-burners, nest-scrapers? More thieves and children of thieves? It would be broodseasons before the nests just replanted were ready for young again; in the meantime they would have to nest elsewhere, which meant unfriendly seasons contesting for marginal sites with the others who roamed the grasslands. And would they come back, eager for the great nestmass, only to find more monsters?

An elder troop overheard their keening and swept them up. No monsters had been seen after that earlier sky-scar. Chances were it had been a scouting raid, no more.

No one ever looked.

Many broodseasons. Monsters are hasty. No need. No one ever looked. That from a youngling as enthusiastic this way as the machine-enthusiast had been. They all knew that, as they all knew everything about each other.

Too far. The desert. The thornbrush. Then too wet, and trees too tall. Worse than cities. The final insult, strong enough to discourage anyone but this youngling, who had the hunter's own determination to follow any trail where it led.

Stinking trail, one of the oldest finally said. No good at the end. Empty belly, can't eat monsters.

They had tried, only to be spectacularly sick in the burnt grass.

Nestmass, said one of the shy younglings. Many grumbled at that. If the shy ones started, the whole People might turn aside, and that at a time when new nests must come first.

Go . . . drummed the lefthand, passing the drumming from troop to troop on that flank, and then through the center. Go, go, go. Seek, seek. Take enough, but not too many.

After nesting? The youngling troop were not that eager to wander into dryness and salt and thorn and then swamp and tall trees for inedible monsters.

Now go, drummed the lefthand. Now, now, now. GO.

The youngling troop split, and split again. The enthusiast, not so enthusiastic now, but like any hunter intrigued with a new quarry. The shy youngling, only a broodseason from needing a nest. A few more of the raucous type which the older troops were glad enough to see leaving. And the elders who, on second or third thought decided that it might be an adventure, who had heard about the fishing on that more southern coast, who had a relative who had seen the sky-scar. With them, in the gourds and sacks and pouches of a nomad People, went their knowledge, their skills. However far they went, however long it took, the People relished travel, relished the chance to learn, the flavor and fiber of novelty.

As they went they discussed the monsters, reminding each other of every last detail, all that had been seen, heard, smelt, tasted (ugh! that disgusting flavor, turning the belly), surmised. Inbrooders, like the grasseaters they hunted? Likely. Two-formed, one with sticks and one with holes. Two-everything, except where on the ends of arms and legs the little bits stuck out in fives. Odd number, fives. Sacred to some, mostly fisheaters. How well could they see with those two eyes in the flat face? Well enough to aim fire tubes; they'd noticed that. Flaps on the side of the head: might be ears. Or tasters. Little ones big-headed, otherwise similar. Only a few little ones, most big ones. Big ones all dark-hairy on top, shades of earth-color. They passed the images back and forth. Yes. They would all know a monster if they saw one again.

The question of sense took longer. The monsters had sense enough to recognize threat, but so had most creatures, even the very stupid. Quick response meant nothing; the People knew that Carriers had little sense, although they responded quickly to anything, even training. Some of those things had been machines, some very large machines, but how hard was it to build a machine to carry dirt? Any child could do that.

It moved on its own.

It didn't. It had a spell cast on it.

It didn't. A monster guided it.

Who saw? The answer to that quelled all doubt; a monster had guided the machine that moved the dirt (and the nests! Filthy thieves!) and although no one had seen the twisted sinew or string, it must have been in there somewhere.

We should have looked harder.

Machine-lovers look at machines.

They would, too. That distraction shrugged off, they went back to considering whether monsters had sense. Had they known they were robbing nests? How could they not, with the People's sigil in plain view, the braids and coils of grass that warned of nestmass and named the nest guardians. If they were not blind, they must have seen. If they had sense, they must have understood.

The arguments went back and forth, across the open grass, until someone scented game, and drummed a short signal.

SIX

Loneliness weighed on Ofelia like stones. She struggled through each day, forcing herself to work in the gardens, forcing herself to check on the animals. Too many times she came back to herself and found that she'd stopped what she was doing to stand gape-mouthed, rigid, listening for sounds she knew she could not hear.

She didn't understand it. It hadn't been like this when the others left, her own son and daughter-in-law, people she had known most of her life. Then she had felt free. Then the empty streets and the quiet houses had given her chances she had never had before. Then no voices had been welcome, and over the days even the memory of them had fallen away, leaving her mind at peace.

Now she felt trapped, confined in a narrower place than she remembered. The empty streets might be full of enemies; the quiet houses gave hiding place to her fears. She could not forget the strange voices, voices of people she had never seen, crying out for help, crying out in fear and pain. And death.

She had not cried long when Humberto died, or the children. She had not cried at the thought of her own death; death was death, and it came to all, and there was no help for it. But now she cried, feeling the wobbling of her face, the wet tears, the runny nose, the spittle that ran down her chin – the ungraceful tears of the old – for people she had never seen, and had not wanted to see. They had come so far to die, and she had not wanted them.

It made no sense. When the tears finally ran out, she wiped her face with a rag – it had been a scrap of fabric from the center, carried home without noticing – and peered into the street. Nothing. Yesterday and the day before and the day before that, nothing, and nothing would be there tomorrow or the day after or the day after that. She lived in the center of nothing, in a moment always suspended between the eternity behind and the eternity before. It had never bothered her, and now it did.

Slowly, as slowly as the retreat of pain from a serious injury, the loneliness wore itself out. The fear remained. Something had killed all those people, and would kill her if it found her. She had been ready enough to die alone on this world, when she chose to stay. But she had believed age would kill her, or accident. Not malice.

She felt fragile, exposed, helpless. There were a few weapons in the storehouses, but she knew they would not save her. No one could be alert all the time; she was human, she had to eat and sleep and use the toilet. One person alone, even with the help of all the machines, was not a human presence. If those things found her, they could kill her easily. She had no doubt they would, as quickly as they had killed dozens of people younger and stronger.

But the fear wore itself out too, more slowly than loneliness. Days at a time she managed to forget – not trying, but simply immersed in the irregular routines of her life.

They had not found her yet. They had not killed her yet. And she still enjoyed things, and still wanted things.

She retrieved the beads she had dropped from under the sewing tables, and strung them again. She made and painted more beads, added the slimerod cores she had dried, the seed pods of this plant, tufts of long hair from cows' tails caught in brush . . . she wasn't sure what she was making, only that she liked the patterns of chunky things and thin ones, color and texture and line. When she put the construction on her body, she realized it needed a bit more here – another length of beads – and something else there to balance the weight and keep it from slipping off her shoulders. She looked in the mirror. Odd how seldom she'd done that, not since before the other landing. She had not wanted to see her expression; she had been afraid that she might frighten herself. But now the figure in the mirror hardly looked human.

She stared. She felt the same – mostly the same – and in the mirror her own face scowled at her, the familiar scowl with which she had always greeted her mirror-self. Her eyebrows were thinner and whiter; her white hair a tousled bush of silver. But the inner self that had been so intent on stringing beads and feathers and wool and cows' hair and seedpods, that had been so sure where to lace this string to that, and how to hang the tassels – that self had not imagined how she would look in anything but the old drab workshirts and skirts and bonnets of earlier years.

Indecent, the old voice said. Amazing, the new voice said, with approval. Her body was old, wrinkled, sagging, splotched with the wear-marks of nearly eighty years . . . but hanging on it in weblike patterns were the brilliant colors and textures of her creation. When she shifted her weight from her sore hip, the whole mass swayed, as if she were the breeze. The big beads across the back rolled in the hollow of her back, comforting. The plant fibers she'd used across her shoulders scratched itches she always found it hard to reach.

She stood looking a long time, then carefully took the garment off. It would not be comfortable for many of the things she needed to do, but she liked the way it felt. She would wear it often, she knew. In the meantime, she tied on the wrap she now wore most of the time, and made herself grin into the mirror. Rosara would not have approved of this, which left her legs bare, which had nothing underneath it but her raddled skin. Defiantly, thinking of Rosara, she stuck a finger in the pot of red paint she had used on the beads, and streaked it across her chest. Black paint: spots on her cheeks, on her forehead, on the sides of her thighs. Blue: a narrow line down her nose. She began to giggle; she had not imagined how much fun it could be to treat her body as the material of art. She made green hand-prints on her belly, on the front of her thighs, one each on buttocks. She splashed yellow on hands and feet. Then, leaving yellow footprints, she walked out into the street, unafraid, unthinking, for the first time.

It was drizzling, a warm drizzle that hovered as much as fell. Ofelia walked up and down the street, touching the doors of the houses she passed, leaving hand-prints splotched yellow and green. Suddenly she wanted to mark them all; she ran back into the center, snatched up the pot of yellow paint, and strode from house to house, touching every door. By the time she was halfway through, it was more than a game; fear returned in a rush, demanding that she finish, insisting that something dire would come if she stopped for anything, if she were interrupted, if the paint ran out before the last door was marked with her sigil. Breathless, her legs aching, she ran from door to door, house to house, even the toolsheds, the storage sheds, the waste recycler, back to the center, every door in the center . . .

The panic subsided. Thunder muttered outside, and the drizzle thickened to rain. She remembered other times of strange feelings before storms, forebodings, crazy feelings, wild actions. It was just the storm. When it was over, she would feel better.

Wind slapped harder rain against the center windows. Ofelia looked down at her decorated body, and laughed. What a mess. She couldn't go to bed like this. The rain would wash off the paint. She went outside and let the warm rain flow over her, scrubbing at her spots and stripes with her yellow hands, until she stood in a rainbow puddle. How odd that the colors didn't merge into one muddy mess . . . for a moment her mind caught on that oddity, as the colors avoided each other and made rings and blotches on the ground. Then a closer peal of thunder sent her dashing across to her own hand-marked door. Warm rain it might be, but she felt cold now.

Inside, she dried herself and began humming. Memories of childhood naughtiness tumbled through her mind. Mudpies, messes in the kitchen, the time she had used colored chalk to make her sister's foot look swollen and infected . . . they had both thought it was funny, but her mother had been first scared, then furious. Her cheeks felt hot even now, remembering the slapping she'd gotten for that. Silly, silly, silly . . . she had been a silly child, and she was a silly old woman, but it had been fun. Painting herself had been fun, and she would do it again. Why not? If she was going to be killed by some strange animals, she might as well have what fun she could first.

After the storm, the cattle were unsettled. Ofelia squinted across the meadow to the river, trying to count the restless animals. Fourteen . . . no, thirteen, she had counted the red one with the black face twice . . . no, fourteen, because there was the rusty-black one with the white spot. And the bull. She couldn't see the calves in the tall grass. The sun was out; she had put on a wide hat tied with a long narrow piece of pink, and a blue cape beaded with green and yellow in flower patterns. She didn't like it that much now, but that meant she didn't mind if it got dirty while she hunted for the cattle.

One of the cows shied and broke into a bouncing trot away from the river; two more followed, moving faster. Ofelia caught a glimpse of a calf's head between the cows, then the rest of the little herd lunged away from the river, grunting. The bull swung around to confront whatever had spooked them. Ofelia could see nothing. Halfway to the buildings, the cattle slowed and milled uneasily. Ofelia walked past the calf pen, angling upriver where the dust wasn't so bad. The cattle watched her now, ears wide; the bull moved away from the river to rejoin the herd. She counted again: black-faced red cow, solid red cow, rusty black, brindle with white spot, plain brindle, red-and-white, rusty black with white spot . . . fourteen cows, one bull, at least one calf. From a distance she heard others, probably the younger bulls, who ran in a clump together.

She really needed to know how many calves there were. She angled nearer the herd, not directly at it. A dark red calf, paired with the black-faced red cow. And there, another one, brindle with white legs, beside one of the brindle cows. The cows shook their heads; she kept her distance, trying to see between bodies and legs and wide ears. Was that another? Yes – a lighter red calf, tucked into the middle. Ofelia walked back to the village, keeping an eye on the cows to be sure none of them charged her. The black-faced red cow had a bad temper.

On the far side of the buildings, the sheep were grazing peacefully, the lambs scattered like bundles of wool, sunning themselves. Ofelia walked out among them, rubbing the hard little heads and noticing that none of them had disappeared in the past few days. In the forest, something screeched, the usual midday screech that she had learned to ignore. Even the sheep ignored it, hardly twitching their ears. One of the lambs woke, lifting its head. It looked around, shook its ears, and rolled over, then folded and unfolded its legs quickly and stood, emitting a faint bleat. One of the ewes looked up and replied; the lamb gamboled over to its mother and began nursing. Within a minute or two, the other lambs were up and nursing too.

Back among the buildings, she noticed that the rain had not obliterated all her wild handprints on the doors. Some were still bright, unblurred; others had half-melted away, clearly dissolved by falling water. One looked smeared. Ofelia stared at it – how had that happened? How had something stroked across it, almost like another hand wiping it out . . . ?

A gusty breeze billowed her cape out behind her, and she laughed at herself. She had been wild and crazy, dancing around; it had been wet. She had certainly done it herself, in her haste. She had slipped, and put out her own hand . . . slowly, she raised her hand to the smear. The right height, perhaps, if she'd slipped in the wet. If she'd caught herself there, it could have happened. She didn't remember it, but she did remember slipping and sliding a lot as she hurried from house to house, desperate to mark all the doors.

She felt cold anyway. She wanted the sun on her shoulders. She took off the blue cape, and folded it over her arm, untied the hat and held it in her hand. The sun's heat eased her, calmed her. It was all right. The animals were all right, and she was safe, and she would take a long nap this afternoon. In fact – she looked around. She had long since slept in other beds than the one she thought of as 'her own.' On a day like this, with the wind in this quarter, her own bedroom would be muggy and unpleasant. Two houses down, though, she knew of an east-side bedroom with two windows. Since she opened the houses only when she was in them, it would have stayed shady and cool in the morning.

On this door, the yellow hand-print had dripped only a little. Ofelia pushed the door open and went inside, leaving it open behind her. Dim light came from the shuttered windows; she smelled a faint mustiness. She really should air the houses out more often, she thought. She opened the bedroom shutters and felt the mattress on the bed. Not damp at all; something else must have been damp. Possibly clothes left in a closet. She tried to remember whose house this had been, but she wasn't sure. On this side of the settlement, some houses had been lost to the two big floods; people who survived the flood had insisted on moving to the higher side, and younger people moved into the rebuilt houses.

Not that it mattered now. Ofelia lay down on the bed and stretched. While she liked the familiar hollows and humps of her own mattress, it was sometimes nice to sleep on a different one. Her hips felt a little too high, her shoulders a little too low, but she was tired enough to doze off anyway. When she woke, the light outside had a pearly quality; the sun must have gone down. She was aware that she had been dreaming, a vivid dream involving colors and music and movement, but it vanished so fast that she could not retrieve any of it. She stretched again, and stood up slowly. Again that musty smell; her nose wrinkled. Perhaps she should leave the lights on in this house, to dry it out.

She closed the shutters, turned on the lights, and went out, shutting the door behind her. In the twilight, colors and shapes seemed to float, unrelated to daytime geometry. Ofelia blinked, shrugged, and walked back home. With such a good nap behind her, she would have the energy to work on her beading tonight. Or even the log . . . she felt a little guilty when she realized how long it had been since she added anything interesting to the log.

The current date surprised her again. Had it been that long since the other colonists had come . . . had died? Ofelia sat a long time, wondering what to write. She had been lonely; she had been frightened; she still didn't want to think about what had happened.

They were not my people, she wrote finally. *But I am sorry, sorrier because I did not want them to come. And their families think they died alone; they do not know someone is here to grieve for them.*

Then she scrolled through the calendar, making short notes when anything caught her notice. Her back ached; her hip had stiffened. She turned off the computer finally, and pushed herself up. How it hurt to move when she had been still too long! It seemed impossible that she could get older, *feel* older, but she was definitely stiffer than when Barto had left.

In the sewing room, she eyed her beadwork with distaste. If she sat down again, she would stiffen into place. But she wasn't sleepy yet. She leaned on the table, pushing the beads around idly. When she was young, she had had a necklace of brilliant blue beads streaked with silver and copper. She had left them behind, for her sister, when she married Humberto. He had never liked that necklace; he had suspected it was a gift from Caitano. He had been right, though she never admitted it to him. She wished she knew how to make such a beautiful color. The fabricator had color settings, but its version of dark blue was a dull, muddy color, nothing like the color she remembered.

She touched the dried cornhusks; they rustled under her fingers. Twisted into fat, stiff ropes, cornhusks might be the edging she wanted for the new cloak. She could dye them – she stopped, her skin puckering suddenly with alarm. What . . . ? Not a sound, though her ears strained to hear past the pounding of her own blood. Nothing to see when she turned slowly, eyeing everything around her. Nothing. Nothing, but – she was still alert, still certain of danger.

That smell. The same smell as at the other house. Musty, she had thought, and yet when she came to think about it, not the same as mildew. A *thicker* smell than mildew. Her heart hammered in her chest; when she put her fist to her side she was not surprised to feel the rapid throb on her chest wall. She had to swallow, though her mouth was suddenly dry.

'I am here,' she said to the darkness outside, the silence, the emptiness. Her voice sounded odd, scratchy like a bad broadcast. 'Come out if you are there.' She had no idea who, or what, she was talking to. Ghosts of the slain? She did not believe in ghosts, exactly, although she had seen Humberto once, six months after he died. He had been wearing a white suit, and a blue hat; he had been smiling at another woman, and when she said his name, he vanished. But did ghosts smell? Humberto had not smelled, as a ghost; he had merely slid, an immaculate and dimensionless image, across her sight that one time.

Ofelia held her breath a moment, then breathed in, not quite sniffing. Yes, whatever this was smelled, and smelled different. New. It was most likely an animal, something from the forest grown bold enough to venture into the town, though the forest creatures had never done so before.

With what confidence she could muster, Ofelia walked out of the sewing room to the front door of the center. Light spilled out the doorway from behind her, and her shadow stretched away from her feet. She could see nothing but the light patches on either side of her shadow. Inside the door were the switches for the exterior lights, rarely used even when the colony had been there. Now she turned them on. Only two of the bulbs came on; the others must have been damaged by storms. But in that skewed light, she saw something move, down the street.

A monster. An animal. An alien.

A deadly alien, which had already killed humans.

Ofelia could not make herself walk out into the street, or back into the center. She could not even turn off the lights. She looked the other way. Something else moved there, a dark shape against darker night. It came closer, a massive bluntness, manylegged, eyes glowing in the light . . .

Cows. Ofelia sagged against the doorframe as several cows strolled up the lane. Between them, a calf pranced.

One of the cows, with a switch of her tail, slapped the handprint on a door. So that had been cows. And the smell – was that cow? Hard to tell, but the cows added a ripe, complex odor to the lane.

'Cows,' Ofelia said aloud. The cows startled, ears wide, seeming almost to lean away from her voice. She wanted to laugh; she wanted to butcher the cows for scaring her so. 'AAOOH!' she bellowed, without knowing it was coming, a bellow from her gut that hurt her throat coming out. The cows ducked, whirled, and galloped off, loud thunder of hooves in the lane. 'Stupid cows!' Ofelia yelled after them. Full of righteous indignation, she flicked off the lights in the center, and stalked across to her own house. Now that she had spoken, she found she wanted to keep talking, to feel words in her throat again, to hear her voice in her outside ears, not just in her head. 'Silly of me to be scared of cows. I should have known they came into the streets at night – there's no gate, after all.' But even as she said it, she wondered . . . she had never found manure between the houses, and why would they come? If they foraged in the gardens regularly, she'd have found damage from that.

Her voice dried up suddenly, as if she had had only so many words to say, and now they were gone. The cows came into the town. The cows came in and the cows don't come in and the cows came in because . . . because . . . because they wanted to because something scared them away from the river.

It hurt to be so scared again the same night. Her ribs hurt from the beating of her heart, from the painful clench of her breath. She stood in the kitchen, unable to move in any direction, until a cramp in her foot stabbed her with such pain that mere terror was forgotten. She leaned her weight onto the cramping foot, and her breath sobbed in and out, and finally the cramp eased. She was tired and she hurt all over. If the aliens wanted to kill her, they could do it while she was asleep.

Her foot cramped again once she was in bed, and she rolled out clumsily to stand on it again. She was too old for this. Familiar anger warmed her. She was too old, her foot hurt too much, things were too hard and it wasn't her fault. When the cramp eased, she got back into bed and pulled the bedclothes over her. Then she remembered she hadn't barred the door to the lane. She never did, but now . . . if there were aliens . . . Sighing, muttering a curse she was surprised to remember, she got up again and went out to bar the useless door.

She had to peek out. In the darkness, she heard the distant sound of cattle grazing, the rhythmic ripping of grass. A light breeze moved between the houses and stroked her body. She could see nothing, nothing at all, but the sparkles that she knew were inside her eyes. She stood until she shivered, then shut the door, barred it carefully, and went back to the bed. On the way, she stubbed her toe on something left out of place – she was not about to turn on the light again tonight – and she came to the bed in the mood to dare bad dreams.

Instead, she had good dreams. She could not remember them, but she did remember that they were good. She had slept late; sunlight striped the kitchen floor from the garden door. She scowled. Garden door? Had she blundered around in the dark barring the front door and forgotten the kitchen door to the garden? Surely it had been shut all along.

She couldn't remember. This had happened before, her thinking she had shut something that was open later, or opened something that was shut later. And it wasn't new; it had started even before Barto left. She hated not remembering; it made her feel foolish. She got up and looked for the toe-stubbing object of the night before. That, at least, she would put out of the way, while she remembered it.

She couldn't find anything between the front door (still barred: she hadn't botched that) and the bedroom door that could have given her toe that nasty clonk. The chairs were neatly pushed under the kitchen table. Nothing . . . unless she'd lost her way entirely, in the dark, and had stubbed her toe on the doorframe to her old bedroom. And if that had happened, surely her hands would have felt the wall.

She looked from the open kitchen door to the bedroom door, from window to window, back to the chairs and the table. Nothing was out of place. In the bright morning sunlight, with the rich growing smells of her garden coming in on the breeze, she could not believe that anything had been really wrong in the night. She sniffed. No strange smells, though the scent of cow was strong. When she opened the door to the lane, she saw cowflops dotting the lane like stepping stones.

She fetched the garden cart and the light shovel, and spent the morning picking up cow manure for the compost trench. The cows were back in the meadow, grazing peacefully as if nothing had ever bothered them. It was much easier to get the manure off the lanes than out of the grass; she told herself that if the cows would only come into town every night, she could manure every garden plot every season and keep the waste recycler topped up. Of course, she didn't want to spend every day picking up manure; she didn't like the smell of it. When the trench was full, she put the rest of the manure into the waste recycler, then showered to get the smell off. At the center, she noted in the log that the cows had come into the streets at night. It probably meant nothing, but it was a change. When she checked the weather display, she saw one of the big sea-storms – the first of the year – far out in the ocean. That was more dangerous than any imagined aliens. She jotted down a list of chores to finish before the storm could arrive – if it did. Repairing shutters, doors, making sure nothing was loose to blow free in the winds. She might spend the storm in the center this time, she thought. She could move a mattress into one of the sewing rooms. The one from her old bedroom would do, and it was nearby.

It was also too heavy to carry by herself, and the lane was damp, smudged with the remains of the cowflops. Ofelia glared at the stains. She was not about to drag her bed through cow manure and then sleep on it, even days later. And the garden cart still smelled of manure, too. In the waste recycler's storerooms were larger, heavier carts once used for hauling; Ofelia fetched one of those. It wouldn't fit through the front door. She dragged the mattress to the door, wrestled it onto the cart, and then pulled the cart to the center. The center's door was wider; the cart just fit through it . . . but not through the inside door to the sewing room. Ofelia dragged her mattress off the cart and left it where it was. She was too tired now to drag it into the sewing room.

By the time she got the cart back to the waste recycler storage, it was twilight, and she felt grumpy and ill-used. Stupid storm, stupid cows, stupid mattress, stupid cart. Stupidest of all, the people who built doorways too narrow for carts to get through them. And stupid Ofelia, because she had not checked the garden today, and the slimerods had probably cut through half the tomato plants.

She went outside in a rush, and found no damage, but a crushed slimerod core between the tomatoes. A fresh one, still glistening. She picked all the ripe tomatoes she could find in the gathering darkness, and took them inside. She was not going to think about that slimerod. Perhaps a cow had stepped on it. Perhaps a sheep. Perhaps a murderous alien planning to cut off her head . . . but at the moment, she was not going to worry about it.

She took a shower, and the streaming water soothed her irritation as well as her muscles. When she came out, and toweled herself dry, she felt like putting on some of her beads. White ones, red ones, brown ones. Then she remembered that she had not made dough that day; she would have to start supper from scratch. She dipped a handful of flour, a finger of shortening, a dash of salt, a little water. Beneath her hands, the dough formed into a plump, firm ball, from which she pinched smaller lumps. She reached out one hand to the stove and set the griddle to heat. Then she rolled the little lumps into flat rounds with her second-best rolling pin. (Rosara had taken the best rolling pin, and she still resented that, though Rosara was probably still in cryo, on her way to someplace she wouldn't like – worse punishment than Ofelia would have given anyone.)

She crumbled sausage into a pan, chopped onion, and started them frying. She would not have pork sausage much longer; she had finally eaten her way through nearly all the pork in the freezers at the center. Eventually, she would have to butcher a cow or sheep. She should do that while she was still strong enough, she told herself. She had told herself that last winter, too, and then she had gone on eating the frozen meat on the grounds that it might spoil and that would be a waste. The truth was that she liked pork sausage. If only the pigs had not disappeared . . . the colonists had finally butchered the remainder when it became obvious that the pigs, unlike the sheep and cattle, would not stay in the terraformed area near the settlement.

When the sausage and onion were half done, Ofelia flicked the rounds of dough onto the hot griddle, and flipped them with a twig, then onto her plate. Another minute or two for sausage and onions; she sliced the fresh tomatoes as she let the meat sizzle, and added sprigs of mint and basil.

She had never grown tired of good food. Some old people did; she could remember them complaining about the lack of flavor, or simply not eating, but she was luckier than that. A bite of warm tomato, then of hot sausage and onion in flatbread, a nip of mint . . . yes. And tomorrow, she would finish planning for the storm, if it came. She would go back to her regular checks of the machines; it had been several days since she inspected the pumps. She would make sure everything was ready for the storm. She would even wrestle that be-damned mattress into the sewing room.

SEVEN

In the morning, the sea-storm had moved closer. The weather monitor projected its track; if it did not swerve away, it would romp right over the settlement in four or five days. It wasn't as big as the storm two years before, but it would grow until it reached shore. She walked out over her mattress. She could drag it into the sewing room later; if she stopped to do that now, she might be distracted by her beadwork.

Outside, the weather was clear and bright, with the spurious calm that Ofelia had learned preceded the squalls. She looked at her list. The pumps first, and then the other machines. She would take a pad along to note which buildings needed repair. Dayvine had overgrown the pumphouse door, its brilliant red flowers and delicate seedpods draped elegantly from the roof across the opening. Ofelia yanked it loose, and pulled the door open with difficulty. Inside, the pumps throbbed, the same steady rhythm she was used to. All the gauges were normal. She wondered how high the river would go in the rains. If it rose too high, she should shut off the pumps, but she could do that from the center if she had to.

The door jammed on the vines again when she tried to

shut it. Grumbling, Ofelia sawed at the tough vine stems and cleared them away from the door, then shoved the door shut and barred it. She hated to cut dayvine; the flowers would wilt within a few minutes, even if she got them to water. Still, for the few moments of beauty, she twined the severed stems around her neck and arms. She would throw them in the waste recycler when she reached it.

The cattle this morning were grazing steadily, as if anticipating the need to store up fuel before the storm. Ofelia remembered how some had been lost to the last flood. Should she try to drive them up into town, even shelter them in one of the buildings? Would the doors and garden gates hold, even if she could get them into one of the few walled courtyards? No. She would stick to her list.

All the machines were in working order, but she knew a number of light bulbs had burnt out. That was a resource she could not replace once the stores were gone. Her attempts to get the fabricator to make light bulbs – they were on its menu – had never worked, and she didn't understand the machine well enough to know why not. Rather than replace bulbs now, she removed those that might be damaged by the approaching storm. That left no outside lights on the center or waste recycler, but she rarely used them anyway.

After a quick lunch, she took her tools and began to repair shutters and doors that seemed likely to break loose in a high wind, leaky roofs and sagging eaves. She found more than she had expected. She tried to remember when she had last worked on them, fighting off the guilty feeling that she should have checked every single house, door, and shutter every day. That would have been impossible, she knew. She would have had no time to garden, sew, or anything else. Still, in the oppressive weather before a major storm, her old voice harassed her, talking of duty and pointing out that she had not really needed to make all those pretty necklaces.

Yes, she had needed that. She had needed it all her life, without knowing that was what she needed. The joy of creation, of play, had been the empty place unfilled by family and social duties. She would have loved her children better, she thought now, if she had realized how much she herself needed to play, to follow her own childish desire to handle beautiful things and make more beauty.

In this argument, she passed the afternoon, mending a half-dozen loose shutters and refitting the latch to one door from which the catch had come loose. Not until that door did she stop to consider how many of the things she'd fixed looked more damaged than worn. This latch, for instance. The colonists had found the native trees to produce hard, tight, straight-grained wood. It held nails and screws both; it required sharp tools for working. In forty years, most of the original attachments had not loosened. In her own house, the hinges and latches still fit tightly. What usually went wrong was a broken louver, where something heavy hit it, or metal fatigue in the fittings themselves.

Here . . . here something had pried the latch loose. When she looked, she could see the little gouges in the hard wood, showing a fresh surface next to the weathering of the rest. A cold chill shook her body. She tried to talk herself out of that panic. Some animal had done this. Some animal from the forest, one of the clever climbers. She had seen how they could grasp and pull, how they poked into things with long-nailed fingers. They had been slow to come into the village after the colonists left, but they had come at last. That would explain all the little oddities of the past few days.

If it were the creatures who had killed the other colonists, they would already have killed her. So they were not here, and the treeclimbers were. She had not seen them because they were shy. They were not so shy in the forest, but that was their natural place. Of course they would be shy here, and they would have better hearing than she did, and maybe better eyesight. They could easily keep out of her way.

She tightened the screws that held the latch, and checked the fit. It caught snugly. Then she made herself go into the house. Empty, as she'd expected. The scuffed dust on the floor fit with her idea of forest animals; it could even have been scuffed the last time she came through. She went out, latched and barred the door, and told herself she would not give in to the temptation to come back later that evening and see if it had been disturbed. Time enough tomorrow, when she would have to mend the shutters at the next house. One slat had broken away completely; she could see that a limb of a fruit tree touched it even with no wind.

Why did she even bother to maintain the other buildings, she wondered as she went back to the center. She didn't need them all; she had long since outworn the half-guilty pleasure of sleeping in other people's houses, using other people's bathrooms. She used four or five houses regularly, depending on the weather, but the others were just something else to look after. It was the old guilt, which insisted that she be responsible for everything, that things must be conserved in case of later need.

She would not waste the next day or so fixing houses she didn't care about. She would make sure of her own and the few others that were especially cool in muggy weather, exceptionally snug in the rare cold spells, or handy for a shower if she had been working nearby. She would let the rest go.

Panic gripped her for a second. If she let the wind and rain begin to erode the buildings, she might end up old and feeble, helpless and exposed in the storm herself.

If she fell off a roof or ladder while trying to keep everything in repair, she could end up in pain, helpless, and exposed while the buildings stayed healthy. The new voice – it still seemed new after these years – which had urged her to wear what felt good on her body now urged her to conserve her strength and health with the same care she lavished on buildings. They existed for her. She owed them nothing except what made them serve her better.

She felt uncomfortable with this argument. If she extended it to living things, she did not like it at all. But tools and buildings? A little breeze tickled the backs of her legs; when she looked up, the cloud wisps warned of the storm coming. The breeze did not die, but continued a steady push. She imagined herself on a roof tomorrow, or even a ladder . . . no. She would let it go. Her own roof, at dawn. The center's roof, perhaps.

In the morning, despite a thick mugginess, a slow unrefreshing movement of air proved the storm's location off to the southeast. Ofelia placed a ladder carefully and climbed up to check her own roof. The fabricator had produced rooftiles of some composite material, lighter than clay tiles but tough and long-lasting. The colonists had re-roofed only five years before they left, as much from prudence as need. As Ofelia expected, the rooftiles were sound, uncracked. A few had loosened; these she beat down into place with new spikes.

From her roof it was easy to see across the sheep meadow to the brush and forest beyond. The sheep were down at the far end, near the shuttle field, a dirty grayish mass. She could not see most of the meadow near the river; it was hidden by other buildings. But she could see part of the shuttle field, now mostly overgrown with terraforming grasses.

She climbed down, dragged the ladder to the center, and climbed up again. The center's roof was more complex, since it covered a larger building and had been designed to gather rainwater as well. In the early days, the colonists had not known how easy it would be to purify the river water, and they had depended on rainwater stored in cisterns.

Ofelia hated climbing around on the center roof. Parts were steeper; the valleys where angles came together were slippery and difficult. The roof had not leaked in the other sea-storm; she could probably let it go this time. A stubborn sense of duty took her up to the first ridgeline. It felt harder than the last time she'd climbed up. She got a knee across the ridgeline and sank down to rest. Her heart thudded; her breath came short; she could not see as well as she wanted.

When she looked back across the roof of her house to the sheep meadow, she saw movement in the brush. She sat motionless; she could not have moved if someone had prodded her. Out of the brush came a trio of reddish animals smaller than the sheep. Tails high, they ran across the grass, disappearing behind her house.

Climbers. Her breath came back with a rush as she recognized them. Forest climbers, as she'd thought. One appeared on the roof of her house, long arms busy . . . was it prying up her roof tiles? A long slender paw to its mouth – it was eating something that nested there. Sweat broke out, relief. The climbers had never been a menace. She had nothing to worry about unless they pried rooftiles off, and even that was not a serious threat.

She waved her own arms, and the climber froze, tail stiffly raised. 'Shoo!' she yelled. The climber jerked as if shot, then scampered over the roof and disappeared. Moments later, all three appeared again, racing across the grass to the brush. She caught little glimpses of red bodies moving between the scrub, then they were gone.

There was something to be said for climbing on roofs after all. She felt lighthearted, childish again, and had to remind herself firmly that she could not caper here. She looked around, and saw nothing else interesting. The center's rooftiles all fit snugly; none were cracked. The only real danger would be a stoppage in the cistern overflow outlets. Slowly, carefully, she climbed back down the roof, and the ladder. She could check the cistern overflows from the ground.

The weather monitor displayed the storm's track and projected course. The first squalls should hit the next day, and the main storm on the day following. Ofelia dragged her mattress the rest of the way into the sewing room, and put it under one of the tables. She felt restless; she could not settle to her beadwork or any other activity. She had gathered in the food – she would make a last couple of rounds through the gardens until the storm closed in, since the vegetables would continue to ripen. But otherwise – she watched the cap of clouds cross the sky, a great arc that hour by hour closed over her world like a lid, first white and then darker and darker gray.

The first squalls were actually a relief. Ofelia was in

the center; she stood by the door to the lane and watched the wind drive the rain before it. She wished the center had a second floor, a place from which she could see farther, perhaps even to the forest. She wondered if the big trees bent and swayed like the small ones in the village. She wondered how the forest climbers survived such storms . . . did they stay in the trees, which must be swaying back and forth, or did they huddle on the ground?

All day the squalls continued, the breaks between them shorter and the wind never completely still. Ofelia laid out the project she intended to work on, and between squalls went back to her own house for things she had forgotten: seeds she had collected, ends of yarn from old projects, her favorite yarn needle, her best thimble.

She was going to make another of the network garments . . . this one more festive than the last. She put on the first, to remind herself where she wanted to make changes. She wanted something that made her feel like the storms: something that evoked wind and rain and lightning and thunder.

Beating the scraps of metal into bell-shapes had taken longest. She could have had the fabricator mold bell-shapes, but then she could not have listened to them, choosing the shape that fit the sound she wanted. Far back in her memory lay a field-trip to a costume museum; the guide – docent, her mind said, casting up the old word along with the memory of sound – had shaken the costumes made for carnival wear, and she had thought then how like rain some of them sounded. Now she had small thin cylinders to crimp onto fringe . . . it tinkled coolly. Yes. Bigger, rounder shapes of copper gave a mellower sound, water trickling into deep water.

The weather monitor beeped its main storm warning

while she was still playing with the sounds, still making tinkling fringe and tonkling strings to hang from her shoulders. She went in and turned off the warning signal. The storm would strike full force the next morning. She should sleep while she could.

It was surprisingly hard to sleep. Although she'd napped in several houses, she had not spent the night in any but her own after the first few months alone. She had become used to the bigger bed, the wider mattress. The center had its own set of night noises, and outside the squalls rolled over, boisterous and loud. She finally slept in spite of herself, and woke late to a steady sustained roar. It was still dark outside; she checked the weather monitor and found that the storm had accelerated slightly, coming onshore several hours before the prediction.

Dawn came slowly under that blanket of cloud and flying water. Ofelia wasn't really hungry for breakfast; she went back to her project, trying not to hear the noise outside. But the wind's noise rose and rose; even the center shivered from time to time in the gusts. Was her house all right? It was tempting to open the door and look, but she knew better. She quit working with the metal dangles – she couldn't hear their various tones – and went back to painting and stringing beads.

Her ears ached slightly as the pressure dropped and dropped. She felt tired, and finally lay down again in midmorning. Silence woke her. She went to open the door. There it was again – the eerie center of the storm, with bright sunlight shining from a deep blue sky. Later in the day than last time; it was afternoon. Ofelia walked over to her house. Windblown rain had pried its way around the front door seals, leaving a wet patch on her floor, but she found no other damage.

She went back outside. It was as beautiful as the other times she'd seen it. To the east, sunlight, turned the entire cloudface to a snow-and-silver-and-azure sculpture, as decorative as a pile of meringue. Ofelia splashed along the lane, keeping a cautious eye on that eastern rampart. This storm had seemed slightly stronger than the other. That should mean she had a little more time to roam, but she intended to be safely under cover again before it hit.

Down the lane to the right, she saw a pile of debris, a tangle of mud-gray and brown, streaks of bleached white. What had that blown from? She picked her way to it, enjoying the squish of mud between her toes.

Eyes stared back at her, great golden brown eyes whose pupils widened enormously. The pile stirred; a noise like the cooing of an entire flock of pigeons came from it. Ofelia stared; she could hardly breathe. That sodden mass of – of what she could not say – it had eyes – it was big – it—

From a distance, a rhythmic drumming that could only be intentional. The pile produced a weaker drumming of its own. Communication. Ofelia knew what this had to be. The aliens, the monsters, who had killed all those people. They had found her at last; only the storm had saved her, and only if it killed them. This one, at least, she could outrun back to the center. She hoped. Maybe the storm would kill them all. She turned. At the far end of the lane shapes moved. Upright, taller than she was, they danced nearer, high-stepping as the cows through shallow water. They fit no pattern she had seen, or imagined. They were earth-colored, streaked in beiges, browns, pale and shifting grays. Ofelia could not tell if that was skin, or short fur. Their faces – if those were faces – stuck out like birds' faces, but they had no feathers, and no wings. Like her, they had lower and upper limbs in pairs, but – but it was wrong. Ofelia backed against the wall. She could not outrun these. Elemental fear dragged at her bowels; her mouth tasted foul suddenly and her vision blurred.

Whatever they were, they looked at her, directly *at* her, in the way of people, not animals. Big eyes, fringed with stiff lashes. Three of them stopped to stare at her; four others moved to the fallen one and, with much noisy bird-like chatter, helped it up. It seemed weak; it leaned on them. It had what might be fingers, she saw now, though they made a very odd looking hand.

She glanced back at the ones staring at her. They looked nothing like the forest creatures she had seen. Taller, leggier, long toes tipped with hard blue-black nails. On their bodies, beaded straps held sacks and gourds in the arrangement Ofelia associated with pictures of soldiers. A short fringed leather skirt hung about what must be their hips. But aside from long sheathed knives, they carried nothing she recognized as weapons.

She shifted her weight; one of those watching her uttered a raucous noise that caught the attention of the rest. All of them stared at her; she felt she might melt in the regard of all those eyes.

The light failed suddenly, as the approaching cloud wall cut off the sunlight. Ofelia glanced upward. It was close – she should get back to the center now. The creatures also looked up at the rumble of thunder. She took a step sideways. Instantly their heads snapped back to stare at her, and several of them made that raucous noise. She wondered if they understood about the storm, that it was coming back, that it would hit with full force when it did. If only she could get into cover, and leave them outside, the storm might still blow them all away.

The injured one coughed, a sound so close to human that Ofelia had to look. Its supporters patted its back, for all the world like humans. It hawked and spat, a gritty spittle. Ofelia glanced sideways. She had barely time to get to the center, if she went now – but only a few meters away was the door to one of the other houses. If she could make it that far . . . she took another cautious step. Again the quick response, but the creatures did not move. It was as if they merely commented to themselves on what she did.

Emboldened, she took another step, and another. Thunder grumbled louder; one of the things drummed again. Two more drummed, and then the entire group. Their pupils contracted when they drummed. Ofelia moved crabwise, watching them; they seemed to ignore her now. A fine mist of windshredded rain cooled her skin – the storm would be on them in a few seconds. She was at the door – she struggled to lift the bar, to open it, to drag the bar with her inside. She took a last look at the little group in the lane. They were all looking at the sky, as if worried. Stupids. They would be blown down the lane to crash into something if they stood there.

Killers. Aliens. Troublemakers. She hadn't wanted them, any more than she'd wanted the other colony. But she would feel guilty if they died because she barred them out – and if they survived, they would be angry.

'Hey!' All the heads turned her way. 'It's coming back.' She knew they wouldn't understand her words, anymore than she would have understood their noises. She pointed at the sky. 'Whoooo. Bang.' She made a whirling motion with her arm. The creatures looked at each other and back to her. 'Come on,' she said. She swept her arm inside.

The two supporting the injured one moved toward her; others made throaty sounds. 'Hurry,' she said, as the light darkened, as she heard the howl of wind on the other end of the village.

In a rush, they dashed to the house. She had just time to duck out of the way as they came through the door, all eight of them, the injured one limping. Wind and rain roared down the street outside; the door tore itself out of her hands and banged wildly. Wet wind swirled inside. Ofelia grabbed the door again and pushed; she felt warmth beside her as a creature joined her. And when the door finally shut the storm outside, another of them picked up the bar and set it across the brackets.

Then she was alone with them in the dimness, in the loud fury of the storm outside. Ofelia reached for the light switch, and touched strangeness instead; the surface felt slightly warm, and bristly, like the stem of a tomato plant. Beside her the creature grunted and caught her hand in hard-nailed fingers. Ofelia yanked back; she felt her skin stretch but the thing did not let go.

Panic would not help. She reached carefully around with her other hand, and found the switch. In that sudden light, she saw all their eyes change, the wide pupils narrowing sharply. The one who held her moved its face closer to hers, then released her hand. Ofelia shook it, and looked; the grip had reddened, but not broken, her skin.

She could smell them, in here. It was the smell she had noticed before, the one she had lacked a name for. Up close, in the bright indoor light, they looked larger and more dangerous. Their narrowed eyes and beaky faces looked ill-tempered; their long limbs with the hard-nailed digits suggested both speed and cruelty.

She needed to use the toilet. She was not going to disgrace herself here, in front of them. She took a step toward the middle of the room, and the one who had grabbed her hand before now grabbed her shoulder. Again a soft grunt.

'Let go,' Ofelia said, without heat. 'I'm just going to the other room.' A deeper grunt from one of the others, one wearing a string of some bright blue stones, and the one holding her shoulder let go. Slowly, trying to look harmless, Ofelia made her way around them – they did not move aside – to the bathroom door. She could hide in there, she thought suddenly, until after the storm. And if this house had a bathroom window, she could even escape.

The bathroom door had only the simplest latch, and it opened inward. The storm battered the shutters of the window; it shook in its frame. Ofelia sat down on the toilet, her brief calm over. If the creatures wanted in here, they could get in easily enough, and it would be hours before she could get out the window. If she could; it was a high window, and she didn't relish the thought of clambering up on the toilet to get out of it.

When she was through, she sat on the toilet lid until she heard something bumping at the door. Fear cramped her again. But better to go out than to have them drag her out; it had always been so with Humberto. She opened the door. One of the creatures stood there with its head cocked. Could it want the toilet? Of course not – they could not know what it was. Ofelia opened the lid . . . but what if it thought that was drinking water? Perhaps it would not hurt them, perhaps it would kill them. She would try to make it clear there was another source.

She edged past the creature and went to the kitchen

end of the main room. She turned on the water in the sink. All their heads came up; she felt pinned in place by the intensity of their gaze. The one who had been peering into the bathroom now came to her side. She demonstrated: the twist of the controls to turn the water on and off.

The creature reached out to the controls; its hard nails slipped on the metal control. Ofelia put her hand out to help, and the creature slapped her aside, hard enough to sting, but not a damaging blow. Ofelia glared, but years of marriage to Humberto suggested that the best thing to do was stand there looking subdued. Anger throbbed in her. She had not wanted to be in this situation again, where someone could bat her aside.

The creature continued to struggle with the control; one of the others made a sound, just loud enough to hear over the storm. The one struggling stopped, shook itself, and fished a short length of what looked like suede from one of its pouches. Wrapping that about the control to give itself purchase, it turned the control easily. Water spurted out; water ceased. Raucous sound now, from several of the things. The first one fumbled at a strap, unfastening a gourd, then held it under the stream of water. When the gourd overflowed, it handed it to one of the others, who sniffed and tasted cautiously.

All this time it left the water running. Ofelia risked another slap to reach out and turn the water off. Again they all looked at her. Then one of them looked at the light bulb overhead and jerked its snout at it – an unmistakable gesture. Ofelia walked to the light switch, and demonstrated that. More loud noises . . . discussion, she was sure. Another, not the one at the sink, came to test the switch for itself. This was easier for a hard fingernail to work. Lights on lights off lights on. More noise.

Suddenly something hit the house from outside, a blow that shook the walls and shattered the shutters in one of the bedrooms. Wind howled through, wet wind that smacked her face like a damp towel. The creatures scattered to the main room's corners, out of the direct blast of the wind. Ofelia huddled near the front door and wondered what had hit them. When she ventured to peek into the bedroom, she saw the floor already slick with water, and the window full of tree branches.

It would only get worse. Ofelia could see a bedstead, a soggy mattress, a crib. She splashed across the floor, worked her way to the outside wall. Water streamed off the tree limbs and down the wall, but the wall itself held. Lightning flashed outside; she heard a startled yelp from the doorway. When she looked over, two of the creatures were watching her. One of them lifted its foot from the puddle near the door with an expression she was sure meant dislike of wet feet.

Typical. They would let her do the work. She didn't want to. She made her way back across the floor, pulled the bedroom door shut, and latched it. With the wind behind it blowing it shut, the weak indoor latch should be enough. A wicked draft came under the door; it would blow water under it soon. She looked around for something to stop the draft. The creatures watched her still. She finally found some dish towels in a drawer, and rolled them up to stuff under the door.

It was getting dark now. She was tired and hungry. If she had been in the center, she would have had plenty of food. It was their fault, she told herself. If not for the stupid creature that got itself blown around in the storm, she might have been safe in the center, and they might all have been storm-blown . . . or at least sheltering somewhere else.

She could have had a last day or night of peace – as much peace as the storm allowed – before her death. She could at least have had food and a familiar bed, and something pleasant to do. Instead, she was stuck here with – she counted – eight aliens, murderers, and no food, and no comfortable bed. There was the other bedroom, but . . . it occurred to her then to look for the damaged one, the one whose plight had gotten her into this mess.

She could not be sure which it was. Three of them lounged together on the worn bench, but none looked as bedraggled as the sodden heap she'd seen in the street. When had they found the towels that now lay in dirty piles on the floor? She was too tired to think how long it had been, or exactly what they had done. Even as panic told her that they would kill her in her sleep, that she must not sleep, exhaustion dragged her down. Either she would die, or she wouldn't, and either way she would sleep.

EIGHT

Ofelia woke in a panic, sure she was suffocating. It was dark, too warm, too damp, and something stirred against her in the darkness. She gasped, found she could breathe, and even as that panic eased remembered that she had fallen asleep in a houseful of aliens. In the light. She forced herself to lie still. She could feel something along her back, something warmer than the air, something that felt . . . alive. She blinked, but saw only the wandering bright spots that haunted her eyes at night anyway. What had happened to the lights?

Thunder muttered in the distance, but the storm's roar had died; she could hear the steady drip of rain off the roof. The main storm must be past. But where was she, and when? Her back and shoulder hurt; her bad hip stabbed her when she tried to move, and she bit back a gasp.

The creature beside her stirred; she was aware of its sudden alertness. It made a sound like water coming to a boil in a kettle, and she felt it move closer. She tensed . . . some part of it touched her lightly, felt along her body and paused on her chest where her racing heart felt as if it would burst free. Then the touch vanished. Ofelia blinked, surprised. What had it been feeling for?

As she lay there, she began to pick out vague shapes in the darkness. Light seeped through the shutters; it must be past dawn. Her stomach growled; she needed to use the toilet again. She would need the lights, or she'd step on some of the creatures, and she didn't want to do that. She tried to stretch, and her hip stabbed her again. Stupid hip. She would need it to run with, if she got the chance. Slowly, she moved her leg back and forth until the pain eased.

When she turned on her side to push herself up, the creature beside her roused again. She could see the dim shape looming, taller even sitting than she was. But it didn't touch her. Slowly, because that was what she could do in the morning after sleeping on the floor, she clambered to her feet. Now she could see the other shapes slumped in corners, huddled together . . . and she could walk between them.

The one who had been at her side watched her, the great eyes gleaming in the dim light. She walked across to the bathroom, shut the door behind her, and used the toilet. The flush was loud, in the quiet aftermath of the storm. She heard startled noises from the other room; when she went back out, they were all awake, all looking at her.

She could not be as afraid now; her body was more interested in food. Her stomach growled; one of the creatures made a similar sound. Was it hungry? Or was it mocking her? She made her way across the room to the door, wondering if they would let her walk out, and she would go back to the center and bar them out of it. Then she could eat breakfast, and . . .

Of course they would follow. She turned on the lights; as they all blinked, their pupils contracting, she unbarred the door and opened it. Soft warm rain fell steadily from high clouds. She could smell rotting vegetation, cow manure, even wet wool. She took a step outside. The rain was so warm it felt more like a second coating of sweat than a cleansing bath. Ofelia looked back. Two of the creatures stood in the doorway, watching her.

'I'm going back,' she said. And walked away.

That raucous sound, from more than one of them. Ofelia looked over her shoulder. One of them moved out into the rain, shook itself, and kept walking after her. Not running, just walking, stepping high through the puddles. Ofelia walked on, ignoring it. She was hungry, she was tired, her hip ached, and she wanted to be back in her own space. Even if they were going to kill her.

At the center, she found water draining out the front door. Had she forgotten to close it when she came out to walk around? Or had the creatures found it and opened it? She walked into a mess. Wind had driven the rain all the way back down the central hallway; water had run into adjacent rooms and soaked the mattress she'd left on the floor in the sewing room. Apparently the interior doors had blown shut, though, and prevented worse damage.

She would have to sweep out the worst of the water before she could cook in the center. Perhaps her house was dryer. She went back out the door, nearly colliding with the creature who had followed her, and across the lane. Inside her house it was dry . . . until she and the wet creature following her came in and dripped on the floor. Ofelia toweled herself off and handed dry towels to the creature. It took the towel and held it aside, looking at her with those great eyes.

Muttering, Ofelia took the towel back. Worse than a child. Surely it knew it was wet; surely it had seen her dry herself off. She reached out very slowly and ran the towel along one of its upper limbs. It shivered, but did not move. She tried to hand the towel back, but it didn't take it. And it was still dripping on her floor. Stupid creature. How had they been smart enough to kill the other colonists? She touched its other upper limb with the towel, and when it didn't resist dried its front and back, and finally its legs. Then she wrapped the damp towel around its feet, sopping up the puddle it had made.

It grunted. What did that mean? It twitched its lower limbs and grunted again. Ofelia glared at it. Was it too stupid, or too lazy, to get its own feet out of the towel? 'Take it off,' she said. It grunted again, and jerked its . . . she had to think of it as a leg. 'Stupid baby,' Ofelia said, and bent down to take the towel away. 'Stupid, lazy, inconsiderate . . .' Luckily it could not understand her speech. She was out of the habit of holding her tongue.

At least it was drier, and not dripping on her floor. She moved to the kitchen, turned on her stove, and pulled out her canisters. She needed bread, and meat, and vegetables. She would make flatbread first. She had a handful of flour when something hard touched her shoulder; she jumped, spilling the flour.

'Idiot!' she said. The thing grunted; it let go. 'I'm cooking,' she said, as if it could understand. 'I'm hungry, and I'm cooking.' She got another handful of flour, the shortening, the salt, the water, and mixed them. The dough in her hands felt comforting, a familiar presence she understood better than most. Knead, knead, flatten, knead, knead, flatten. Pinch off bits, flatten them, roll them, lay them on the griddle. Already her mouth watered; the smell of the dough alone had done that. The creature, when she looked around, had retreated to the front door, its eyes

fixed on the hot griddle where the flatbread steamed. Afraid
of fire, was it? That might be useful, but not until she'd
eaten. She opened the cooler door and took out a chunk
of sausage. The first flatbread was done; she rolled it
around nothing but her hunger, and ate it so hot it burned
her tongue. On the second, she remembered to spread
some jam she had made that spring. Better. The sausage
sizzled now; she sliced potatoes to fry in its fat. She looked
for the creature, and found it in the middle of the room,
staring with apparent fascination at the cooler door. She
opened it again, watching the creature; its eyes met hers
and it grunted.

'You can't leave it open too long,' she said, and shut
the door. She wondered if it was hungry too, and thought
of offering it food, but when she turned around again, it
had disappeared. Only the damp towel on the floor proved
it had been there.

She had finished a meal, and gone back across to the
center to sweep out the water when they came back. The
rain was lighter, though still steady; she swept the water
out into a lane streaming with it, the side ditches brim-
ming. She didn't see them until they stood in the doorway
as she swept toward it, three or four of them at once. They
didn't move. Ofelia pushed the broom toward them.

'Get back.'

They still did not move. Rude. She pushed the broom
hard, and a cascade of dirty water rolled over their feet.
One squawked, and backed away; the other two didn't.

'I'll do it again,' Ofelia said. When they stood there,
stupid as cows, she thought, she pushed another slosh of
water over their feet. Two more squawks, and they all
backed up, glancing at each other. She went back down
the hall. When she came to the door again, they were

back, but this time they moved aside before she pushed
the water out.

And this time they followed her inside. She ignored the
wet smack of their feet on the floor; it didn't matter, this
floor was dirty and wet already. She wished they would
dry themselves, rather than stand around in her way dripping, but she wasn't about to stop and find towels for
them. They moved out of her way as she came past with
the broom, but otherwise simply stood watching her work.

Lazy and spoiled, she decided. Rude, lazy, and spoiled.
If they had mothers, their mothers had never taught them
to help out around the house. If they had houses. She
paused at that thought and looked at them. Surely they
had houses. Intelligent animals built dwellings, it was one
of the ways you knew if they were intelligent. Who wanted
to be out in storms and blown about and rained on? Not
these things; she had seen one injured by the storm. So
they had to have houses, and if they had houses someone
had to clean them. And they should know how.

On that, she went to the storage closet and pulled out
a mop and a broom. If they were going to kill her, they
might as well earn the privilege. She dragged the mop and
brooms back up the hall; the creatures stood there, passive.

'Here,' she said, holding out the broom. One of them
reached out and took it. She held out the mop to another,
and it also took it, in the way of a child who is not sure
what it's for. She could teach them. She had taught her
own children. And she was not about to become the
unpaid housekeeper for a band of aliens.

'Like this,' she said, demonstrating the push of the
broom. The one holding the broom looked and looked, with
those wide eyes, and then looked at its companions and
grunted, a series of little grunts ending in a high squawk.

They squawked back. Ofelia made assumptions. 'Yes, I *do* expect you to use it,' she said severely. 'The floor is wet. You are bigger than I am, and stronger. Push the broom.'

The creature holding the broom made a tentative pass at the floor, waggling the broom exactly like a child. 'Harder,' said Ofelia. 'Push it harder on the floor.' She demonstrated again. The creature pushed a little harder, not hard enough but a start. 'Go ahead,' Ofelia said, waving her arm at a puddle where the floor was uneven. It glanced at her, at its companions, and pushed the broom through the puddle, not very effectively.

'And you,' Ofelia said to the mop holder. 'Like this.' Since she had no mop, she put her hands over its grip on the mop and forcibly moved it into the right position. 'The mop sops up the water,' she said. Even if it couldn't understand, she felt better explaining aloud. When there were people there, you talked to them. Under her hands, its hands felt big and bony, harder than human hands and oddly constructed. 'When it's full of water, you wring it out,' she said. It stiffened when she tried to raise the mop to wringing height, resisting her direction. It churred, and the other two grunted in reply.

Ofelia looked at its face, and saw that its eyelids were almost closed. Something was wrong. She let go of its hands on the mop handle, and its lids raised. It grunted. Well. Perhaps she could find another broom. She handed her broom to the third creature and pointed to the puddle its companion was more stirring than sweeping. Then she went back to the closet for another broom.

With gestures and nudges, she had them pushing water more or less toward the door, while she herself mopped. She didn't like mopping, but she also didn't like wet floors. Outside, the post-storm rain continued steadily.

She was hungry again when the rest of the creatures showed up, and noisily interfered with what 'her' creatures were doing. That was what it seemed like, anyway. The newcomers grunted, squawked, and gabbled; the ones holding the brooms dropped them. They all stared at her, and again she felt the pressure of all their attention. She did not like it. She wished they would all kill her, or go away, anything but bother her by looking at her like that.

The floor was merely damp now; she didn't really need the help. 'Go on,' she said, sweeping at them with her arm. 'Let me alone, then.' Instead of that, the newcomers came all the way in and dripped; new puddles formed under them. 'Idiots!' Ofelia said. 'Babies!' She picked up the mop again and pushed it at their feet. Behind her, the ones who had been sweeping gabbled at the newcomers, who gabbled back. The newcomers stood their ground; she had to flop the mophead against their long dark toes with the thick black nails, and push past them to wring it out into the lane. They made no move to help her, or to get out of her way.

Just like them. They would. The complete meaning of that pronoun – the source of her experience – she did not bother to consider. When she had mopped the new puddles, she wrung out the mop a last time and propped it by the door. They were discussing something – possibly how she would taste, she thought – and ignoring her. She was still hungry. Down the central hall, past the rooms for machines, was the center kitchen and its pantries. She gave them a last disgusted look and walked away. Behind her, she heard startled noises, and the click of toenails on the hard floor. It took her a moment to think why she hadn't noticed it before – it had been too noisy during the storm, and she'd been talking to them here. The center pantries held staples: flour, sugar, salt, dried yeast, baking powder and baking soda, dried beans and peas, and freezers less full than they had been of meats and other perishables. Ofelia had turned on the kitchen lights when she came in; now she turned on lights in the lefthand pantry. She was too hungry to wait for dried beans to cook. She looked in the freezer. Every household had contributed some finished dishes, for emergencies: casseroles and stews and soups. She had eaten little of that in these years, because she liked her own cooking. Now she took out a packet Ariane had contributed; it had her name and family name on it, and the contents: lamb stew. Ofelia put the packet in the kitchen's quick-thaw machine, and rummaged for a saucepan to cook it in. By the time she found the pan, the packet was soft. She opened it and put the lumpy cold contents into the saucepan.

As she heated the stew, the creatures came into the kitchen. They were like children, prying into everything. They tried the water controls of the sinks – so they had remembered what she taught them in the house. They opened cabinets, picked up and put down everything they could move, and even turned on the light in the other pantry. One of them came to her side, and very slowly touched her hand on the stirring spoon. It grunted softly.

As long as they weren't actually killing her, she might as well be polite. 'I'm cooking stew,' she said. 'That's a spoon, this is a pot, this is a stove.' As she spoke, she pointed. Did they understand pointing? The creature dipped its head low over the pan, then jerked back as the stew bubbled. 'Hot,' Ofelia said, as she would have to a toddler. 'Be careful, it's hot.'

A crash behind her made her jump, and she whirled around. One of the creatures had tried to take plates out of a cabinet, and had dropped several. Now it stood stiffly, arms away from its sides, while two others advanced on it slowly. Ofelia giggled before she could stop herself. It was so much like a child who'd had an accident, being scolded by siblings. She didn't really mind about those plates; they were dull beige with a brown stripe, a pre-programmed design in the fabricator, and she had never liked them.

She turned back to the stew, which was hot enough now, and turned the stove down. She would need a bowl. If she remembered right, the small bowls were at this end of the china cabinets. She opened one, and found serving bowls; in the next were the small bowls. The creatures watched as she took out a bowl, and then a spoon from the drawer underneath. She poured her stew – Ariane's stew, actually – into the bowl.

She tasted it. Ariane was a good cook, but she had been more conservative with this dish, meant for the community as a whole, than at home. Ofelia would have added more marjoram and more pepper. Still, it was good enough, and she was hungry. She looked at the creatures, who were now exploring again, all ignoring her except for the nearest, and decided to eat where she was, standing up. She finished that bowl of stew, and then another, and put the remainder into the cooler, in the cooking pot she'd used. Then she started for the sink with her dirty bowl and spoon.

They still hadn't cleaned up the broken bits of plate. Ofelia looked at them, and sighed. One of them looked back, and churred. 'It's your mess,' Ofelia said, without much hope that this would make any difference. It grunted. 'Not my mess,' Ofelia went on. She didn't want to stoop down and pick up those pieces; she was already tired and sore. She walked on past and turned on the water in the sink. One of the creatures came close and peered at her while she washed the bowl. Didn't they wash their dishes? Or didn't they have dishes? Ofelia put the bowl upside down to drain. When she turned around, one of them was trying to pick up the pieces of plate in one hand, and hold them in the other.

Perhaps they didn't have trash collectors. Ofelia opened the cabinet under the sink, and got out the trash collector. She took it over to the creature and mimed putting the broken pieces in. It stared at her a moment, then dropped them in. Ofelia smiled, and it stepped back, its pupils dilating. Was it scared? Ofelia looked away, and found the others watching. Was it embarrassed? She couldn't tell. And she wanted to go home and take a nap, before she tackled the rest of the cleaning. Although she really should get that soggy mattress up off the floor. Her joints ached at the thought of heaving it up.

She started back down the passage, and heard behind her the clicking of many toenails. Drat. She couldn't leave them here alone in the center. What if they got into the control rooms and started pushing buttons? What if they broke the machines she depended on? She turned around, and there they were, close behind her, bright-eyed and bouncy.

Go away, she wanted to say. Go away and let me sleep and maybe later I can think how to deal with you. Go away and leave everything as it is, don't touch anything . . . It wouldn't work. It didn't work with toddlers, who never cared how sleepy you were, or how much you needed to get done, or how dangerous the machine was they were determined to explore. These creatures were not toddlers to themselves, but they were as dangerous, even if they didn't mean to kill her.

She would have to stay awake. She wondered if she could make locks for the doors she didn't want them to open. Their hands were not as dexterous as hers; they had fumbled at first with the water faucets. She suspected that they would interfere if they saw her blocking their way. Even as she thought that, one of them opened the door to the control room and squawked loudly.

No. Ofelia pushed past them, using her elbows even as they squawked and grunted. Then she faced them, arms spread. 'Get out of here,' she said. 'No.' It was like talking to a new puppy, or someone else's baby: they were staring past her at the colored lights, the gauges, the monitor screens flickering with status reports. They grunted at each other and pushed forward.

'NO!' Ofelia stamped her foot; they stopped as if she'd hit them with something heavy and stared at her. 'This is not for you,' she said. 'You'll break it. You'll ruin it.'

The one in front gave a long rolling churr and waved its forelimb at the room.

Ofelia shook her head. 'No. Not. For. You. Dangerous.' She wondered how to mime danger to them. Did they know about electricity? 'Zzzzt!' she said, pretending to touch something and then jerking back, shaking her hand.

'Zzzzt . . .' It was the first sound of hers any of them had copied. What did zzzzt mean in their language? More importantly, would it stop them from poking around in here and destroying things? Ofelia tried to remember childhood lessons in electricity. Lightning was also electricity; they had to know about lightning. Could she get that across?

The one in front slowly extended its long dark nails toward one of the control boards. 'Zzzzt . . .' it uttered, more softly than Ofelia had, and yanked its limb back as if stung. Ofelia nodded; at least they had that right.

'Yes – zzzzt. Hurts you. Big ouch.' She felt silly, talking to them as if they were babies just reaching for trouble, but it had worked.

The creature extended its limb to her, not quite touching. It tilted its head to one side, presenting her with more of one eye than the other. 'Zzzzt . . .' it uttered again, and then touched her very gently on the chest.

Ofelia frowned. It meant something, she was sure of it. It wanted to say something to her . . . but she could not think what that meant. She rehearsed it in her head. She had tried to convey that the things in here could hurt if you touched them – and the creature had copied her actions, which might mean it understood, although she had known plenty of children who couldn't learn from a pretense like that, who had to be hurt themselves before they understood that fire would burn. Then it had uttered the sound, while almost touching her, and then had touched her.

Was it saying that she might hurt it, the same way as the machines? That she did hurt? But no – they had touched her already, and as near as she could tell, it hadn't hurt them. They hadn't jerked or jumped back or shown any other sign of pain. If they showed pain the way people did.

'Zzzzt . . .' the creature uttered, repeating its earlier sequence. Then it seemed to point to the machines behind her, with an emphatic little stab on the end of the gesture. 'Zzzzt.' Then it pointed at her again.

Oh. Ofelia laughed aloud before she could stop herself. Of course. It wanted to know if the machines would *zzzzt* her. Or it wanted to see her get a *zzzzt*. Or something that connected her with the machines and the action she had claimed they had.

She held up one finger; the creatures stared at it. 'The wrong place will go Zzzzt,' she said. She walked over to the outlet where the cables linked to the power system. 'Here it will make anyone go Zzzzt.' Again she pretended to touch it, made the noise, and jerked back. 'But here – IF you know what you're doing, I can touch it.' As she spoke, she mimed: finger tapping head . . . knows . . . a careful approach, looking all over the control board before deciding which button to push . . . a careful touch with one finger on one button. No zzzzt. The lights blinked; she had enabled a warning circuit that put all the center lights on slow flash.

Squawks and grunts and gabbles, restless stirring in the hall behind the frontmost creatures. Ofelia prodded the button again and the lights returned to a steady glow. While she was there, she touched other controls, storing all monitor displays for later analysis, disabling all but the board she was using, choosing the most resistant of systems to run things. Just in case they got eager and tried to poke around, she could prevent much of the trouble they'd cause. They would be unlikely to hit the enabling sequences with random attempts to get something to happen. And she would disable this board when she was through. Let them have another scare first. 'If you aren't very careful,' she said. 'If you just swipe at the controls, bad things will happen.' She laid her hand on the board, carefully across the emergency alert panel. Sirens wailed outside, higher and higher; bells rang in every room in the center; the lights changed to a different flash sequence, from normal to brighter and back. Ofelia turned it off, and locked the board down. 'And that's why you shouldn't mess—'

But they had. At least half of them had left stinking

piles on the floor they had just cleaned. All of them stared
at her. She didn't have to know their language to know
they were angry. Ofelia glared back. It wasn't her fault.
She hadn't meant to scare them that much – only to
convince them to leave the controls alone. And they'd
dirtied the floor.

'I'm not cleaning that up,' Ofelia said. 'Get the brooms.'
It would take mops. It would take . . . but it didn't. One
of them grunted something especially emphatic, and the
guilty parties – as Ofelia saw it – bounced away at high
speed, to return with scoops that she recognized too late
as the big stirring paddles from the kitchens. Oh well.
They could be sterilized. She didn't care that the biochemistry wasn't supposed to be compatible: she was not going
to use stirring paddles that had picked up alien waste until
they'd been properly disinfected.

The creatures picked up their messes and went down
the hall in the direction of the outside door. Perhaps she
should have told them about the toilets. She looked back
at the ones still staring at her. Perhaps she should not
upset them any more. A lifetime's experience reminded
her that upsetting those who outnumber you and have
weapons is a bad idea. It was because they hadn't hurt
her yet . . . she had begun to think of them as harmless,
or at least not immediately threatening.

The cleanup crew returned; she noticed that the stirring paddles looked clean, as if they'd been scrubbed in
the rainwater. Looks weren't everything; she'd put them
through a hot water cycle. With a little shudder, the others
relaxed; their intent gaze left her, and Ofelia felt herself
relaxing too. Perhaps they weren't going to kill her. At least
not now. At least not if she kept them pacified. If they had
been children, she would have cooked something sweet,

but they had not seemed attracted to the food in the kitchen.

She moved toward the door, and the creatures moved back. They followed her down the passage, and into the sewing room where her wet mattress lay under the long work table. She counted – all of them. No one was lurking in the control room, tinkering with the switches.

As in the kitchen, they moved around, looking at everything making soft noises that she could not help but assume were language of some sort. Ofelia squatted down with a grunt of her own and tried to drag the wet mattress out from under the table. It had absorbed enough water to add kilos to its weight, and it stuck to the damp floor beneath it. She yanked harder, wishing she had had the sense to prop it up on something in the first place. Of course, she hadn't meant to have the door open and rain blowing in. She still couldn't remember whether she herself had left it open when she went out to walk in the calm at the heart of the storm. Not that it mattered, really.

She tugged again and again, and the mattress resisted. Suddenly, four bony odd-shaped hands with long dark nails gripped it; it slid suddenly towards her and she fell backwards. The mattress landed on her feet. She looked over; two of the creatures, still holding the mattress, were watching her. 'Thank you,' she said. It was important to thank children, if they were trying to help, even if they got it wrong. That way they would keep trying. She dragged her feet out from under the mattress, levered herself up to a squat again, and tugged. They tugged. With her guidance, they got the mattress out from under the table and up on end, propped sagging against a wall.

Ofelia put her hands to her back, and sighed. Tonight she would sleep in her own bed, if she was still alive, and rest. She looked around. One of the creatures was poking at the loose beads; another had picked up her beaded and fringed netted garment and was shaking it softly, listening to the sounds it made. Children! Always into things, always moving things, always making messes.

'That's mine,' she said. The heads turned, the eyes stared. It wasn't quite as bad now; she knew they could stare very well without doing anything else. She took the garment from the one who held it – it released it to her without resistance – and then realized they could have no idea what it was for. 'It's a dress,' she said. She might as well show them; it wasn't as if they were people, who might make comments about her handiwork.

She wriggled into the garment, enjoying as before the feel of it against her – she had finally gotten that set of beads in just the right place, and the itchy place just under her shoulderblade now had an automatic scratcher every time she moved. Her hands moved without her thought, touching the beads, the bits of bright color and softness and smoothness and texture.

'That's better,' she said.

'Zzzzt . . .' said one of them, pointing its long hard fingernail at her.

'No. Not zzzzt. I made this.' Her hands spread, then she picked up a loose bead and threaded it onto one of her twisted-grass strings. 'I like to make things.' She picked up another bead, a tiny spacer, then another larger one, and showed them. They all approached; she sensed real interest.

NINE

Ofelia finally elected to sleep in the control room. She simply could not be sure that the creatures would leave it alone otherwise. Not that they couldn't push her aside, if they chose to, but so far they hadn't. She collected an armful of dry fabric from the sewing rooms, and spread it on the floor for a mattress. She had slept on worse. The night before, she reminded herself, she had slept on the bare damp floor with a roomful of aliens.

She shut the door in their faces. They made noises through the door, and she ignored them. She spread her material next to the door, and lay down, grunting with exhaustion and aching joints. She really was too old for this. She could not think of a time when it would have been easy, but now she resented it with additional vigor. She had been living exactly as she pleased since the other colonists left, constrained only by what she thought of as real things: weather, the needs of her garden crops, or the animals.

Now she was sleeping – or rather, not sleeping – on a hard floor instead of her own bed simply because some pesky aliens that reminded her too much of demanding children couldn't be trusted to stay out of the control room. Like children, they could do immense harm without even knowing it, and unlike children they offered no compensations: she had no desire at all to cuddle them. If she slept, she would wake up stiff and sore. If she didn't sleep, she would be exhausted in the morning, and there they would be, bright-eyed as children, who always got the sleep they needed, no matter what happened to the adults.

It was the end of her life. It was supposed to be simple. She had been so sure she'd worked it out at last. The end, she'd assumed, would be unpleasant, but at least it would be *private*. No one would disturb her; no one would wake her up, demand things from her.

She dozed for awhile, waking as uncomfortably as she'd expected, but unaccountably happy. From outside soft sounds came through the door . . . rhythmic sounds, harmonious sounds. Music? Were the alien creatures making music?

She had never thought of aliens as making music. She had never known any musicians at all. Music came from boxes: from cube players, from transmitted entertainment. Sometimes she had seen, in a cube drama, someone actually making music, and far back in her life, in the primary school, the children had been taught music appreciation. She could still remember the field trip to the symphony rehearsal. But no one she knew could play an instrument. Everyone sang, of course. Some better, some worse, but all mothers, she supposed, hummed to their babies. All couples in love sometimes sang along with favorite songs, strolling down a crowded street . . . she and Caitano had. But Humberto had told her she couldn't carry a tune, and after that she sang only for the babies, tuneless murmurings that soothed them. The other women

had sung, sometimes, as they worked together, but she
had never joined in.

How did those creatures make music? She tried to think
of the things they carried on those straps slung around
them. Sacks and gourds, mostly, and the long knives in
their sheaths. No instrument she had seen a picture of
would fit into those shapes. Were they just singing and
pounding the floor?

She edged off her inadequate pad of cloth and cautiously
opened the door a crack. She could not see them; they
must be down the hall somewhere. But she could hear
better, and what she heard had a lilting, laughing quality
that made her chuckle even as she told herself it was
ridiculous. DA-dah-dah DIM-duh DIM-duh DIM-duh . . .
and a tune that tickled her ears. It wasn't quite right, she
thought; perhaps they all sang flat, the way Humberto had
said she did, or perhaps their music was simply that
different. But it was music, and she had to know how it
was made. She told herself that her joints hurt too much
to go back to sleep.

She opened the door wider and put her head out.
Nothing to see. Light spreading from the open door of
one of the sewing rooms. A faint whiff of unpleasant odor
from the floor, where they'd cleaned up their messes. And
that sound.

Slowly, silently, Ofelia crawled down the hall toward
the light. Now she could hear complex under-rhythms,
little sounds much like seeds in a seed pod, or a handful
of beads. A haunting, breathy sound carrying the tune, a
sound she identified with no instrument she knew. And
something else, something that tingled in her ears.

When she peered around the door, they were all sitting
in a ring; they had pushed the long tables to one side.

She could not see much, but she could see that one of them had a set of tubes up to its mouth. It must be blowing them. The elbows of one with its back to her moved, and a tangle of notes rang out above the melody. Ofelia felt tears burning her eyes. What *was* that? Suddenly the others began to chant something, more or less along with the instruments. One held up a hand, and they lowered their voices abruptly; several glanced in the direction Ofelia would have been had she been in the control room. If they had been humans, that would have been awareness of someone sleeping, someone who should not be disturbed. But these were aliens. What were they thinking? She crouched against the wall of the hall, not looking, just listening. Their voices together had a roughspun quality, more like thick crochet or knitted fabric than fine weaving. Her ears liked it, as her hands liked thick soft yarn better than thin thread.

She did not know she had gone to sleep in their music until she woke to find them standing over her. She had fallen asleep half-sitting against the wall; she had a crick in her neck, and her mouth felt dirty and used. She blinked up at them. One still held the handful of tubes. It blew into them now, soft breathy sounds, notes that might have been no more than the wind around corners except they were so pure. Then the creature cocked its head to one side.

Was it asking if she'd heard? Or if it had woken her? Or if it had put her to sleep? She had no idea. She liked the sound. She reached out, meaning to gesture *Go on*, and the creature handed her the tubes.

There were seven of them, polished, tied together with braided strips of grass almost as fine as thread. Ofelia bent her head to look closely at the work. Someone had made those narrow strips, then braided them – evenly, she noticed – and then braided the braid with others, and wrapped the tubes. The tubes themselves felt light, like the bones of birds or stems of great reeds. They had been stained a deep vermilion, so she could not tell what color they had been. Unless that was the color. They smelled like the creatures themselves, a pungent but unclassifiable odor.

The creature's hand came close now, pointing to one end of the tubes. Ofelia saw little notches carved in the tubes. She blew experimentally into the end of one; a sound came out, not musical at all but breathy and harsh. She tried another with the same result.

'I'm sorry,' she said, handing it back to the creature. 'I can't play it.'

Was that satisfaction on its face? It blew a ruffling flourish, triumphant, then stared at her.

Ofelia grinned. 'It's lovely,' she said. 'I wish I could do that.'

She looked at the others. One held a gourd covered with a network of laces strung with beads. It shook the gourd, and produced the light rattling rhythm she'd heard. It held the gourd out. Ofelia took it, and shaking it remembered a rhythm from her childhood, a song she and Caitano had danced to. She felt her toes wiggling as she tried to match the memory with present sound. A deeper drumming joined her; she looked up, startled. One of them bounced a stick – a stick that looked remarkably like a bone – against its torso. She lost her rhythm, found it again. Now one of them clicked long black toenails against the floor. The one with the collection of tubes blew into them again.

Ofelia concentrated on the rhythm she was trying to make, but she kept losing it in the confusion with the other sounds. Finally she quit trying, and simply shook the gourd back and forth. Around her the creatures made a variety of sounds, all of which wove together in ways she enjoyed without understanding. when her arm got tired, she quit shaking the gourd and just listened. She had not ever imagined what it would be like to make music in a group . . . it was fun, she decided, but it would be more fun if she knew what they were doing.

When they stopped, she grinned and handed up the gourd to whichever one would take it. Then she shook her arm, to explain why she had quit. She thought she might look for some of the old cubes, the ones the colonists had played for recreation nights, and let them hear what human music was like. Most of the cubes were gone, of course; people had combined their cube libraries when they came, but reclaimed favorites when they left.

Tomorrow. She was too tired tonight, too ready to go back to sleep. She got to her feet, grunting a little, then shuffled back down the hall to the control room. They watched, but did not follow. She shut herself in, lay down on the thin pallet and wondered if they would keep making music. If they did, she did not hear it. She woke when one of them bumped against the door, woke all at once in a fright, her heart racing. But they didn't try to push their way in. It was nothing like that other time, the time she woke to the bump on the door and it was the shadow in shadows pushing his way in, wanting her, wanting her despite her refusal. Ofelia sat still until she regained her breath. Not the same at all. Now that she could hear something other than the blood rushing in her own ears, she could hear them down the hall, grunts and squawks.

She looked at the chronometer before she opened the door. Midmorning already; she had had plenty of sleep.

When she opened the door, sunlight streamed in the open front door. No creatures. Ofelia closed the control room door behind her and went to look in the kitchen. Another mess – one of them had broken a jar of kilfa and the pungent smell of the green berries filled the room. Ofelia grumbled to herself as she swept up the spice and the glass shards. Like children indeed – you had to keep after them, after them every time.

But they seemed to be gone. They weren't in the sewing rooms, or the hall, or the assembly room where Ofelia had heard the colonists debating which destination to choose. When she looked out into the muddy lane, she saw tracks leading away eastward, but no creatures.

They would be back, but in the meantime, she could check on her own house and garden. The mud in the lane squished between her toes; in the ditches, the water trickled clear at the bottom. It was a hot, muggy day, typical of the weather after sea-storms; the sun felt like a soggy hot towel on her shoulders as she walked across to her house.

There on the floor were the blurred marks left by the one who had followed her inside, the wet towels, already mildewing, she had used to dry it. Ofelia hated the mildew smell. She took the towels outside and spread them on the garden fence. This time it had not blown over. The plants, flattened by wind and rain, were beginning to recover, lifting a few leaves above those still beaten flat. Ofelia picked the tomatoes that hadn't been turned to mush, gathered a handful of beans, and four ears of corn. She had pulled most of the cornstalks upright again when shrieks erupted in the forest.

Now what? Ofelia noticed that the sheep were ignoring the din, nibbling placidly at the meadowgrass nearby. The shrieks and yelps came nearer. She could see nothing, but whatever it was must be in the lower brush now. Then it came nearer – a troop of the treeclimbers, tails high, loping toward the village and screaming. The sheep lifted their heads, ears stiff. Behind the treeclimbers – on either side – were the aliens, their high-stepping gait now lengthened into an easy, efficient run. They were herding the tree-climbers . . . herding them to the village. The sheep bolted, scattering with frightened noises of their own.

As she watched, one of the creatures lengthened its stride, caught up with a treeclimber, and caught it by the neck. At once, it slung the treeclimber around, like a child swinging a doll by the arm, and at the same time drew its long knife with its other forelimb. No, Ofelia wanted to cry. No. But it was far too late; the knife finished what the snap of the neck had begun, and the dead treeclimber twitched, its blood draining out into the grass. Two more had been killed; the surviving treeclimbers made it to the village, where they raced up to the rooftops and chittered wildly.

Ofelia unclenched her fingers from the fence. So the creatures hunted. She had known they could not eat human food. They would have been hungry after the days of storm. And those were only treeclimbers.

Yet . . . it was hard for her to reconcile her memory of the night before, making music with the creatures, with this: with the creatures lapping the blood as it flowed from the necks of their prey, with the quick, efficient gutting of the carcasses. Would they eat them raw? She couldn't stand to see it if they did, yet she could not look away. The little troop had formed again, the dead treeclimbers slung by their tails from the belts of those who had caught them (she thought – she was just beginning to know the differences between them).

They saw her. One of them waved a bloody knife, as if in greeting. Or threat. Ofelia swallowed. Behind them, the pile of innards had already attracted a swarm of black buzzing things that Ofelia knew were not really flies. She turned away and went inside her house, but did not shut the door. She hoped they would leave her alone (that bloody knife) but if they didn't, she did not want to be surprised by a knock on the door. She looked at the orange-red tomatoes, the green beans, the green husks of corn over the yellow kernels. She wasn't hungry.

Through the window, she saw them pass, highstepping over her garden fence, walking through as if they owned it. Most went on over the lane fence, but one looked in the kitchen door and squawked.

'I saw you,' Ofelia said. 'Go away.' As if it understood, it turned away. Then it swung back, and pointed at the vegetables on her table. 'You can't eat that,' Ofelia said. 'That's my food.'

A grunt. A complicated movement of the upper limbs that she thought might be like a shrug in meaning, and it left, hopping nimbly over the lane fence. She could hear its feet squelch in the mud.

Where were they going, muddy-footed, with bloody prey slung from their belts? Not to center—! Ofelia looked out to see. They were strolling along the lane, pointing at one of the treeclimbers that squatted on a roof-edge. They were strolling east, toward the shuttle field. Her stomach turned, remembering the bloated corpses the Company reps had left.

All day she told herself it was only natural. Of course they had to eat, and of course nothing in the village could feed them, any more than she could eat the fruit of the great forest trees. Why shouldn't they hunt? Humans hunted, if they lived on worlds with game they could eat, and they ate farm animals elsewhere. She herself liked meat. She didn't like killing, but then she hadn't learned how early enough. These things had been hunting from childhood, she supposed. It didn't mean they were killers, really. Killing things to eat was not the same thing as killing them just to kill.

But the treeclimbers were just as dead. And she had not seen them eating the treeclimbers. Suppose it had been only sport, only for fun. She shivered. Those long knives . . . had that been how the other colonists died? No, because she had heard explosions. They had spoken of other weapons.

She had seen no weapons but the knives, no tools but the musical instruments. Were these the same aliens that killed, or something else? And how had they lived here for forty years without meeting them before?

In the afternoon, she went back to the center, secured the door to the control room as well as she could, and latched the other doors, including the outside door. Then she went back to her house. It was not secure – nothing was secure – but she wanted to sleep in her own bed again. If it was the last night, very well: she would be comfortable for that night, at least. No more sleeping on floors, whatever happened.

She had stretched out on her bed, her body happily finding its hollows and bulges again, when she heard them coming back up the lane in the dark. Grunts, squawks, more of the low churring that sounded like contentment. The one with the set of tubes was blowing into it again; she could hear the notes above their gabble.

She knew when they came to the locked center by the

chorus of squawks. Anger? Disappointment? Who could tell, with aliens? Thumps against that door. Would it hold? More gabble. Then, inevitably, thumps against her own door, followed by a trill from that odd collection of tubes. Ofelia felt a rush of hot anger. They had the whole village to live in: why did they have to bother her? Why couldn't they let her rest? Didn't they know she was an old woman, a tired old woman who needed her sleep?

Of course they didn't. She had no idea how old they were. Grumbling, she got off the bed, turned on the light, and went to the door, in no humor to cooperate with them, whatever they wanted.

The one with the instrument held it up, shook it, and then gestured to the center. It probably meant it wanted to hold another musical night there. She didn't. She wanted to sleep in her own bed, all night long, without interruption. And she wasn't about to turn them loose in the center without her supervision.

'Sleep somewhere else,' she said. 'All the houses are open.' Except hers; she stood in the door determined not to let them in.

The one with the instrument shook it again, pointed again, and this time held out two of its long-nailed digits. Two? Two *what*? Two musical evenings, two nights, two of the creatures? Now it pointed at the instrument, and then at the center door, then held up two digits.

'I don't want you in there alone,' Ofelia said. 'You'll make more mess.' The many eyes blinked at her. The creatures did not go away; they did not move. She knew if she shut the door, they would bang on it again. She knew she could not get to sleep until they were satisfied. It was as bad as having the family again. She knew she had given up a long moment before she was ready to admit it to them. 'All *right*,' she said. 'But you're not spending the night there.' They would, and she couldn't stop them. She would have to decide where to sleep, and her body had already made that decision. She needed her own bed.

When she opened the center door, two of them slipped past her and darted into the sewing room on the right. The rest stayed in the lane. In the light streaming out from the hall, Ofelia saw that no tree-climber bodies hung from their belts; they must have eaten them. She shivered. The two creatures reappeared, one with another bundle of tubes, and one with the gourd hung with strings and beads. They waved these at the others, and with a series of rapid grunts the whole company moved off down the lane, east-ward as they had come.

All they had wanted was their instruments. Ofelia could hardly believe it. She turned off the lights, relatched the door, and watched as the shadowy forms melted into the darkness farther down the lane. Back in her own house she lay a long time awake in her bed. Who could imagine how aliens thought? Who could imagine why they did what they did? The music she enjoyed, but the killing . . . so quick, so easy, so casual . . . though she had seen people kill like that, the quick twist of the neck for chickens, the quick thrust of the knife for sheep, for calves. But not at a run, not loping across the grass. She could not help but imagine herself, her old stiff body in a shambling, hope-less run, with the creatures chasing her, laughing to each other, enjoying the chase, until one of those hard-taloned hands caught her by the neck, and one of those long sharp knives emptied her belly onto the grass.

The soft music trickled in through the closed shutters of her windows. They had settled somewhere nearby, perhaps in a corner of some garden, and now they made music. She imagined the comfort of having full bellies after several hungry days during the storm, and heard that in the music. Not that it made sense. She fell asleep at last, arguing with herself about whether it made more sense to sing or sleep after a feast. Her dreams terrified, but never quite woke her.

Morning. Still muggy, but less so. A stronger breeze from the sea, damp but fresher. Ofelia woke comforted by her own bed, by the familiar shapes and smells of her own room. The terrors of the dreams translated quickly to the comfort of her own space, her own time.

She went into her garden before the sun was high, for the first time in too many days. The tracks of the creatures didn't bother her; they had mashed only two bean plants and one of the green squashes. She busied herself restaking the tomatoes, raking away the rotting leaves, loosening the soil. She found a little yellow tomato, one of the sweet ones, that she had missed the evening before, and put it straight into her mouth. Sweet, juicy. A grunt across the fence; Ofelia looked up to see one of the creatures watching her. How had it come so silently? She kept turning up leaves, looking for crawlers, for slimerods, for aphids, for another ripe yellow tomato. A slimerod halfway up the stem; she picked it off and cracked it.

The creature squawked. Ofelia looked at it. It held out its digits.

'You want the slimerod?' She could not believe that. Slimerods were slimy, itchy nuisances. But she walked over and dropped the slimerod into that waiting hand. The creature grunted at her, and flipped the slimerod into its mouth.

Ofelia tasted bile at the back of her throat. Eating a *slimerod*. 'That's disgusting,' she said, even though she knew it couldn't understand. Its expression didn't change. She wasn't sure what its expression meant anyway. She went back to her work. When she found another slimerod, she looked over her shoulder. There it was, watching her. She held up the slimerod. It reached out; this time she gave it the slimerod uncracked. Again that flip of the hand, that quick crunch and gulp. Utterly disgusting. Yet slimerods were native here, so something must eat them. Why not these creatures?

She found another slimerod under one of the squash plants, already halfway through the stem. Dratted thing. She pulled it out, handed it to the waiting creature as it leaned over the fence, and then pulled off the unripe squashes. The vine would die; she would save what she could. She could pickle the little squashes just like cucumbers, at this stage. Sometimes she even ate them raw, though most were too bitter. She nibbled the end of one. Not too bad. The creature grunted sharply, and when she looked up, its eyes had narrowed, just like the one with the mop. Distress? Well, she had been distressed when it ate the slimerod. Defiantly, she bit a larger chunk from the squash, only to find it too bitter after all. She swallowed with difficulty, tossed the rest of the squash across the garden toward the compost trench, and smiled at the creature.

It did not move for a long moment, then seemed to shake itself slightly before turning to walk off. Westward down the lane, she saw three others, walking with that high-stepping easy stride that made her think of them all as exuberant children. Ofelia shrugged and went back to work. She had a lot to do, and today she really must check on the animals.

The sheep, when she found them, were huddled at the

west end of their long meadow, ears twitching nervously. When she tried to approach them, they broke into a panicky run as if she were a wolf. She didn't try to chase them; she knew better. Instead she tried to count . . . were there as many? It seemed so, though in the flowing mass of gray backs and twinkling feet she could not be sure. Had the alien creatures been tormenting them? It seemed possible, but she had no proof. She went on around the west end of the village to the river meadows. The river had risen, spreading out from its banks. The cattle, unlike the sheep, seemed calm, spread out grazing between the pump house and the old calf-pen. Ofelia counted them; none were missing.

Back in the village itself, she began to make her rounds looking for damage from the storm. Broken shutters, damage to roofs, fallen trees. From time to time she saw the creatures in the distance, but none of them approached her. She couldn't figure out what they were doing, but if they didn't bother her or the animals she really didn't care.

By nightfall, Ofelia had surveyed the village and knew all the repairs she would have to make. She remembered that she had considered letting some of the buildings go, not worrying about them any more, but that had been pre-storm depression. She never had any energy before a big storm. Now it was over, and she could not imagine just letting things slide, no matter how tired she was.

She opened the center to check the weather monitor. No storms approaching, though far to the east another whirl of clouds might become one. Two storms in one season were very rare; it had happened only twice in forty-odd years. Probably that storm would veer away and go somewhere else. She hoped so.

She unlocked the keyboards to enter a brief report on the past few days. How could she say this? Even though she knew no one would ever read it, she didn't want it to be as crazy as it was. 'In the middle of the storm, I went out and there was an alien in the street.' That sounded like an entertainment cube, something made up by the crazy people. She wasn't crazy. They were real. How could she make them sound real?

Clicking in the hall. Of course they would have come in; she hadn't closed the door. She looked around. One was watching her, its eyes bright and interested. Of course they were real. It held the gourd with the beaded strings wrapped around it; when she met its gaze, it shook the gourd.

What was that? Invitation? Explanation? She didn't know. She didn't really want to think about it; she wanted to get this into the record in some way that made sense to her, that might make sense to another human, even though another human wouldn't see it.

Her experience in writing about the colony's past was not enough. She could tell about the loves and hates, the betrayals, the quarrels, because she understood them fully. She knew exactly how the wife felt when the husband was jealous for no cause – or with cause. She knew how the human feelings acted on each other, flavoring the simplest interaction with complicated swirls of hidden meaning. But these? It would be like writing about animals, and she had never written about animals. It would be like writing about animals that could think, and she had never known animals that could think.

She waved dismissively at the creature; it withdrew. Was it understanding her gesture, or just not that interested in what she was doing?

'In the middle of the storm . . .' She read what she had written. 'Alien' was the wrong word, really. These were native animals, like the treeclimbers. What was the word for that? She didn't know, and she wasn't going to ask the dictionary function now. Aliens would do for the moment, or native beings. Creatures.

'I thought it was a pile of trash, and then it looked at me.' That sounded sufficiently crazy too. But that's what she'd seen, a pile of trash with eyes. Let them laugh at her, the ones who might read this if anyone ever came to find out about those who had died.

Slowly, with many corrections, she tried to put it down. It was not, as she'd hoped, a short task. For it to make any sense at all, she had to put in her feelings, her inferences, her assumptions. She had to put in everything she had done, and everything they had done. She had to try to reproduce the sounds they made . . . no, she didn't. The automatic recorders would have recorded some of it. She could insert that into her own record, if she could retrieve the right segment.

When she leaned over to the other control board, to enter the search criteria for the segments she wanted, her back cramped. She gasped with the pain, and a squawk from outside let her know that the creatures were still observing her, as much as she was observing them.

It was late. It was very, very late and she would sleep late in the morning and feel groggy and miserable half the day if she didn't go home and go to sleep now. She shut the boards down, resetting the alarms, and got herself upright with many pops and creaks from her joints. Three of the creatures were sitting in the hall when she came out. She shut the door behind her, retied the latch she'd improvised, and said firmly 'Let it alone. It's not for you.'

They said nothing, only watched her as she went down the hall.

Would they follow? No. They wanted to be in the center without her, and she was not strong enough to get them out. At the moment she didn't care. She wanted sleep, in her own bed, and if they destroyed all the machines that had helped her stay alive, then she would die. But she would not worry about it now.

TEN

The next morning, Ofelia woke with the sensation that she had been fuzzy-headed for days, missing things she should have seen. Aliens, yes. Intelligent aliens, yes. And they hadn't killed her yet. They had . . . *studied* her. They had arrived before the storm, how long before she could not know. The houses she had found open, the things she had found moved . . . they had moved them. They were not thinking of her as prey, or as an enemy, but as something interesting.

She did not have to fear the chase, the long knives.

Unless they were like some people she had known.

She could not know that. She could not know anything, unless she studied them as well. She had no idea how to do that, but she could try, as she had tried to understand Sara's third child, who had been born without the gift of speech, who had mewed and screamed.

They did not scream. When she went out into her garden, one of them was there, carefully looking among her plants. She suspected it wanted more slimerods, but it would not find them among the maize rows. She found one under the tomatoes, a favorite haunt, and called to the creature.

'Here's one.' It looked around; she pointed to the slimerod. It came, picked it up deftly, and flipped it into its mouth. Ofelia managed not to shudder. 'We call them slimerods,' Ofelia said. She realized that she had not really looked at the creatures more than she had to. She had resisted thinking of those taloned digits as fingers . . . of the collection of them as hands. Yet they functioned as her hands functioned.

Now she looked. Four digits, not five. One, as in her own hand, broader and thicker, angled to oppose the others. This made the hand look longer and narrower than it really was. The wrist too was different, though she could not define it. Did the creature have two bones in its lower arm, or only one? One bone in the upper arm, or more? Were the bones *bones* or something else?

Four fingers, she told herself. Four-fingered hands. She watched, as the creature turned over more tomato leaves itself. The long, hard talons didn't interfere with precise, delicate movement. It didn't tear the leaves; it didn't miss turning any of them.

She looked down at the creature's feet. All she had seen at first were long feet with splayed toes. Now she noticed four toes, three almost parallel and one angled aside, all with heavy dark toenails blunted at the tips. No . . . the angled one had a narrow front, almost spike-like. This creature, placidly squatting in her garden and turning up leaves, had its feet flat on the soil, but the tracks she had seen didn't show the heel. How, then, did it walk? On its toes? She turned away and looked over the lane fence. There were two of them far down the lane; she couldn't tell.

She wasn't a . . . whatever it was that studied animals or aliens. She didn't know how to do this.

It grunted, and she turned back to it. It held a ripening tomato in the pincer of its digits; it had not bruised the tomato nor broken the stem.

'It's not ripe yet,' Ofelia said, shaking her head. Gesture might be easier than words; certainly she had learned none of their words yet. Assuming the grunts and squawks were words, and she had to assume that now. She spotted a ripe tomato on another plant and touched it. 'This one is ready. Ripe.' She nodded, then pulled it off. The creature looked at her a long moment, then let go of the one it had touched. Ofelia put the tomato in the basket and then picked a handful of beans. The creature touched the beans, then the tomato. Different. Of course they were different, beans and tomatoes. Green beans, orange tomato. Long skinny beans, fat round tomato. 'Beans,' Ofelia said, touching the beans. 'Beans.' Then the tomato. 'Tomato.'

The creature grunted, making no attempt to say the words.

'Beans,' Ofelia said again. 'These are beans. Tomato.'

A series of grunts, none resembling the words she had spoken. Why should she expect words? They were aliens; they might not be able to make the same sounds. Terran animals couldn't. Besides, she had more work to do. She picked more beans, aware of the creature watching her closely. When she had as much as she wanted, she stood, grunting. Did the creatures think her involuntary grunts and groans were attempts at speech? She couldn't tell. This one had not reacted in any way she could detect to the noise she made.

It followed her to the door of the house, but did not come in. She rubbed her feet on the doorstone, scraping off the bits of mulch that clung to them. The creature watched that, head tilted. She did not shut the door, but she glanced that way often. She put the beans in the drawer of the cooler; she would cook them in the evening. The tomatoes went in a bowl on the table.

When she opened the containers of flour, salt, sugar, the creature leaned in the door. Ofelia decided to make raised bread instead of flatbread. Yeast breads had always been a festival bread, made but once or twice a year. The waste recycler was capable of maintaining a yeast culture, but the flatbread was familiar, and so much faster. She had not made yeast bread since before the colonists left. Could she remember exactly how much sugar? She really should look it up.

When she took down the stained little book that had been her mother's, she glanced again at the creature. Would it understand reading? Did it have any similar system for making words last? She paged through the book. Some people insisted that there was no need for hardcopy cookbooks, but Ofelia liked this one. It reminded her of her mother.

She put the lump of yeast culture from the cooler into warm water with a pinch of sugar and flour. Sugar, salt, fat – she could use the fat she'd saved from the sausages. Rosara had not approved of using that fat, but Ofelia saw no reason to make the waste recycler clean it. She melted the fat and strained it into her big mixing bowl through a clean cloth cut from one of Barto's old shirts. Then she mixed the fat, the sugar, the salt, with warm water and tested it with her wrist. Warm enough, cool enough.

She glanced at the door. Two of the creatures now, both watching intently. Ofelia scooped flour into the big mixing bowl, stirring with a wooden paddle. She didn't measure the flour; she knew that by feel. The lump of yeast culture had softened, was beginning to bubble in its little cup of water and sugar. She poured it in and kept stirring. When it was smooth, she worked in more flour, and more, until the dough pulled away from the bowl. Now flour on the table, plenty of it – her mother had said there was no use making raised bread if you were going to worry about wasting a little flour – and she turned the dough out.

It was fun to knead. This was something else she had missed, without realizing it. A few of the women had made raised bread more often; they had said they enjoyed it. At the time, Ofelia had thought of the mess it made, the flour drifting onto the floor, their hands sticky with dough. Now, her fingers sank into the warm dough, enjoying its resilience, the way it pushed back against her. She turned it, flattened it, rolled it up and flattened it again.

The creatures chittered. Ofelia looked at them. One had cocked its head, and now lifted a foot, as if to step forward. Was it asking permission? She chose to think it was.

'Yes, come on,' she said, sweeping a welcome with one floury hand. It came to the table, and leaned over, peering closely at the bread dough. One taloned digit hovered over the dough. She could see the dirt around the long, dark nail, and who knew what else under it? 'You have to wash,' Ofelia said. She nodded at the sink, and when the creature didn't move, she sighed. Just like children, who never believed they were that dirty. She brushed the flour off her hands, and reached slowly to take the creature's arm. 'Wash,' she said. 'Over here.' She led it to the sink, and nodded again.

It looked at its hands, and then at hers. With only a little fumbling, it turned the water on and held its hands under the flow. It eyed Ofelia. She didn't want to get her hands wet, not when she still had more kneading to do, so she mimed scrubbing. The creature blinked, but complied, and she could see the dirt coming away from its nails. Ofelia turned off the water when she thought it was clean enough, and handed it a dishcloth.

'Dry off,' she said. As if it could understand, it squeezed the cloth in its hands, drying them well enough. Then it followed her back to the table. Again it extended a tentative digit. Ofelia nodded this time, and it poked at the dough, giving a sharp *Eerp* when its digit sank into the dough and came out sticky. Ofelia grinned, and went back to kneading the dough.

The creature touched the dough more lightly, then very slowly moved its digit to her face. What? Ofelia felt herself frowning. Again, very slowly, the creature touched the dough, and then this time her mouth. She couldn't figure it out. She put her own finger on the bread, lifted it to her mouth – oh. Of course. Eating. It wanted to know if this was food.

'Yes, but not yet,' she said. How to explain bread? She made an attempt anyway, moving her hands to show the dough growing fat, the second kneading, the second rising, the shaping into loaves, the baking. The creature's expression didn't change. Well, it would have to observe, that was all. The dough had gone silky, the way it should, firm and responsive under her hand. She covered it with a cloth, cleaned her hands, and remembered that she had meant to cook a pot of beans. She opened another container, poured out the beans into a cooking pot, and covered them with water.

The creature watched closely as she did this, then reached out to the cloth-covered dough. 'Let it alone,' Ofelia said sharply. 'It needs to rise.' Again, she mimed the enlargement of the dough. The creature pulled its hand back.

She had more work to do. She needed to air the house, sweep the floor. She eyed the creature but it didn't go away. Well, then, let it watch. Ofelia went to work, and the creature watched. It moved away when she came toward it with the broom, staying out of her way, but not departing. When the bread dough had risen, and she punched it down, the creature stood beside her. It skipped back a step when the dough whoofed out its excess air, then came forward again as Ofelia kneaded and shaped the dough into two round loaves. She put the cloth back over the loaves, and checked the beans. They had just begun to soften.

By the time the bread had risen the second time, Ofelia had her house cleaned to her satisfaction. Now, with the creature watching closely, she turned on her oven, and when it was hot enough, she put the loaves into it: The creature seemed fascinated by the hot gush of air from the oven when she opened it. Ofelia waved it back – it could not know what part of the stove got dangerously hot. Then she showed the creature the cooler. Like a small child, the creature stood in the cold flow of air from the open door until Ofelia pushed past to shut it.

'You can't waste it,' she said. The creature looked at her, and Ofelia was sure it wanted to argue, as her children had. She had no intention of arguing. She wanted to find some way to communicate with these creatures, some sound they could both make. 'Cooler,' she said, laying her hand on it. 'Cooler – makes things cold.' The creature stared, as always. She moved to the stove. 'Stove,' she said. 'Makes thing hot. Hot . . . cold.'

The creature fumbled at the cooler latch, opened it, and waved its hand in the direction of the downward flow of cold air. The sound it made was neither *cooler* nor *cold*, but it did begin with a harsh consonant that Ofelia thought might be an attempt at a 'kuh.' Somewhat to her surprise, it closed the door.

'Cooler,' Ofelia said again. 'Cold.'

'Kuh.'

Well, it would do. It was a start. Babies started that way, one sound at a time. It moved to the stove, held its hand safely above it. Now what? Should she say 'stove' or 'hot'? She had always said 'hot' to babies, but these weren't babies. It grunted, clearly impatient. She might not know the words, but she had a lifetime's experience with impatience.

'Hot' she said, emphasizing the initial sound. 'Hot.'

'Kuh.' It patted at the cooler.

They knew nothing. They would not know that flour came from grain, and the grain from grasses, from the seeds of wheat grown in the little walled plots to protect them from sheep and cattle. They would not know about cutting the grain, beating the gathered stalks to release the seeds, winnowing the seeds to remove the chaff. Or perhaps they did know that much; perhaps they harvested this world's equivalent of grass in much the same way. Ofelia wondered how much they did know, and how she could find out. Were any of those things hanging from the belts and straps the equivalent of sickle and shears?

She remembered that in the first years of the colony, long ago, the colonists had had to do it all by hand. The machines were too busy fabricating parts for other machines, for building materials, for cloth and crockery. She and the others had cleared and weeded and harvested with hand tools that gave them blisters and sore backs. Later, the fabricator had turned out little harvesters that fit even in the smallest enclosures and could cut the grain faster than women with sickles. The fabricator could convert rough grain to coarse or fine flour, with the waste material remade into a variety of forms. Even though she had grown up in a city, with store-bought foods, she had been almost awed by the little machines, the first harvest that she didn't have to do all by hand.

Would these creatures be awed? Did they believe in magic? Or would they take it all for granted?

The conversation begun when the People first found the city ran alongside a dozen others. Was this the same kind of monster? It wore no clothes on its feet, and little on its body. Yet it had the short soft toes of the invaders, thieves, nest-destroyers. It had five of those toes, and five on the upper limbs. It had white hair instead of dark on its head, but the same arrangement of holes and protuberances.

It is the same. There is the scar where the flying monsters landed.

It is not the same. It is alone; it has white on top.

It is interesting. It does things strangely.

It is a monster, what did you expect?

It is not a hunter. Is it prey?

We cannot eat it. We can watch it.

Soft skin. Wrinkles. Things hang loose.

Things! Ornaments, seed-eater!

Ornaments. It had ornaments hanging on it, ornaments it changed from day to day. What did that mean? A way of counting, a way of responding to the weather? Who could tell? Worth watching, worth learning from. If more came, they would know more about them.

And so much else to learn from. All those tools,

containers, fasteners, noisy boxes, picture boxes. They had drummed to an agreement that no one would touch or handle the obvious triggers except for those the monster demonstrated and offered to them: the light, the water. Hot boxes, cold boxes.

If it had not been for the monster's ornaments, they might have believed monsters cared only for boxes: they lived in boxes, kept things in boxes, cooked food in hot boxes, kept food in cold boxes, had pictures and noises in boxes. Some of the People carved boxes of bone or wood, or made them of the skins of grasseaters. But sacks and gourds were more comfortable to travel with. Only those who chose to live in permanent nest grounds had big boxes.

That picture box. It is like the bird's seeing.

?

The bird, the high bird – higher and higher. Things look small, but the bird sees far.

That high?

The flying monsters scarred the sky. What if they actually cut through it? That far up, they could see all the world at once.

A flurry of arguments about the shape of the world, recapitulating every theory known to the People. The world was flat. The world was not flat, but round like a gourd. It was not round like a gourd, but a rough lump like a stone. No, like the root the burrowers preferred: the gods had hidden the shape there to show that it was sacred. The arguments died down when the eldest, ignoring them, swept a clear space on the ground. They all understood that, and gathered around.

Grass laid in a careful pattern reproduced the gullies between the boxes; the whole array less than a handspan across. The eldest crouched, one eye close to the pattern, then stood, slowly. They watched, saying nothing. So much was obvious; it had been agreed already. Bird's seeing, high seeing, makes small, sees far. So?

Now the eldest swept an arm around, snapped a finger-click, swept the arm again. Estimate! Heads cocked. The young hunter crouched, trying it himself. Here, the monster-box-nests. Here the gullies. So – a grass-joint wide, and when on the braced toes, so much less – then – they knew already the conversion from distance to familiar sizes. So many paces, so hard a throw, to hit the darting burrower. So hard a run, if the grasseaters have that much start. No word for such long distances, but a conversion – that was easy enough.

Less than a day's run across the grassland, more than a day's travel in the too-tall trees. Eyes widened. A day's run UP? They peered into the blue sky, at the puffy clouds. How far then were clouds? How large? Estimates came as effortlessly as breath: if that is a sprint at top speed, then the cloud is larger than five grasseaters, but if it would take a handspan of sunturning, then it is . . . it is the size of a hill. Someone named the hill, and someone else argued for another hill.

Some monster thing up there watching, a monster bird with big eyes. It would have to have big eyes, to see so much, and in the dark. They had seen that the picture moved in the dark as well. The picture itself was never dark.

A picture, the eldest reminded, is a made thing. The choice of the maker, if it is to be light or dark.

A maker up there? A monster still in waiting?

It watches what we do with this monster. It will learn from us as we learn from it.

It knows we killed the monsters.

A shiver through them all. The monsters had been wrong, had been thieving nest-burners, but ... if the monsters could walk UP that far, and stay and watch, perhaps ....

Nests first! said the fierce young one who would soon require a nesting ground. Lose nests, lose People.

Comforting murmurs. Nests will be. Will find nests. A nest for you, for the younglings. Always nests. Nests ...

Nest here. The brashest of them looked around at the monster boxes. Right hand drumming, no agreement. The brashest twisted a neck suddenly too thick for the straps of the travel harness, and looked away. Sorry. No offense meant. Sorry.

The eldest stretched, one long arm after another. Enough now. Relax. Safe here. Rest.

One by one they settled. The eldest opened a stoppered gourd and removed the whistler. The brashest stretched fingers. A few slow notes, up and down. Someone shook the gourd, and seeds and beads shivered, danced, made a rhythm. Long toes curled, tapped on the dirt. Another whistler, wavering at first until the tones met, clasped fingers, and danced together. Now the voices.

Good hunting, good hunting. New hunting, new hunting. The music curled around familiar patterns, engulfing new learning, shaping it to the arch and spring of the known. Monster, monster, dancing, dancing. Monster, monster, boxes, boxes.

'Kuh,' said the creature when it came in the kitchen. Ofelia grinned. So it could remember. She had thought it would. They were not stupid, after all. She went to the cooler and opened it. The creature came to stand beside her. Ofelia scraped some of the frost off the inside of the freezer section with her fingernail and showed it to the creature. It sniffed, its eyes disconcertingly focussed on her instead of the frost.

She felt the shock of its tongue on her finger before she realized it – she had been looking back at its eye, not at her finger. The dry rasp startled her; she felt the air gusting out of her, and jerked her hand away. Its eyelid blinked; it too pulled back with a little burst of air that felt warm on her hand.

Warm. Warmblooded. She had known that. She had felt the heat of their bodies against hers that stormy night. But she had not been so aware of the warmth of their breath. Her hand was across her mouth before she knew it; she could only think of the smell of her own breath, how it might offend. That breath, its breath, had an odd smell, but it wasn't bad.

It was looking at her now, at her finger. Its tongue came out again, and licked what she had to think of as lips. Not so soft and mobile as human lips, but not like the skin of its face. Browner . . . a purplish brown on this one. The tongue, too, was darker than the bright pink of human tongues. It had felt stiffer, dryer, than a child's tongue.

Now, as she watched, the creature reached into the cooler and scraped off some of the frost with its talon. It licked that off with quick little strokes of its tongue. Then it scraped up another lump, and reached toward Ofelia, holding its hand in front of her mouth.

What did it mean? Ofelia looked from the hard dark fingernail with its coating of melting frost, to the golden-brown eyes, and back. Did it expect _her_ to lick _its_ finger? It moved the finger closer to her lips. She swallowed, watching the first drop of water ooze down from the cap of frost.

Courtesy overcame caution. She put out her tongue and touched it gingerly to the frost. Cold, of course. Under the frost, her tongue felt the hard, smooth surface of the nail – talon – whatever it was. Like her own nail; her tongue felt nothing disgusting, only a hard smooth surface topped with cold.

'Kuh,' the creature uttered.

'Kuh,' Ofelia agreed. Her children had liked to eat the frost in the freezer; most children did, in hot weather. She turned away, found a shallow bowl and a wooden spoon, and scraped more of the frost into the bowl. She handed it to the creature, who took it and stood there as if it had no idea what to do next. At least it couldn't expect her to lick its fingers if they were all engaged in holding the bowl. Perhaps it didn't even know the frost would melt into water.

Meanwhile, the cool air was chilling her feet and ankles, and the open door wasted electricity. 'Don't stand in the door,' Ofelia said, and gently nudged the creature away so that she could close it. It moved back, holding the bowl but not looking at the frost. Instead it watched her. She wished it wouldn't. She had had enough for the moment. She poked her finger into the bowl. 'Cold,' she said. 'You can eat all this, if you want.'

It turned its head, then set the bowl on the table, and picked up another finger-tip of frost. She watched as its tongue came out – dark, yes, and more bristly than human tongues, and dryer – and licked at the frost. It looked at Ofelia. She sighed, and took a fingerful of frost she didn't particularly want, just to be polite. If that's what it had meant. It dipped another fingerful, and licked it dry, then paused. That must be what it had meant. Take turns. Did it think she was trying to poison it, or was it being polite?

She had no idea. The cold felt good in her mouth, better than she remembered. She let the frost melt on her tongue, trickle down the sides of her mouth.

The last of the frost had melted before they had taken many turns. The creature dipped its finger in the water and touched it to the long protrusion she now thought of as its nose, above the mouth. Then again, to touch the lids of each eye. It pushed the bowl a little towards her. Ofelia, frowning, put her own finger in the cold water. She didn't know what the gestures meant; she was half afraid to copy them, but she was also afraid not to copy them. What was she saying, if she touched water to her nose, to her eyelids? It would be something about smelling, something about seeing . . . but what? She put her wet finger on her nose, then on her eyelids.

The creature grunted, and walked out of the kitchen without looking back. Now what? Had she insulted it, or was it running off to tell its friends what she had done? She went to the door to see. It hopped over the fence between the lane and the garden and started down the lane. Now she could see that the high-stepping stride was mostly on the toes, with the heel knob touching down only occasionally.

Ofelia shrugged to herself. She had raised bread to eat today; she didn't have to worry about the creatures all the time. She cut herself several slices off one loaf and ate. It was good, from the hard crust to the soft, yielding inner crumb.

Were the creatures like bread? She had touched them several times now, and she still wasn't sure. Their skin – if it was skin – felt harder than hers, but no harder than the calluses she remembered on feet and hands. Were they soft inside? Were their muscles as soft as human muscles, or hard like their skin? Did their shape come from bones in the middle or the hard skin on the outside?

She found herself looking at her bread with new attention. Her science lessons had been a long way back, and no one had seemed to care much whether she really understood living things. A special class understood that, just as a special class understood spaceships or government. What they cared about, all they really cared about, was that she learned to do what she was told and not make messes. Even when Humberto insisted that they both take night classes to qualify as colonists, the instructors had not cared whether she understood the machines she was taught to tend and repair. Follow the instructions, she was told. Follow the diagrams. It's no harder than making a dress from a pattern, one of them told her. Even homemakers like you can do that. She had clenched herself around the pain of his scorn and proved that she could, indeed, follow the diagram accurately.

Of living things she remembered scattered words and images: cells, with skins called membranes around them, endoskeletons like humans and exoskeletons like flies. Cells were round or oval, with more round shapes inside. They looked rather like the holes in the bread, except smaller. She remembered watching a cube presentation of dissection, the way the instructor's knife slit the trembling rat up the belly, the oozing blood that made the boys in class snicker and say cruel things. Some girls had looked away, but she had seen the intricate tangle of intestines, the bright pink lungs, the little dark red pulsing heart.

She had felt her heart pulsing, the first time she had really noticed it, and imagined someone looming over her with a huge knife ready for her belly. And it had happened, but not to her, when her childhood friend had needed her belly opened to have her child. Donna had never forgiven her for not coming to the hospital to visit; Donna had guessed that it was something more than packing to leave.

But the creatures here and now – she made herself quit sending mental apologies to Donna, who had probably died by now, on that distant world where they had been childhood friends – these creatures fit none of the categories she had been taught. She knew she had not learned them all; in her school children had been taught only the biology they needed, that of the living things immediately around them, a small selection of the original rich Terran biology.

These were not plants, she was sure. So they were animals: insects, fish, mammals, birds, reptiles, amphibians. They weren't insects, because insects didn't have warm breath. They weren't fish, because they lived on land and breathed air. They might be amphibians, though they didn't look much like frogs or toads, and she could not tell if they laid eggs. Birds? Birds had feathers and wings, beaks and not mouths. People raised flightless birds for meat, but even those had feathers and small wings. She had seen them. These creatures had no feathers, and no wings; they had mouths, with teeth. Reptiles? Reptiles had scales, were not hot-breathed, were much smaller. Mammals? Mammals had hair and gave milk: she saw no hair on them, and nothing that looked like breasts.

On other worlds where animal life had been found, people had made new classifications, but Ofelia knew only that they existed. She had no idea what they were, or what features had been used to make them. She didn't know what their cells looked like or their blood (could she even call it blood if she saw it? Or were they dry inside? No, because their mess had been wet.)

Ofelia chewed her bread slowly, trying to pull out of her memory information that had not been stored securely in the first place. It was a long time before she realized she could probably find more information in the computer tutorials.

ELEVEN

<Archives of the Consortium, Report on the Attempted Recolonization of 3245.12 after the failure of the Sims Bancorp Ltd. colony and the subsequent loss of license.>

Study of documents entered in evidence by Sims Bancorp at the time of the hearings indicated that the failure of their colony might have been due, in part, to a poor choice of location. Subsequent follow-up was certainly a factor, in that losses resulting from climatic conditions were not replaced, but had the colony been planted appropriately, it might have made at least moderate progress. According to meteorological records, recurrent cyclonic sea-storms with associated flooding caused loss of life, loss of live-stock, loss of equipment (boats, other vehicles) and crop failures.

For this reason, Zeoteka O.S. chose to place its newly licensed colony in the North Temperate Zone, close to but not in the flood plain of a river (see attached charts and scan data.) It was believed that weathersat data indicated the site chosen for the colony's shuttle field had not been flooded in the 42 years of observation.

The colony insertion followed standard practice as specified in the 14th edition of the Unified Field Manual.

Captain Gian Vasoni, commanding the cargo vessel *Ma Jun Vi*, logged several days' observation. Clearance of the Sims Bancorp tropical colony had been completed on schedule; that colony site was clearly visible on broadband scanning. Infrared spectra indicated that the powerplant had not been properly shut down, but there was no activity indicative of remnant population.

Sims Bancorp has claimed that by their records the plant was shut down, but that there were native animals in the region which might, in the intervening time, have accidentally turned it on: the abandoned machines had not been destroyed because there was believed to be no intelligent native life (see original survey data).

Captain Vasoni authorized survey shuttle flights to provide current data about the proposed colony site. The flights recorded data similar to that of the original survey. Temperature, humidity, gas mix, were all within limits. There were small herds or bands of wild animals moving nearby but none within five kilometers of the planned shuttle field. Nor was there any sign of purposeful activity that would have suggested the presence of intelligent, let alone hostile, life forms to nonspecialist personnel. No xenotechnologist or equivalent was available for consultation.

Upon completion of the required survey flights, Captain Vasoni then authorized the retrieval of colonists' capsules, and the first unmanned landings of heavy equipment robotics. Site preparation proceeded normally, and the first shuttle flights containing colonists landed uneventfully. As the facility was extended, and assembly of the prefab shelters began, the ground controller reported the sudden appearance of massed wildlife to the east (sunrising).

The massed wildlife initially appeared to be a stampede of some kind, perhaps frightened by the noise of the shuttles. The ground controller fired smoke cartridges to deter the wildlife. It became apparent that the wildlife were hostile, and were attacking the landing party. It is not known for certain what weapons were used (see attached military analysis) but some of them were definitely projectile and explosive. One shuttle was lost on the parking pad to a projectile which exploded on impact with sufficient force to breach the fuel tanks and explode the fuel. It is assumed that this was not an aimed hit; whatever these creatures are, they could not have had experience with shuttles before.

Captain Vasoni quite properly refused to send additional support to the ground party. Court records show that Captain Vasoni had no resources for a military ground action, nor experienced personnel with which to conduct it. Morever, Captain Vasoni realized that the actions of the putative wildlife reflected possible intelligence as defined in Section XXXII, Subsection 14, of the General Treaty on Space Exploration and Development, and that the regulations governing Alien Contact now superseded all others. Unfortunately, those colonists already on the ground were overrun by the creatures, with great loss of life. Captain Vasoni faced considerable resistance aboard ship to abandoning the personnel on the ground; it became necessary to avert a mutiny by forceful means.

Because of the delay resulting from loss of personnel in both the attempted landing and the mutiny, and the delay caused by lengthy adjudication, the full story of this tragic affair has only now come to the attention of the Bureau of Alien Affairs. Clearly it is imperative that we send an experienced Contact team to assess the native (?) culture and its technological level. Since the Sims Bancorp colony left behind a number of advanced devices prohibited on non-treaty worlds, we must be concerned with the fate of that equipment. What little data we have suggests that the native (?) intelligent (?) culture responsible for the recent debacle is a social nomad living in one region only, and herding the local equivalent of grass-eating cattle. Since neither grow in the tropics, it may not yet have found the Sims Bancorp site. But if it should, and if that powerplant is indeed functional (as Captain Vasoni's data suggest) then we have a crisis. Such an aggressive, hostile species must not be handed advanced technology too soon.

Authorization 86.2110. Alien Contact, Secondary. Team Leader: Vasil Likisi. Mission definition: assess for

1) intelligence
2) social organization
3) technological level
4) hostility index.

If suitable, attempt to gain level-one agreement to the General Treaty. At all events, secure Sims Bancorp colony powerplant and other prohibited technology.

'It was stupid from start to finish. I don't care what they said, I'll bet Sims knew all about it – they were pissed enough to be losing the license.'

'It's not in any of their internal datastream. I say they didn't know, and the critters just hit I-critical about the time the first survey was done.'

'Poppycock. They had to know. Unless no one reviewed the weathersat's recordings – look – there – you can't call *that* undisturbed ground.'

Kira Stavi sat back and listened to the bickering. Vasil Likisi, experienced team leader her left little toe. Vasil Likisi corporate bootlicker was more like it. Vasil holding forth about Sims . . . and hadn't he once worked for ConsolVaris, one of Sims' minor acquisitions? She looked at the display instead of getting into the argument that Vasil clearly wanted to have with Ori . . . Ori could handle it. And the display had its interest. Although it had no legend, she knew from experience that the purple and yellow streaks were enhanced-contrast thermal-emission spectra. Regular streaks and blobs, too regular entirely. Vasil was right about that, at least.

Ori brought up the point she would have, the point he had tried to bring up before. 'Is it possible that we're seeing a species at emergence?'

'Impossible,' Vasil huffed. 'It's those clods at Sims—'

'I don't see why it's impossible.' Ori's voice didn't go up, but he had not been intimidated by Vasil, and he made that clear. 'Just because we've never observed it before doesn't mean it can't happen. In theory, it has to happen sometime.'

'The odds—'

'Make no difference now. What matters is what is.' Ori could never leave out his Pelorist tags. Vasil went redder, if possible. Kira decided it was time to cool things off.

'What about the thermal source at the old Sims site? Are we quite sure that doesn't imply illegal occupancy?' Vasil scowled, but held his peace when Ori turned to her.

'They said not.' Ori rubbed the bridge of his nose. 'It did surprise Captain Vasoni, but there was no organized movement. He did look for that. Here—' He touched the display, and it shifted location, then scale. The shuttle field's original outline had blurred already – tropical vegetation,

Kira reminded herself, could do that in a short time. Buildings still crisply upright – well, they would have made them stout in the first place. A cluster of hotdots here, labeled sheep, and another near the river, labeled cattle. Those were the right size, and temperature, and perhaps livestock could survive without human care that long.

'Has anyone asked the vets?'

'Oh yes. And the original herd sizes. That's well within possible limits. They won't survive another decade without care, but they're well below the carrying capacity of their pasture, and they can forage in the village gardens as well.'

'We have one hotspot in the village itself,' Vasil said, but more calmly. 'Vasoni wasn't scanning it the whole time, so we can't be sure it's the same one, but whatever it is isn't human. Wrong patterns. The Sims colonists reported a treeclimbing, dexterous species in the nearby forest, which came into the settlement at first. If it were Terran, it would be a monkey. The experts think this is one of those. It's smaller than the big fellows up north.'

'Mmm.' Kira wasn't convinced. 'Anyone check the personnel list of the Sims pickup?'

'As well as we can. The colony database they brought with them could have been doctored, of course, but they claim to have accounted for everyone. A few of the elderly died in transit, as you'd expect. We could confirm if Vasoni had had the sense to get a fine-grain visual of the old colony beforehand, but by the time he realized he needed one, he had a mutiny to deal with.'

'Well, then.' Kira hoped to get them back on the real problem, the aliens. 'Any ideas on where these folks would fit on the Varinge Scale?'

That brought them back all right. Scowls from both, sighs, the sort of thing that made her wonder why she stayed in the service at all. Teamwork, ha!

'No artifacts,' said Vasil. 'We don't even know if they have metal.'

'And our ship leaves in less than ten days, and we won't learn anything more until we come out of FTL at the beacon and can strip it. Vasoni did have sense enough to put a permanent watch on the area.'

Kira looked at the rest of the list. A specialist in linguistics, of course, though so far the record of the alien linguistics staff was something below encouraging. By picking alternates with slightly different specialties, they could cover a fairly broad range of biology, technology assessment, linguistics, anthropology . . . but something this important really needed a larger team. Particularly when the team leader was a political appointee who had used his degree, such as it was, in corporate and government service. The problem was the capacity of the transport vessel. No one wanted to waste the time it would have taken for an ordinary ship to crawl inward from the jump point to the planet they wanted . . . which meant squeezing them into a military ship that could make the inward transit in days, not months.

And that meant putting up with a military presence. Kira wondered what the others thought about that. After all, these things had killed the colonists, all of them, so they were certainly dangerous. The military could protect them. On the other hand, the military tended to think they were in charge of things, even when they weren't. This was supposed to be a scientific and diplomatic mission.

They all loved the coolers, Ofelia discovered, especially the frost that formed on the freezing compartment walls.

Twice she came into her kitchen to find the cooler door open, and one of them scraping away with its horny fingernail, while a second held the bowl. The first time, the one holding the bowl dropped it, exactly like a guilty child, when she came in; they both bobbed a little, and sidled out. The second time – was this a different pair? – they both stared at her coolly and went right on eating frost until she pushed them aside and shut the door firmly. The difference in reaction struck her as very human: some recognized rules to observe, even as they broke them, and some didn't care.

She was glad she had disconnected the coolers in nearly all the other houses. She would have to have spent all her time checking cooler doors. It wasn't just the waste of electricity; it was the wear and tear on cooler motors. At least they didn't mess with the motors. She had managed to convince them – how, she wasn't sure – that they must not take things apart. They did turn the lights on and off, and the water, but that did no harm. She had worried that they might start up some of the vehicles down by the shuttle field, but they hadn't. Perhaps those vehicles wouldn't work now anyway, sitting out in the storms all this time. She had not tried to start them since . . . she couldn't quite remember. Before the creatures came, anyway. Perhaps that was why they hadn't experimented.

They were not as bad as children, really. Endlessly curious, as children were, but unlike children they understood limits. The worst was not being able to settle to her own pursuits any more without being aware of their curiosity and attention. When she tried to paint beads, one of them was sure to stick a talon into the different paints; when she tried to string beads, a large beaky head hung over the work, watching. When she crocheted, one of them would reach to feel the yarn, 'helping' by taking it off the ball and holding it slack. She had no way to explain that she needed the slight tension against the ball to gauge the tension of her stitches. If she tried to work on the log, they clustered in the door, watching as the words scrolled across the screen.

That was like having children around, never being allowed to settle to anything in peace. When she knew someone watched her, noticing her choice of colors, textures, shapes, stitches, words, she could not concentrate. Even when the creatures didn't interrupt intentionally, their very interest was an interruption.

She tried to get them involved in projects of their own, as she would have with children. If only they would settle to something, then she could get on with her own activities. She offered dull beige beads from the fabricator for them to paint, bits of cloth and colored yarn. But although they would twine the yarn into twists and curls, and even dip the beads in color, they would not settle to any of it. Just when she thought they were engrossed, so that she could mutter to herself as she worked out what she wanted to do next, there they would be again. Clustered around, hanging over her. Watching.

Outside, it wasn't so bad. In the open, they didn't seem quite as large; she didn't feel their presence as overpowering. She grew used to having one of them in the garden with her, eager for the slimerods she tossed it. They no longer knocked down the corn, or trampled the ruffled leaves of gourds and squash. They followed her as she made her regular tour of the meadows to check the sheep and cattle. Eventually the animals grew used to them, and quit shying away. It could be almost companionable, walking along on a breezy day with one or two of them.

She found herself talking to them quite naturally, and imagining the meanings of the grunts and squawks she got in return.

But inside, they were always a nuisance: slightly too big to share the working spaces comfortably, yet determined to learn what she did and how. She felt constrained, crowded. They would not attempt entry if she locked a door against them, but she could not relax inside, wondering what they were getting into outside. That, too, was like having children around. She had more than once used the bathroom for sanctuary when her children were little, but she had never stayed long. She knew too well what might happen . . . at least with children. With these, she didn't know; she could only worry.

The near-nesting one decided first. It is a guardian. It is a nest-guardian.

Right hand drumming wavered, steadied. It cannot be; these are not nests.

Nests were. Quick gestures evoked the picture-machine and its images. Nests were . . . the guardian stays.

Left-hand drumming. It is so, these were nests, and it is so, that this could be the guardian . . . the only guardian left.

Old . . . it must be so old. Shivers of shoulders, a courteous glance at their eldest, so much younger than the eldest of their People, but an elder still.

And, the near-nesting one added, it knows so much about all those boxes and things that light and move and speak . . .

If it is speech.

It is speech. It answers them.

Things that talk.

That in a tone that expressed hunger better than words, a visceral growl. They all straightened a little, breathing faster: game in view. Things that talked, that did things, things they could recognize as useful, to move water, to make heat and cold, to draw pictures and make noises. More dangerous things like those the invading monsters had used to destroy the nestmass. They could taste that bright blood, that wriggling intelligence.

It would nourish the young, the near-nester said. That went without saying, but a near-nester always said the obvious, and repeatedly; that was how to tell they were close. That knowledge in the monster's head, those things, would nourish their young if only . . .

It cannot be eaten, the eldest reminded them. It is monster; it will not nourish. A quick flurry of right hand drumming, then left hand, then confusion of rhythms as they worked it out. Of course it could not be eaten; guardians were *guardians*, not prey.

Not eaten. Not eaten but . . . tasted? No. A lurch to the rhythm, of the nausea they had felt tasting the dead monsters at the nesting grounds. *Breathed*, said someone finally. A vast gasp, as they all tried that idea. Breathed. Yes. As they passed new things to each other, breathing them into the air and catching them in again, so they could breathe the monster's wisdom.

Its speech. Who will learn to breathe it?

A harsh, guttural exhalation from all of them. A soft flurry of knuckle-beats on belly and breast, mouths open, trying out the sounds.

It is hard. That from the youngest. Eyes rolled.

It is a monster; it would not be easy.

The singers would do better. Eyes rolled that way. No true singers had come with them; none had been interested enough, not with the story of the invasion and war to sing.

Who will go?

Silence. Without drumming, they knew their choices now, and their decision formed in silence. One stood, then another. A moment's pause, then a third stood.

It is too important. We must have all three legs of the stool.

Left hand drumming, slow and sad, but without any flutter of weakness.

Tell the monster?

Show the monster. We will learn.

In the morning, the whole crowd of them – if that was indeed all – waited outside her house. Ofelia looked them over, wondering what was coming. Three of them came nearer, and one at a time curved over until their heads were at the level of her waist. What was this?

'Do you need something?' she asked. Bowing, it must be, and what did bowing mean to them? No answer, not even the grunts they were now producing regularly in response to her speech. 'Want cold?' She opened the door wider and waved them in. They didn't come. Instead, the others moved apart, and let the three begin to walk away down the lane.

Puzzled, Ofelia followed. Were they trying to lead her to something that needed repair? When they turned into the lane that led to the river side of the settlement, she was sure of that. It must be the pumps – although water had spurted out of her faucet and shower normally that morning. Perhaps they wanted her to show them how the pump controls worked. She had been expecting them to want that.

The three walked on past the pump house, with her

behind them, the others trailing. It reminded her of processions, of something ceremonious in which she did not know her part. Past the pump house, down the meadow into the tall grass by the river. Ofelia slowed. She didn't like to walk in the tall grass; it cut her feet and made fine stinging lines on her bare skin.

Now the three stopped, and turned to face her. They bowed again. One of them approached, and touched one of her necklaces with its talon. A soft trill. Then a wide-armed gesture, as if waving to the whole area, then a jerk of the head to the river. Certainty flared in her mind: they were leaving. All of them? She turned to look at those behind. They stood in a ragged line, unmoving. Were they going to try to make her leave? She couldn't. She couldn't eat their food – they had to know that.

The one who had touched her necklace did so again, this time slipping the talon under it, delicately, hardly grazing her skin. What? Did it *want* that? And why? Ofelia lifted her hands to the necklace, and slowly lifted it over her head. It was the one with slimerod cores among the beads she had made and painted; the colors of this one were greens and yellows with a few blue beads. Not her favorite; she didn't mind giving it up, if that was the question.

She held it out, and the creature took it, looking in her eyes as if memorizing her face. If it was leaving, perhaps that's exactly what it was doing. When it finally looked away, it stowed the necklace in one of the stopped gourds hanging from its shoulder belt, pushing the stopper in firmly. Then another bow, and the three turned away.

She had not seen them near the river before; she did not know if they could swim . . . she felt a stab of fear for them, as if they had been her children after all. Things lived in the river that ate other water-creatures; the colony had once lost a child to something scaly with large teeth. Then she saw the slender boat move out of the reeds, into the river, and realized all over again how alien they were, how adapted to their world. They had made a long narrow craft of a something – skins? – sewn around a framework of bent wood. The seams formed a brickwork pattern; she wondered what sealed them from the water. And the paddles – long double-bladed paddles, the tips of the long blades pointed, dipped in and out of the water, moving the strange craft along the surface of the water as quickly and easily as one of the water-striders.

The colonists had had nothing like that; she had never imagined something like that. The colony boats had been one-piece shells, large enough to hold twelve adults, square on the ends, with a small engine mounted on one end. She remembered helping to build the launch site for the boats, that first season. The fabricator could not make anything that size, so when the last boats were lost, they had done without. It had not occurred to anyone to build something this small. Ofelia stared at it, trying to imagine wrapping cowhide around a wooden framework. Perhaps it could be done . . . if someone thought of it first.

She looked back at the ones left behind; they watched intently until the craft reached the far shore of the river, a tiny sliver it seemed, and with a last wave their companions disappeared into the forest there. Boat builders. Boat designers. They must have built that boat after they got to the river; she could not imagine them carrying boats like that across the grasslands where they lived.

Even if she had spoken their language she would not have had to ask why they left. They had gone to tell the others about her. They hadn't killed her (yet, she tried to keep in mind), and they had now learned enough to go tell others. Would the others come? Or would all of these eventually leave? That was a thought – maybe they'd go away and leave her in peace once more, to pursue her own life the way she wanted, without having to pay attention to them.

For a moment she gave herself up to contemplation of that possibility, that blissful state, but she didn't believe in it. Her peace had already been shattered, by the new colony, then by the creatures, and she knew, as if she sat on the committees where the decisions were made, that eventually someone would come to investigate the creatures who had killed humans.

Her creatures were still there in the morning. She had thought they might desert her, move on, hunting in the forest perhaps, now that they had sent word back. But they stayed close, almost as obtrusive as the whole group had been. Very gradually, she found herself mimicking their grunts and squawks, cautious, fitting her mouth into the strange shapes. They stared, and grunted or squawked back, and she did not understand. It just seemed more comfortable to make the sounds they made, as she might have done with babies.

They had become individuals, though she did not know what the individuality meant. She had no sense of male or female, old or young, or any social role. Her names for them came from what she noticed. The player, whose blowing through their tubular instrument she liked best. The killer, who had swung its knife at the treeclimber . . . she wished that one had gone away with the others, but it hadn't. The gardener, who did not garden, but accompanied her most often, appreciating the slimerods.

Days passed. The player painted and strung a necklace of beads . . . blues mostly, with a few green and yellow ones. It could not hold the brush as she did, in those hard slippery talons. Instead, it pared a sliver away from a twig, slid the bead down onto that stop, then dipped the whole bead in the paint. Ofelia watched, amazed, as it waited for the excess paint to run off then upended the twig (neatly holding the painty end in the very tips of talons) so that the bead slid off onto a waiting stand, this made from a larger branch fixed to a base with its twigs uppermost. Bead after bead, dipped the same way, released to land on another of the empty twigs . . . the branch began to look like the holiday trees Ofelia vaguely remembered from the public buildings of her childhood. To her further surprise, the creature pared a separate dipping twig for each color of paint. Children had to be taught to clean a brush after using each color . . . these were not children. Nor were they human, though that became harder to remember as the days passed.

When the beads dried, the creature strung them on twisted grass, not the cord Ofelia offered. And when it had finished its work, it held the completed necklace out to her, hooked on one talon. A gift to replace the one she had given? She could not be sure of anything but the intent. She took it, and put it on. It bobbed at her, and made one of its noises; this one sounded happy, she decided. She smiled and said her thanks aloud, as she would to a person.

The one she thought of as the killer roamed the meadows: Ofelia feared for the livestock at first, but day after day none were missing. When she walked around to check, the killer walked with her, stopping at times to scratch with its long talored toes at the tallest clumps of grass. Once it even threw itself down in the tall grass near the river, and rolled on its back like the chickens having a dust bath. Ofelia grinned before she caught herself. It looked ridiculous, wallowing in the grass like that, even without feathers to fluff. She could not imagine what it was doing, unless the grass eased some itch.

The gardener continued to help her find and exterminate slimerods. It seemed to have no other interest; it was often missing from the group that plagued her in the center, hovering when she tried to settle to some task. Several times she found scratch-marks in the dirt around the plants, as if it had cultivated or weeded while she was not there. Perhaps it was only gathering slimerods, or perhaps it understood what her hoe and rake were for.

She heard the sound from inside, where she was drying herself after a shower. A long, rhythmic cry, several voices. Her heart lurched, then raced. In the lane outside, she heard a nearer, answering cry, and then the quick click-and-thud of the creatures running.

Their friends – their families? – must have arrived. Ofelia finished drying between her toes, very slowly, so that she could think. It would be different again. She was tired of difference, but the world had never yet shaped itself to her measure. How many had come this time? And would they, like her creatures (she almost allowed herself to think *friends*) allow her the freedom to do what she wished?

She put on the necklaces she had left on the kitchen table. It did not feel like enough. She opened her door and saw nothing in the lane. Down by the river she heard excited voices, then the cattle. She considered. The garment she had been working on, ribbonlike strips of cloth in brilliant colors ... or the sea-storm one, or the cloak she had embroidered with flowers and faces? The voices came nearer. The cloak: it took less time to put on, and she had it here at home. With the cloak over her shoulders, and her necklaces layered over it, she felt she still lacked something. Bracelets around her wrists, yes, and the bit of crocheted netting that she had once put over her head: the creatures had widened their eyes at that, she recalled.

She went out, along the lane to the turning and then toward the river. She would meet them, not wait at home. It was her place, after all. The cloak lifted a little from her shoulders in the breeze; she peered down it at the upside-down faces with their staring eyes. She could not quite remember why that one had three eyes, and why she had run a double row of eyes down either side, between the faces in front and the flowers behind.

Ahead, a cluster of the creatures coming up from the river. She recognized her necklace on one of them – had the original three returned? And newcomers, one much darker than the others, and one wearing a skyblue cloak that came halfway to the ground. She paused beside the last house. They were moving now, coming toward her, carrying sacks. Food? Equipment? And the new ones – at least the one in the blue cloak – moved more slowly than the ones she was used to.

Close to, they were obviously the same kind of creatures, but she felt a different intelligence. She had never noticed much organization among her creatures, never been sure who was in charge. Except when going off to hunt, they had seemed to drift through the days intent on nothing but following her, studying her. Now she noticed that her creatures had shifted to the back of the group; the cloaked creature went first, as if it had the right.

Her heart pounded; her blood hissed in her ears. Was it fright or excitement? She stared at the cloaked one, trying to find some clue in its features. Under the cloak she could just see criss-crossing straps and slings, hung with the same sort of gourds and sacks she was used to.

It halted some five meters from her. The others halted behind it. The breeze tugged at her cloak, lifted its cloak in a ripple. It moved its hands out slowly, turned them up, spread its fingers. That she could recognize: empty hands, no threat. She did not have to believe it to answer. She spread her own hands, palms up. It brought its hands together, talon to talon, posed as carefully as the devotional figurines she remembered from her childhood. Again she imitated the pose. Whatever these creatures meant, it was not what her people meant. She had never believed in what her people meant. Guilt stabbed for a moment, then she drove it away. These creatures could not know that she had never believed.

The cloaked one spread its arms now, in a slow gesture that evoked the village behind Ofelia, and then seemed to wrap it into a tidy package, which it handed her. If she had any understanding at all, that meant 'This whole place is yours.' Or it might be asking. Ofelia, remembering a childhood song, drew a big circle in the air with her hands, swept a hand from that to the horizon, and then repeated the wrapping-up gesture the creature had used. She handed the invisible package to the cloaked one, as if it were both large and precious. This whole world is yours, she meant to say.

Behind the newcomers, her own creatures bounced a little, though the cloaked one showed little reaction for a long moment. Then it looked around, and gestured to the other creatures. Two of them – one her own player, and one new – brought out instruments and piped a thin tune against the wind. Then the drumming began.

She had known they had drums of course. She had heard drumming before, night after night. But she had not imagined how they did this, or how it would affect her.

TWELVE

Their throats swelled, bulged into grotesque sacs; their arms twitched; they seemed to vibrate all over. And from the distended throats came the sharp pulse of rhythm. Ofelia felt it shaking the air, rolling through her body as if she were one of them, much louder than the drumming her creatures had done before. The soles of her feet itched with a different, unmatched rhythm, as if an army marched in step with each other, out of step with music. When she looked, the creatures were stamping in unison, but not in time with the higher drumming.

She didn't like the feel of the discordance; her body wanted to move with one or the other, but could not move with both. Or could she? Her feet twitched; she felt the discordance move into syncopation, and her arms lifted, swayed . . . she moved into what she felt as both dance and song, though she had never danced so before, and had no idea what her movements sang to the creatures who had begun the music.

Beat and beat, step and step again. Now the cross-current of rhythm steadied; she found she was marking the accented beats, and their feet matched hers. Which had changed? She could not be sure. She felt breathless, and yet light-footed, ready to dance a long way.

Her creatures moved from the rear of the group, moving to flank it like wings. Ofelia looked from one to the other. Player, Hunter/Killer, Gardener, the others for whom she had found no name. They danced a step nearer. Ofelia moved back; they moved forward. Comprehension came with a quickening beat, with the unison movement of their feet toward hers. They would not enter the village without her lead, her . . . permission?

A moment's rebellion: what did she want with all these creatures, who would plague her even more than the ones she knew? But the music held her, steadied her. She could not stop them if they wanted to come, and this way they would come at her pace, at her will. She turned a full circle, one arm extended: this, too, may be yours.

Then, to the combined drumming of vocal sacs and feet, she led the way into the village. Behind her, the drumming steadied to a single pulse she felt in her entire body, as if the earth itself pulsed. She led them up the lane, past the shuttered homes, past the place where she had seen the first storm-battered one, the house where they had sheltered together. She came to the turn, the lane past her own house, and then to the center. Here her breath stabbed at her; she stopped, leaning over with her hand pressed to her side.

The drumming slowed, became softer and more vocal, almost a song, almost words. Her creatures approached. Were they concerned, or merely hungry? Ofelia put out a hand to steady herself on the wall. It could be funny . . . here she was, the center of attention, the attraction that had drawn alien creatures across thousands of kilometers, and because she was just an old lady she might die of excitement and waste all their time. The thought made her chuckle against the pain; the chuckle made her cough.

When she could draw an easy breath again, they were all waiting, silent, poised in a circle around her. The cloaked one faced her, head tipped to one side.

'I'm fine now,' Ofelia said. 'It's just that I'm old.'

It blinked. Then, slowly, it leaned over the way she had, pressed its hand to its side the way she had, and coughed. The cough had the stagy quality of a child who has just learned about social coughs. Then it held its hand low, and raised it in short steps to her present height . . . and fluttered those long-taloned fingers along a horizontal path, dipping and rising as if to mark intervals. It held that hand still finally. The other hand rose to meet it, matching fluttering the same way, a little distance beyond it, then dropped suddenly. Then both hands down, and the creature bobbed its head.

Ofelia stood thinking. If she had done that, what would she mean? She put her own hand low, and began the sequence. Growth, of course. Then the level fluttering would be adult life, and the sudden drop, death. Her heart raced suddenly. She felt dizzy. Was it a question or an observation, that she was close to death? She could not tell how old they were . . . how could they tell she was old?

She continued the sequence, wondering what the little dips in the horizontal flutter meant to the creatures – she had no idea whether they marked time by seasons, years, or something else – but continued the horizontal longer than the cloaked creature had. She wanted credit for every year she'd lived. The short period from now – the still hand – to the final decline she gestured differently, waving her hand more widely. She didn't know what the creature would understand, but what she meant was uncertainty.

She might die today, or a year from now, or three years; she could not know.

The creatures were silent until she finished, then the ones she knew began talking. The cloaked one silenced them with a gesture. It took a step nearer Ofelia, and slowly extended a talon to her cloak, pointing to the three-eyed face on it, and then, very slowly, to her eyes, and back to the face on the cloak.

No, she couldn't explain that. She didn't know herself why she had put three eyes on that face. She shrugged, and spread her hands. They wouldn't understand, but what else could she do? After a long moment of silence, Player squawked something at the one in the cloak, who grunted back. Then Player touched Ofelia's arm, gently, and nudged her toward the center door.

She wanted to say it was her door, and she would decide for herself when to let them in. She wanted them to go away, all of them, for she could tell that this was going to mean more work, more interruptions, less privacy. She glared at Player, who had locked eyes with Bluecloak, as she now thought of it. Bluecloak grunted something at Player, who stepped back at once. Bluecloak bowed.

She might as well get it over with. Ofelia opened the center door, and waved them in.

Only Bluecloak followed her. Here, in the confined space of the passage, she could hear its breathing, the click of its nails on the floor; she could smell its scent. Ofelia moved slowly, opening the doors on either side as she headed toward the back of the building. Sewing rooms, control room, storage, the big communal kitchen. At each door, Bluecloak paused and looked in. Ofelia named the rooms, but did not enter them; Bluecloak did not enter either, but followed her.

In the kitchen, she turned the water on and off, remembering how that had fascinated the first creatures. Bluecloak hissed, but otherwise did not react. Perhaps they had already told it about the water that came from the walls. Then she opened the big storage freezers; Bluecloak leaned closer, waved cold air up onto its face. Then it picked at the frost with its dark talon, and tasted it, just as her own creatures had.

'Kuh . . .' it said. Ofelia stared. Had one of her creatures carried that word to this one? Had they really understood that her words were language?

'Cold,' she said. Then she patted the side of the box. 'Freezer. The freezer makes cold.'

'Kuh . . . ghrihzhuh . . .' The second sound, clearly different from the first, sounded like nothing Ofelia had said. She tried to remember her exact words. Freezer. Freezer makes cold. Was that an attempt at 'freezer'?

'Freezer,' she said, stretching it out. 'Freezer makes cold.' Slowly, distinctly.

'Ghrihzhuh aaaaks kuh,' Bluecloak said, separating each word as carefully as she had. Did that mean it was trying to say what she said? She wanted to think that. She had believed it of children.

'Freezer,' she said again. She opened it again, reached in, and took out a package of food. She held up the package of food. 'Food in freezer.'

'Dhuh ih ghrihzhuh,' it said. It reached in and took out another package. 'Dhuh . . .' Clearly a question, but the intonation was the opposite of her own, dropping instead of rising.

'Food,' she agreed. Of course it couldn't understand 'food' yet. But Bluecloak seemed so much more responsive than the original creatures. Was this why they had brought it? If they were anything like her own people, if the first ones who found her were scouts of some kind, then Bluecloak might be a specialist of some kind. A specialist in languages?

Bluecloak put its package back in the freezer and turned away. Ofelia replaced her own and shut the lid. Bluecloak had moved to the row of sinks. It touched the faucet control. Of course it would want to know more words; children learning to talk were that way too. They didn't want to practice until they got one word right; they wanted to learn the names of everything they saw.

Ofelia turned the water on. 'Water,' she said, putting her hand in it. Bluecloak put its talons in the water.

'Yahtuh,' it said, producing a sort of gurgled snarl at the beginning of the word.

'Waah-ter,' Ofelia said, again stretching it out. Bluecloak moved its talons from the water to the control.

'Aaks yahtuh . . .' with the dropping intonation that she suspected meant a question.

Ofelia tried to back her mind up: if 'ghrihzhuh aaaaks kuh' meant 'freezer makes cold' then maybe 'aaaaks' was the closest it could come to 'make.' In that case, it had just said 'make water.' Ofelia felt smug. It wasn't that hard, to someone who had dealt with generations of babies learning to talk. She was too old to learn their language, but they could learn hers.

'Make water on,' she said, turning the control to strengthen the stream. 'Water on.' She turned it off. 'Make water off. Water off.'

'Aaaaks yahtuh on.' Ofelia was surprised; the 'on' sounded quite accurate. Why couldn't it say 'make' if it could say 'on'? Bluecloak tapped the control. 'Aaaaks yahtuh on.'

Ofelia turned the control again. Bluecloak dipped its head. Approval? Agreement? Thanks? She didn't know.

'Aaaaks yahtuh awk.' Make water . . . awk? Off. Ofelia turned the control.

'Water off,' she said. Again that bob of the head, then Bluecloak turned away, clearly searching the room for something it expected. Something the others had told it about, no doubt, but which of the many things? Ofelia decided on the obvious, and went to the door. When it followed, she pointed out the light switches, then up to the ceiling lights.

'Lights,' she said. Then, with a touch. 'Lights off. Lights on.' Its 'l' trilled, a wavering sound prolonged beyond anything Ofelia had heard before. 'Llllahtsss.' The word ended in an explosive tss. 'Llllahtsss on. Aaaaks lllahtsss awk.' Ofelia turned them off. Bluecloak reached out and turned them back on, repeating its new phrases: 'lights off; lights on.' Then it tapped the switch itself, not hard enough to trigger the control.

'Switch,' Ofelia said. 'Light switch. Switch turns lights on and off.' She said it slowly, a careful pause after each word.

The creature attempted a sound. Ofelia recognized only the 'chuh' of the word's end; whatever the creature had heard and tried to reproduce didn't resemble 'swih' at all. The creature cocked its head at her, and she tried again. 'Switch' did not lend itself to the slow stretching she had used on the other words: when she tried to slow it down, her own version didn't sound right to her.

This time Bluecloak produced 'khuhtch.' That must be the best it could do. Ofelia could accept that, for now. It was a lot closer than she'd come to making most of their sounds.

'Khuhtch aaaaks lllahtsss.'

Ofelia translated as she would for a toddler's speech. Switch makes lights? Now how was she going to explain that the switch didn't make the light, but controlled it? Did she need to explain that yet? If she didn't, she'd have more trouble later on – she knew that from experience. She'd already gone astray when she'd agreed that the faucet controls made the water on or off.

Suddenly the task of teaching the creatures her language looked hard again. She needed the simplest words human children learned by themselves, the no and yes of every mother's discourse.

'Switch makes the lights *on*,' she said. 'Switch makes the lights *off*.' She demonstrated again; Bluecloak looked at her with slightly widened eyes. Now she went very slowly indeed. 'Switch not make light.' Bluecloak blinked. 'Not make light,' Ofelia repeated. 'Make light on. Make light off.'

'Nnnaht.' A cock of the head. Then Bluecloak touched its talons to the light switch again, and turned the lights off. 'Lllahtss awk. Nnnnaht lllahtss.'

'Not lights,' Ofelia agreed, in the dark room. She turned the lights back on. 'Switch makes lights on. Makes lights off.'

'Aaaks lllahtss on. Aaaks lllahtss awk. Nnnnaht aaaaks lllahtss . . .'

'That's it,' Ofelia said. It was going to work after all. It was quicker than a child, quick to realize what 'not' meant. But it was walking back to the freezer. Ofelia followed.

'Ghrihzhuh aaaaks kuh.'

'Freezer makes cold, yes.'

Bluecloak moved to the sinks, and tapped the faucet control. 'Aaaks yahtuh.' Ofelia shook her head. 'Makes water *on*. Makes water *off*.'

Bluecloak waved its hand under the faucet. 'Nnnaht yahtuh.'

'That's right,' Ofelia said. 'Not water now.' She touched the control. 'This makes water on.'

'Aaaks yahtuh naht.'

'That's it. It doesn't—' She realized it couldn't follow that yet. 'Not make water, make water *on*. Like lights.' She was amazed at the quickness of its thinking, the way it checked its understanding.

Now it gestured, as if throwing something outward. 'Aaaks lllahtss.'

Oh. It wanted to know what did make the lights. She was too tired to deal with this; it would take days and days and days to explain the powerplant, electricity, wires, tubes . . . even if she could remember it all, which she couldn't.

Perhaps it would understand the pictures in the control room, though the others hadn't seemed to catch on. Ofelia led the way to the control room. Behind her, she heard a click. When she looked back, Bluecloak had turned the lights off. Amazing.

The control room, with its many banks of switches, keyboards, display screens, and light panels, brought a hiss from Bluecloak. Ofelia brought up the maintenance manual for the electrical supply, and scowled at the illustrations as she scrolled past them. All too complicated. She knew what they meant, but they would confuse another human, let alone one of these creatures. She turned to say something to Bluecloak, and saw that it was staring at the screen.

'Aaaks . . .' Its hand gestured up, rolling, as the screen display scrolled. *What makes move?* Ofelia wasn't ready for this. She didn't know how to explain the scrolling image to children, let alone to an alien creature who didn't speak her language. She worked her way out of the maintenance manual, ignoring Bluecloak's noises, and found the education files. Here, at the simplest level, with the clearest illustrations, she might find something Bluecloak could follow.

There was the sketch she remembered, a cutaway of the power plant, showing the connections to the other buildings. 'Power plant,' said Ofelia, pointing to the drawing. 'Makes electricity.' No, that was too hard. 'Makes zzzzt. Zzzzt in wires.' She moved her finger along the lines. 'Zzzzt makes light.'

Bluecloak's unreadable expression could have been anything from eager comprehension to total confusion. It reached a talon to the screen, pointing to the blocky drawing of the power station. 'How-huh laaant.' Close enough. Power plant. Then Bluecloak moved back, to the door, and waved a circle.

'Oh – where is it? I can show you.' Ofelia heaved herself up, locked the controls with the drawing still on the screen, and headed for the door. Bluecloak, unlike her first creatures, moved aside readily. She led the way outside. The other creatures were huddled in the lane, noisily discussing something in louder voices than she'd heard before. At the sight of Bluecloak, they all fell silent. Bluecloak uttered a single complex squawk, and two of them fell in behind it.

Ofelia did not hurry. She had already done that dance; her knees crackled. Besides, she wasn't sure she should show Bluecloak the power station. Right now her creatures respected the limits she had set; they respected her, because she could make the lights work, the water flow. They had never asked to see the power station; they didn't understand how everything worked. Surely Bluecloak couldn't possibly understand, just from looking . . . but what if it did? What if these creatures could use the tools, the machines? If they could control that themselves, if they didn't need her, what would happen to her?

Bluecloak seemed in no hurry either. It stopped outside the first doorway, and churred. One of the creatures answered. Bluecloak tipped its head toward Ofelia. It had to be a question. The logical question was whether this was her house. But the others could have told it that. Perhaps it wanted to know what this was.

'House,' Ofelia said. Whose had it been? She was surprised to discover that her memory of who had which house had blurred. Surely it hadn't been that long. Tomas and Serafina? Luis and Ysabel? Still thinking, she unlatched the outer door and pulled it open. Inside, the house was dark and smelled musty. Ofelia ducked into the cool dimness, and made her way to the windows, where she opened shutters. When she turned around, Bluecloak stood poised at the door, head cocked.

'Come in,' Ofelia said, gesturing. Bluecloak stepped in, its toenails clicking on the tile floor. Ofelia opened the other doors, showing Bluecloak the bedrooms, the closets – there, a scrap of rotting cloth that pricked her memory and reminded her that this had been Ysabel's closet, the scrap part of an old coverlet that Ysabel had cut up for rags before the colony's removal. The bathroom, with its shower head – Ofelia turned the water spray on and off to demonstrate – the garden door from the kitchen. Bluecloak followed her, attentive. One of the others touched the cooler – one of those Ofelia had disconnected long before – and said 'Kuh,' then grunted. It opened the door; Bluecloak uttered a sharp squawk, and it shut the door as if its fingers had been stung.

Or as if Bluecloak were its parent, and it had disobeyed. Ofelia digested that thought. Was Bluecloak an adult, and were these others really children? She liked the idea that Killer might be an undisciplined child, but she had not failed to notice the long knives the newcomers also wore, even Bluecloak.

Bluecloak touched the cooler gently, and looked at Ofelia. Asking permission? She nodded, then reached out to open the door herself.

'No cold now,' she said. 'Cold off.'

'Kuh awk,' Bluecloak said. Cold off. It looked the box over; Ofelia held her breath. It could not know what made the box work or not work. It had not had time enough with the cooler at the center. It could not . . . Leaning over, Bluecloak peered behind the cooler. With a glance at Ofelia, it leaned lower, reached, and came up with the end of the power cord. 'Aaks kuh,' it said, with the falling intonation that Ofelia now thought meant a question.

She felt colder than the cooler had ever been. How had it caught on so quickly? Small children learned . . . but they saw someone plug and unplug appliances. These creatures had no electricity . . . did they? They could not have understood, with no common language, how it worked. Yet Bluecloak's questions were so direct . . . it must be smarter than she had thought. Smarter than humans? She didn't want to consider that question.

'Bzzz makes cold,' Ofelia said. Should she give a label for the cord? She might as well; it would be easier to talk about if she did. 'That's a cord,' she said, touching it. 'Cord. Bzzz in cord makes cold.'

'Zzzz . . .' Bluecloak said. 'Howhuh laaant aaaks zzzzt.' It paused, giving Ofelia time to arrange *Power plant makes electricity* in her mind. 'Zzzz in cort, zzzz aaaks kuh.'

Yes, electricity in the cord made the cooler cold, but how had it figured out that the electricity traveled in the cord? It should not have been obvious. It could not have seen the wires behind the coolers in the center; they were hidden by the bulk of the boxes. Ofelia nodded, forgetting again that they did not understand nods.

Bluecloak flipped its cloak back, and opened a mesh bag hanging from one of the straps around its body. From the bag, it took a thin cylinder as long as Ofelia's forearm. She thought it looked like wood or thick-stemmed grass. Bluecloak lifted it with one hand, and blew into it, holding the other hand before the open end. Then, very gently, it took her hand, and placed it before the open end. She felt the stream of air. But why?

Bluecloak spoke, a rapid gabble she couldn't follow. Then it slowed. A breathy whushing, a pause, then 'in' and a talon tapped on the cylinder. Air in cylinder? Ofelia nodded, hoping that was right. 'Yahtuh in . . .' a guttural squawk. Ofelia blinked. Water in . . . something. Air in the cylinder, water in the cylinder? In something like the cylinder? In a pipe, she would say . . . had that been their word for pipe?

'Pipe,' Ofelia said. 'Water in pipe.' Her breath came short; she could not believe the creature was making these connections.

Bluecloak tipped its head to one side. Was that their nod? It repeated the sequence: [Whoosh] 'in' gesture to cylinder. 'Yahtuh in kye . . . kye . . .' It must be trying to say pipe. Ofelia tried again. 'Pipe.'

'Kite.' It tapped the cylinder again, preventing another correction. 'Yahtuh in kite . . . zzzz in cort.'

It had the whole idea. Like air in a tube, like water in a pipe, electricity flowed through cords, cables, wires.

Ofelia had known children who found that hard to grasp, who had insisted that electricity could not flow, because wires were not hollow. And this creature had figured it out with no more than a few glances at the appliances and cords, at the elementary sketches of the teaching programs.

Ofelia felt cold all over. These were dangerous creatures; they had killed humans. And she was exposing them to human technology . . . at the rate this one was learning, it would not be long before they were building their own starships.

She could not stop them, either. Even before she had known they were there, they must have acquired enough information to be dangerous. By the time she realized they were learning too much, they had already learned it.

Her mind cycled through the reasoning, discussing with the old voice whether or not it was her fault. The old voice accused, as always; the new voice defended. The old voice frayed, audible at last as the separate strands that had formed it: her mother, her father, the primary teacher who had been incensed when she learned too fast, the secondary teacher who had been incensed when she turned down the scholarship; Humberto, Barto . . . even Rosara.

The new voice . . . she thought the new voice sounded like herself, but younger. But how could she be sure? It insisted she was not to blame. It went on to point out how exciting this was, what an opportunity.

Ofelia burst out laughing, and Bluecloak shied away. 'Sorry,' Ofelia said, pulling her mouth back to its normal expression. Bluecloak could not know why she laughed; it might not know her laughter was laughter. Could she explain, even to herself, why she was laughing? Just that the internal argument seemed so silly, both the worry that she was responsible for endangering the whole human race, and the newer voice's enthusiasm for learning about an alien race.

Whatever she learned would be of use to no one; she would be dead and if the others came back they would pay no attention to anything she tried to leave behind . . . assuming the creatures would not destroy it. For a moment she was shaken with grief and despair as sudden as the laughter. Death, that she had not feared, now stood at the end of the lane: darkness, and nothing beyond. She had not known she counted on leaving her memories as glosses on the official log – something that would survive her, whether anyone read it or not – until she realized that those additions might not survive.

With the grief, every ache in her body made itself known, as if her nerves transmuted emotion to physical signs. The heavy stutter of her heart, the sharp pain in her hip, in her knee, the burning beneath her ribs. Exhaustion dragged at her, and she fumbled behind her for one of the chairs that still stood around the wide kitchen table. She pulled it toward her, scraping its legs across the floor; Bluecloak stiffened and spread its arms a little away from its body. Ofelia sat heavily. It would pass; it always did. In a few minutes her breathing would ease; she would think of something pleasant, and help it along.

She glanced around the kitchen, out the garden door she'd opened. This was one of the gardens she had not kept up, beyond the odd shovelful of terraforming inoculant from the recycler. Runner beans with creamy flowers had gone rampant, sprawling over the whole space, reaching up with waving tendrils for the supports she had not supplied. The breeze set the tendrils waving even more wildly, and sent a gust of bean-scent through the open door.

Ofelia breathed it in. Yes. Always something to overcome the body's momentary collapse, if you only gave it a chance. A color, a scent, a scrap of music. She waited until she was sure her heart had settled to a steady rhythm, then pushed her chair back and levered herself up. She really should shut the house up again before she left, but she was very tired, and if she was to make it to the power plant, she could not spare the energy.

When she turned to the front door, Bluecloak churred. Ofelia looked back. It had its hands on the garden door; it swung the door a few centimeters, then cocked its head. As clear as words, she thought. Do you want me to shut the door? Ofelia nodded and gestured with her hands, one the closing door and the other the wall it closed against. Bluecloak shut the door, and then, as she watched, the shutters. At the front door, it shut the door behind them, and fastened the latch.

She would have been surprised except that she had been surprised too many times that day already. She was old, she reminded herself. She didn't have that many surprises left.

THIRTEEN

In the powerplant, Bluecloak peered around at the readouts and warning signs just as a human might who had wandered into so strange a place. The big greenish-gray boxes and cylinders, the glossy black insulators, the steady thrum . . . Ofelia had not really seen or heard it in years, not since it was new to her, when she and the other adult colonists were taught how to run and maintain it. Now it looked almost as alien to her as the creatures themselves. She could not imagine how to explain any of it to Bluecloak; she could remember the words, but she had never really understood it. The waste recycler provided fuel; the powerplant converted that fuel to electricity as long as someone made sure the parts all worked.

'Zzzzt,' Bluecloak said. It walked carefully toward one of the greenish rounded humps; Ofelia fended it off.

'No!' she said. 'Hurts you.' She mimed touching the machine and yanking her hand back.

Bluecloak stared at her a moment, then looked around again. Its throat sac pulsed. Slowly, with obvious care, it moved to the other machines, staying at the distance Ofelia had indicated. It shivered suddenly, then leaned to one side. Ofelia watched, baffled. It leaned to the other side, then stood upright again. It extended one arm, hand open, toward the machine, but with no intent to touch it. It looked almost like someone warming hands before a fire, searching out the comfortable level of heat.

Ofelia stood still until the ache in her hip forced her to shift her weight, and then walk around. Bluecloak still stood by the machine, holding out first one hand then another. She was bored. What was it doing? She was thirsty, and possibly hungry; she knew she wanted to use the toilet.

Moment by moment her irritation increased; she had felt an obligation to this creature as her guest, and then a fascination with its quick learning. But if it was going to stand there doing nothing, she had better things to do.

She hoped it wouldn't fry itself to a crisp in something. It wasn't likely; the powerplant had been designed with a colony in mind, with the expectation that children might occasionally get inside without supervision. Touching the casing wouldn't even give it a shock. With a final dramatic sigh, Ofelia headed for the toilet down the hall.

'I'll be back in a few minutes,' she said. Bluecloak didn't move or answer. Fine. Let it be rude; she would take care of herself. In the hall, the other creatures moved out of her way. None tried to follow her into the little room; they understood now that she wanted to be in these places alone.

Sitting on the toilet, she calmed down and told herself that Bluecloak might not intend to be rude. Perhaps it was fascinated by the faint hum she could barely hear. She could remember, as a young woman, standing and listening – it had sounded clearer then, with her young ears, even loud – soothed by that even, steady sound.

When she came out, she went back to the main room,

and found Bluecloak still in the same place, still moving its hands slowly toward and away from the machine. That couldn't be healthy. Perhaps its ears were more sensitive than hers, perhaps it had some animal reason to respond more strongly to those sounds, as the sheep and cows responded to sounds she could not hear at all. She looked back at the doorway to see the other creatures clustered there. Were they worried? She was.

She went up to Bluecloak. Its eyes seemed glazed; it didn't seem to focus on her. She touched its arm gently. It jerked away as if she had transferred a shock, and grunted. Then it looked at her. 'I was worried,' Ofelia said. 'It was so long.' She thought it would not matter what she said, if she said something quietly. 'I'm hungry,' she went on, and mimed putting food in her mouth. 'Time to eat.'

Another soft grunt, then it looked beyond her to the others and began talking in its own language. When it turned back to her, it leaned a little to her and said 'Zzzzt . . . kruzh.' Kruzh? Ofelia had no idea what that meant.

'I'm hungry,' she said again, and again put her hand to her mouth. This time when she turned away, it followed.

She had not meant to take it into her own house, but it followed, and her own creatures had already gone in. They had been doing that for some time now; unless she shut the door against them, or pushed them out, they wandered in and out as if it were their house. Bluecloak watched as she took cheese from the cooler, as she went outside to pick fresh greens, as she mixed and cooked the flatbread and wrapped it around shredded cheese and sliced tomato. She had become used to eating in front of those who were not eating – clearly, the creatures could not eat her food – but Bluecloak's presence bothered her.

'I wish I could share with you,' she said, before taking the first bite. Then it occurred to her that perhaps it could use salt . . . salt was inorganic, a simple compound. She uncovered the salt bowl and took a pinch of salt on her palm. She reached across the table. Bluecloak leaned closer. Then it put one talon into the salt on her hand, and took it to its mouth.

'Salt,' Ofelia said. 'If you can use it—'

It wet its talon this time and touched her palm again. Against the dark shiny talon, the salt grains glistened. This time she could see its tongue touch the talon, a quick swipe that wasted no single grain. She felt stupid for not having realized before that the creatures might be able to share salt with her.

Bluecloak reached out and took her hand gently. Ofelia waited. It opened its mouth, and showed its tongue, then briefly dipped its head toward her hand and came back up to stare at her. It wanted to lick the salt off her palm, that was clear enough. Ofelia wavered. She would rather give it more salt in a spoon or saucer . . . and yet she wondered what it would feel like. She was old; she might not have another chance to find out.

She moved her hand slightly toward Bluecloak, and nodded. At once it dipped its head again, and licked the salt off her palm. It tickled, then rasped more than tickled, and finally tickled again. Then Bluecloak withdrew its tongue, and pressed its firm mouth against her palm before releasing her hand.

Ofelia realized only then that she had held her breath; it gusted out of her. If Humberto had done that—! But that was ridiculous; this was an alien creature, a monster, and she was an old woman. A nervous giggle wormed out of her, and then she remembered her food. She bit into it roughly, as if she could destroy that feeling, that sudden thought. She almost choked on that mouthful before she made herself slow down and chew properly, carefully. It would be truly silly to choke herself in front of Bluecloak, who would not understand, who might even feel responsible. If these creatures had such notions.

She ate the rest of her food with exaggerated care. By the end of the meal she was so tired she felt she could put her head on the table and sleep through until morning. She wanted a nap; she needed a nap. How could she convey that to this creature, even if it was smart enough to figure out that electricity ran in wires just as water ran in pipes?

Bluecloak stood, and pointed at the ceiling. What now? It ran its arm through an arc that Ofelia recognized as the sun's path. Then it began again, stopping its arm high, and closed its eyes. Slowly, eyes closed, it moved its arm down to what Ofelia thought of as late afternoon, then opened them.

It takes naps, she thought. And after all, it has already traveled today. Of course it is tired too. Ofelia nodded, then closed her own eyes a long moment. When she opened them, Bluecloak was going out the door into the lane, leaving her alone. The other creatures clustered around it, chattering like children released from school. Ofelia watched them go into the center, and hoped she'd remembered to shut and latch the control room door. She was far too tired to go check.

Ofelia woke with the memory of that day, and awareness of the things she should have found a way to convey. It had asked how old she was; she had not asked it how old it was. It had asked so much, so many intelligent questions, and she had not thought of hers, even the old questions, until now.

It was only age. She could not be expected to remember everything, think of everything, do everything.

That old defense felt shaky. This was not some supervisor, for whom a shaky old woman was just a nuisance, who could get his questions answered elsewhere, or any time. She was the only person available; she had to think clearly, or . . . or she was not sure what, only that it would be worse. How worse, or what kind of worse, she didn't know.

She had not wanted more responsibility. She had not wanted more tasks. But the world, her mother had often said, does not shape itself to your wish, any more than dough mixes itself when you're hungry. That was truth; she had never found it otherwise. Unlike the more hopeful things she had read, in school and the literature of Sims Bancorp Colony Division, her mother's bleaker statements had always matched reality as she lived it. So now to mix the dough, and hope – she could not be sure – the bread would be edible. Sighing, she got up and went in search of Bluecloak.

She found the creatures where she expected, in the center's hall. Bluecloak bowed to her; Ofelia bobbed her head in return. It pointed to the door of the control room. Ofelia shook her head – her creatures had learned to understand that meant no, and she now believed they'd told Bluecloak everything about her. Ofelia went instead to one of the doors she had not opened since the colonists left. This had been the primary schoolroom, and she thought some of the teaching models might be left.

Bluecloak followed, as she expected. So did one of the others. Ofelia searched the cabinets along the walls, and found the model she had hoped for. If you turned the little crank, part of it rotated on a shaft, and in some way that Ofelia had never quite understood provided a weak current that would light a tiny bulb. If the bulb still worked. She knew the names of all the parts; she knew how to fix it when it went out of adjustment, but she had never understood *why* spinning little magnets past bundles of wire called brushes made a current in the wire connected to the bulb. She could recite what the training tapes had said, but it didn't make sense.

Still, it was the best she could do. Ofelia pulled out the model, and removed its dust cover. It was difficult to dust; she remembered that well enough, and if it was too dusty it didn't work right. She pushed at the crank. It didn't move; it had always taken a strong arm to turn it at the speed required. She pushed harder, and the shaft moved grudgingly, with a gritty noise.

It hadn't always been this hard. Was she really so weak she couldn't turn a child's toy? Ofelia peered at it, and suddenly remembered the safety lock. Where was the release? There. She prodded it, and finally got it free. Now the shaft turned, faster and faster, as she cranked. Once it had made a tiny, characteristic noise, but she couldn't hear that now. She kept her eye on the bulb . . . was that a weak glow?

'Turn the light off,' she said to Bluecloak, as if it could understand. It reached out to the switch and the room light flicked off. Now they could both see the little orange glow. Ofelia pushed harder, and it brightened to a weak yellow.

'Aaaks Illahtss,' Bluecloak said. It touched her hand with its talons, and Ofelia let go the crank. Before it had slowed, Bluecloak was pushing, faster and harder than

Ofelia had managed. Had it used a crank before? Usually little children had trouble learning how to make that round and round motion, rather than the back-and-forth that came so naturally. The light brightened, orange to yellow to almost-white. By that light, Ofelia could see Bluecloak's other hand, held near the dynamo, moving closer and back as he had in the powerplant. He could get a nasty shock . . . but he didn't try to touch it. It was as if he felt his way along a surface she could not see.

Ofelia decided it was time for more light on the subject. She walked over and turned the room lights back on. Bluecloak's great eyes seemed to flash gold as its pupils contracted. It released the crank, and the shaft slowed, the light dimming until it could not be seen in the room's lights. Both hands now hovered about the dynamo, fluttering in and out. Curious, Ofelia came and put her own hand beside Bluecloak's. She felt nothing. Of course not; there was nothing to feel.

Nest guardian, the singer-to-strangers had said at once. Wearing the holy symbols, the eyes of the body and the eyes of the spirit, this is the one who births the minds of the nestlings.

I hope you have showed respect, the singer-to-strangers added after a pause. No one had interrupted; no one would interrupt a singer engaged in the ticklish matter of bringing harmony between strangers. Only the nest guardians were more sacred. The singer waited, until the impatience of the youngling near nesting burst out in a flutter of toes that produced a soothing answering rhythm from the group.

Of course we showed respect. Of course we knew . . . .
Not from the beginning.

I knew. That discourtesy passed unremarked; younglings approaching a first nesting were expected to be hasty and abrupt. The singer-to-strangers throbbed a rhythm more complex than the others, and the youngling settled back, mouth slightly open. Yes . . . it would not be long, and then this one would feel better.

A nest guardian, the singer sang. And where are the nestlings?

Gone away, one of the hunters ventured. The monster – the nest guardian – moved that way. The hunter moved in imitation of the old woman's gestures, the sweeping arm that indicated the village, the walking fingers that must mean others of like kind, then the upflung arm and pointing finger.

It has a winged hunter far above, another said. A winged hunter with good eyes, that tells it how the world looks – it tells of storms coming from far away.

It can walk the air without wings?

We have not seen it do so. But the flying monsters we did see, near the nestmass . . . and the little monsters were swallowed within.

Its people travel far, the singer mused. And when they return, heavy for nesting, they will know of us. The singer shivered, and gave a single resonant throb. The others shivered as well. Those who returned with the singer had told of the longer and more sober discussion that followed the successful elimination of the nestmass marauders. It had been less skill than luck, the leaders had decided; the monsters of the sky had not expected trouble, and that by itself suggested a measure of their power.

We are juicy leapers too far from the burrow, one of the hunters said. Known, visible, no place to hide. Hunted by those who could see from far above, even with no hills

near; hunted by those who could scar the very sky with
the speed and power of their passage. Leapers have teeth,
one reminded.

But fall to the knife anyway, another said. As teeth to
the knife are our knives to the weapons such skymonsters
might carry.

The nest guardian's people will return, the singer said.
If they are the same people as the ones we killed, then
. . . it will be difficult to drum harmony.

A long way, and no travel camps between, one of the
youngest said. It had been a hard journey both ways, and
this one had had a thorn in the left foot, making most
steps painful even after it was out. Perhaps they are not
the same beings at all.

They are the same in some things, the singer said. No
one argued with this. The singers, along with the surviving
nest guardians, had examined the dead monsters carefully;
the singer would have noted details that escaped a hunter
in the battle. The difference, the singer went on, is mostly
age, and the garments of the nest guardian. These creatures
change with age, as all do. The long grass of their heads
bleaches like grass in the coming of cold; the skin dapples
and loosens. If they are like us, they become slower of
movement.

This one's skin is so hot, one of the hunters said.

I do not know about the others; they were all dead.
But certainly this is a hotblooded creature, more like us
than like the flaked skins. Has anyone seen it swim?

No. It does not swim, but it sprinkles itself with water
daily . . . sometimes more than once, in the hottest
weather.

Unclothed, another added, it has attached sacks here
– the hunter rubbed the chest – and yet we have never

seen anything in them, or any opening.

The singer tapped left toes. Yes, so had some of the dead ones, but those were not empty. I saw one slashed by a knife; it was the creature's self inside, all part of its body. One of the nest guardians looked at many such, and noticed that the larger ones went with the kind with an extra hole between the legs.

Nest-ready! cried the one who was.

Perhaps. These are monsters, after all. The nest guardian thought perhaps it was a way of storing fat for the production of young.

We could ask this one, a hunter said.

The singer drummed again, this time with the right toes, disagreement. It would be intrusive to notice that a nest guardian has not completed the change. What if it became angry? Refused to talk with us?

Perhaps it talks with us only because it has no nestlings to instruct?

It is too quick of mind to mistake us for nestlings.

It is alone, said the one nearing nesting, in a quavering voice. It is alone, and its people have abandoned it.

The others drew near, drumming softly with left toes, with left fingers, soothing, reassuring . . . you are not alone; we are here, your people . . .

But I have no nest guardian for *my* nestlings! That in a wail that drew involuntary squeals from some of the younger ones; neck sacs puffed and flared in the bright orange of menace.

The singer took over, drumming a stronger rhythm, and shifting to the traditional counterpoint of the nestchant. Here is safe nestmass, here is safe place, here your nestlings will be guarded. A powerful guardian is here, the singer continued, powerful against the new dangers, more powerful than those you knew before. The nest-ready shivered again, then slowly relaxed into the comforting hands of the others.

It will guard my nestlings? Half question, half statement.

Singers did not lie, but they created new truths with their songs, new ways for the People to drum agreement.

Guardians are wise, the singer said. This guardian is very old; this guardian nourishes our minds as well as those of the nestlings. This guardian will guard your nestlings; I will sing it so.

The nest-ready fell asleep, in the abrupt way of those carrying young, and the singer gestured to the others for silence.

They did not know what the monster called itself. The singer considered that so wise an old one would surely have a preferred name. It had been withheld out of courtesy, not grasping; this one, like all guardians, was generous to all needs. The singer was sure the guardian would agree to protect their nestlings. Almost sure. Unless its own people came back, when its duty to its own nestlings might take precedence.

The singer leaned against the wall, remembering the feel of the guidestone. Guidestones! So strong, in the building where the zzzzt came from. Among the People were those who would ache to find such . . . though he doubted the guardian would say where they came from. Such a treasure. And the smaller guidestones, in the little machine. Those interested in making new devices could copy that, if they had the chance. The singer was sure that zzzzt alone would not give the People mastery of all the monster tools, but if they could make zzzzt themselves — whatever it was — then they could make their own tools.

The singer's mind drifted, as it often did, along the dream paths of night, where the drumming shifted sides as often as the dreams. A day of marvels, indeed: seeing a monster alive, hearing it speak, realizing that it was indeed a nest guardian, most sacred of mortal beings. It walked in the singer's dreams less awkwardly than in reality; it moved swiftly and gracefully, more smoothly than the People with its flat-footed gait. It wore the guardian's cloak, all covered with eyes to signify that the wearer saw with all eyes: outward, inward, high, and low.

Ofelia found, in the next days, that she was under a curious scrutiny, both more intense and less constant than before. Bluecloak must be very important, because the other creatures acted on its slightest whim. And its whim included her. When Bluecloak saw one of the original creatures walk into her kitchen as if it owned it, and open the cooler to get a fingerful of frost – something it had done all along – Bluecloak said something in their language and the startled intruder sprang back half its length. Bluecloak said something else, and the creature sprang forward to shut the door and give Ofelia a look she had no way to interpret. Then it edged out past Bluecloak, and went off down the lane.

'I didn't mind that much,' Ofelia said, out of politeness, because she had in fact become tired of the creatures coming in so casually for frost-scrapings. She had often wished they would learn manners and wait to be invited. Now Bluecloak simply looked at her, standing beside the lane door. 'Thank you,' Ofelia said finally. It tipped its head and withdrew.

Within a couple of days, she realized that the other creatures no longer came into her house, and Bluecloak came in only when a wave of her arm invited it. If she wanted a few hours alone – and she still did – they did not intrude. She could cook her meals in peace; she could even, she discovered, shoo them out of the sewing room she preferred, and work on her jewelry again without those inquisitive eyes on her.

It felt comfortable. She relaxed in this new privacy, realizing how she had missed it in the time they had been with her. All over again, this time in familiar sequences, she felt her muscles relaxing, her mind relaxing. It was not quite like having the planet to herself, but it was better than it had been when the creatures first arrived. She no longer felt smothered by their presence.

And she could have companionship too. She had never in her life experienced companionship with the opportunity to shut it out when she needed to be alone. Bluecloak seemed to understand, or perhaps these creatures did not intrude on each other all the time as humans did. When she looked, peering from her new privacy as if from behind a veil, she saw that they seemed to let each other alone at times . . . not as she remembered people doing with each other in the village, grudgingly or angrily, but as if it were natural for any of them to desire time alone. When they were ready for companionship they returned, as she did with more willingness than she had expected ever to feel.

She realized that she was willing because Bluecloak's lively interest, both in learning and in teaching *her*, made it worthwhile. Day by day – almost hour by hour – she found that Bluecloak understood her better, and she understood it. Bluecloak now understood – she thought – that humans bore their young inside, and birthed helpless infants. That the things on her chest were organs to nourish those infants. She understood – she thought – that the creatures made some sort of nest, but whether they laid eggs or had babies she could not determine. Her questions to Bluecloak about that didn't seem to get through.

It would have bothered her more, if she hadn't been reveling in her new – if limited – freedom. It was still a nuisance to have them around, because she knew that they could intrude even though they didn't. Her privacy depended on their courtesy, not on herself, and in the time alone she had enjoyed most of all her freedom from anyone else's decisions. But she could shower in peace, singing if she wanted to, without listening for the click of their talons on the tile. She could sit muttering over a tricky bit of crochet, without those great eyes peering at her, the hands hovering as if to mimic the motions of her fingers, until their interest made her own hands clumsy.

And when she wanted companionship – when she wanted to listen to their music, or let Bluecloak try out its rapidly increasing store of words and expressions – they were there. Quiet, polite, and eager. She didn't mind being the center of attention when she could choose the time. In the evenings, when they played music, they offered her any of their musical instruments. She usually shook the gourd with its seeds, but she had finally coaxed a note – breathy but musical – from the handful of hollow reeds. They listened when she played music cubes for them; they even tried to sing along with the children's songs, and came surprisingly close to the melodies. She tried to hum along with their songs, but worried that she would sing the wrong notes; it was easier to keep a rhythm on the gourd.

Bluecloak and one of the others seemed determined to

learn to read; they encouraged her to read from the children's books in the center schoolrooms. She explained about letters and numbers, and soon saw them tracing letters in the air, on walls, in the dust of the lane. They seemed to learn very fast, but she had no idea how fast adults could learn letters if they had not been to school as children. She wondered if the creatures had any written language of their own. Again, her questions to Bluecloak didn't seem to get through. Did it not understand, or did it not want to answer? She couldn't tell.

FOURTEEN

Aboard the *Mias Vir*, en route to former Sims colony #3245.12

Kira Stavi reminded herself frequently that she had not expected this trip to be pleasant. It didn't need to be pleasant; it was a chance to meet the first alien intelligence ever found on a colony world. On any world, for that matter. What did the usual shipboard nonsense matter, with that in view?

Still, it was annoying. All of them had superior academic qualifications – that went without saying – so there was really no need for the covert pushing and shoving, the back-biting, the attempts to impress. They'd all get publications out of this, no matter how it turned out – material for a lifetime's maneuvering in the academic or bureaucratic jungle. They were not competing with each other.

Except that they were. Primary and backup teams, two sets of paired specialists, eight active minds each determined to make or complete a reputation out of this trip, and too much shipboard time with too little to do besides worry about how the others might frustrate that ambition.

The primary team alone could generate, Kira thought,

a storycube of problems. Bilong Oliausau had to impress them with her knowledge of neolinguistic AI, and her sexual attractiveness. Ori Lavin, normally a calm, pragmatic Pelorist, almost a caricature of that sect, had reacted to Bilong as if to a shot of rejuvenating hormones, and sleeked his moustache every time she undulated by. He had engaged in one fierce argument after another with Vasil, most of them unnecessary. Vasil, for his part, interpreted 'team leader' to mean that both Bilong and the lion's share of transmission time were his by rights.

Kira didn't care about Bilong's behavior – she even had a sneaking sympathy for the girl, off on her first long expedition, given a place on the primary team only because the director of the linguistics faculty had chosen this inauspicious time to collapse with a richly deserved bleeding ulcer. Kira had heard about the almost-mythical Dr Lowaasi, who went through secretaries and graduate assistants with equal voracity. Rumor had it that the linguistics faculty cheered as the ambulance drove away. Anyway, it was no wonder Bilong seemed immature and unstable, and threw herself at Vasil while flirting over her shoulder with Ori. What really upset Kira was the way Vasil hogged the transmission time.

Kira reminded herself that her own position was secure. She had tenure; she had a high citation index, and after this it would go even higher. The xenobiologist on the backup team, whose unpronounceable name everyone rendered as Chesva, respected her without embarrassing hero worship, leaving Kira free to do the thinking, and treat Chesva as a normal assistant. Whether the creatures were intelligent or not, whether they signed a treaty or not, she would have exclusive access to the biota . . . wish fulfillment for a xenobiologist. She had samples already –

Sims Bancorp had deposited the requisite samples with the colonial office decades before – but samples were no substitute for observing living organisms in their native ecosystem. All she had to do was survive the voyage without committing assault on her team members.

She reminded herself of this day after tedious day, through the intermediate jumps and the long insystem crawl to the planet. She reminded herself that it would have been worse – it would have taken longer – on most ships. Although it was tempting to think that a larger team would have been less difficult, she knew from previous field experience that large teams could offer just as many opportunities for interpersonal unpleasantness. Here, the small size of the team would force them to cooperate once they were on the planet. And she, the only one presently acting like a responsible adult, would make sure of that.

When they were close enough, she joined the others at the wardroom viewscreen. Blue, white, tan, dark green . . . polar caps, mountain ranges, forests . . . no wonder someone wanted to colonize it, she thought. If it had been purpose-built for humans, it could not have been closer to ideal.

'Needs a moon,' Ori said, as if reading her mind. Sometimes he could; they had been on several expeditions together. Kira took it as a sign that he was getting over his infatuation with Bilong. She smiled at him without saying anything.

'We're going to sit out here for awhile and really look at things,' Vasil said. He had said this before, more than once; Kira felt her shoulders tighten now. She didn't like being treated as an idiot who couldn't remember. Perhaps that was what he was used to; unlike the others, he had no academic appointment. She tried to convince herself that this explained his attitude. 'We're going to launch a low-orbit scanner,' he went on. Kira could have repeated his next words with him; she did it silently, careful not to move her lips. 'And only when we know what we're getting into, will we decide where to land.'

The obvious place was the old colony site, since their mission included shutting down that powerplant. Vasil knew that. The shuttle pilot knew that. Kira glared at the viewscreen and told herself she'd feel better when she got out of the ship for awhile.

She watched the launch of the low-orbit scanner, and then went to the lab to put the first transmissions through her own special filters. She didn't expect the analysis of atmospheric gases to have changed from the baseline data filed before Sims Bancorp was issued the first development license, but she would be more comfortable with her instruments than the tension in the wardroom.

Chesva followed her. 'Would you like me to do the atmospheric stuff, and let you get right to the surface data?'

'I don't think there'll be any surface data for awhile, but we can check the response of the visuals.'

'I'll load the old data for comparison.' They knew it by heart, but the computer would catch subtle changes they might miss.

'Thanks,' Kira said. She wished Chesva were on the primary team with her . . . but then she might have had someone like Bilong for her backup. Better this way, probably.

The atmospheric data began to show up on her screen. She pulled up the old, and had the computer highlight any changes. Nothing showed. Just as she'd expected.

'What about that old weathersat?' Chesva asked. 'Do we have the access codes?'

'I'll check.' Kira ran through the expedition manual, which was supposed to contain a precis of all relevant data, including enabling codes for any equipment Sims Bancorp had left behind. 'Yes – and I'll just give it a shove—'

The weathersat's computer obligingly dumped a long file of weather observations, graphics and all. Kira called up the current image. Blue water, swirling white clouds in streaks along the wind patterns, a mass of clouds lumped up over something on the western side of the image. She muttered her way through the selection tree to pull up information about that. Mountains, it turned out to be.

Chesva had moved over to her workstation. 'Do you suppose the weathersat has any idle scanners? If so, maybe we could get an early peek—'

'Good idea. Have you ever peeled this kind of system?'

Chesva grinned. 'Actually, yes. And it nearly got me drafted into the military.'

'Sounds like a good story,' Kira said. 'But in that case, why don't *you* fiddle with this, and I'll watch and learn.'

Chesva explained as he went along, but Kira was more interested in the incoming data than in the way he convinced the weathersat to realign scanners and antennae to pick up and transmit the data he wanted. By the time he had it running to his satisfaction, the weathersat's area of observation was moving toward the nightside.

'Handy that the powerplant's still on,' Chesva said. 'It's the thermal peak there which has let the weathersat stay in position all these years.'

'Really.' Kira wasn't that interested. She could see the bright dot on the infrared herself. Around it were the softer, dimmer blurs of buildings radiating heat absorbed from the sun, distinctly different from the ground only on the side where shadows had cooled the soil . . . they all seemed to have one sharp edge, and the rest blurry.

'Now if we can just get the magnification working—' Chesva said. 'Ah. There. Now what do you suppose *that* is?'

A visible light scan, this time, the low slanting rays of the setting sun making bold shadows . . . there were the buildings of the abandoned colony, arranged in neat rows, the forest ramparts with their longer shadows . . . and something moving between the houses.

Kira felt a shiver run down her back. Animals. Probably only animals, either the surviving domestic animals abandoned by the colonists, or the forest animals they had described. The aliens had been thousands of kilometers away; the colonists had lived there forty years without seeing anything dangerous. But the shadows they cast were long, upright.

'Thermal sources,' Chesva said. 'Whatever they are, they're warm-blooded, but not as hot as the power-plant.'

'Upright,' Kira said. She was glad to hear that her voice was steady.

'Yes.' His voice was as calm as hers. They were professionals, academics, adults . . . but her heart pounded. She knew . . . she *knew* these were not cows or sheep or monkeylike forest climbers. These were the ones who had destroyed a colony – blown up a shuttle – and now prowled about, learning entirely too much.

Sunlight vanished from the scene, and without the stark contrast of sun and shadow she could see nothing, not even movement. On the infrared, she could still see the buildings radiating their stored heat. At a little distance, two clumps of brighter dots might be cattle and sheep.

And between the blurred shapes of the buildings, she could see little pale dots moving. Abruptly they disappeared.

'Went inside something,' Chesva said. 'One of the buildings.' She heard him swallow. 'They're really *there*.'

'We're theorizing ahead of our data,' Kira said, trying to sound professional. Chesva snorted.

'You know we're not,' he said. 'We just got more data than anyone else has had.'

'Yeah,' Kira said. 'I think so.'

Suddenly the visual scan changed. Lights sparkled on the dark screen.

'We know so,' Kira amended. 'They've figured out the lights—'

'Wouldn't be hard,' Chesva said. He sucked his teeth, his only irritating habit, and then went on. 'It wouldn't take digits, necessarily. A hand-swipe – if those are standard toggle switches. A tentacle. Even a beak.'

'Bipedal,' Kira said. 'Those upright shadows.'

'Not necessarily *bi*,' Chesva said. 'But I agree, they're upright. Let's pull up one of the earlier frames and really go over it.'

'You do that. I want to watch this—' Kira waved at the screens. Lights. The computer said four lights. She put a trace on the IR pattern that had moved, the little dots that had crossed the street and gone inside. Now that she had a moment to think, she called up the village street plan furnished by Sims Bancorp, and decided that the – indigenes, she had better think of them, rather than aliens – had gone into the multipurpose building that housed the control and monitoring functions, the rainwater storage tanks, schoolrooms, communal workrooms, and so on.

The computer bleeped; when she glanced at the visual display, another light had come on. She looked back at the village plan. Falfurrias, Bartolomeo et u. et m., it said. She translated the archaic notation: et ux et mater, 'and wife and mother.' Originally built and occupied by Humberto and Ofelia Falfurrias. She looked up the evacuation report. Bartolomeo and Rosara Falfurrias had been taken up on shuttle 3-F; Ofelia Falfurrias on shuttle 3-H.

Kira wondered why they'd been separated. She had always assumed families were transported together. Not that it mattered, really. She did wish they had an arrival manifest for the Sims Bancorp colony transport, but it hadn't yet arrived where it was going. She wrinkled her nose, glad that she didn't have to travel on the old, slow, sublight ships. Cryo made such travel possible, but nothing could make it efficient.

'I've got another light source,' she said to Chesva, who merely grunted. She glanced over, and saw that he was doing something to a single frame of the earlier visual data. His screen changed color, the images shifting to more contrasting hues.

Kira went back to her own investigations. Something – she was sure it was the same indigenes that had wiped out the second colony at landing – was in the buildings, and using at least the light switches. What else could they be using? She glanced at the Sims Bancorp material to remind herself what was down there. Waste recycler, which provided fuel for the basic powerplant producing electricity for the lights, the coolers, the fans, the pumps. The vehicles . . . some electrical, some running off biofuels. No aircraft, thank the Luck. No surviving boats . . . Kira wondered what had happened to them. With the electricity on, the indigenes could make the stoves hot and the coolers cold, but they couldn't get into real trouble. She hoped. Like most colonies, this one had had few weapons, and the evacuation teams reported that they'd removed them.

Of course, they'd also reported turning off the power-plant. Kira had another cold feeling, along with the certainty that 'What else?' was a question that should have been asked long ago. She checked the low-orbital scanner. It was behind the planet now, probably still doing its first run of pre-programmed tasks. She no longer cared about atmospheric gases, about tidal reflectance data.

'Aha!' Chesva said. 'Come see *this*.'

Kira moved over. It was a single motionless screen, again visual, but not what they'd seen before. For one thing, the sun was higher, the shadows shorter, and in the other direction.

'Midmorning,' Chesva said. 'I threw in some search parameters based on those few frames we had, and this is the best I've found so far.'

'Why was the weathersat doing an optical scan? It was turned off when you queried, wasn't it?'

'Probably one of those things put its foot on the controls,' Chesva said. Clearly he didn't care how the weathersat had come by its images, now that he had them. Kira felt the same way.

'Two legs,' Kira said instead of commenting on the unlikelihood of some animal stepping in the right place and then stepping there again to turn the same scan off.

'Yeah . . . you were right about bipedal. The theory's always said it's more likely. Two upper limbs, too – the shadows show that clearly. But look here—' He pointed to a shorter figure among the others. Shorter, its proportions familiar. Human.

Kira choked back all the rude expressions she knew, and said instead, 'Vasil will not be happy about this.'

'No,' Chesva said. He grinned at her. 'But it should get his mind off Bilong, don't you think?'

There was now no question of landing anywhere but the Sims Bancorp shuttle strip. They had been lent a military-grade drop shuttle, supposedly impervious to anything but 'extremely advanced technology,' the military pilots said. The pilots had come with the shuttle, along with a small contingent of 'advisors' who had not mingled at all with the scientific and diplomatic specialists during the voyage.

The shuttle had made several reconnaissance flights after the low-orbital scanner showed no evidence of technology that could blow them from the sky. Evidence of lower-level technology filled the datastrips and cubes. Stone buildings – obvious permanent settlements – clustered on the rocky coast far north and east of the Sims Bancorp colony, and troops of nomads accompanied by herds of quadruped grazers in the grasslands west of the settlements.

'I'm not surprised they missed the nomads,' Vasil said. 'They could be other migrating animals, nothing special. They don't seem to build fires, or structures. It's only that we know to look for them. But how they could have missed those cities—!' He shook his head dramatically.

Kira refused to restart the discussion of critical points and emergence, gradualism versus cultural discontinuity. They didn't have the historical data they needed to determine when the indigenes had achieved the cognitive and cultural complexity needed for this level of technology, and they couldn't get it up here. Down there, if Ori and his backup were good enough, might be the data they needed to settle the question. Instead, she concentrated on biota: the four-legged herds the nomads accompanied . . . hunted? Herded? Herbivores, surely; only abundant plant growth would support that mass of flesh. Prey animals, certainly, with those eyes set on the sides of longish heads, eyes that could see behind and around. Were the indigenes the only predators? She looked for, but did not find, something equivalent to canids.

'Boats, with rowers, and sails,' Ori said, gloating over the pictures taken of the coastal settlements. 'They can work wood – I wonder if it's all as hard as the stuff Sims exported from the tropics. We have to have metal for that. If they have metal tools—'

Kira looked at the creatures themselves. Indigenes, she reminded herself. She couldn't tell what they were most like, mammals or reptiles or birds . . . they had no visible hair or feathers, but their surface looked more like skin than scales. Their gait, with its long-legged, bouncing quality, reminded her of ratites, the large flightless birds of old Earth, but the obvious joint in the leg faced forward, like the human knee. Large eyes, placed slightly more to the side of the head than human eyes; they would have both binocular and monocular vision, she suspected. Four-toed, four-fingered . . . an opposable digit on the hand, and one of the toes looked as if it were almost opposable.

'Look at those buildings,' Ori said, breaking her concentration for a moment. 'And I'd swear those are pipes – maybe just hollow reeds or something, but tubes to carry – yes! Something just came out of that one.' Kira had looked just too late; she saw the tubes, but not whatever had been in them.

Memnin, the anthropologist on the backup team, spoke up. 'I'm noticing how aware they are. Did you notice, Ori, how they looked up at the shuttle? No panic, no real surprise, and that one there—' he pointed at a corner of the image. 'It's sketching something, I'd bet.'

Bilong and Apos, the linguists, stood in the corners watching. They had nothing to do, since the scanners had not picked up any sound. Apos looked alert, but Bilong pouted. Kira wished again that Bilong hadn't been chosen for the primary team. Apos might be younger and less experienced, but at least he wasn't trying to make trouble.

Several days of overflights and data analysis – enough new data to keep an entire faculty busy; Kira felt she was drowning in it – and finally the military pilots agreed that they could risk a landing at the old colony. They insisted that everyone wear protective gear, hot, heavy, clumsy, and unfamiliar to the civilians. Kira was sure the military advisors were laughing at them. They probably did look ridiculous, she told herself, trying to see the funny side as she struggled with the toggles and slides that held the thick panels together. At least they were going to see the real world at last; it was worth this inconvenience on the way.

Unfortunately, from her point of view, the military version of a shuttle had no viewports, nor any of the other amenities of civilian shuttles. She had expected to watch the approach, seeing for herself how the atmosphere changed color and affected the look of the landscape. The exterior cameras would capture that for later analysis, but that didn't make up for not seeing it herself. She had to sit staring at the back of Vasil's head all the way down, her rump going numb on the hard seat, her ears assaulted by the roar and rattle. She had no idea how far along they were until the pilot's announcement that they would be landing in two minutes. The shuttle dipped, swayed, and shuddered in the disconcerting way of all shuttles, and Kira very consciously did not clench her hands. She hated this; she couldn't even see the runway. Then the seat smacked against her backside, and she felt the uneven rumble of the wheels rolling on the rough, overgrown surface.

At first view, the abandoned colony looked exactly like an abandoned colony. They had landed at local dawn, and a hazy pink light glowed from the walls of the shabby little one-story houses. Nothing moved. Parked in a ragged row beside the shuttle strip were the colony vehicles, streaked with rust, tires deflated. Tough grass, and even a few shrubs, had encroached on the runway itself. A moist warm breeze stirred the grass and carried the strange alien smell of a different world.

The shuttle skin popped and hissed; Kira could hear nothing more at first, until her own ears popped. Far off, something groaned horribly; she jumped. Ori said, 'That must be the cows,' and she could have kicked herself for not recognizing the sound. She was the xenobiologist, after all; she was supposed to know animals. Vasil started down the ramp, but one of the advisors stopped him.

'We aren't sure yet,' the advisor said. Sure of what, Kira wondered. They were sure the indigenes were here, and at least one human. They had speculated endlessly about that human, seen only on the weathersat visual scans: who was it, how had he or she found this place, and why? Some drunken crewman left behind after the colony was evacuated? Some exploring entrepreneur come to salvage the leftover equipment? Someone who wanted to claim the planet for himself?

'Somebody—' said another of the advisors. Despite Vasil's arguments, they had brought weapons along. He might be the team leader, the future ambassador, but they had traveled on a military ship, landed on a military shuttle; he had not been able to change the captain's orders. 'To defend the shuttle,' the captain had said to Vasil; Kira, standing behind him, had seen his ears redden. He had told the others he would take care of it, meaning get rid of the weapons, but his bluster had gotten him nowhere. Now the advisors had their weapons out. Kira was not surprised.

'Don't do anything,' Vasil pleaded. They ignored him. Kira, sweating in her protective suit, ignored him too.

'One individual,' the advisor said. He was speaking into a mic more than to them. 'Appears to be human, female . . .' Then in a tone of surprise, '*Old*. An old woman, alone.'

Kira couldn't see what they were seeing; the advisors and Vasil, all in bulky suits, blocked her view up the village lane. They could have moved enough to let those behind see, but they were all standing foursquare, as if intending to be as obtrusive as possible. She looked sideways instead, back down the runway with its ragged rows of grass, to the river – a surface gleaming in the early light – then the other direction, where a distant green wall was the forest. Kira could not tell this second-growth forest from the uncut primary forest a little to the west, even though it had shown up clearly on the scans from space.

'She's . . .' A long pause, almost a gulp, then the advisor found the right official phrase for it. 'Inappropriately attired. Wearing . . . uh . . . just some sort of cape-like garment and some beads. Barefoot. Uh . . . this individual may be disturbed . . .'

Kira couldn't stand it. She was the assistant leader of this expedition, and they were ignoring her. She pushed forward, not too carefully, and Vasil staggered into the advisor, who almost went over the edge of the ramp. She didn't care; she wanted to see. And there, walking slowly toward the shuttle, came a scrawny little woman with an untidy bush of white hair. Barefoot, yes, and wearing an embroidered cape over her tanned skin . . . some kind of garment slung around her hips. And beads.

She didn't look disturbed, not like the senile clinic patients shown in newscubes to remind people to take their anti-senility pills. She looked annoyed, like someone who has had unexpected company drop by on a day when she had planned to do something else. It was this very assurance, the way she planted her gnarled old feet carefully on the ground, one after another, that silenced them all, Kira thought. The old woman was not embarrassed by her odd attire; she was not impressed with them.

They stood, sweating in their protective suits, as the old woman walked slowly up to the foot of the ramp. Kira tried to make out the design embroidered on the cape, and suddenly realized it was faces – faces and eyes. Too many eyes. The old woman tipped back her head and glared at them with her bright black eyes.

'This was *not* a good time,' she said. 'You've upset them.'

Vasil shook himself into action first. 'By the authority vested in me—' he began. The old woman interrupted.

'I said it wasn't a good time,' she said. 'You could have listened when I tried to talk to you.'

'Talk to us?' Kira asked, cutting off Vasil's angry sputter.

'Yes.' The woman's head bobbed, then came up again. 'But you folk have done something to the weathersat, so I can't get it to listen.'

'*You* took those pictures?' Ori asked. 'You made it do the visual scanning of this location?'

'Of course,' the old woman said. 'They wanted to see what it looked like, not just the weather. It helped them understand.' They. Kira shivered as she realized what the old woman must mean by they. Perhaps she was crazy, if she had been showing them the technology. Surely even an uneducated old woman knew better.

'By what right—!' began Vasil, just as the senior advisor said, 'Under whose authority—?' The two men glared at each other.

'Who *are* you?' asked Kira, into the moment of silence.

'Who are *you*?' the old woman asked, without answering the question. If she was senile, perhaps she had forgotten her own name.

'We won't hurt you,' Kira said, trying to sound gentle and patient. 'We want to help you—' That sounded stupid, even to her, and she was not surprised when the old woman made a scornful noise.

'I don't need help,' the old woman said. 'If you're one of that other lot, you're in the wrong place.'

'That other lot?' Vasil got that out, silencing the advisor with another glare.

'Come awhile back, tried to land – you must know about them.'

'Yes,' the advisor said, this time beating out Vasil. 'What do you know about them?'

'Heard it on the com,' the old woman said. 'Heard them coming down, heard them calling for help.' She clamped her mouth together, then said 'Heard them die.' She looked down.

'Didn't you try to help?' Vasil asked. Kira was cheered to find that someone could say something stupider than she had. Did Vasil really think that this frail old woman could have stopped a massacre that had happened thousands of kilometers away? The old woman said nothing, just kept looking up at them. Vasil turned red, and cleared his throat. The advisor, Kira noted, looked amused.

'Have you been here all along?' Kira asked, since no one else broke the silence.

'Of course,' the old woman said. 'Forty years and more, by now.'

'But Sims Bancorp said—'

The old woman grinned. 'Company wasn't going to waste time hunting down one old woman they didn't want anyway. Already charged my family extra for me being overage, figured I'd die in cryo.'

Kira shivered. She had not imagined that kind of crassness, even from Sims Bancorp. Surely it was against the law – but who would enforce such a law, out here in the frontiers?

'So I stayed,' the old woman said. She was still grinning; it looked grotesque.

'On purpose?' Vasil asked, as if he still couldn't believe it. The old woman scowled now.

'Yes,' she said shortly. Kira wondered how – how had she survived all alone? Or had someone else stayed behind? But she could not ask that angry face.

'Well,' Vasil said, doing his best to get back in control. 'Whatever your reasons, you are in violation of the order to evacuate, and by your actions you have jeopardized the position of Sims Bancorp—'

The old woman muttered something Kira could not hear, but from the expression on her face it had not been complimentary.

'—And you have presented us with an unnecessary dilemma,' Vasil went on. 'What are we going to do with you?'

Kira was not surprised when the old woman gave the obvious answer. 'Let me alone,' she said, and turned away.

'But – but you must understand the seriousness of the situation,' Vasil said. The old woman turned back. 'I'm not stupid,' she said. 'I understand – but you came at a bad time. Now go away.' Then she turned and walked off, the long fringe on the back of her cape brushing the backs of her crooked tanned legs. The back of the cape had a single large face on it, in glittery embroidery; the overlarge eyes had long eyelashes like rays extending to the margin of the face. Kira felt uncomfortable, as if the eyes were staring at her, and more uncomfortable for having that reaction. She was not a primitive; she shouldn't be affected by such obvious symbolism.

'Come back here!' Vasil ordered, but the woman did not turn around. Vasil turned to one of the advisors, but Kira tapped his arm.

'Let me try. She's a woman, after all, and if she's been here alone for several years, she may be overwhelmed by all of us.'

'Ma'am, I don't think—' began one of the advisors, but Kira had already started down the ramp. 'You want an escort?' asked the advisor.

'No – she's not going to hurt me,' Kira said. She was finding it surprisingly hard to walk down a ramp in the protective suit. She fumbled at its fastenings, and opened the front seam. As hot and humid as it was, that wouldn't help much, but anything—

She made it to the foot of the ramp without stumbling, and then found that the suit's weight slowed her so that she could hardly overtake the old woman – and the old woman had a twenty-meter lead. Already she was at the end of the lane, between the first houses.

'Don't get out of our sight,' the advisor called. 'If you go too far—' She waved vaguely backward, meaning she had heard and would do what she thought best. Admittedly, she probably shouldn't get out of their sight, when she knew the aliens – no, the indigenes – were somewhere in the area.

'Please—' Kira called to the old woman. 'Wait for me. They'll stay back, but one of us must talk to you.'

The old woman stopped and turned slowly, as if she were stiff. Kira tried to take a longer stride, tripped, and nearly fell. Now she could see the old woman's expression clearly. The dark eyes sparkled with amusement.

'Sorry,' Kira said, out of breath. 'But – we really do—'

'It's a bad time,' the woman said again. This close, Kira could see the remaining dark strands in the white hair, the warts and patchy discoloration of a lifetime's unprotected existence in open air and sunlight. The old woman's hands were wrinkled and weathered, the knuckles swollen and distorted. She should have looked sick – any individual feature Kira noted had pathology all over it – but the general impression was one of vigor, both mental and physical.

'Which is your house?' Kira asked. She would have to be firm, she knew that. With the ignorant – and colonists like this had almost no education, not real education – and the wavering old, it was necessary to be firm. 'We can go there, and you can rest, and we can talk.'

The old woman just stared at her, eyes no longer sparkling. She sighed. Then she scratched the back of one leg with the dirty toes of the other foot. 'It will be hot today,' she said.

A local custom, to start with the weather? 'Is this the hot season?' Kira asked, hoping courtesy would engender trust.

Another long stare. 'You'll sweat in that thing,' the

woman said, pointing to Kira's protective suit.

'Yes.' Kira made herself laugh. 'It was the advisors. They were afraid someone would shoot us, or something.'

'Advisors . . . Company advisors?'

'No, the military.' The old woman's expression did not change; Kira felt she was talking to a computer with a defective I/O subroutine. 'Let me explain,' Kira said. 'When the other colony was attacked, the orbiting ship went back and told the government—' Never mind the delay caused by the mutiny; she didn't want to overload the old woman's capacity. 'And then they decided to send us to assess the situation.'

'To kill the aliens,' the old lady said, as if it were the most natural thing in the world.

'No!' Kira surprised herself with vehemence of her answer. 'Not to kill, to study. To see if they can become allies. We did want to dismantle the powerplant, so they wouldn't have access to our technology . . .'

Now the old woman was smiling, but it was not a nice smile. 'They are very smart,' she said. 'They understand it.'

Kira hoped she had misunderstood. 'Understand—?'

'The powerplant. Electricity. Machines.'

Impossible. This old woman didn't know what she was talking about; she herself couldn't understand all that. She probably thought being able to move a switch was the same thing as understanding. But perhaps she and the other colonists had known of the indigenes before, even though they hadn't reported it for some reason. 'Did you know about them before – before the evacuation?'

'No. We never saw such creatures, not in all my years here, until after that other colony tried to land.' She scuffed one foot in the dirt. 'Then they came. They found me.'

'And you showed them everything?' Kira could not keep the tone of disapproval out of her voice. Even an ignorant colonist should have known better than that; she was sure that was part of the lectures given all outgoing colonists. If anyone found an alien intelligence, it was to be reported, not allowed contact with human technology.

The old woman ducked her head, and shrugged, much like a guilty child hoping to escape punishment. She probably wasn't too bright – possibly mentally ill, or why else would she have stayed behind? Ignorant, disturbed, and a little slow, she had probably seen the indigenes as something interesting. A wonder they hadn't killed her.

'Come on,' Kira urged, being consciously gentle again, charming, as she would have been to a slow child. 'Show me where you live; let's have a little chat.'

Now the black eyes were opaque as obsidian, and the old woman's body seemed to settle, as if she'd turned to stone. 'It's a bad time,' she said. 'Come back later.'

'You don't have to worry about cleaning up, if that's what you meant,' Kira said, imagining the kind of housekeeping this woman might do, she with her cape and loincloth and bare feet. She probably hadn't washed a dish in the years she'd been here; it would be squalid and horrible, but . . .

'It's not that,' the old woman said. 'It's just a bad time. Come back later.' She turned away again. 'Tomorrow. And don't follow me.' She walked off, slowly and steadily. The morning sun had burned through the mist, and revealed all the varicose veins on the backs of the old woman's legs.

Kira stood staring after her. She had not had anyone snub her like that since childhood. She hoped she was not one of those academic terrors who demanded deference beyond their rights, but a little common courtesy . . . she fought down the irritation. She was hot and sweaty, that was all, and the old woman wasn't quite right in the head. What could you expect of someone who would choose to stay behind, alone – although the old woman hadn't said that. Perhaps she had had another companion, another old person who'd stayed and now was sick. That would explain a lot.

Kira watched as the old woman kept going, up the street – hardly more than an open way between the houses, not paved at all, though it had a ditch to either side. The old woman turned aside, finally, entering what seemed to be a gap between the houses, or a garden. From here, Kira couldn't see for sure. She turned, and lumbered back to the shuttle, uncomfortably aware of the warmth of the sun. Sweat soaked her clothes inside the suit already; she could smell herself. It would be stifling by midmorning, and she didn't like to think about the afternoon.

'And what did you accomplish, Kira?' Vasil asked. He sounded very sure she had accomplished nothing.

Kira stopped at the foot of the ramp, and deliberately unfastened the rest of the protective suit. She clambered out of it, nested the segments and folded them, then looked up at the others. She could feel a faint breath of breeze on her wet clothes.

'She still says it's a bad time for her, and we should come back tomorrow. She thought we came to kill the indigenes, because they killed the people at the other colony site.'

'Did you make her understand our mission?' Vasil asked.

'I tried. She's not too bright, ill-educated, and as the advisor said, possibly disturbed. Very old, I would say, but not senile in the usual sense. Not that much there to start with.' As she said this, Kira felt a guilty twinge. Was the old woman really stupid and crazy . . . or was she taking out her own discomfort on someone who had made her uncomfortable?

'She has no right to tell us to wait,' Vasil said.

'If we want her cooperation,' Ori said, 'it would be wise to wait. This is her space, in one sense. She has been here a long time. Speaking as an anthropologist—'

Vasil glared at him. Bilong heaved a dramatic sigh that got the attention of both men. For once, Kira approved – anything to forestall another turf battle: Vasil hated it when Ori called himself an anthropologist rather than a technology assessment specialist.

'It is too *hot* for these suits, and no one is shooting at us. We might as well be comfortable.' Bilong began peeling out of hers with conscious grace. Kira glanced at the military advisors, who looked disgusted, but said nothing.

FIFTEEN

Ofelia had finally understood from Bluecloak what the odd behavior of one of the creatures meant. Pregnant, needing a nest. She eyed the creature; she still could not tell male from female, not with those little skirt things. She presumed they had some sort of organs under there but her curiosity didn't run that direction. The creature about to give birth certainly didn't have the hugely swollen belly she associated with pregnancy.

It had scratched out a hollow in the tall grass by the river, but the others had discouraged it. Ofelia could follow some of the explanation now: big biting things that lived in the water might eat the nestlings. The grass in the sheep meadow, while far enough away from the river, wasn't tall enough. The pregnant creature scratched at it with obvious distress, kicking the loose bits away.

Despite the progress made with Bluecloak, Ofelia had great difficulty understanding what the creature needed in a nest site. Tall grass for cushioning? She offered a bundle of soft cloths, which the pregnant one snatched away and threw into the air. The others retrieved them, bringing them to Ofelia with averted faces, as if expecting her to be angry. Ofelia knew better than that; if the creature was

about to give birth, she – it – would naturally be edgy
and irritable. Tall grass for concealment? From what?
Bluecloak gestured to the air; Ofelia looked up, seeing
nothing. Bluecloak made wings of its arms, mimed a
soaring hunter that might swoop on young. That made
sense, except that Ofelia had never seen a winged thing
big enough to bother the creatures. Maybe that, too, came
from the far north.

Why not give birth inside, in one of the houses? She
tried to convey this with gesture and the few grunts and
squawks she could now make. Bluecloak stared at her, and
she wondered if she'd said something rude by accident.
Then it led the way to the center, to the schoolroom. It
fumbled through the books on the shelves until it found
the one it wanted. Ofelia took it. This was now a familiar
routine. She could page through the old textbooks more
easily than it could, especially if she had a clue – ah, yes.
This one told of a child whose aunt took care of her while
her mother went away to work in the city.

She turned the pages, looking for the picture she
thought Bluecloak would want, the one it had chosen
many times before, where the child waved goodbye to her
mother and the aunt had a hand on her shoulder. Sure
enough, Bluecloak's talon came down on the page when
she opened the book to that picture. It tapped the book.

'I'm looking,' Ofelia said.

'Uhoo,' Bluecloak said, its version of 'you.' It pointed
at the aunt. It had done that before. Ofelia thought it
meant that she had cared for other children than her own,
and that was true.

'Yes,' she said. 'I've done that.'

It made the sound she now thought of as the pregnant
one's name, though she couldn't ever get it right herself:

'Gurgle-click-cough' was the closest she could come. Then it pointed to the departing mother. That was clear enough – Gurgle-click-cough was going to be a mother. It pointed again to the picture of the aunt and to her. And she was to be the aunt of Gurgle-click-cough's baby? She felt her face growing warm. It could only be an honorary position, but – but it was nice of them to trust her.

'Nesst . . .' Bluecloak gestured around, clearly meaning inside a building. 'Uhoo aant.' If Gurgle-click-cough nested inside, Ofelia would be the aunt? Clear enough, but . . . that sounded like an obligation more than an honor. 'Aant iss . . .' another unpronounceable cluster of sounds that Ofelia tried silently, only to find her tongue wandering around the roof of her mouth looking for the place that worked. Bluecloak said the word again, and again, until she tried it aloud. Then it said it again, while she tried to shape her pronunciation to what she heard.

When she had come as close as she could – it still sounded like 'click-kaw-keerrrr' to her – Bluecloak called in the others, and spoke briefly to them. They enacted a pantomime of the soaring hunter, the creeping hunter, the hunter that leapt from behind things . . . Ofelia watched in amazement and delight. She had not realized how many things might hunt these efficient hunters, and she had not realized how cleverly they could mimic other creatures. Did they mimic her like that, when they were alone? She had no time to think about that, for Bluecloak was making sure she understood. The click-kaw-keerrrr, equivalent to the aunt in the storybook, protected nestlings from the various threats, and between times held the nestlings, soothed them, sang to them.

It seemed to Ofelia more the mother's role than the aunt's, unless all their mothers went away after the birthing. Why would that be? It also seemed that they would expect a lot from her for letting the pregnant one nest in one of the buildings. Did they really expect her, all alone, to take care of a baby she knew nothing about? Bluecloak halted the performance with a gesture, then spoke again. 'Alll click-kaw-keerrrr-llluk putt uhoo click-kaw-keerrr ost.' The mix of languages confused her for a moment, then she worked it out. All of them were sort of click-kaw-keerrrs, but she would be the most click-kaw-keerrr, if she invited the pregnant one to nest inside.

She wondered then what obligations she had taken on when she invited the original group inside in the sea-storm. Perhaps that explained their familiar behavior, and the odd moments of respect. Still . . . she could not see a pregnant creature, even an alien, give birth in a place it thought dangerous, when she had a place it might find more comfortable.

But which place might it find more comfortable? They had all spent time in the center, but the center rooms were big, cluttered with machines. The size of the nest-cavity it had scratched out in the tall grass suggested to Ofelia that a closet in one of the houses might suit it better. She led Bluecloak to the house next to the center, and offered the closet in the main bedroom. It smelled a bit damp, but airing would help. At least it was not the wet season. She still had the armful of cloths; she mimed putting them on the floor.

Bluecloak conferred with those who had trailed along, the language far too fast for Ofelia to follow. Some moved away immediately, to begin opening windows. One left the house; she could hear it running away up the lane. To tell the pregnant one? Ofelia wasn't sure. She wasn't sure about anything except that she was about to become an aunt. And a click-kaw-keerrr, which she hoped would be within her ability.

The ones in the house began to clean it, using the brooms from the center. When they took the brooms back, they disappeared for a time. Ofelia went to the herb garden she maintained three houses down, and came back with clean-smelling herbs. She had seen the creatures leaning over these plants as if they, too, enjoyed the scents. Already one of the others was back, with fresh-cut tall grass which it spread on the closet floor. The pregnant one came in, stepping warily through the door. She – Ofelia could not think of a pregnant creature as 'it' – grunted when she saw the closet with its layer of grass. Two others arrived with more grass, and the pregnant one went into the closet and began trampling the grass in a pattern that resulted in a compact coiled arrangement looking very much like pictures of birds' nests. Ofelia noticed that she hardly touched the grass with her hands. This went on until the nest rose half a meter above the closet floor. Then the others brought finer grasses and other fine-leaved plants that looked softer than the coarse tall grass used so far. This the pregnant one worked into the interior of the nest. Then the pregnant one stepped out and churred at Ofelia.

'Uhoo nesst,' Bluecloak translated.

Why did they want her to get into the nest? They all did; they all stood there looking expectant. Ofelia stepped in, and was surprised at how springy it was under her feet. The bowl shape held her toward the middle; she realized how comfortable it would be for a nap. She sat down, and they murmured soft sounds to her. So that was what they wanted? They wanted her to pretend to sleep, perhaps? Or did they make a nest for aunts, and then a nest for the pregnant mother?

She curled up on her side, and wriggled around. Very comfortable indeed. Suddenly something sharp poked her side. She sat up, and felt around with her fingers until she found the cause – a stone about the size of a chicken egg, with sharp angles. *That* didn't belong in a nest, and how had the pregnant one missed it? She held it up, scowling at them.

Their left toes drummed; she knew now that meant approval. The pregnant one snatched the stone from her and held it aloft; the drumming deepened, including fingertips on torsos, and finally the pregnant one's throat sac.

Obviously, they had planted the stone in the nest for her to find, but why? It was just an ordinary stone. One of them held out a hand to her, and helped her out of the nest. The pregnant one clasped her wrists and bent her head; she felt the dry, ticklish touch of a tongue on her hands. The pregnant one released her, and the others did the same, even Bluecloak. Her hands tingled from the touch of so many tongues.

Her stomach recoiled, knotted in fear. She was in over her head; she was committed now to something she did not understand. What if she made a mistake? What if she did something that hurt the baby? She looked around for Bluecloak. If she could read their expressions at all, Bluecloak looked satisfied, even smug. The others looked relaxed; the pregnant one stretched out in a patch of sun on the floor and one of the others squatted beside her, running its fingers lightly along her back.

Then Bluecloak urged Ofelia out of the house; the others left the pregnant one and her – birth attendant? best friend? husband? Ofelia didn't know – alone in the house. Two of the creatures settled outside the house, squatting in the lane, and pulled out their long knives. The rest went back to the center, Ofelia with them. Behind her, she could hear the ring and rasp of sharpening; it made her shiver. She was hungry for lunch, but she was even hungrier for knowledge. She still didn't know whether to expect eggs or a a wiggly baby. She didn't know why those knives were being sharpened . . . to guard the pregnant one and the baby from predators, or to carve up a clumsy, ignorant aunt if she made mistakes?

She was just opening her mouth to ask Bluecloak, when an alarm went off in the control room. Ofelia jumped, then led the way there, heart pounding. It was the wrong season for sea-storms, and that morning she had seen nothing in the gauges to indicate any problem.

The gauges were still steady, still in the safe range for all functions. The flashing red light was on the weathersat board. Which meant someone had queried the weathersat, which meant another ship had arrived.

She had known it would happen someday. Eventually someone would come to investigate the attack on that second colony, and the creatures who had made it. That was why she'd set the alarm as she had, so that she would know when to hide. She had even explained that to Bluecloak, as best she could; she wasn't at all sure that the creatures understood space flight, or how far away things were. She had hoped she wouldn't be alive when the other humans came, but she was.

And far worse, the pregnant one was nesting. Ofelia had no idea how long it would be before she gave birth or laid her eggs or whatever, but she knew it was a bad time for the other humans to come.

She conveyed this to Bluecloak: others like herself were coming, were in a boat – they had agreed on the term –

far up in the sky. They would come down – she was sure
of that – and they would most likely come down here, at
the shuttle strip. She had no idea how long it would be.
They might sit up there for days looking at things through
orbital scanners, making sure they would be safe. They
might already have been there for days, in which case it
was no use trying to get the creatures to conceal themselves in the houses because they had already been seen.
Besides, if they could strip the records from the weathersat,
they would find plenty of evidence that Ofelia and the
creatures were both living here.

And what if they decided the creatures here knew too
much, and killed them? Ofelia felt a cold sweat break out
all over her. She could not let that happen. She would
not. She did not know what she could do, but she would
not let that happen.

First, could she find out something about the ship that
had arrived? She queried the weathersat herself, but got
no answer. Apparently the people on the arriving ship had
pre-empted all local requests. That might mean they didn't
yet know she was here, that she used the weathersat, or
it might mean they didn't care.

She turned to Bluecloak again, and tried to ask how
long it would be before the pregnant one – she stumbled
over Gurgle-click-cough – delivered. Bluecloak's answering
gestures were not reassuring. It might be today, or
tomorrow, or the day after. It was Gurgle-click-cough's
first birth, and its timing was more uncertain than for a
subsequent one. Ofelia understood that well enough; it
was the same with humans. She conveyed that to Bluecloak
fairly easily.

More difficult was the concept that the arriving humans
presented a special danger to Gurgle-click-cough and her

young. Bluecloak cocked its head to one side; its right
toes tapped the floor. She had tried to explain before that
the humans killed far to the north were not the same as
those who had lived here, and the ones who lived here
went somewhere else, very far away. Now she tried to say
that the ones coming were more like those who had been
killed, not like her.

'Nesst click-kaw-keerrr,' Bluecloak said, as if that would
end the discussion. 'Aant.'

'It doesn't matter,' Ofelia said. 'They won't care.' She
tried to think how to say *that* in gestures, but when she
looked at Bluecloak it was standing rigid, its throatsac
swollen and pulsing, its eyelids partly shut. Then it
blinked.

'Nesst click-kaw-keerrr nnot kkaerrr?' A pause. 'Kkilll?'

'Not kill,' Ofelia said, hoping it was so. 'But they won't
care about me. I'm not one of them. Not their . . .' what
was the word Bluecloak had used about its people? She
opted instead for gestures that included her, Bluecloak,
others who lived here, as opposed to others who lived
someplace else.

'Uhoo,' Bluecloak said, pointing to make it clear. 'Click-
kaw-keerrr.'

She was the click-kaw-keerrr; whatever click-kaw-keerrrs
had to do, she had to do. She was uncomfortably certain
that this meant she was supposed to protect Gurgle-click-
cough and her young from the other humans . . . or die
trying.

She chose to interpret the hollow feeling in her belly as
hunger, and went back to her house to cook something.

They had seen the white streaks of the shuttle's flight;
they had heard the brief transmissions between the shuttle

and the orbiting ship. Ofelia wondered how much the creatures understood of this. She herself couldn't follow much of the talk; the accent was strange, and the utterances perhaps intentionally cryptic. She thought of trying to use the colony transmitter, even keyed it once, but the signal had to go through the weathersat, and she couldn't get it locked open. Apparently, they were still using the weathersat themselves. She felt a guilty relief. In her inmost heart, she still hoped they would simply go away.

Meanwhile, Gurgle-click-cough had settled into the house next to the center – not in the nest itself yet – and the others brought her food and sat with her. She seemed larger to Ofelia, her lean form now bulging under her kilt. She rarely left the house, and had no interest in the news. Every time Ofelia visited, Gurgle-click-cough leaned against her and licked her hands. Ofelia felt helpless and protective all at once.

On the third day, Bluecloak roused her before dawn when the voices came again. Ofelia hobbled across to the center, stiff as she always was in the early morning, and grumpy with being awakened in that last sweet deep slumber before she would have awakened on her own.

'They're landing this time,' Ofelia said. 'They're coming here.' She had known they would – it was the only reasonable thing for them to do, and they must by now have noticed that a human and some of the creatures were here – but she had hoped very much they would do the unreasonable thing and go away.

Bluecloak's throat-sac expanded, and it thrummed at her.

'I know,' Ofelia said. 'I have to do something.' What, she had no idea. She listened to the pilot of the shuttle describing his descent, his plan for landing. They would make one low-altitude pass to look again at the colony and check for weapons. It would be noisy, then, worse than just landing. They had made a low-altitude pass the day before, scaring all the creatures, sending the sheep and cattle into panicky stampedes around the meadows. Ofelia looked at Bluecloak, pointed up, and covered her ears.

Far in the distance, she heard the approaching growl of the shuttle. They would circle out to sea, then come back and land. She would have to go meet them, and say . . . what? What could she say that would keep them from bothering Gurgle-click-cough? She stood up, only then realizing that she had come from her bed wearing nothing at all but the string of beads she rarely took off these days.

And she had no idea where her dress was, the only dress that strange humans would find decent. Or shoes . . . she had thrown that last pair of shoes in the recycler, she remembered.

As fast as she could, she hobbled back to her house through the predawn twilight, and grabbed the green embroidered cloak that had impressed Bluecloak. At least one of the peoples here would find it appropriate. The shuttle thundered overhead; she did not go outside to look at it. She used the toilet, splashed water on her face, scrubbed at her teeth, swiped at her flyaway hair with both hands. Then she wrapped a length of cloth around her hips, and looped more strands of beads around her neck. They might think she had gone native, but at least they would recognize an effort made to look festive.

This took longer than she wanted; she had to use the toilet again. Now she heard the great roar of the shuttle approaching, descending. She went out her front door, and shooed the creatures back into shelter. If there was only one old woman, she did not think the other humans would shoot first – and if they did, at least the creatures might have a chance to escape.

She saw the shuttle angling in, but ignored it to look in the doorway of the house where Gurgle-click-cough was. The two creatures on guard waited just inside the door, looking tense even in the dimness. They could have turned the light on, Ofelia thought, but when she reached for the switch, one of them caught her wrist. She heard a wheezy rasp from the closet. Ofelia sighed. Naturally it would happen now, at the worst possible moment. And she would not get to see it, because she had to go deal with her own kind. It seemed as unfair as the rest of life.

'Good luck to you,' she said softly.

'Click-kaw-keerrr,' they all replied in soft chorus. As if she could forget that responsibility. By the time she reached the shuttle strip, the sun was just up, shining right in her face, making it hard to see anything but a great dark blur that stank of scorched plastics and oils. Ofelia squinted into the light, moving slowly over the rough pavement where grass was doing its best to reclaim its domain. No one called out to her; no one came toward her.

When she got into the shadow of the shuttle, she could see them clumped on the ramp above, all wearing bulky suits that would be intolerable later in the day. Ofelia could have laughed at them, but then they would think she was crazy. They might think that anyway – with their eyes on her, she was far more aware of how she must look. She felt herself going hot, but perhaps they wouldn't notice with her dark tanned skin and the early light.

Two of them held weapons, and looked past her to the village with professional intensity. The unarmed man in front was probably the one in charge. He had that expression, of one used to telling others what to do. She had forgotten how much she disliked that expression. Beside him, crowding him, stood a woman who looked as disgruntled as Ofelia felt. Remembered resentment gave her the courage to speak first.

'This was not a good time,' she said. She put into it all the reproach of the experienced mother. 'You've upset them.' No need to specify who was upset; they would know.

The man puffed out his chest; he didn't like it that she had spoken first. Ofelia didn't care, and she didn't listen past the first '. . . authority . . .' She interrupted, telling him again that it wasn't a good time. 'You could have listened when I tried to talk to you,' she said. They didn't have to know that she'd only keyed the transmitter once.

This time the woman answered. Her voice sounded mature, but she was certainly younger than Ofelia. Perhaps middle-aged, but it was hard to tell with shipfolk, who hardly ever saw weather. Ofelia answered her, trying to think ahead to what would impress this woman. She wasn't afraid of the man who thought he was the leader, that was clear. Perhaps this woman would be sensible, and listen. The men, of course, did not; she had hardly started talking to the woman when two of them interrupted. But their voices clashed over each other, and the woman spoke again.

'Who are you?' she asked, as if she had a right to know.

Ofelia turned the question back on her – would she recognize that as the insult it was? – and the woman did not answer, but reassured Ofelia that they had not come to hurt her, but to help her.

Help! She had not asked for help; she didn't need help;

she needed them to go away and let her alone. She snorted before she could stop herself, and the woman looked embarrassed, as if she realized how preposterous that was.

She made it very clear, spelling it out. 'I don't need help.' And they might as well know that she knew about the other colony. 'If you're here about that other lot—'

The man interrupted, and then the armed man; it was as if they had a contest on, which could ask questions the fastest. Ofelia answered, shortly. She was not a schoolchild in a contest; they might at least have had the courtesy to come down to her level, offer her a seat, before pouncing on her with all these questions. The creatures, alien as they were, had shown more courtesy.

'Didn't you try to help?' the unarmed man said finally. Ofelia glared at him, wishing boils on his posterior and head lice to his children. One moment he questioned her as if she were a stupid child, and the next he thought she had magical powers and could fly thousands of kilometers to rescue healthy young people from disaster? Ridiculous, insulting . . . she ran through her store of invective, in grim silence, until he turned red.

The woman spoke again, asking how long she'd been there. Another stupid question, if less insulting; it was just possible, Ofelia thought, that some silly old woman with a spaceship might have crashed here, or even come here prospecting or something. She explained, briefly; she enjoyed the shock on the woman's face when she told the truth about the Company's attitude towards old colonists. Didn't know everything, she didn't, no matter what fancy job she had. Wait until she was old enough to face her company's scorn . . . then she'd know. But the man broke in again, this time scolding her for being there. Like the Company, he thought she was just a nuisance, just something to be dealt with. The old resentment boiled up, making a bad taste in Ofelia's mouth. That one had not even been a colonist, was not due the respect she had paid to the men who worked with their women to build the village she lived in. She had not liked all of them, or all the things they did, but the slackers had died early on, one way and another, and the men who had been evacuated had earned her respect if not her affection. This one, with his smooth ship-bred skin, hiding in that protective suit as if one old woman were a threat to his safety . . . She probably was, she thought.

'Let me alone,' she said, with more bitterness than she intended. He glared back at her, and began trying to convince her of the seriousness of 'the situation.' She could have laughed; he didn't know himself how serious the situation was.

'I'm not stupid,' she said, putting an edge on it; his eyes widened. Would it help to say again that they had come at a bad time? Probably not, but she said it anyway. 'Go away,' she said finally, and turned and walked off, feeling their gaze on her back as if the embroidered eyes were crawling over her skin.

She heard clumsy footsteps and an argument behind her. From the voices, it was the woman following her. All right. Let the woman come, down on the same level where she wouldn't get such a crick in her neck trying to talk to her. She kept walking, hoping to lead the woman clear into the village, where the others could not hear them. Of course there were sound pickups, she knew that, but at least they might not interfere as much.

When the other woman called, politely enough, she had made it to the end of the lane. Not as far as she'd hoped, but better than standing beside the shuttle. From here, the creatures could see her, if they wanted. She turned.

The woman had more weathered skin than she'd expected, as if she'd spent much of her life outside. She had a thick mop of caramel-colored hair, cut short but shaped with care. Her gray-green eyes were trying to look earnest and friendly, but Ofelia distrusted them. Something about the woman exuded authority, not the natural authority of experience, but the authority of position. And she was out of breath, probably from wearing that heavy protective suit and trying to run in it. Ofelia took a deep breath and smiled at her.

The woman started to speak, but Ofelia interrupted her. She had to understand that Ofelia had a message more important than hers. 'It's a bad time,' she said firmly. She let the other woman's eyes rove over her, inspecting her hair, her face, her body, her strange clothes. Would she believe Ofelia made sense, if obscure sense, or would she dismiss her out of hand because of her age, her strange appearance?

The conversation teetered back and forth, never quite finding a balance where both women could be comfortable and exchange the information Ofelia was sure the other both wanted and had to impart. Ofelia learned, as she expected, that they knew about the creatures being here. The woman was shocked that she had cooperated with them – but what did she expect? That Ofelia would have killed them all off by herself? That by herself she could have kept them from learning? The other humans had a lot to learn about the creatures.

She saw the moment when the other woman's attitude shifted, when she decided that Ofelia was negligible, probably crazy. She kept trying to get Ofelia to take her home, to let them have a cozy chat. Ofelia was not about to go into any enclosed space with this young, strong woman in her protective suit. Finally she had to be rude to get the woman to go away. She saw in the woman's expression that she recognized the rudeness, that it hurt.

Fine. Let it hurt. Maybe she would be more careful next time. And maybe – just maybe – she would convince the others to stay away until tomorrow. By then, if Ofelia guessed right, Gurgle-click-cough would have had her young, and perhaps in the night – if they were very lucky – they could get the mother and child away to safety.

SIXTEEN

Ofelia went to her own garden first, in case the woman followed or watched where she went. She was not going to lead them to the nest-house. She poked among the rows for a few minutes, not really seeing the plants. When she looked back, from the corner of her garden, she could not see anything of the shuttle but its tall tail sticking up beyond the roofs. The lane behind her was empty; the woman was out of sight, presumably on her way back to the shuttle.

She went in through the kitchen door, and felt the emptiness of her belly as hunger. She had cold flatbread from the night before; she rolled it up and stuffed it in her mouth so fast she almost choked.

That would be silly, to choke herself at a time like this. She spit out half the mouthful, chewed and swallowed the rest carefully. Then she ate it all, slowly, trying to concentrate on the flavor and not what had happened.

They had not looked the way she expected, those people. She had become used to the creatures, to the narrow big-eyed faces, the long graceful legs with the bouncy gait, the long four-fingered hands with the hard black talons. These people looked pale, soft, squashy as dough, with little eyes sunk like raisins in their broad faces, with soft hands sprouting too many soft-tipped fingers like tentacles.

She avoided the mirror; she did not want to remind herself how like them she looked. When she had eaten, she went back out her kitchen door and looked around the corner of the next house down the lane. Nothing. That didn't mean none of them had sneaked into the village, to hide between houses. But curiosity tickled her; she had to know how the delivery was going. In the low sunlight of early morning, she walked across the lane and down to the house they had chosen.

Inside the door, the two guards were drumming softly; she could see now that their throat-sacs were distended. They said nothing to Ofelia, and made no move to stop her as she went on through to the bedroom. Here were two more of the creatures, including Bluecloak. Where were the others? Ofelia hoped they were staying safe under cover somewhere. They had closed the shutters on the morning side of the room, and half-closed the others, to make a quiet blue shade. In the closet, it was even darker, but she could see the hunched form of the laboring mother. Hissing, gurgling, occasionally letting out a loud *chuff* . . . she was in the midst of the process, whatever it was. Ofelia sat down on the bedframe to wait.

Her back hurt and her eyes felt gritty; she had been wakened too early. Before she knew it, she dozed off, leaning against the wall. She woke to a chorus of hisses and squeaks. Bluecloak stood by the closet door, its throat-sac bobbing in and out, vivid orange in the shadowed room. It was a minute or so before she realized that the chorus – the multiple voices – came from inside the closet. Whatever it was had been born.

Ofelia pushed herself up, wondering if she needed to apologize. Bluecloak's great eyes stared at her, and a moment later Gurgle-click-cough peered over the edge of the nest. Invitation or warning? She looked outside instead, at the glaring sunlight near midday. No sign of the other humans, and from this window she could not see the shuttle's tail anyway. She went back to the living room, where the guards squatted by the door, their knives out, and glanced down the lane. Nothing. That woman must have made them stay at the shuttle, or at least not come into the village.

Ofelia went back to the bedroom. Now Gurgle-click-cough was leaning out of the nest, one arm stretched out to Ofelia. Ofelia went closer. The smell of birth was never entirely pleasant; she had not expected their births to be any neater than those of humans. Sure enough, the closet now smelled strongly of creatures and their waste, and something else – not unpleasant, this last, but new.

Ofelia leaned closer, and Gurgle-click-cough took her hand and guided it. Something damp, and hot, with a quick pulse shaking its fragile body. It seemed very small. And another one, and another. Gurgle-click-cough moved aside, and now Ofelia could see them. Striped vividly in dark and light, big-headed, the heads mostly eyes, skinny little legs, and arms hardly noticeable, folded against the body. And tails.

They hissed, one after the other, and one of them squeaked. Gurgle-click-cough picked that one up, delicately balanced in her long narrow hand. She reached towards Ofelia, and Ofelia put out both hands to take it. It felt hot, light, perilous. It squirmed the way babies squirmed, the little tail writhing across her wrist. Ofelia almost dropped it, but didn't, and brought it to her as she would have cuddled a human baby. The eyes opened – they were pale gold, with an even lighter rim around the pupil – and it squeaked at her.

She leaned her cheek to it, and murmured, the way everyone murmured to babies. There, there, there, and easy, it's all right, everything's fine, take it easy. It pushed its hard little snout against her breastbone, and she had to giggle. Nothing there for anyone anymore, certainly not an alien that looked far more like a lizard than its mother. Then she felt the touch of that tiny, raspy tongue. Tears stung her eyes. She had always cried when she first held newborns; one corner of her mind was a little surprised that the same reflex worked with these creatures.

Gurgle-click-cough insisted on handing Ofelia each of the young, one at a time, and each of the young licked Ofelia on wrist or hand or chest, as she held it. Bluecloak approved; its throat-sac throbbed softly.

'Click-kaw-keerrr,' it said.

'Click-kaw-keerrr,' Ofelia answered. Of course she wanted to protect these little ones, odd as they were; she could wish them no harm. Hard to believe they could grow into the tall bright adults she knew, but then human babies were red, slimy, squalling little messes right after birth. She supposed an alien would find them every bit as unlikely precursors to adults as these. She looked again at the squirming newborns; she could not tell one from the other, at least not in that dimness.

In the afternoon, at the hottest hour, when Ofelia was stooped over her own kitchen sink washing out the soft cloths which Gurgle-click-cough had used after all, one of the creatures let out a squawk, and bolted into Ofelia's house. 'All right,' she said. She knew what it had to be.

The humans had not waited until the next day, as she'd told them. She hadn't expected them to, but at least they had not interrupted the birth. She glanced out her kitchen door and saw them coming along the lane. The woman she had talked to before, now in cream-colored slacks and shirt, with a big hat on her head, accompanied by another woman and two men in variations of that outfit, and two obviously dangerous men in the dark protective suits, with weapons. The armed men had faces even redder than the others, dripping sweat under their helmets.

Ofelia pulled all the ice trays from her cooler, and emptied them into her largest pitcher. She had already squeezed the juice of lemons and limes; she poured this into the pitcher with water and sugar. Hot humans were grumpy humans; if she could get them comfortable, they might listen to reason.

When she went out the door to invite them in, they were halfway to her house, peering curiously into the houses on either side. She didn't want them to find Gurgle-click-cough yet; she called out, and they looked at her.

'Come have juice,' she said. They looked at each other doubtfully, then came forward, the armed men making it obvious by their movements and expressions how little they trusted her.

She ignored the armed men, and looked at the others. The woman she had met, Kira. A much younger woman – or a woman who acted younger – who reminded her too much of Linda. The man she had seen, who said he was in charge, and a shorter, stockier man who kept glancing at the younger woman. That kind of thing already! She felt tired before she started.

The two armed men would not come in her house; one stood by either door. She handed them glasses of cold juice, and they stared at her, blank-faced, before finally taking sips. The others crowded the main room, staring around them at her things.

'This is the Falfurrias house,' Kira said, to the others. 'It's on the plat Sims furnished.' She leaned into the bedrooms, looking, clearly unconcerned about Ofelia's privacy.

'Are you sure?' the taller man said. He spoke as if Ofelia were not there, as if she might not know where she was.

'That's right,' Ofelia said. He glanced at her and away, as if he did not like what he saw. She had changed from the green cape to a shirt with fringed sleeves and bands of color across the front and back. It was too hot for this time of day – for this season, in fact – but she was not comfortable with her bare skin in front of these strangers. It made her angry to be embarrassed again.

'It's my house,' she went on. 'I helped build this house. I am Ofelia Falfurrias.'

'You were supposed to be evacuated,' the man said, without giving his own name. Such rudeness. Ofelia felt her dislike harden, as if it were sap drying in the sun. 'None of you were supposed to be here, and this colony's equipment was supposed to be properly shut down. If it hadn't been for you—'

'It's not her fault,' Kira said, again as if Ofelia could not speak for herself. 'She's only an old woman—'

Only. So Kira was as bad as the rest, thinking an old woman of no importance.

'Perhaps we should introduce ourselves,' said the shorter man. He smiled at Ofelia. 'I'm Orisan Almarest, a cultural anthropologist, Sera Falfurrias. I'm an anthropologist; I study the way people and their tools work together.'

'Kira Stavi,' the older woman said shortly.

'Vasil Likisi, leader of this team, and designated representative of the government,' said the taller man.

'Bilong,' said the younger woman, with a wide artificial smile. 'Just call me Bilong, that's fine.'

It wasn't fine. She didn't want to call Bilong anything except what the other women had called Linda. The only one with any manners was the shorter man, Orisan Almarest. That one she recognized with a little nod. 'Ser Almarest.' She gestured at the iced juice on the table. 'Would you like something cool to drink?'

'Thank you, Sera Falfurrias,' he said. She poured him a glass, and he took it and sipped. 'It is very good,' he said.

Ofelia relaxed slightly; this was the ritual she knew. 'The fruit is more bitter this year,' she said. 'You are too gracious with your thanks.'

'It is delicious on such a hot day,' he said. He smiled at her over the glass as he took a large swallow. The others still stood around like untrained children. Finally the older woman moved.

'Thank you for inviting us in, Sera Falfurrias,' she said.

Ofelia smiled the required smile. 'You are welcome in my home,' she said. 'Unfortunately, I have only this juice to offer you.'

'Thank you,' said the woman, with a smile as forced as Ofelia's. She sipped, and her brows lifted. So she had really expected it to be bitter; Ofelia nearly laughed.

'Oh, please may I have some of that?' the younger woman asked, like a child who cannot remember to wait until food is offered.

'Of course,' Ofelia said, pouring it out and handing it to her without other comment, as she would have to a child. The stocky man smiled at her.

'Bilong is our linguist,' he said. 'She will study the indigenes' language.'

'Indigenes?' Ofelia hated herself for asking the moment the unfamiliar word was out of her mouth. All of them but the stocky man smiled in a way that meant they enjoyed her ignorance.

'It's the academic term for anything native to a place,' said the stocky man. 'You and I are not indigenous here, but the creatures who attacked the second colony landing are. At least, we think they are.' He said this in a matter-of-fact voice, as if there were nothing strange in her not knowing. Ofelia appreciated this courtesy even though she didn't trust him. He went on. 'Kira – Sera Stavi – is a xenozoologist; she studies animals alien to human worlds. Of course, that means they are native, or indigenous, where they are. She will study the biology of animals here.'

'They are not just animals,' Ofelia said, looking at the woman.

'No, but like us they are animals in part,' the woman said. Her voice had softened – was it the cold juice, or was she trying to be more polite? 'It is my job to find out how their bodies work, what foods they eat, and so on.'

Ofelia transferred her gaze to the tall man who had been so quick to claim authority. He took that cue instantly.

'I'm the team leader, as I said, and the representative of the government, here to ascertain whether these things are intelligent enough to warrant protection under the law. If it seems warranted, I also have the authority to make an official representation from the government to their government, concerning recent events and our desire for some kind of arrangement whereby our scientists can study them. As you may not know, they are unique in the history of human stellar exploration.'

He seemed ready to go on a lot longer but Ofelia was not in the mood to listen to him. She poured out another glass of the juice and handed it to him as he drew breath. He looked surprised. Finally he blurted, 'Thank you,' and took a sip.

'Please sit down,' Ofelia said. She had just enough chairs, if she herself perched on the stool she used while cooking and chopping vegetables. Slowly, awkwardly, they all sat. Ofelia made up another pitcher of the fruit drink, and refilled their glasses before she sat down herself.

'I have lived here alone since the others left,' Ofelia began. They would know that, but starting with the obvious and known was both polite and sensible. From this known, she could lead them by her own paths to the view she wanted them to see. 'I had come here as a young woman—' She had felt middle-aged then, a mother of three, no longer in her first youth, but now she knew how young she had been. 'My husband and I built this house, and my last children were born here. Then my husband died, and one by one all the children but Barto. When they said we must leave, they told Barto that I would be of no use, that I would very likely die in cryo. They made him pay extra. I did not want to cost him that, and I did not want to leave the place my husband and children had lived and died.'

'Poor thing,' said the younger woman, with such fake sweetness dripping off her tongue that Ofelia felt she could scrape it off and make jam with it.

'You could have died here,' the older woman said, as if accusing her of a crime. 'I could have died in cryo,' Ofelia said. 'Old people die; it is the way of nature. I am not afraid to die.' That was not quite true, but she had not been afraid the way this person meant it.

'It was irresponsible, nonetheless,' said the leader. 'Look at the results.'

Ofelia gave him a blank look. 'Results, Ser Likisi?'

He waved his arm expansively, almost hitting the younger woman in the face. 'These . . . things here, knowing about humans, seeing the technology in use. The government has strict standards on the use of advanced technology in front of primitive cultures.'

'They would have found it anyway,' Ofelia said.

'But you were here to show them how to use it.'

Ofelia had wondered about that, in those first intoxicating moments of communication with the creatures, but then she had had no time to think . . . they were learning so fast. She had finally decided that the creatures would have found the master switches on their own. She had at least taught them to use caution, to respect the machines. She opened her mouth to say that, but the armed man by the front door moved suddenly, bringing up his weapon.

'Halt where you are!' he said, as if he thought anyone in the universe could understand his words.

'No!' said Ofelia. He was going to shoot one of her creatures; she couldn't let him. That was all she thought. She pushed herself off the stool, stumbled as her bad hip stabbed at her, and pushed between the two men in chairs to get to her front door. The broad dark back of the armed man in his protective suit was in her way.

'Move,' she said, poking a finger in his back.

His reaction came so fast she was on the floor before she knew he was moving. Her head rang. Outside, a loud squawk and the rapid thud of feet – the creatures—

'Don't hurt them!' she said, as loudly as she could. 'Don't—'

'They're attacking,' the armed man said. She could see

between his legs. Bluecloak, formally dressed in that blue cloak, throat-sac fully expanded, throbbing. Two of the others, knives drawn, eyes partly hooded by the extra eyelid.

'They're not,' Ofelia said from the floor. Her head ached, and it was going to ache worse, and none of these people had the courtesy to help an old woman up off the floor – she rolled over, glared at the ones in chairs, who were sitting there with their mouths open as if they were children at a play. She tried to sit up, and discovered that her ribs hurt too, and so did her arm, where she had fallen on it.

'Click-kaw-keerrr!' came from outside. Bluecloak's throat-sac pulsed.

'Click-kaw-keerrr,' Ofelia said. At least she could talk clearly enough to reassure them. She got to her knees, shook her dizzy head, and got all the way up. She limped back to the door. 'Let me out,' she said to the man with the weapon. 'They're not attacking; they want to see that I'm not hurt.'

'Could have killed you,' the man muttered angrily. *Stupid bitch* hovered on his lips; Ofelia said nothing. 'Sorry,' he said finally. 'Reflex.'

'Let me out,' she said again. Slowly, still aiming his weapon at the creatures, he moved aside.

'Don't get between us,' he said. 'If I have to blow you away, I will.'

'Don't start anything, then,' Ofelia said. She was in no more mood to be gracious than he was. 'They're not attacking, and they've never hurt me.' Not as much as you have, she thought at him as loudly as she could.

She limped out into the lane, and extended her hands to Bluecloak. It took them gently; its throat-sac shrank. Then it touched her head, her side, with one gentle finger.

Ofelia hissed; it hurt already, and she could imagine the dark bruise swelling on her scalp.

Behind her, she heard the team leader talking to the armed man; she could not quite hear the words, but the tone was angry. So was the armed man's reply. Let them argue; that would give her time. Time for what, she was not sure. Her head hurt a lot; she felt dizzy; she wanted to lie down in a cool dark place and have someone offer her cool drinks.

Bluecloak touched its own head, thumping it with a fist, then making the same jerk-away motion she had used to mime the pain of electric shock.

'Yes,' Ofelia said. 'My head got banged on the floor; it hurts. But I'm all right.'

Bluecloak pointed to the armed man, and made a motion of swinging an elbow back to hit someone.

'Yes,' Ofelia said. 'But I scared him.'

Bluecloak said 'Click-kaw-keerrr.' Ofelia frowned past her headache. What did being a click-kaw-keerrr have to do with being hit by the man at the door? Did he think the man shouldn't hit a click-kaw-keerrr? If so, what *was* a click-kaw-keerrr? Did they never hit theirs?

'He didn't know,' she said. 'I haven't had time to tell them about the babies.' She wasn't sure she wanted to; she remembered having her babies before in the hospital, where some of the staff handled them as if they were dolls or animals. She thought that was how Kira Stavi would handle these babies; she was sure the woman had never borne children.

'Nnot know uhoo click-kaw-keerrr?' Bluecloak asked.

'Not know,' Ofelia repeated. 'He did not know.'

Bluecloak said something to the other two, and they slid their long knives back into their belts. Ofelia still couldn't understand them when they talked so fast, but she did catch the word click-kaw-keerrr in the midst of the utterance.

'Gurgle-click-cough?' she asked. 'And the little ones?'

Bluecloak let out one grunt, and its eyelids sagged shut. Sleeping, was she? Natural, after a birth. Ofelia wondered if she nursed the babies, or if they ate other food. And if so, who brought it?

'Is that their leader?' asked Vasil from behind her. 'Is that why it's wearing that blue thing?'

Ofelia turned, trying not to wince visibly as her ribs and leg twinged. 'This is Bluecloak,' she said. 'I call it that because of the cloak; I can't say its real name.' She turned back to Bluecloak. 'This is Ser Vasil Likisi,' she said. 'He's the leader.' The others were in the doorway now; as they came out, Ofelia said their names: Kira, Ori, Bilong. Bluecloak said nothing, only standing there in the hot sunlight, head slightly tilted.

'You were talking to it,' the young woman said. 'I heard you – can you make it say something?'

Ofelia said to Bluecloak. 'This is the linguist, who will study how you talk.' From the glint in his eye, she thought he had been understanding more of this than he let on.

Bluecloak looked past her at Bilong. 'Uhoo Pihlog.' Ofelia could have laughed at the expression on the girl's face.

'It said my *name*,' she said, almost dancing.

Bluecloak rattled off a long sequence of squawks, grunts, clicks, and other sounds which seemed to delight Bilong; Ofelia suspected it was something as meaningless as the alphabet.

'Are you all right?' the other woman asked. She looked truly concerned.

'My head hurts,' Ofelia said.

'No wonder. I was so shocked I couldn't move – I'm sorry, but I just froze—'

'It's all right,' Ofelia said. The woman must be really ashamed, to say so much. Perhaps she had some proper feelings.

'Uhoo Kirrahhh,' Bluecloak said. It extended a hand, which the other woman took warily.

'Four fingers . . .' she breathed.

'And toes,' Ofelia said.

'Bi-sexed?' the woman asked, as if Bluecloak had not just shown that he could understand much of what was said.

'I haven't looked,' Ofelia said primly. She wasn't going to admit she still couldn't tell. It was quite true that she hadn't looked; it would have been rude.

'Of course, it's not your field,' the woman said, as if Ofelia were an idiot for not knowing. Ofelia's momentary sympathy for her vanished.

The whole team clustered around now, the four civilians staring, pointing, talking among themselves, as if the creatures were statues in an art gallery, or animals in a zoo. The two armed men stood stiffly by the house, glaring at them. It was stupid, out here in the hot sun. Ofelia's head throbbed; she wanted to be in the shade. Her house didn't have enough seats for all these, but the center did.

'You could come into the center, out of the sun,' Ofelia said. 'There are plenty of chairs in the center.'

'That's very kind of you,' the stocky man said, looking around. Of course, they wouldn't know where it was.

'It's over there,' said the older woman, the one who had known Ofelia's house by the family name. She started that way, and Ofelia repressed a desire to hit her. She should have let Ofelia lead her there; it was not *her* center.

Bluecloak touched her shoulder. 'Kuh?' Yes, she thought, cold is exactly what I want. Cold ice on my head, cold drink in my throat. Bluecloak walked beside her, the others still chattering, and Kira Stavi in the lead. Then Kira stopped short. In the doorway of the center, three more of the creatures, standing stiffly and looking at the group with those intense eyes. Ofelia felt the wicked giggle in her throat, and her hand rose to cover her mouth.

'Explain to them,' the tall man said. 'Explain that it's all right for us to go inside.'

Ofelia walked past Kira and the others with Bluecloak. The creatures in the door stepped back, and Ofelia waved the others inside.

'You really shouldn't—' she heard from behind her. The two armed men, she supposed, didn't want their charges to be out of sight and surrounded by alien killers. She didn't want the humans there either, but she had no better idea.

'It's all right,' the tall man called back. 'If they haven't hurt the old woman, they won't hurt us.'

Ofelia pondered all the faults in that assumption as Kira led the way into the left-hand workroom. Why should they hurt an old woman who had never threatened them, once they found out she wouldn't? And why would they not hurt those who did pose a threat? But she was not going to argue. She didn't know how in the first place, and in the second place her head hurt too much.

Bluecloak said something to the other creatures, and one of them walked away quickly toward the kitchen.

'Did you notice,' Kira said to the stocky man. 'They don't walk flat-footed all the time. I'd love to see the bone structure—'

The stocky man nodded, then narrowed his eyes at

Ofelia. 'You're not feeling well, are you, Sera Falfurrias? Perhaps you need to lie down for awhile?'

Nothing she would like better, but not while these people were poking around. Might as well leave a roomful of toddlers to play in the kitchen with no one watching. 'I'm all right,' she said, but she sat in the chair he placed for her. Then the creature came back with a bowl of crushed ice – when had they learned to use the ice-crusher? – and folded a towel around a handful of ice as deftly as any nurse. It put the ice on the bruise; she sucked in air, but it did help after a moment. She put up her hand to hold the ice in place, but there was no need. The creature stood behind her, holding it.

'Well,' said the tall man. She struggled to remember his name. Vasil Likisi. 'It's clear you've made friends with them. How did you teach them to do that?'

'Ahhnt,' Bluecloak said. They all stared at it. It pointed at Ofelia. 'Ahhnt.'

'Aunt?' That was the young woman, Bilong. 'You mean like . . . aunt? Mother's sister?'

Bluecloak took the book that another of the creatures had brought it from the schoolroom, the storybook about the girl who stayed with her aunt. It showed the book to Bilong. 'Ahhnt.'

It fumbled through the pages until it found the picture it wanted, then pointed to Ofelia, and the picture of the girl and her aunt.

'It can't possibly understand,' Kira said impatiently. 'A storybook? Whatever it means by aunt, that's not what we mean by aunt.' She glanced at Ofelia. 'Do you know what it's talking about?'

She did, but how could she explain it to this woman, who was in her way as alien as Bluecloak? This woman so impatient she was already fidgeting, already unwilling to listen to more than a word or two? No. Her head hurt too much. Courtesy demanded some answer, but not a complete one.

'I took care of some children other than mine,' she said. 'I think that's what Bluecloak means.'

'Oh.' The other woman sat back, looking unconvinced.

'How did you tell it that?' asked the younger woman. Her head was pounding. Ofelia shifted, and other bruises stabbed her. 'I – used gestures,' she said. 'And I'm really very tired now.' She closed her eyes.

'Do you suppose she's really hurt?' asked the tall man. When she didn't have to listen to him, his voice still sounded tall and self-important, as if he had a lime in his mouth. He was ready to be annoyed with her for being hurt.

'I hope not,' said the other man. 'She's our best source for understanding this alien culture; she's been living with the indigenes—'

'But she's so—' Ofelia presumed a gesture went with that, and probably a sideways glance to see if she was really asleep or just pretending. 'She hasn't the background,' the tall man said finally. Playing it safe.

'Vasil, you are the most—!' But that was cut off. Ofelia heard the stealthy sound of people rising from chairs and trying to walk off quietly. Let them. She didn't care. She dozed off, and when she woke found that someone had put a row of chairs under her legs, and padded them with a blanket. Her head still hurt, but not so badly.

Bluecloak stood beside her. 'Ghouls,' it said. Her mind wavered. Ghouls? Then she made the transformation: it meant 'fools.' And she didn't have to ask who it meant. It meant the other humans.

Ofelia made no attempt to get up; she didn't want to

move. But she winked at Bluecloak. 'They are fools,' she agreed. And ghouls too, she thought privately.

'Uhoo nnot—' Bluecloak gestured away, meaning those others she was sure. 'Nnot – click-kaw-keerrrr?'

'Not,' she said again, reassuring it. 'They're not my people, and I'm not their click-kaw-keerrrr, not their aunt.'

Bluecloak offered an arm, and she managed to sit up, biting off a groan at the pain in her side and leg. Another of the creatures moved to her other side, and the two of them helped her along the passage. Outside, it was dark, with stars glowing softly in the warm damp wind.

'Where are they?' Ofelia asked. Bluecloak pointed down the lane; she could see a bright glow of light at the shuttle field. Had they gone back to the shuttle? She didn't really care. Bluecloak and the other one helped her to her house, and inside, flicking on the light for her. Bluecloak opened her cooler and clucked at the contents. Ofelia wasn't hungry, and tried to say so, but Bluecloak wasn't deterred. It rootled around until it found some dry flatbread, and offered it to her, sprinkled with salt. It tasted surprisingly good, and her stomach let it stay. Bluecloak poured her a glass of fruit drink, and stood over her while she drank it. She could feel its determination that she would eat. After that, she wanted only her familiar bed. For the first time since Bluecloak arrived in the village, the creatures came with her to the bathroom. She was not embarrassed; they had seen it before, and she was too tired. She glanced in the mirror accidentally and stopped, staring at the purple lump on her head. She looked down at her arm, where the skin over the bruise had torn, leaving a dark crust. Bluecloak's expression, when she looked up at it, was grim. She sensed anger and disapproval, but not of her.

'It's all right,' she said. 'I'm not really hurt.' They offered her support – she was glad to lean on their arms – to the bed, and when she sat down, the other creature bent and lifted her legs gently. Bluecloak moved to the other side of the bed and turned down the cover, then paused, looking at her.

She was so tired . . . but she managed to roll over, into the open bed, and Bluecloak pulled the covers over her as tenderly as any mother.

They were frightening in a way they had never been frightening before – she had no idea what they thought had happened, or what it meant, or what would happen tomorrow. She was too tired to say anything; Bluecloak turned the lights out, and she waited to hear the front door open and close, but fell asleep first.

SEVENTEEN

When Ofelia woke in the pearly light of early morning, she heard soft voices from the next room. She stretched, and then winced as the bruises from yesterday's blow and fall intruded on her. She hurt all over, in more places than she remembered being hurt yesterday. And who was in her front room?

She didn't want to get up. She wanted to lie there until she died, or her body quit hurting, whichever came first. She moved her left arm cautiously up to feel the lump on her head. It felt as large as it had been, if not larger. She let her arm fall back, and imagined the commotion if the humans returned and found her dead. Would they realize they had done it, or would they blame the creatures?

She needed to use the toilet, too. It was one thing to lie here, sullenly determined to die from a few bruises, and another to lie here miserable because her bladder ached with fullness. Besides, if they blamed Bluecloak, what would happen to Gurgle-click-cough's babies?

Even with that thought, when she first tried to sit up, it hurt so much she caught her breath hard and felt tears stinging her eyes. She scolded herself; the old voice was happy to provide the terms she had not used for several years. Coward. Weakling. Sissy. Just a few bruises and you act like a baby.

She tried to make no noise, but she felt shaky and weak from the pain by the time she had pulled herself to her feet. Her arm had bled again in the night, sticking to the sheet, and the bright pain when she pulled it free was too much. A sob came loose in her throat.

The door to her room opened. Bluecloak, throat-sac expanded. It hissed when it saw her, and came to her quickly, offering an arm. Ofelia took it, hating her weakness. It put its finger on the slow ooze of blood, sniffed it, and drummed – she could not tell with what part of its body, but the sound filled the room.

'I'm all right,' Ofelia said, wishing her voice didn't tremble. 'I'll be better after a hot shower.' Bluecloak helped her into the bathroom. She felt better after she'd used the toilet, and the hot shower eased some of the aches, though she knew she would stiffen later. She came out of the hot water to find that Bluecloak had fetched extra towels. It waited, towels in hand, to help her dry off. The mirror had fogged with the steam; she could not see herself, and she was glad. What she had to see, as she dried herself, was ugly enough, dark bruises all along her right side where she had fallen.

It was hard to find something to wear. The garments she had made for this season, that she would have worn, left the bruises exposed and obvious. The old voice told her that was shameful, that it would embarrass her guests, that she must appear to them as if yesterday's blow had done no harm. After all, her old skin tore so easily that any minor injury could make it bleed. It wasn't their fault; they couldn't be expected to realize how fragile she was.

The new voice said nothing; she wondered where it

had gone. She hunted through her closet for a shirt with long sleeves, something that would cover her arms and her torso completely. All the long-sleeved shirts were hot, meant for the rare cool spells in the rainy season. She put one on anyway, wincing at the rasp of the coarser cloth against the tender bruises. She put on the longest pants she had; they came just below her knees.

She felt hot, and breathless, but safer. She looked down at her bare feet. The others had all worn boots. They had not actually stepped on her, but her bare toes now seemed vulnerable, as her bare skin was vulnerable, so that even a gaze could menace it. She had no shoes; she had put her last pair in the recycler, she reminded herself. For a moment, she felt happy; she remembered the little dance of celebration she'd done as she'd put them in, along with the ugly dress Barto and Rosara had wanted her to wear more often.

Bluecloak churred softly. Ofelia tried to smile at it. 'I'm much better,' she said. 'Thank you for your help.' Bluecloak knew 'thank you' – she had used all the ritual courtesies with it, and the creatures had done their best to reciprocate.

Ofelia looked at her bed with distaste. She did not leave beds unmade, or sheets with bloodstains on them, but she did not think she could pull the sheets free this morning. Bluecloak, following her glance, pointed to the bloodstains then touched her arm. 'Uhoo plud?'

'Yes, it's my blood. But not bad. Just a little.' She hoped Bluecloak would understand that.

Bluecloak said something in their language, and another creature came in. Bluecloak pointed to the bed; the creature hissed, its throat-sac expanding for a moment. Then it grabbed the sheets and pulled them off into a heap on the floor. Bluecloak spoke again, and it picked up the heap.

'Where are you—?' Ofelia began. 'Ahshhh it,' Bluecloak said. Then, with great satisfaction, all the consonants emphasized, 'Dddirrrttih! Ig iss ddirrttih, ahshhh it!'

Ofelia recovered from astonishment in time to say 'Cold water!' to the creature departing with her sheets. 'Wash blood in cold water.'

Bluecloak's eyes widened. 'Kuh?' It pointed to itself. 'Mih plud, mih ahshhh in kuh . . . ah . . . ssoo.'

'You also wash off blood in cold water?' Ofelia had not realized they washed their clothes at all, though they didn't stink like people who failed to wash.

'Ahshhh in hah, plud tick.' Wash in hot, blood sticks, Ofelia translated. 'Llihff pron.' Ofelia worried at that for a long moment. She had not heard even Bluecloak make an f sound before, and she didn't think this was 'lif' or 'leaf.' Pron was probably bron . . . brown. Leave brown. Yes.

'Ours too,' she said. She felt hungry now, and in the kitchen found that someone – Bluecloak? – had tried to make flatbread dough and made a mess instead. Bluecloak, when she looked at it, fluttered its eyelids.

'Ssorrrih,' it said.

'Thank you,' Ofelia said. 'It was a kind thought, anyway.' It had also tried to clean up the mess, but it had left streaks of flour, pellets of something that was supposed to be dough, and wasn't. Probably it had watched her making dough and thought it was easy. She scraped the residual mess off, then mixed the dough herself, her hands glad to take up familiar tasks. Bluecloak turned on the stove for her, and handed her the griddle just as she reached for it. Then it closed the containers she had left open, and put them away. She had shared kitchens with women less helpful. As she was laying the flatbread on the griddle, the kitchen door opened, and another creature – not the one who had taken the sheets – brought in two tomatoes and a handful of green beans, handling them carefully.

'Thank you,' Ofelia said again, wondering what was going on. The creatures had been friendly enough before, but they had not gone out of their way to help her. She sliced the tomato, found that Bluecloak had fetched an onion from her bin, and chopped that. Onion fumes made her eyes water – they always had – but she could no more cook without onions than onions could grow without water. Again, Bluecloak anticipated what she would want next and handed her a stalk of parsley, one of cilantro, one of rosemary. She chopped the fresh herbs, mixed them with the tomato and onion, and folded the first round of flatbread around them.

She felt better when she'd eaten. The side of her head was still sore, and she was still stiff, but she didn't feel sick. As if they could sense that, Bluecloak and the other creature left her house while she cleaned the dishes, brushed her teeth, and wrapped a soft cloth around the oozing tear on her arm.

The sun was well up when the humans returned. Only two of them this time, the stocky man – Ori something – and the older woman, Kira. Ofelia had gone back to work in her garden, both because it soothed her and because she had missed several days. One of the creatures was with her, eating the slimerods she found; another had insisted on pushing a broom in her house. The hot sun eased her bruises, though sweat stung in the scrapes . . . and then the creature churred, and she looked up.

'Tuh-hoo,' it said. It held up two fingers in case she didn't understand. What she didn't understand was when this one had learned so much human speech.

'Did Bluecloak teach you that?' she asked. It tipped its head to one side and said 'Uhoo.'

Ofelia didn't believe that; she hadn't spent much time with any of them trying to teach them her words, not since the beginning. But if it wanted to give her credit, that was polite.

'Good morning,' the stocky man said, when he came close enough. 'How are you today?'

'Fine,' Ofelia said. She had a basket nearly full of tomatoes; they were ripening far faster than she could eat them. 'Would you like some tomatoes? They're not very big yet—'

'They're beautiful,' the man said. 'We don't get fresh foods like this on the ship, you know.'

She didn't know; she'd spent her ship time in cryo. But he might not know that.

'Your arm—' the woman said. Ofelia glanced down; the sleeve didn't quite cover the bruise and scab.

'It's nothing,' she said, looking away. She didn't want to talk about it.

'That's—' the woman began; Ofelia saw the man hush her with a gesture. So much for that one's arrogance; she still had to be quiet when a man told her to hush. Ofelia found another slimerod and clicked to get the creature's attention. It came eagerly, and gulped the slimerod down. Ofelia glanced at the humans. They were wide-eyed. The man recovered first.

'You . . . get along well with them,' he said.

Ofelia shrugged, then wished she hadn't. Her shoulder was still sore, and the man might think a shrug was rude.

'They're good neighbors,' she said. 'They don't bother me.'

'You can talk to them?'

'It's not so much talk,' Ofelia said. 'We understand things.' She gestured with one hand. 'We use our hands a lot.'

'Can you tell us which is the leader?' the man asked. 'Is it the one you call Bluecloak?'

Ofelia wondered if Bluecloak thought it was the leader, in the way this man clearly meant. 'Bluecloak is . . . the one good at learning new things,' she said finally. 'Learning words, for instance. I understand Bluecloak best.'

'But is Bluecloak the one in charge?' the woman asked.

Ofelia shook her head, another mistake. For an instant, the world whirled around her, then steadied again. 'Only on some things,' she said, when she could speak again. She knew she couldn't really explain which things; she was only feeling her way into that understanding herself.

'It's a small group,' the man murmured to his companion. 'It may be government by consensus; they may just hash it out.'

'Surely not everything,' the woman said. 'After all, they attacked the colony landing; that had to have organization, leadership. And those coastal cities . . .'

'Cities?' Ofelia said. 'They have cities?' She felt betrayed; Bluecloak had said nothing about cities, any of the times he'd seen the pictures of cities in her books.

'We saw them from the shuttle flights,' the woman said. 'Some of them live along the northern coast of this continent, in what look like stone and wood-built cities. They have boats—'

Ofelia remembered the boats she had seen. But she could not imagine her creatures, the ones she knew, living in cities. Something about their attitude toward this village suggested that they had no settled home. Except the nest-mass.

'We won't keep you,' the man said, as she was wondering whether or not to mention the nestmass. 'A couple of your lovely tomatoes, and we'll be on our way. We'll be surveying the area today, just wandering around looking at things. We won't touch anything of yours,' he added, as if his being here weren't intrusion enough.

Ofelia held the basket over the fence and they each picked out a tomato.

'If it's convenient,' the man said, 'I'd like to interview you later. After all, you were the first contact, even if you weren't trained for it.' He chuckled, in a way that he probably intended to sound good-natured. It did sound good-natured; Ofelia could not have said why it made her so angry. She wanted to hit him, and that frightened her. She had never been one to hit people.

'I am always here,' she said, not quite rudely. He smiled, and nodded at her, and turned away, already biting into the tomato. Ofelia looked down the lane; she saw nothing of the other humans. Maybe now she could go across and look at Gurgle-click-cough's babies.

Her escort of creatures followed her, and exchanged greetings with the door guards; Ofelia noticed that today the door guards had their knives out. In the bedroom, Bluecloak lounged on the old bedstead, singing with eyes half-closed. He rose when Ofelia came in, and reached out to her hands. He lifted them gently, and touched his tongue to her palms.

'Click-kaw-keerrr.' It was greeting and commentary both; Ofelia felt cheered. She turned to the closet. Gurgle-click-cough looked out, alert and calm; Ofelia wondered how she was reading the expression so well. Gurgle-click-

cough held out a hand, and Ofelia came nearer. The babies
were piled in an untidy heap in the middle of the nest,
between their mother's legs. Ofelia could not tell which
striped tail belonged to which set of spindly legs . . . but
she would have sworn they'd grown noticeably since the
day before.

The nest smelled better too. Fresh herbs packed the
inner surface. Ofelia wondered if the Terran-origin herbs
would hurt the babies. One of them opened its eyes, and
peeped, a sharp imperative. Gurgle-click-cough leaned
closer; the tiny mouth opened, and its mother spit into
it. Ofelia almost gagged, but choked it down. Spit? Vomit?
She didn't want to know, really, and it was none of her
business. The baby swallowed again and again, blinking
its eyes. Then it hissed contentedly, and curled up again.
Gurgle-click-cough picked it up, and handed it to Ofelia.
Ofelia cradled it, no longer flinching when it licked her
wrist with its catlike tongue.

Bluecloak said something; Ofelia turned, and he
gestured her over. She sat on the bedstead beside him,
the baby in her lap. It seemed content, and Gurgle-click-
cough was feeding one of the others now. She looked at
it closely, in more light than she'd had yesterday. The bold
stripes on back and tail were dark brown on cream. Its
head was large for its size, but nowhere near as large as
a human baby's. Bluecloak hummed; the baby cocked its
little head at the sound. When the hum became rhythmic,
the baby's left foot twitched in rhythm.

Left foot drumming meant agreement . . . the baby was
learning to agree, or . . . or what? 'Sssinng,' Bluecloak said.
'Click-kaw-keerrr sssinng.'

She didn't know what to sing to an alien's child with
stripes and a tail; the only songs she knew were the cradle

songs she had sung her own children. She started, self-conscious at first until the baby's intent stare took all her concentration.

'Baby, baby, go to sleep . . .' It didn't; it crouched in her lap watching her face, its gaze flicking from eyes to mouth to eyes again. 'Little sweetling, never weep . . .' She had no sense that these babies wept; it seemed almost tingling with eagerness for something . . . for life itself?

She sang herself hoarse, and stopped with a crick in her back and the little creature still watching her, showing no sign of boredom or tiredness. She levered herself up, and carried it back to the nest stiffly. She couldn't possibly do that with all of them . . . but Gurgle-click-cough was asleep herself, and the one Ofelia carried squirmed into the central pile without waking any of the others and closed its eyes.

'Click-kaw-keerrr,' Bluecloak said, and it came outside with her.

Down the lane, she saw the young woman talking to one of the creatures. Ofelia's stomach knotted; she looked at Bluecloak, but it seemed not to care. The creature stood awkwardly, like a halfwit, Ofelia thought, which it was not. The tall man, the one in charge, stood in the lane outside the center, looking west; Ofelia could see nothing beyond him but the lane itself dwindling into grass. He turned, caught sight of her, and frowned.

'I was looking for you,' he said, as if she had missed an appointment. Ofelia did not want to be ungracious, but there was nothing to say to that. They had not looked where she was; they had not called loudly enough to get her attention. That was not her fault. She smiled, as tension and resentment knotted her belly. 'You need to understand how we'll go about our mission,' he said, after a moment. 'We will study and make official contact with these . . . indigenes. I'm sure you think you have already made contact, but after all you have had no training in this sort of thing. You were a . . . a what? . . . housewife?'

Ofelia did not correct him. Whatever she had been, on the work rolls of the company, that was long ago, and it made no difference. Whatever training she had had would mean nothing to such a one.

'It's not your responsibility, is what I'm trying to say,' he went on, his face shining in the sun. 'You did very well, I'm sure, to have gotten along peacefully with them, but now we're here, and we'll take it off your hands.' He took a deep breath, as if to say more, then let it out slowly. 'You do understand, don't you?'

She didn't understand all, but she understood enough. She didn't matter, she didn't count, she was nothing. Exactly right, the old voice said to her. This is how it is; this is how it has always been. Accept it, and they will accept you as what you are. Old woman. Nothing.

'And we'll have to figure out something . . .' he said vaguely, not looking at her. 'About the machines . . .'

Fear chilled her. She needed the machines. 'What about the machines?' she asked, though she was afraid she knew.

He made an impatient gesture. 'Advanced technology. They shouldn't have it. They shouldn't even have seen it. Part of our mission was to shut it all down. I suppose we can find you a place somewhere – it's Sims' fault; they'll have to pay some kind of fine, and that should be enough for a place in some residence . . .'

'You mean . . . leave?' Her vision darkened; she forced herself to breathe. She would not faint in front of this person.

'Well, you can't stay here,' he said, as if that were

obvious. 'Even if we have a permanent mission . . . there's no post for someone like – someone your age, you see. And the need to secure the technology, prevent cultural contamination . . . it will be difficult, even for trained personnel. You can move aboard the shuttle with us; then we can shut down the powerplant—'

'Not now,' Ofelia said, hating the quaver in her voice that left her desire as vulnerable to his will as her naked skin had been to his eyes.

'Oh, not today,' the man said, as if it didn't matter. 'I suppose they've been here for some time; it's not as if we could prevent what they've already seen. But they can't have understood much of it, and the longer we let them have access, the more chance they'll learn too much. When the preliminary work's done . . . then you should prepare to leave.' He smiled, the wide smile of someone whose decisions cannot be changed. 'Don't worry . . . uh . . . Sera Falfurry . . . we'll take care of you. You won't be alone any more.'

He went into the center, his body swinging, satisfied with the power he'd shown. Ofelia could not have moved if someone had poked her; she wished she could be blown away in a gust of wind. She was not so lucky; no wind stirred the leaves. Bluecloak chirped, and she looked at it. It nodded at the departed human.

'Kuss-cough-click,' it said.

'Stuck-up bossy lout,' Ofelia said; she had no doubt they meant the same thing.

In her own house, alone because Bluecloak called the others out and set them as guards at her door, she raged silently, yanking clean sheets onto the bed, slamming pillows down. She would not leave. She had not left before, and she would not leave now. They could not make her.

They can, said the old voice. They will. They know you evaded once; you can't do that again.

It isn't fair, she wailed silently. I worked so hard; I did so much; it's their fault.

It doesn't matter, said the old voice. You are nothing to them; they have the power, and they will take you away. The old voice reminded her how much her protests sounded like those Rosara and others had made, protests she had been contemptuous of, back when she thought she could escape. She raged at that, too.

Finally, exhausted, she lay down and napped, waking to quiet afternoon. She heard voices outside, human voices; when she peeked out the front windows, the two women were walking along side by side, so much like her former neighbors that she almost called out to them.

They were not neighbors. They were enemies who would take her away. They were enemies who would destroy everything she had worked for, the life she had made for herself, the new friends she had found.

The next morning, the shorter man, Ori, appeared at her garden fence to interview her. He was willing to ask his questions and listen while she worked; he even asked intelligent questions about the varieties of beans and tomatoes and corn she chose to grow. Despite herself, she found it easy to tell him which strains had been supplied by the Company, and which the colonists had developed on their own.

'Then you had geneticists among you?' he asked. If he had had ears, they would have been pricked up, alert.

'Not . . . like in colleges,' Ofelia said. How to explain? 'They taught us all what they thought we could use,' she said finally. 'Practical things. How to choose the best progeny for seeds. How to repair the pumps and power plant and waste recycler. But they wouldn't tell us why, on most things.'

'Did that bother you?' he asked, this time without much interest. Ofelia was surprised at her own ability to tell that; she didn't know how she knew.

'Not really,' she said. 'We had much to learn, and little time.' It had not seemed like little time, all those nights in class or studying, when the children were small and she could have been mending or cleaning or simply resting. But in terms of absolute hours, they had had too much practical material to fit in to allow of much theoretical digression.

Ori leaned back, satisfied with her answer; she did not explain further.

'Now – the first time you saw the creatures, what did you do? What did you think? Did you recognize them right away?'

The first time . . . she had to start with the sea-storm, with her attempt to ready the village. That bored him, though he didn't say so; his eyes drifted away, seeing something else entirely, something beyond her head. When Bilong crossed her own view, a minute or two later, she knew what it had been.

She told of that first storm-bound afternoon and night, the first few days. At first he let her talk on without interruption, only urging her to continue when she stopped. But then he wanted to ask questions. How had she first noticed that they were intelligent? How did she know who was in charge? What had she learned of their social structure? How territorial were they?

'I don't know,' she kept saying. 'They don't do it like that—' Whatever it had been, from dividing up food to making decisions to marking rank. The more he asked, the more she felt she knew nothing about the creatures at all. It had never occurred to her to wonder if both sexes had extensible throat-sacs; she tried not to think about their sexes at all. When she said that, shyly, he gave her the smile of an adult to a backward child.

'It's all right,' he said. 'Anthropologists look at these things differently.' The right way, he meant. That he was too polite to say it didn't really take the sting out of it. He asked more, and she told what she knew . . . except about the babies, about being Click-kaw-keerrr. She was afraid someone would harm the babies; she hated herself for the knowledge that humans would certainly kill those babies if they thought it prudent. This man himself, with his gentle voice, she might have trusted, except that his eyes slid too often to the young woman . . . and his rival was the tall man, the cold-eyed team leader that Ofelia did not trust at all.

After that one long interview, Ori did not come back. She saw him following the creatures around, sitting where he could watch them with a sketchpad on his knee. He had told her that the act of drawing sometimes taught him more than the best video clips. He had showed her a few of his first sketches, and she had admired the graceful lines, drawn surely and quickly, that did seem to capture the essence of the creatures' forms and movements. She would like to have seen his sketches of the babies, the alert way they carried their snouted heads on those flexible necks, the brisk swipes of their striped tails.

The team leader ignored her completely, barely nodding as he strode up and down the streets, in and out of most buildings. He talked endlessly into a recorder that hung from his belt. He seemed to be making an inventory of

every item of human origin in the village, even to the
number of tomato plants. He avoided the one where
Gurgle-click-cough nested; Ori had insisted that humans
not intrude when the creatures made it clear they were
unwelcome.

The tall woman took short trips into the forest,
collecting samples of plant life from the intermediate zone
as well as areas of pure native growth. She set out fishing
lines in the river, put out traps for small animals. The
creatures watched her, with expressions that Ofelia interpreted as a mixture of avid curiosity and mild disgust.
Ofelia did not know how to ask what she herself wanted
to know: did they mind another hunter in their territory,
and one that did not even eat the catch?

The young woman, Bilong, seemed to spend most of
her time wandering from man to man; she had a recorder,
and she had placed pickups in the center – Ofelia saw
that, and assumed she had put them other places as well
– to gather language samples. What Ofelia knew, and
Bilong did not, was that the creatures knew exactly where
the pickups were, and amused themselves by standing
under them reciting . . . reciting what Ofelia suspected
were merely lists, possibly even nonsense words. Certainly
their speech then had none of the rhythm and feel that it
had most of the time.

Ofelia went back to her old life, as much as she could,
slipping across to play with the babies – the rapidly
growing and very active babies – when the humans were
not in evidence. Quite often they were not in evidence.
She suspected the creatures of having something to do
with that, of intervening to be sure that the Click-kaw-
keerrr had ample time with the babies.

The babies changed faster than human babies, in those

first days. In this they were more like young calves or
lambs, quickly alert and active. Ofelia had always assumed
that the slow early development of human babies went
with their higher intelligence – that anything which was
born able to run around was also born limited, close to
its adult potential of wit. She remembered parenting
classes, early-childhood-development classes, in which she
was taught precisely this. Children took a long time to
grow, because they had a long way to go; the human brain
had to organize itself, teach itself how to learn. Other baby
animals could be born with more behaviors wired in,
because they didn't have to be able to learn much later.

These babies . . . already their high squeaks sounded
speechlike. Already their busy four-fingered hands manip-
ulated the stalks of grass and sprigs of herb in their nest.
Handed empty gourds by an adult, they put in pebbles,
and poured them out. They squabbled with each other,
shoving and nipping, using their tails to hold one another
down . . . but these squabbles quickly shifted into coop-
erative play, if someone offered a toy. At ten days, twenty
days of age, they were more like children of three years.

Ofelia could not merely observe; she found herself being
used as a plaything, a living obstacle course. The other
creatures handed her the items they thought the babies
should have: gourds, beads, pebbles, bits of string. She
was the one who hissed disapproval when one of them
wound string around its throat. It froze, eyes wide. Ofelia
mimed strangulation, producing a guttural squawk. The
baby blinked; the others, sitting up on legs and tail,
squeaked softly. To her surprise, none of them tried that
again.

If they were like human toddlers, then . . . she wondered
if they could learn letters and numbers. If the other

humans hadn't been there, she would have taken them to the center, would have shown them the books and the teaching computers. She couldn't do that now. Her conscience nagged her; she shouldn't *want* to do that. She should protect human technology from them, and them from human technology.

Water rushed into the sink, startling her out of that reverie. One of them stood on the long faucet of the deep sink, its talons hooked around the cold-water tap, pulling; the other two, braced against the wall, had pushed at the same tap with their feet. Now, as she watched, they reversed their force: the ones who had been pushing hooked their talons over and tried to pull. The one on the faucet tried to push . . . and lost its footing, to splash into the sink. Ofelia heaved herself up, and put her arm into the water. The talons dug in, as the baby climbed her arm, squeaking furiously.

So much for protection, either way. They would have to learn how to use the technology safely; there was no way to keep them from using it.

Although the daily sessions with the babies delighted her, Ofelia felt a steady weight of apprehension. Someday – some one of these hardly numbered days – the team leader would think they had done enough, seen enough, and would order Ofelia to the shuttle. She would have to leave, or die. She had not thought of any way to escape this time, not with her inability to eat the local food, not with the determination of these people to find her and bring her back. She would have to leave, and leave her creatures – her responsibility, the babies – to these others, whom she did not trust.

EIGHTEEN

After days of scant contact with the other humans – polite but distant greetings that made it clear they didn't have time to waste with an ignorant old woman – Ofelia noticed that she had become real to them again. She wasn't sure she liked it. She suspected it meant that they were finishing up their contact work, as they called it, and getting ready to 'make a final determination' (the team leader's phrase) about her, and the colony, and the creatures.

The change began with slightly warmer greetings when they saw her, politely asking how she was, how her garden prospered. The tall woman commented on a necklace Ofelia had made. The stocky man told her he had discovered that Bluecloak was a minstrel or entertainer, a singer. The younger woman began hanging around Ofelia without saying much, just like a pesky child. Ofelia noticed that she had pilfered a necklace to wear, and that she left too many of her shirt buttons undone. After a few days of hovering that nearly drove Ofelia to rudeness, she actually began a conversation. She asked how Ofelia had taught the creatures to speak.

Ofelia explained, as well as she could. She had tried to teach them as she had taught babies – human babies, she repeated, though Bilong didn't know about the others.

'That's not how you teach a language,' the woman said. 'I know you probably thought you taught your children to talk, but human children don't have to be taught – they just learn.' Bilong was trying to be polite. Ofelia could tell that, just as she could tell that the woman was treating her with exaggerated patience, as if she were a naughty child. She herself tried not to resent the rudeness which was not intended.

'Some do,' Ofelia conceded. Most, probably. But had any mother ever been able to resist teaching?

'All of them,' Bilong said, emphasizing it, '—all human children learn to talk on their own, because they're designed to speak human language.'

Ofelia wished she could remember how to do what she had done for so many years, remove herself from the talk and let it pass by, but it was impossible to put that chicken back in the egg. 'Sara's child,' she heard herself saying, even as the old, cautious voice implored her to keep quiet. 'It couldn't talk, no matter what.'

'I meant *normal* children,' the woman said, less patiently. 'But these are aliens, Ofelia – I can call you Ofelia, can't I?'

A girl from this neighborhood has no business getting a swelled head, her father had said. Pride goes before damnation, someone had said. The tall stalk asks for the knife. You are nothing.

'Sera Ofelia,' she said, with the least emphasis.

'Oh – Sarah? I'm sorry; I thought you were called Ofelia.' The woman seemed confused, but willing. Her accent, Ofelia realized, meant that she could not hear the difference between the name Sara and the title Sera. Nor had she paid attention when the stocky man addressed

her correctly as Sera Falfurrias. Ofelia did not enlighten
her. She waited, hoping her face would remember the
bland expressions that had kept her out of trouble before.

'Sarah,' the linguist said. 'Let me explain about alien
languages.' Ofelia waited in silence, but her mind crackled
with comments. 'They aren't like human languages,' the
linguist went on. Oh really? Did she think Ofelia hadn't
noticed? 'Since their biological nature is different, the very
structure of their brains – if we can call them brains, which
is doubtful – determines a different structure of language.'

Ofelia repressed a snort with difficulty. Whatever the
brain had to do with language, some of the messages would
have to be the same. I'm hungry, feed me. I'm hurt,
comfort me. Come here. Go away. OUCH. Do it again.
What is that and how does it work?

'They may not intend any of the same meanings,' the
linguist said, completing the picture of an idiot.

Prudence lost out; she had been too long free to speak
her mind, if only to herself. 'They have to say some of the
same things,' she said. 'If they're hungry. If they hurt.'

The younger woman's eyebrows went up. 'Well . . .
there are a few nearly universal messages. But those are
least interesting; even a nonlanguage species may have
vocalizations associated with hunger or pain. Besides, in
the languages we know, these aren't expressed the same
way. The goetiae, for instance, actually say "my sap dries"
when they mean "I'm hungry," and in one dialect of your
language—' The linguist said 'your language' as if it were
particularly silly. '—the South Naryan, I think it is, no
one ever says "I hurt" – they always use the form "it pains
me."'

Ofelia rubbed her foot a little backwards and forwards
on the ground, reminding herself of that reality. She had

never heard of the goetiae – were they aliens? – but she
had had an aunt who was South Naryan, and she knew
perfectly well that her aunt said 'I hurt myself' when she
fell over something. Did this linguist say 'I hurt' when she
had a backache? Or did she say, more sensibly, 'My back
hurts'? She thought of a question she could ask.

'How many alien languages do you know?'

The woman flushed. 'Well . . . actually . . . not any. Not
truly alien, that is. No one's ever found one. This will be
the first.' As if Ofelia had said what she was thinking, the
linguist hurried on. 'Of course, we practiced with computer
generated languages. The neural modelers created alien
networks, and we practiced with the languages they generated.'

Ofelia kept her face blank. She understood what that
meant: they had created machines that talked machine
languages, and from this they thought they had learned
how to understand alien languages. Stupid. Machines
would not think like aliens, but like machines. The
creatures were not machines – very far from it.

But the linguist was leaning closer, confiding now, as
if Ofelia were a favorite aunt or grandmother.

She did not want to be Bilong's mother, or her grandmother. She had done with these roles, with being a good
child, a good wife, a good mother. She had put seventy-
odd years into it; she had worked hard at it; now she
wanted to be that Ofelia who painted and carved and sang
in an old cracked voice with strange creatures and their
stranger music. The role the creatures had given her was
more than enough.

'It's all this tension,' the linguist was saying. 'I probably shouldn't be telling you this—' Then don't, Ofelia
thought. Don't tell me. I don't want to hear it. '—but

you're wise, even if you don't have an education.' The arrogance in that almost yanked a reply from her, but she managed to squeeze it back. Wise even if she had no education? What did wisdom have to do with education? Besides, she had an education; she had spent hours studying, nights and early mornings studying, long before this child was born. This . . . this chit of a girl who hadn't known how to repair the pumps, who had blithely walked between a cow and her calf.

'The thing is,' the girl went on, in happy unawareness of Ofelia's thoughts, 'they don't like each other and never have. So they're using me as an excuse. One says I'm flirting, and the other one says I'm not flirting, and—'

'Are you flirting?' Ofelia asked. She thought so; why else wear that perfume? Why else swing her ripe young body back and forth like fruit on a vine, every motion declaring her readiness to be picked and eaten?

'Of course not.' A flounce, an outraged glance. Just like Linda, who had always denied with her mouth while proclaiming with her hips. But this was not Linda. 'Well . . . maybe. But not *seriously*, you know. It's not like your culture, you know.' Again that gentle condescension. 'We don't have the same rules—' As if human biology would shift aside for her convenience, as if men were not animals born to respond to smells and motions. 'I do rather like one of them, and there's no reason he shouldn't know it. But that's not really flirting.'

'Do you have sex with him?' Ofelia asked. The girl flushed and scowled.

'It's none of your—' She stopped abruptly and her face changed, as if someone had wiped a thumb across clay. 'Oh, hi Kira. How's the tech survey going?'

Ofelia looked up at the other woman. Older, warier,

than the young one, but still young to Ofelia. She was angry about something; Ofelia suspected it was the girl's antics.

'There's a staff meeting in twenty minutes, Bilong, and you're supposed to have the preliminary analysis ready—'

'I can't – it's too soon – all I can do is discuss the raw data—'

'Then do that.' Kira stood there, as threatening as a sea-storm wall cloud until the younger woman got up and walked away, her shoulders stiff.

'You are angry?' Ofelia said. She leaned back against the sun-warmed wall and hoped she looked old and stupid.

'She is not supposed to waste her time talking to you,' Kira said. 'She has work to do.' Ofelia waited. She had seen just this maneuver in older children who chased young ones away. What they really wanted was their own chance at the mother or grandmother.

Kira sighed, the kind of dramatic sigh that meant she too was going to confide. Ofelia let her eyelids sag almost shut. Maybe she would change her mind if Ofelia looked stupid enough.

'You're not a chatterbox,' Kira said. Mistake. This woman had wanted a safe confidant, and for that purpose stupid and quiet would do well enough. Ofelia opened her eyes but it was too late to pretend alert garrulity. Kira's mouth quirked. 'And I don't think you're half so dim as you pretend, either. A stupid woman couldn't have survived alone so long.' Good observation, if unflattering. Just once, Ofelia would have liked people to see her as she was, not as their ideas painted her.

She looked at Kira, the short hair so carefully shaped that it must be a style of some sort, the smooth young-woman skin just showing the first lines of age. Who was this person, really? 'I don't think I'm stupid,' she said.

Kira's eyes widened, then narrowed

'No. I can see that. What I can't see is why you chose to stay behind.'

'No,' Ofelia said, mimicking Kira's intonation. 'I can see you don't. But you are too young.'

'You didn't want to die aboard the ship, in suspension?'

Ofelia shrugged, annoyed. They always came back to death, these young ones; they were obsessed with it. She tried again to explain. 'It was not about death. It was about life. If I stayed, I would be alone—'

'But no one can survive isolation,' Kira said, interrupting Ofelia as she had done before, as they had all done. 'You must have been terribly lonely. It's lucky for you that the indigenes showed up when they did.'

It would do no good to argue that she had not been lonely. She had tried that, and they had looked at her with such pity, and such certainty.

'Perhaps I am crazy,' Ofelia said.

'Your psych profile didn't show anything before,' Kira said. So they had snooped into her personnel file, something she had never done herself. Again the slow anger burned. What right had they? They were not her people: not family, not friends, not fellow colonists, not even someone she had gone to for help. 'It's not . . . normal,' Kira said. 'Wanting to be the only human on the whole world – that's not normal.'

'So I am not normal,' Ofelia said. Silence would not work with this one; she knew that already.

'But why?'

Ofelia shrugged. 'You did not like my answers before; you told me I didn't understand. Should I tell you the truth I know, or try to guess the untruth you want?'

Kira's eyes widened. Surprise, the old lady has teeth. 'You don't have to be so – so vehement. I only wondered.' She sounded offended. Fine. Let her be offended. 'I wanted to be alone. I had not been alone for years. It didn't bother me to be alone as a child, and it didn't bother me this time either.'

Kira gave her perfect haircut a little shake, warding off that understanding. 'Was it because your husband and children had died here? And you felt close to them?'

Ofelia sighed, and pushed herself away from the wall, standing slowly. These people felt almost as alien as the creatures, and they had less interest in understanding her. 'If you don't listen, you can't hear,' she said, tugging her ear for emphasis. They would make up their own minds anyway, and nothing she said would change that.

She walked away, around the far end of her house, and out into the meadow. Kira followed her a few steps, bleating something incomprehensible. Then she fell behind. Ofelia did not turn to look, but she could feel Kira's stare on her shoulderblades.

Out among the sheep, the blessedly silent sheep, who ignored her at this time of day, Ofelia hid in plain sight from the other humans. She used the basket she had brought to gather sheep droppings. She spread them along the outer margins of the meadow, supporting the terraforming grasses with their mix of bacteria and fungi, maintaining the meadow's boundaries.

The newcomers hated the droppings, hated anything that smelled alive: 'stank of organics,' is how they put it. They wanted nothing to do with her while she was doing work they considered dirty. After that first rapture over fresh tomatoes, they had recoiled from the discovery that she did not sterilize the sheep and cow manure, the kitchen garbage, that went into the compost trench and then into the soil. They accepted no more tomatoes, and refused the cooling fruit drink – although they would pick fruit themselves, and then scrub it in the kitchen sink in the center.

She was tired of the newcomers' silliness about dirt, tired of their busyness, tired of the way they interrupted her without apology, talked as long as they wanted to, and then walked off, leaving her as casually as they would leave a building. She was behind in her garden work; she could not enjoy sewing or crocheting or making jewelry when at any moment someone might come interrupt her, with that expression which meant they thought she was especially silly to be making things now, when she would have to leave. They seemed to go out of their way to make her feel unimportant.

The contrast between their behavior and that of the creatures could not be ignored. The old voice, smug in its certainty, told her that was to be expected. She could mean nothing to the humans; they knew how to rate humans, and she came at the bottom. The creatures could not know. They might like her because she had been their first human; they might value her for the novelty. Whatever the reason for their respect, they could not value her for anything important; they didn't know what was important.

In the sun's heat, the droppings had dried quickly; Ofelia did not mind picking them up, although the stooping bothered her. Her head hurt now only when she bent over, as if all the blood rushed into that swollen knob and pulsed there. Maybe it did. The shirt she wore pulled across the shoulders. The old voice told her how old she was, how weak, how useless. The new voice said nothing, but lived like a cold knot in her heart. She tried to ignore the old voice, and kept on working. Maybe if she stayed away from the other humans, the new voice would speak to her again. She missed it.

A shadow, a blur of motion: one of the creatures. She looked up, attempted the chest grunt of greeting, and got one in return. This creature wore one of her necklaces draped over its own accouterments. When it had her attention, it tapped the basket and gurgled its question. This one rarely attempted human speech.

'Sheep droppings,' Ofelia said, as if the words had been clear. 'For the grass. It feeds the grass.'

The creature moved slowly to one of the sheep, which lifted its head to stare. Even more slowly, the creature leaned down, yanked loose a tuft of grass, and offered it to the sheep. The sheep accepted it docilely and its narrow jaw worked back and forth. The creature touched the sheep's throat, then lightly ran its hand down the body to the rump. Ofelia could follow that: food goes in here, and goes through . . . When the creature tried to lift the sheep's tail, the sheep yanked away and moved off briskly. The creature gaped its mouth at Ofelia – laughter? annoyance? – and then pointed at the sheep's rump, then droppings on the ground.

'Yes,' said Ofelia, nodding vigorously.

The creature turned to her, presenting its own rump, and lifted the decorative kilt to point to an unmistakable orifice. Ofelia looked away. She didn't really want to see what a creature hole looked like, but she had already registered that it had the predictable puckered appearance.

'Yes,' she said. 'It comes out a hole in the back.' They

must know that, from their observations of her; she suspected them of watching at times when she had been unaware of it. She hoped they could get off this topic quickly, but the creatures had a way of sticking to something as long as it interested them. They should know this already; it had been impossible, in the early days, to keep them from knowing what happened when she used the toilet. This one had come with Bluecloak, so perhaps it had never seen . . . but it should have known, from talking to the others. She knew they discussed her.

'Utter uhoo,' the creature said. Other you meant the other humans; none of the creatures would attempt the word human. 'What about the others?' Ofelia asked. She had become used to the creatures understanding more of her speech than she did of theirs.

It pointed to its mouth, then her mouth . . . its rump and then the sheep droppings.

'Oh – you mean you wonder if the other humans do this too?' What a silly question. Of course they did. She nodded vigorously. 'Yes. They do.'

'Nott ksee,' the creature said. Ofelia thought about it. The other humans still lived in the shelters they'd set up down at the shuttle field; they had moved out of the shuttle itself only in the past few days. So perhaps the creatures had never seen them eat or excrete.

Now the creature tapped its nose, and sniffed elaborately. 'Nnnott sssane.' Ofelia understood that as 'smells crazy,' which made no sense in terms of what they had been talking about. The creature tried again. 'Utter uhoo—' then a big sniff, '—nnot saamp.' Sane . . . saamp . . . same. Other yous smell not same? Yes, that could be it.

Ofelia gestured to reinforce her own words. 'You think the other humans smell . . . not like me? Not the same?'

'Eeeyess.' It touched her shirt, then its own kilt and belts. 'Nnnott saamp klote-ss.'

True enough, the others didn't wear the same clothes; they wore long-sleeved billowy shirts and long pants, shoes, all in muted colors.

'Saamp utter uhoose purrrt nessstt passs.' The same as other yous – other humans who purrrt – burrrt? – nest-something. Burrrt sounded close to hurt. Ofelia set the basket down to have the use of both hands. Had those luckless colonists hurt the creatures' nests? Was that why they'd been attacked?

'Burrrt?' She mimed pounding, kicking.

The creature looked around, as if confused. Then it said 'Hah-ahttt. Purrrt aaakss hah-ahtt.' Hot. Purrrt makes hot.

'Burn!' Astonishment and horror both hit at once. Where had it learned the word 'burn'? Had she used it, in warning of the hot stoves? She couldn't remember. And the other humans had *burned* the nests? Burned the babies?

She thought of the mechbots dropping out of the sky to scrape away whatever grew, to make the flat landing place for shuttles . . . if that had been nests, if it had caught fire from the mechbot exhausts, or perhaps they even fired the heaps of grass and roots . . . and nestlings.

She knew her face must be a mask of horror, and the creature stared at her, recognizing her shock.

'Utter uhoo,' it said again, this time with a decisive jerk of the head. 'Nnnott saamp. Nnnott . . .' and it rattled off a quick sequence of its own language, in which Ofelia thought she heard click-kaw-keerrr.

However bad they were, these humans had not destroyed the creatures' nests and children. She had to defend them. But she couldn't figure out how to unmake that confusion – not confusion, she realized now, but settled antagonism. And why hadn't Bluecloak told her, when it was teaching her, learning from her, when she had played it the tapes of the other colony's death?

Had it been a wish to spare her pain, or a deeper mistrust?

'Click-kaw-keerrr,' she said, that being the word which usually settled them. 'Gurgle-click-cough?'

The creature touched her head, delicately. 'Uhoo *kud* click-kaw-keerrr.'

She might be a good click-kaw-keerrr, but she still didn't know all her responsibilities . . . responsibilities to both people, she thought suddenly. She didn't want this – they weren't going to listen to her – but she could not leave the humans ignorant of what she'd learned. She needed to find out more first, though, and that meant finding the best source.

'Bluecloak?' she asked the creature. 'Where is Bluecloak?'

It tipped its head toward the forest – the *forest*? What was Bluecloak doing in the forest? The most likely thing was hunting, and although Ofelia no longer feared the long knives for herself, she didn't really want to see Bluecloak butchering treeclimbers. But the creature with her had started walking that way, and Ofelia followed. She dumped her basket of sheep droppings at the edge of the meadow, and stepped carefully through the taller weeds and scrubby growth in the intermediate ground.

She had intended to visit the forest more when she lived alone, but she had always been too busy in the village. After seeing the hunt, that time, she had not wanted to go in among the tall trees with the creatures. Now, it felt no different from following the creature anywhere. Cooler, perhaps. She watched the creature move, its high-stepping gait constrained in the forest by the coils of roots and vines. It led her a way she had no reason to know, but when they came to the place where she had sheltered, she recognized it as if she had left it only the day before. There was the fallen log, there the curve of root where she had put her sack of food.

And there were the creatures she knew, nearly all of them. Bluecloak, formally cloaked. Gurgle-click-cough. Her three babies, hedged about with the bodies of four creatures, who had stretched out to form a living playpen within which the babies tumbled and sprawled. They squeaked when they saw Ofelia, and staggered over to someone's legs, where they bounced up and down on feet that seemed bigger every day.

As Bluecloak greeted Ofelia, she saw two of the creatures slip away, back toward the village. Long knives gleamed in their hands. Had they planned a massacre—? She would have gone, but Bluecloak had her hands.

'Nnnott killll,' it said, as if it had read her thoughts. Her expression, most likely; human faces were so mobile, so flexible. 'Nnot killll utter uhoo. Yahtch.' Not kill, but watch. Keep them away from this meeting, which the creatures had carefully held far from the scanners and recorders that had been planted all over the village by the industrious Bilong.

Ofelia realized that the one who had talked to her in the sheep meadow must have been waiting for that chance. She wanted to know how long – surely they had been in the village the day before – but that was not the most important question.

Bluecloak's throat-sac swelled abruptly, and it began thrumming. Soon they all were, fingers and toes and bodies, in a complex of rhythms that had the babies lurching from one side of their enclosure to another, their little feet twitching first in one rhythm then another. Finally it all steadied; Ofelia could feel it all through her body, could feel her own toes tapping, her own heart slowing to match the left-hand drumming that meant concord.

Then silence, abrupt, into which the babies' squeaks sounded loud. Ofelia put out her hand to them, and they ran to her, licking her wrist, grabbing with their little fingers, so much weaker still than their toes, though apt for manipulating everything they got hold of. The talons felt like tiny pins.

When Bluecloak spoke, Ofelia could hardly believe it. He sounded exactly like Vasil Likisi, down to the accent and the pomposity. 'I have been empowered by the government . . .' He stopped, and rattled off a long string in his own language. Ofelia stared.

'But you—'

Now in the voice she knew, the one which changed some sounds of human tongue. 'It izh kud cahpih, ss?'

Better than a good copy; better than some recordings Ofelia had heard. 'You can . . . can you do that all the time?'

'Nnno. Cahpih foyss, eehess, hut he ssay. Ssay die thoughtss, aaakss utter ssondss.'

Ofelia did not understand. If he could copy Likisi's voice so exactly, even to the accent and tone, why couldn't he say the words right when he said his own thoughts? For the first time, she had something to ask Bilong – assuming Bilong would listen, and then understand the question – but she didn't have Bilong handy.

Bluecloak didn't wait for her to understand. It went on, now uttering a phrase in Kira Stavi's voice, and another in the flat monotone the military advisors murmured into their suit mics. Finally it repeated the song Ofelia had sung to the babies, in a voice she realized must be hers, though it sounded breathier, more like an old woman's voice than she heard it inside. She had never heard her voice recorded. Maybe she did sound like that, and Bluecloak had been accurate with the others.

'Do you understand all that?' Ofelia asked. 'Or just—'

'Eehess,' Bluecloak said. 'Know peeninks.' The meanings, he meant, but how? How could he understand so much, when she had learned so little of their language? She had known they were smart, but this -- Bilong had made such a fuss about how hard it was to learn other languages, even human language families.

'All of you?' Ofelia asked.

'Alll know. Nnnott all tsay.'

If they understood it all – they couldn't really, but if they did, if they thought they did – then what they had heard, in these last decems, must have given them a very . . . strange . . . idea of humans.

Ofelia sat on the pillow one of them produced from behind the log. Her mind ran from one corner of her brain to another like the babies now playing chase in their playpen. How long had they understood? How much? And why this meeting now? What were they planning? What would they expect her to do?

One of the babies squeaked, trying to climb adult legs to get to her. Gurgle-click-cough picked it up, licked its neck, and handed it to Ofelia. She cradled it, letting it lick the insides of both wrists, and then curl into a ball on her lap.

'Ahee,' said Bluecloak, pointing to itself. 'Thry aaakss clearrr tuh uhoo hut he hoo-ahnt.' Ofelia found she understood this much easily; she was reshaping the words almost without thought to the sounds she knew. They wanted to make clear to her what they wanted? That was what she most wanted to know, right now . . . and *then* she could find out more.

Only occasionally in the next few hours, did she have to ask Bluecloak to repeat or clarify what it said; the combination of near-human language and gestures conveyed more complicated meanings than she had thought possible. Much as she disliked the team members, she kept thinking that they should be here instead of her – or with her. They had the education, the training, to understand what she struggled to grasp. She was being given the knowledge they had come so far to obtain, knowledge the creatures still withheld (they made that clear) from the team.

'You should tell them,' she argued, early in the session. 'They're . . . official.' How could she explain official? How could she explain that no one would listen to her, that she was nothing in that social order? But Bluecloak interrupted firmly. They would tell her, and she must pay attention. She could do nothing else.

Ori would be intrigued by the creatures' social structure, she thought, the combination of nomadic hunting and herding for most adults with permanent, safe child-rearing locations in which the young, protected from predators and the rigors of migration, could be tutored as well as protected by the wisest of the adults. The special positions within the troops: singer-to-strangers, war leader, wayfinder, and click-kaw-keerrr. Then the loose confederacy of most troops, the constant testing of opinion with right and left-hand drumming. They had no concept of disobedience; dissenters could always leave, with any who drummed the same rhythm, and the world itself defined error and right.

Now Bluecloak explained more about her special position and his. Click-kaw-keerrr: more than aunt, a combination midwife, infant nurse, preschool and elementary teacher . . . and protector. Singer-to-strangers: those who made contact with other troops, and negotiated the sharing of lands and duties, bringing the drumming into the left hand if possible.

Kira and Ori both would have wanted to hear about the creatures' understanding of their world's living beings . . . how they classified the plants and animals, how they had learned to use them, how they bred their grass-eating herd animals, how they replanted the ruined nestmass.

Ofelia realized that she was dividing what Bluecloak said into what this one and that would like to know – but Bluecloak wasn't thinking that way. To Bluecloak, all 'mind-hunting' was the same, each scent-trail leading to a different prey, but all the same in the joy of the hunt. She remembered how even the first of them had seemed so eager to learn, like young children before they are taught that most curiosity is idle, useless.

She pulled her mind back to what Bluecloak was saying. For a people like this, there could be no single government; nothing they did, in fact, resembled anything she knew about governments. Bluecloak sang for some large fraction of the People (she heard the capital of that now, and accepted it) who roamed the plains, but singing for them did not mean ruling them. And while Bluecloak had sung to (different from singing for) some of the People who lived on the stone coast, this did not mean that agreement had come.

Ofelia had to hear more about the people on the stone

coast; the humans, when asked, had cut her off. Bluecloak
explained, and in the process Ofelia understood why the
idea of water and electricity in pipes had come easily to
them. Their People ran water, other liquids, and particu-
lates like sand in pipes of wood and hollow reeds, and
brewed things in gourds made of clay or burnt sand. They
had no electricity – yet – and their water pumps ran on
water or foot power . . . but the idea of pumped water
was not strange to them, even to the nomads.

But the core of what Bluecloak wanted to say had to
do with the colony that had destroyed their nestmass, and
which they had killed in shocked revenge . . . and these
new humans, who had come because of that, who now
wanted to make their rules for the People, what they could
learn and what they could not. Nestmass – which meant,
Ofelia thought, the nestlings and nestguards as well as the
nests themselves – were untouchable in the People's own
culture.

Bluecloak understood – they all understood – that
perhaps the strange monsters from the sky hadn't known
what they destroyed. But that was an excuse no click-kaw-
keerrr would accept from a nestling. To see the end of a
deed in its beginning was the prime virtue – to lay a trap
where only prey, not allies, walked, was the first lesson of
the stalker. In all the lessons of hunting that continued:
go hungry rather than kill and eat the last mother of the
prey. Go thirsty rather than take water of those who will
be eaten. Leave sweet fruits on the tree for the climbers
you hunt.

Ofelia understood that, but not the lengths to which the
People took it. She had no training in logic; she had been
taught only enough math to use the necessary manuals and
work the necessary machines. She remembered seeing

Bluecloak hunched over the old math textbooks; now it held one out, pointing to a long proof. That, it explained to her, was easy; its People thought in longer and more winding trails than that.

'But you . . .' There was no way to say tactfully that for such smart people, they hadn't got very far. No real cities – well, she hadn't seen the ones of the stone coast yet. But no vehicles, no big machines – she remembered something from the doomed colony tape about a catapult that threw something explosive. No big metal machines, no mechbots. No computers.

'Papiess,' Bluecloak said. If she understood him, if he understood what had happened, they considered themselves a young People, almost babies. They had once been other, only ten or twenty generations back. With the math book, with stones laid out in rows, Bluecloak conveyed that their recent ancestors could think along only few-step chains, whereas they could think along many-step chains. Something had happened; they didn't know what. Someday they would figure it out, but in the meantime, they had other things to deal with.

Such as intrusive humans who wanted to set limits to their learning. Which brought them back to nest-guardians.

The good nest-guardians, Bluecloak explained, wanted the nestlings to learn all they could about everything, to be ready for – eager for – new things. Bad nest-guardians wanted to make life easy on themselves by keeping the nestlings content with sameness. These humans, Bluecloak said slowly, watching Ofelia's face. They destroyed nest-mass. Now they want to keep us from learning new things. They are bad nest-guardians. Not like you. And they do not properly respect you. It sounded as if these were equally bad.

Ofelia thought of all the times she had resented the questions her children asked, the times she had resented the intrusive curiosity of the creatures. She had been snubbed that way herself; she had been kept from learning all she could. Once she had believed that necessary. You couldn't let children waste their time that way; they would never learn discipline if they weren't made to learn what they needed. In her memory she saw the bright faces, the sparkling eyes, heard the eager voices . . . and she remembered how they had changed, how she had changed, all that curiosity and eagerness settling into a mold of passive obedience, more or less sullen depending on how much the child had to abandon.

'I was not a good nest-guardian for my children,' she said. The baby in her lap stirred, and grabbed her thumb with both its hands. She looked down, and stroked the line of knobs along its back.

She was a good nest-guardian now, Bluecloak said. And mothers were not nest-guardians anyway. Only the old, those who were no longer nesting mothers, who understood things, were nest-guardians. Perhaps she had not had the right nest-guardians to help her.

'Not fathers?'

'Nnott.' No more explanation. Ofelia could see where mothers – grandmothers – if they were still physically strong and able, would know things about babies and children that the men she knew would not. But these were not human, and she could not assume that their fathers had limitations. If they even had fathers . . . Bluecloak had still not explained how they reproduced.

They trusted Ofelia, Bluecloak went on. She was a nest-guardian; she had proved herself so with Gurgle-click-cough's nesting; the nestlings accepted her. Bluecloak could sing for her, but only the nest-guardian could make the agreement when all the People could not drum together, because of distance.

'Agreement?'

'Or not agreement.' What followed took her breath away; she felt as if she'd been hit in the chest. She was their nest-guardian; the People would deal with other humans only through her. She must make the other humans understand this, now that she understood.

'But that won't work. They won't listen to me. Besides, they say I must leave,' Ofelia said. 'They say they will take me when they go.'

'NO!' All of them, throat-sacs expanded. The baby in her lap came wide awake, wrapped legs and tail around her arm, and squeaked loudly. She soothed it automatically with her other hand.

'I don't want to go,' Ofelia said. 'I want to stay. That's why I stayed before, but—' But she was only one old woman, and they were four strong younger adults, and two military advisors, and the pilot – they could carry her off kicking and screaming, if it came to that. Or just give her a shot, put her to sleep, and she would wake up – if she did – somewhere else.

'Nnot go!' Bluecloak said loudly. 'Ssstopp tim.'

Were they saying they would protect *her*? Looking at them, she did not doubt they would try. But had they believed anything she'd told them of the humans' weapons? Bright as they were, they would have no chance against those chunky firearms the military advisors carried, the weaponry mounted on the shuttle itself, let alone what the ship aloft might have. She didn't want them to die for her; she wasn't worth it.

She tried to say that, and Bluecloak hissed; so did all

the babies, like a multiple leak in an air line, three slightly different notes.

She was worth it; she was their nest-guardian, and the nest-guardian was the most important position the People had. All the eyes, adult and baby, stared at her as the toes drummed agreement. She: nest-guardian. She: important. Tears burned her eyes; she had never felt such affirmation.

The toes stilled, and Bluecloak went on, as if explaining one plus one to a small child. What she had to do was make those other humans understand. They must let the People learn; they must help the People learn; they must be respectful of Ofelia and all nest-guardians, and all nest-mass. And the People would deal only with Ofelia . . . if Ofelia were taken away, they would not deal at all.

Demands Ofelia understood, though she was not used to them from this direction. The creatures – the People – had been so reasonable before, so childlike . . . she pushed that thought back. Children demanded; she had demanded, when she was a child. The part of her that stayed behind had not been the oldest part, but the child part, the part determined to get its own way, to grow its own way . . . or, as these People would say, hunt its own scent-trail.

She could imagine how the team members – especially pompous Likisi – would react to all this. They were supposed to listen to *her*, to the person they thought of as a nuisance, almost an embarrassment? Her old voice embroidered this design at length, as the People sat waiting for her response. She had no education; she had no profession; she had no powerful family. She was bringing a message they would not want to hear; neither messenger nor message would please them, and she would be the one to take the brunt of their displeasure. They would laugh at her; they would be angry; they would ignore her.

The baby in her lap sat up, and tapped its right foot. She glanced down, and it stared at her, still tapping the right foot. Disagreement. Dissent. What was it disagreeing with? The bright eyes stared into hers, unblinking. Ofelia sighed.

This time, with this child, she would do it right. This time she would give what she had never really wanted to withhold. 'You,' she said to the baby, feeling a real smile relaxing her face. 'You want me to do the impossible, don't you?'

Now it blinked, once, and the left foot drummed. Impossible. Do it. It couldn't possibly understand; it was only days old. But other humans thought she couldn't possibly understand, because she was too old, too stupid. Maybe all the humans were wrong – she about this child, the others about her. But these are aliens, the old voice argued. No. These were people, people with babies and children and grandmothers who took care of the babies, and she could not refuse the eagerness in those bright eyes, the desire in those little taloned hands.

It was impossible, it was all impossible, and she might as well get on with it. Impossible things didn't get done by sitting around in the shade playing with children.

Nonetheless, before she left, she played with all three of them, even bending down so they could explore her hair, which seemed to fascinate them most.

NINETEEN

When she got back to the village, in the hot afternoon, she
still couldn't quite believe what had happened. The old
voice insisted she couldn't possibly do what the creatures
wanted. She had no talent, no training, no letters after her
name. She was too old, too stupid, too ignorant. She closed
her eyes a moment, and the babies' golden eyes stared at
her from the darkness behind her eyelids. She had promised the babies . . . she, the click-kaw-keerrr. She had to
do it, possible or not.

She could not even find the team members at first. They
weren't in the center, or in the lane. They hadn't been in
the sheep meadow, and she didn't see them in the part
of the river meadow visible from the lane angle. She looked
into a few houses, but saw no one. It was too hot to walk
all the lanes, look into all the houses and gardens. Could
they be eating or resting in their own shelter? Ofelia walked
down the lane, and saw the military advisors hunched
over one of the old rusty trucks. One of them spotted her
and nudged the other. They both stared.

She didn't like to turn her back on them; they made her
uneasy enough when they were in front of her. She came
nearer, slowly, cautiously. She wasn't even sure which one

had hit her. They were both so big, so much the same shape, and their expressions seemed fixed in wary contempt.

'What do you want?' one of them said, when she was close enough. He spoke loudly, as if he thought she was deaf.

'I wanted to speak to one of them,' she said. 'Ser Likisi, or—'

'They're not here,' the man said shortly, cutting her off. He turned back to the truck.

'Do you know when—' Ofelia began; again he interrupted, this time without looking at her.

'No. They don't tell *me* their schedule.' After a moment, she realized he was not angry with her, but with the others. He didn't like them. She had suspected that before, but she had seen these men only in company with the others, where they would naturally mask their feelings. 'I'm sorry to have bothered you,' Ofelia said formally. That got another look, this time of mild surprise, from both men.

'It's nothing,' the other man said, not as loudly. 'Was there anything else?'

'No,' Ofelia said. 'I just wanted to talk to them.' But curiosity held her. 'What are you doing to the truck? Do you want to use it?'

They both laughed. 'No, grandma,' said the second one. 'It's past that. But bossyboots told us to dismantle the engines, just in case those lizards could learn to use them.'

Ofelia blinked. Bossyboots? Was that Ser Likisi, who certainly deserved that or a worse nickname, or Sera Stavi? And lizards? Was that how they saw the creatures?

'Shut up!' said the other one. He glared at Ofelia. 'You won't go telling our noble leader what we call him, will you.' It was not a question, but a command. His voice was heavy with threat.

'No,' Ofelia said. 'I won't tell him.' Nor would she tell these two how much she agreed with them . . . or should she? 'He's very . . . sure of himself,' she said, making it obvious that she could have said it another way. The two men looked at each other and laughed.

'You could say that,' the milder one said. 'You don't like him either? He was a Sims corpsucker, I heard; switched to government work when he got his ass in a crack—'

'Kedrick!'

'Never mind, Bo, this little grandma isn't going to tell any tales. She doesn't like lickspittle Likisi any better than we do, do you?' Ofelia grinned, but said nothing. Interesting how little humans varied, from one organization to another. She had heard comments like this before, from disgruntled colonist-trainees. 'Want a little . . . refreshment?' the man asked her, miming a drink.

It had to mean something contraband; they would have something illegal, all such men did. She remembered how quickly after the colony's Company advisors left someone had rigged a still to make alcohol from whatever they grew. She remembered the arguments, the fights, the smashing of one still, and the quick reappearance of foul-tasting fiery liquid passed from one to another in little flasks. . . .

'I'm too old,' she said, but she smiled at them. Men like this – she had known men like this all her life, even though these men would not have recognized the resemblance. 'But thank you,' she said. One did not dare to act superior to men who dosed themselves with illegal substances.

"S all right, grandma,' the loud one said. 'Just you don't go tellin' peerless leader, huh?'

'Of course not,' Ofelia said. 'Not that he listens to me anyway.'

They regarded her tolerantly. Clearly she was no threat, and she was behaving just as an ignorant old woman should. 'Of course he doesn't listen to you,' the quiet one – Bo? – said. 'He's the team leader, isn't he? He doesn't listen to anybody but maybe the oversoul of the universe—'

Ofelia wanted to ask if anyone still believed in that, but she knew better. Never ask about religion; it makes people angry.

'I guess you had it good, here by yourself?' the quiet one went on. 'All the machines working, all the food for yourself, huh?'

'It was very quiet,' Ofelia said. 'But yes, the machines made it easier.'

'That bitch Kira said you were mucking about with the official log. Writing stories or something? Were you some kind of writer or something before they sent you here?'

Ofelia shook her head. 'No, Serin. I did not write anything before. The log – I was reading it, and it seemed boring, just names and dates. I thought no one would ever see.'

'So you spiced it up. Kira says you put in about love affairs and stuff—'

Ofelia realized that he wanted to read it . . . that he wanted to hear about the sneaking around, the betrayals, the fights . . . and yet he had no excuse. She grinned, an intentionally complicit grin, the dirty-minded old woman to the dirty-minded younger man. 'It was like a storycube,' she said, lowering her voice and glancing around as if to be sure virtuous Kira were not in hearing. 'You must understand, Serin, how isolated we were. And the stress—'

The man snorted. 'Stress! What do civvies know about stress? But sex—'

'Well, of course there was sex,' Ofelia said, in the most

insinuating voice she could produce. 'We were here to breed and enlarge the colony. No birth-limits, bonuses for every child above four. And there are some who stay more – more comely, you understand.' Was she being too obvious for them? No. The loud one had put down his tools and was leaning on the side of the truck, ready to hear more.

'I don't know if I should be telling you this,' Ofelia said with fake piety. 'Sera Stavi doesn't like it that I added to the official log, and perhaps—'

The loud one said what Sera Stavi could do with her opinions; it did not differ from the things the men in the colony had said. Not for the first time, Ofelia wondered if humans had thought of anything really new in the past ten thousand years. Had they only wandered the stars because they were tired of their stale jokes and curses?

But she began on a juicy story that wasn't even in the log, because the creatures had come and she had never finished – the story of the young girl Ampara and her teasing ways that had half the grown men – let alone the few boys her age – upset for half a year.

'And what did she look like?' the loud man asked. The other, quieter one had continued to work on the truck, banging loudly to indicate his annoyance with his lazy co-worker. Ofelia grinned even wider, until her jaw hurt.

'You expect me, an old woman, to know how to tell you that?' But that was only the teasing, part of the ritual of storytelling. She went into explicit detail, more than she knew of her own knowledge, remembering what such men liked to hear about abundant soft hair flowing down long supple backs, about curves and round firmness and soft moistness. He was breathing fast now, and she was running out of ideas.

'Look out!' the quiet man said suddenly, in his professional voice. 'They're coming.'

Ofelia stopped short, and turned slowly. Ser Likisi and Kira Stavi, striding along as if in a walking race, and both looking grumpy.

'Sera Falfurrias!' Kira sounded annoyed with her, and Ofelia wondered why.

'Yes, Sera,' Ofelia said meekly. She stood with her hands folded in front of her, the servant ready for orders. Inside her head, the new voice mocked her.

'What are those things up to, do you know?'

'Up to, Sera?' Ofelia asked.

'The indigenes. They've disappeared, all but one, and it's not communicative. Have they gone back where they came from, or what? I saw you going into the forest with one this morning, so don't tell me you have no idea.'

Her first plan frustrated, Ofelia went after a side issue. 'Why would you think I lie to you, Sera?'

'I didn't say that,' Kira began, impatiently.

'Excuse me, Sera, but you said—'

Kira stamped the ground like a cow beset by flies. 'I only meant that *if* you were going to say you didn't know, I had already seen you – oh, never mind.' She glared at Ofelia; behind her, Ofelia saw the loud man's mocking grin.

By then Ofelia had thought what she could say. 'They had found the place I hid when the colony was evacuated,' she said. 'I had left something behind, and they wanted to know if it was mine, or yours.'

'Oh.' Kira did not want to believe it; Ofelia could tell she was in the mood to disbelieve anything Ofelia said, but that was so ordinary. Reluctant belief; her brows relaxed. 'Well. We just wondered.'

Ofelia thought of embroidering that tale, and decided against it.

'I guess they saw me go out in the forest to take tissue samples . . . they might have thought I left equipment behind.'

'I believe that's what they thought, Sera,' Ofelia said.

'Did you want something in particular?' Likisi said. 'Or were you just keeping our guardians and advisors company?' He made it sound as if she had been doing bad things with them, and even though she had been retailing filthy gossip, Ofelia resented it.

'I wanted to speak with you, Ser Likisi,' she said. 'And with Sera Stavi, if that is permissible.'

He rolled his eyes. 'Oh, very well. But if you're going to argue about staying, you might as well save your breath and my patience.'

'That's not it, Ser Likisi,' Ofelia said. She was trying to sound humble, but it came out less humble than she intended. The woman Kira glanced at her sharply, but said nothing.

'Oh, come on,' Likisi said. 'Come inside – it's too hot out here.' He led her past the truck and the advisors, who both looked as if they were sucking lemons, through the doorseal and into the big softsided shelter.

Inside, it was stuffy despite the rushing sound of the aircooler, and not as cool as a shady room in one of the houses. Likisi flung out his arms.

'Ah – that's better.' Then he flung himself down on a padded bench. 'Kira – be a dear and get us something cold, will you?'

Now it was the other woman who looked as if she'd bitten a lemon. But she bit back what she wanted to say, and instead asked mildly what Sera Falfurrias would like.

Ofelia politely refused anything twice, then accepted water. Kira disappeared around a partition. She had not asked Likisi what he wanted; that meant she had fetched drinks for him before.

Likisi watched her between narrowed lids. 'What is it now? Were you wildly curious about this shelter? Do you want to know how much you can bring with you when we leave?'

'No, Ser Likisi,' Ofelia said. He had not asked her to sit down, and she stood, hands folded in front of her. The air moved by the aircooler fans dried the sweat on her back, and chilled her.

'Here—' Kira handed Ofelia a glass of water with ice blocks in it. 'Sit down, for goodness sakes. You don't have to stand there.' She handed Likisi a glass of something purplish; and took her own glass of clear liquid to one of the chairs arranged around a low table. 'Here – sit by me, if you want.'

Ofelia walked over and sat. The chair squirmed under her, and she jumped up, glaring at Kira.

'Sorry,' the woman said; her expression said she meant it. 'I didn't realize – these chairs adjust to each person who sits in them. Please – forgive me.'

Ofelia sat back down, her back stiff. The chair squirmed under her buttocks, her thighs, trying to make her relax. It was hard to sit stiffly, and she felt her resistance giving way. As she relaxed, the chair molded itself to her. It was comfortable, she had to admit. She sipped her water. It tasted cold and flat, nothing like the live water she was used to. 'Thank you, Sera,' she said politely. 'This is very nice.'

'They use similar furniture in geriatric residence units,' Kira said. 'It prevents sores.'

'How interesting,' Ofelia said. She still had no plan for how she was going to convince them. She sipped again. 'Sera – the . . . indigenes, you call them . . .'

'What about them?' Likisi asked.

'I think they are upset. By you.'

He laughed. 'I rather expect they are. They ran off the first humans they saw easily enough, and now we're back. And they've seen the technology here – while that's regrettable, in a way, it's also made it clear to them that they have a long way to go before they can compete with us.'

'We won't hurt them, Sera Falfurrias,' Kira said. 'We know they didn't understand what was happening, when they attacked the colonists. It was all very unfortunate; they aren't really so bloodthirsty. They're quite intelligent, as you said, and when Bilong completes the linguistic analysis, and we can actually talk to them, explain what we know—'

Misunderstandings hid in those words like seeds in an orange. The People had understood; these people didn't.

'The colonists,' Ofelia said. 'They destroyed the nests.'

'Nests?' Likisi stared at her. 'These indigenes build *nests*? That's not what Bilong said.'

'Bilong said she thought the colony landed at a special place, some kind of sacred ground or something,' Kira said to Ofelia.

'It was nests,' Ofelia said.

'They didn't know that,' Kira said. 'They couldn't – they had no idea there were intelligent indigenes.' Clear in that was the unconcern about the nests of less intelligent indigenes. Ofelia felt ashamed.

'Whatever . . . nests, sacred ground . . . it doesn't matter; what matters is that we understand why they reacted so violently. If they're afraid of vengeance, they need to know that we have no wish for more violence, so long as they are peaceful.'

She could not jump up and scream *Fools!* at these two; it would do no good. To say that the deaths of the nestlings and nest-guardians didn't matter . . . to believe that the People were afraid of human vengeance . . . to think that the power lay with them and not with those who belonged here . . . fools they were, whether she named them so or not.

'It mattered to them, that it was nests,' Ofelia said quietly. Then she stood; she could not stay in the same space with them any longer.

The doorseal behind her rasped, and she jumped. It was only the other two, returning from wherever they'd been.

'Led us a merry chase,' Ori said. 'I *think* it had something to do with demonstrating hunting techniques, but I'm not sure. I'm parched. Hello, Sera Falfurrias . . . forgive me for not greeting you first.'

'You would not believe how many palatals they can produce,' Bilong said. She patted a gray case hung at her side. 'I got good recordings this time, very clean sound. When the waveform subroutine's through with it, we ought to have a complete – or almost complete – phonetic analysis.'

'That may be why our mighty hunter didn't catch anything; it was too busy producing pretty sounds for Bilong's box.' Ori sounded grumpy; if he had been following one of the creatures assigned to keep him out of the way, he had had a hot and miserable day, Ofelia was sure. It would be better to wait until he was not in this mood. But she was here, and when would she have the chance again to talk to all four of them? She could almost feel her own left toes twitching: now.

She held her silence. What good was a nest-guardian's experience if you ignored it? Experience said they would not listen now, not with one of them excited and the other one miserable.

'Perhaps you would come to dinner,' she said. 'I have not yet had the honor of entertaining you in my home.'

'What?' Likisi, looking blurred around the edges (what *was* that purple stuff?) gaped, then remembered his manners. 'Uh – thank you, Sera, but not this evening, I think. Ori's exhausted, and frankly I am too.'

'Another day?' Ofelia asked. 'Tomorrow or the next?' The creatures had made it clear that they wanted the confrontation as soon as possible. They were ready. She did not understand all they intended, but she trusted them.

'Tomorrow would be very nice,' Kira said. 'Perhaps you would allow us to bring treats from the ship?' Ofelia saw through that; they didn't trust the food she raised in the garden. Anger made her stubborn; she felt heavier, as if she were a rock resisting movement.

'It will all be carefully cleaned, Sera,' Ofelia said. 'I have cooked many years.' And I am still alive and healthy, she did not add.

'Of course,' Ori said, sighing. 'We are too concerned about these things, Sera Falfurrias. We will be honored to eat with you.' The others looked even less enthusiastic, but they did not argue.

'Thank you,' Ofelia said, and escaped to the late afternoon sunlight. The two advisors were still bent over the truck, but they were talking, not doing anything. When they caught sight of her, they stood up as she passed; the loud one grinned but said nothing.

All the way up the lane to her house, the old voice told

her what she had said wrong, what she should have said, and how it would never work. The new voice held its peace, but she knew it was stirring things, down where she couldn't quite see or hear, but only feel. Left hand and right hand. Bluecloak was waiting, as she had expected. 'They did not listen today,' she said. 'They told me they intended no vengeance because the People killed the colonists. They thought you were afraid of that.' A single tap of his foot; she didn't have to look to know which foot. 'They expect to make the rules for your people and mine to know each other. They think you will accept this.' She grinned at him. 'They think you have no choice. They do not understand, but they will. Tomorrow, I will feed them in the evening. It is what they expect old women to do – feed them, care for them, listen to them.'

Bluecloak's speech sounded even clearer this afternoon; she had no trouble following his accent when he asked how much she'd told them.

'Not much,' Ofelia said. 'They were hot and hungry; they didn't listen well to what I did say. And I need to find out more.' What weapons were on the shuttle and the ship above, for instance. What orders had been left with the ship's captain. If it came to force, they were doomed. It must not come to force. It must be done by persuasion.

Early the next morning, Ofelia went into her gardens to gather the fresh foods. She watched with amusement as several of the People kept the other humans busy and away from Ofelia. She had uninterrupted time in the gardens, time to plan what to make with what she had, lay out the table and prepare the meal. It had been so long since she cooked anything but what she herself wanted to eat. She tried to think what would appeal to these younger ones, these strangers. She put chunks of the hard-shelled squash on to boil; she would make two kinds of little pies, one squash and one fruit. She had put away packets of sweetened berries in the freezer. She took the berries, and a lamb roast from the meat section.

Although she had invited only the team itself, she carried a jug of fruit juices down the lane to the advisors, who today were working on another vehicle. 'I have only a small house,' she said, looking down as if ashamed.

'That's all right,' the quiet one said. 'Thank you for this.'

'I don't suppose you have time to finish that story?' the loud one said, not quite asking for it. Ofelia hoped he was the one who had hit her; he would be easy to dislike. Reason said the quiet one was just as dangerous, but she felt a sneaking admiration for someone who was courteous without need.

'I'm sorry,' Ofelia said. 'I have cooking. Later I can bring little pies—'

'There's the pilot, too,' the loud one said. 'He wouldn't mind some of this stuff—'

'Don't—' said the quiet one.

'I would be honored,' Ofelia said.

She went away, before they could say more. She expected that they would put the fruit drink into one of their machines and make sure she was not trying to drug them. She would not be so foolish, but they would not know that. She did not look back to see if they drank it or not.

In her house, she made the pastry, rolled it out flat, and shaped the little rounds. Into each she put a spoonful of sweetened fruit or spiced cooked squash. She put the little pies in the oven, then went to the center for a large serving platter. If she had thought ahead, she could have had the fabricator make prettier dishes, or she could even have painted designs on some. How could she have thought ahead, with those people pestering her?

The pies were done early enough that the house did not get too hot. She would bake the roast in the house next door, or in the center. Ofelia set the pies on racks, then moved the kitchen table into the other end of the main room. She went back to the center, and found a length of heavy material in blue which would serve as a tablecloth. On it, the plain dishes looked almost festive. The dayvine flowers would not stay fresh when cut, but she made a centerpiece of herbs and fruit.

She had just time to hurry down the lane with a tray of little pies, one of the loaves of bread she'd baked, a pot of jam, a length of hard beef sausage, some fresh fruit, before the final rush of cooking. The advisors and the pilot – she had not seen the pilot before – were doing something to a third vehicle, but they noticed her quickly. This time, they came forward to take the tray.

'Thank you,' the quiet one said. 'This is very kind of you.' He took one of the pies. 'I hope your head feels better . . . it was unfortunate that you startled me that way.'

Ofelia smiled at him. She still wished it had been the other one, the one she could not have liked anyway. 'It does not hurt now,' she said. 'I did not mean to startle you.'

'Of course not,' he said. He bit into the pie, and his expression changed from polite neutrality to surprise. 'This is really good,' he said, as if he had expected to bite into a bitter lime.

'Excuse me,' Ofelia said. 'I must get back to the cooking.

I'm making a roast—' She gave enough details to make them thoroughly jealous of the ones who were coming. She could see the envy and dissatisfaction rise in them like bubbles in bean soup. They eyed the tray with less appreciation now that they knew what they were going to miss.

When her guests arrived, she had it all laid out on the serving dishes. The sliced tomatoes and onions in vinegar and oil, with rosemary and basil making a wreath around the whole. The roast lamb, which had been rolled in crushed herbs . . . it was unfortunate how baked rosemary looked like bits of burnt insect, but it smelled good. And when she sliced it – her guests sucked in their breath. She had boned the roast and laid it flat, then stuffed it with cheese and vegetables and herbs. Each slice made its own unique design.

She herself had no appetite, not only because she had nibbled as she cooked. She was on her feet more than sitting, as she fetched new dishes, and took away those they had finished.

'I had no idea you could do this, Sera Falfurrias,' said Likisi, when he saw the slices of stuffed roast lamb. 'Were you the cook here, for the whole colony?'

'No, Ser Likisi. After the first time, before we had houses, each family cooked for itself. We all cooked some extra to store in the center, for those who might be sick. We used the big kitchens to cook for the school, or special times when more workers were needed in the fields.' Or during the floods, or the epidemics, but she didn't say that.

After the first cautious nibbles, all four of the team had begun eating as if they had not eaten in days. By the time Ofelia brought over the remaining little pies, they were leaning back in their chairs with the half-sleepy look of those whose bellies are overfull. Just as she'd hoped. Ofelia took away the messy serving dishes and platters, and cleared the dirty plates. She offered them little plates for the pies, then sat down herself in the chair she'd hardly used all evening.

Her legs ached, and her back; she had been working too hard to notice until now. Aches never killed anyone. Wars did. She smiled at her guests, and they all smiled back, their mouths full of sweet pies. They were as mellow as they were going to get. Beyond them, in the twilight, she saw Bluecloak and two others go into the center.

This time when she began talking, she had their silence, if not their full attention. She began where she had begun the day before: the indigenes were upset, because they thought the humans did not understand what had happened. The attack on their nests had caused the attack on the colonists, but the indigenes were not worried about retaliation.

'They believe their action was just,' Ofelia said. 'They will not tolerate more intrusion.'

'Surely you told them there was no question of further colonization?' Likisi said, looking at Bilong.

'I tried,' Bilong said. 'I thought I'd gotten it across.'

'You see, Sera Falfurrias,' Likisi said to her, 'they are protected under our laws – no one will try to colonize here – but they can't just go around killing people because they're upset—'

'The colonists killed *their* people – their children and nest-guardians,' Ofelia said.

'But that was an accident,' Likisi said. 'They must understand that – the colonists made a mistake, but what they did was deliberate. We can accept that it was also a mistake – no one is howling for revenge . . . well, some are, but the government won't allow it. But they can't use violence against us again. And we will be sure they don't have the technology to do us any real damage, until they've matured enough not to use it.'

Ofelia felt as if someone had crocheted her insides into one big complicated knot. She forced herself to go on. 'But from what you and the others have told me, they have cities far north of here, and boats with sails. How can you keep them from learning on their own?'

Likisi laughed. 'It will take them years – centuries – to get to a real industrial base. It's unfortunate that they came down here and found out about electricity, but they'll have to figure out how to make generators and batteries . . . it took humans thousands of years, and they won't figure it out in less. Anyway, as long as they can't get offplanet, they can't do us any real harm.'

Humans had not had the finished product to look at, Ofelia thought. How long had it taken the humans who didn't invent the new things to learn to use them? To make and repair them?

Bilong spoke up. 'I don't understand, Sera, how you know all this. You haven't really studied the language—'

'I have lived with them longer,' Ofelia said. 'They want to talk to me.'

'Yes, but you can misunderstand so much,' Bilong said. 'For instance, that word I've heard you say . . . I did an acoustic analysis, and you don't say it anything like they do.' Bilong took a breath and produced a 'click-kaw-keerrr' that sounded right to Ofelia. 'That's how they say it, and what you do is – "click-kaw-keerrr" – can you hear the difference?' Ofelia couldn't. She wasn't sure there really was any difference; Bluecloak understood her well enough when she said it.

'My point is,' Bilong said, leaning on the table with both elbows, 'you don't really understand them; you just think you do. And they came when you were all alone, probably even psychotic from the solitude, and you think of them as friends. They aren't friends; they're aliens. Indigenes, I mean,' she added with a quick glance at the others.

Ofelia looked out the window. It was dark outside, the brief tropical twilight was over. If she knew anything about humans, the two military advisors and the pilot, sure that their nominal bosses would be away for hours, would have accompanied their lesser feast with whatever illicit drink they had offered her the day before. If they had any form of amusement, entertainment cubes or hardcopy, they would be gathered around it now. It was too early to worry, too early for 'anything to happen.' They would be more alert later, when they might be expecting their boss to return.

What she could not know was what kind of safeguards might be on the shuttle itself. She had explained to Bluecloak the kinds she knew about, the little beams of light or sound that reacted if interrupted, the pressure plates, the locks that required known palmprints or retinal patterns. Bluecloak had not seemed concerned. And that was not her problem now. 'They are very intelligent,' Ofelia said. 'They learn very fast, even as babies.'

'Babies! What do you know about their babies?' Kira sat up straight, and put down the pie she had held.

This was the part that scared Ofelia most. She had not wanted to admit that the People had babies here, but Bluecloak and Gurgle-click-cough had insisted. She must tell her people about the babies; they must see the babies.

'They have cute babies,' Ofelia said. 'Very affectionate, very quick to learn.'

'You've *seen* their babies?!' all of them at once, practically. 'There are babies *here*?'

'Why didn't you tell us?' Kira asked.

'You didn't ask me,' Ofelia said, with great satisfaction. Just as anger flowered from the remains of surprise, she stood up. 'Come along, if you want to see them.'

Nothing would have stopped them. They crowded her heels across the lane to the center, where Ofelia knocked on the closed door. Bluecloak opened it; she winked at Bluecloak and led the others in. When they were all inside, she shut the door behind them.

'Why are you shutting the door?' Likisi asked.

'We don't want the babies to run out in the street,' Ofelia said, as she led them down the passage to the schoolroom. She could hear the others following her. Ahead, light spilled out the schoolroom door, and she could hear the squeaky voices of the babies.

TWENTY

Ofelia did not know herself exactly what Bluecloak had planned in the way of demonstrations. What she saw – what they all saw – exceeded anything she had imagined. One of the babies, perched on Gurgle-click-cough's lap, poked at the controls of a classroom computer. On the display, colored patterns swirled. Two of the adults were hunched over a couple of gourds, fiddling with wires that connected to . . . Ofelia blinked . . . they had connected half the room's electrical demonstrations to their gourds. The other two babies played on the floor with models of gears and screws, constructing something intricate. Ofelia wondered what it was, and if it would work when it was done. 'Oh . . . my . . . God.' That was Likisi; Ofelia had not suspected him of any religious beliefs. 'They're – they're using a *computer*?'

Bluecloak came forward; he had shut the door behind them, silently. 'Iss dun.'

'But how did he learn – did *you* teach them? After we warned you?' Likisi glared at Ofelia. Bluecloak stepped between them forcing a confrontation.

'Huhooaht hooeee sssee, hooeee aaak.' Bluecloak said, waving its arm to encompass everything in the room.

'It means,' Bilong said to Likisi, 'what we see, we make. They do, I mean. He says they can make anything they've seen. They can't really, but—'

'Aaakss zzzzt!' Bluecloak said, and spoke in his own language to the creatures with the gourds. Ofelia held her breath. She could hardly believe it would work again; it had seemed too much like magic the first time.

The lights went out, and before the startled humans could exclaim, a string of smaller bulbs flared in the center of the room. The room lights came back on, and the one beside the gourds puffed its throat-sac twice at the humans, then moved a switch and the little lights went off.

'That's impossible!' Likisi said. 'They've used an extension cord – a hidden battery—'

'The battery is the gourds,' Ofelia said. Bluecloak had explained it to her. 'They brew some stuff that works like the acid in a liquid battery—'

'They can't *do* that – there's no way—'

'It could be.' Kira went over to look. 'If they've come up with an acid—'

'They make explosives, you know,' Ofelia said. 'That shuttle—'

'Zzzzt inn ssky,' Bluecloak said. 'Sssane zzzzt inn ires, aaakss lahtt, aaakss kuhll, aaakss tuurn . . .'

'You told them!' Likisi rounded on Ofelia. 'You had to tell them this; they couldn't have figured it out. They don't even have a *government*—!'

'Government and science aren't mutually necessary,' Ori said dryly. He looked more amused than alarmed now, and clearly he enjoyed Likisi's distress. 'Frankly I don't think Sera Falfurrias has the background to set up this demonstration.' He turned to Ofelia. 'Tell me, Sera, what kind of "brew" would it take to generate electricity chemically – do you know?'

'Batteries use acid,' she said. 'It's dangerous, and it makes fumes.'

'Yes. As I thought. And I suspect, Vasil, if we analyze what the indigenes have in their flasks, it will not be the same as the acid Sera Falfurrias may have seen in batteries. As I've tried to tell you several times since we came, these indigenes are quite unlike other cultures I've studied.'

'Well, they're *aliens*!' Likisi said. 'Of course they're different.'

'Excuse me.' Ori turned away from Likisi and went over to Kira. 'Have you any idea what's in there?'

'This plant – I have no idea what it is, or where they got it—' She held out a handful of leaves and some orangered globes smaller than plums. 'I have no idea how they make the liquid from it—'

'It doesn't *matter* how they do it,' Likisi said. 'It only matters that they're aliens, and they didn't have electricity when they met up with Grandma here, and now they do. It's her fault—'

Ofelia flinched away as he loomed over her; perhaps he didn't mean to hit her, but she knew that tone, that attitude. Then long, hard fingers closed around his arms, and two of the People held him . . . not so much still, as unable to break free. The other humans froze, staring, then their eyes slid to Ofelia's face.

'Bluecloak is the singer for most of the nest-guardians of the hunting tribes,' Ofelia said, ignoring Likisi's struggles and the others' expressions. She hoped she was using the right human words for the concepts Bluecloak had conveyed so carefully. 'Singers are not "entertainers"—' That with a pointed look at Ori. 'Singers make contact between the nest-guardians who want to make agreements about nesting places or hunting range; they are what we would call diplomats. Nestguardians are the only ones who can make agreements binding on the People.'

'The . . . rulers?' Ori asked. Give him credit; he was more curious to know the truth than annoyed that he had been wrong.

'No. Not rulers . . . exactly. They are in charge of the young – from the nest to the stage where they begin roaming with the People – and so they are the ones who decide what is important, what must be taught, what agreements must be kept.'

'I don't see how that works,' Kira said, frowning. 'If they stay behind, at the nests with the babies, how can they know what the others decide?'

Ofelia had no idea how they knew, or if they knew. She went on as if Kira had not interrupted. 'Bluecloak came when the first ones here reported that I was the same kind of animal as those they'd killed, but also different. Because I am old, and have had children, and because I stayed behind when my people left, they think of me as a nest-guardian for humans. For *my* humans.'

'I suppose that's reasonable,' Ori said. 'In their terms, anyway . . . they had to fit you into some category.'

'And now I'm a nest-guardian for them as well,' Ofelia said.

'What? How?'

'When these babies were born, I was there; they accept me as click-kaw-keerrr—' At this, the babies all looked at Ofelia and squeaked; the ones on the floor ran to her and leaned against her legs. She squatted slowly, her knees creaking, and they grasped her hands. She felt the now-familiar touch of their tongues on her wrist.

'Imprinting . . . chemotaxis . . .' Kira said softly. 'They've imprinted on her.'

'Which is why I can't leave,' Ofelia said. 'I'm their click-kaw-keerrr, the only one they have. Ordinarily, they'd have had several, but it's too late for them to get another—'

'But these others could have—' began Kira. Ofelia shook her head.

'No. Only the mothers past nesting can become nest-guardians; no one else. I was the only one available, and they asked me . . . I agreed. Who wouldn't want to care for these—?' She smiled down at the big-eyed babies who looked back at her with the trust and eagerness she remembered so well from her own children. She would do better by these, she promised herself. And them.

She looked over at Likisi, red-faced and sweating; though he no longer struggled, every line of his body expressed resentment and anger.

'I'm sorry, Ser Likisi, for your embarrassment, but you see I had to tell you this, convince you. I cannot leave, even if I wanted to leave, and I don't. These babies need me; I'm the only one who can do for them what the click-kaw-keerrr must do.'

'They're *aliens*,' he said hoarsely. 'You can't do whatever it is – you're only an ignorant, interfering old woman.'

The ones holding him expanded their throat sacs and throbbed. Likisi paled; Ofelia could see the sweat break out on his face.

'They respect and trust nest-guardians, Ser Likisi,' Ofelia said. 'They do not like those who don't.'

'But—'

'Be *quiet*, man,' Ori said. 'You're messing this up.' He sat down where he was, by the tangle of wires and little bulbs, then looked at Ofelia. 'Please go on.' Likisi said nothing; Ofelia felt the shift of power within the team, and hoped it was final.

Her knees hurt too much to keep squatting like this; she sat down, and the babies crawled into her lap. 'What they said – what Bluecloak told me – is that they accept me as the nest-guardian for them as well as for humans. That means I'm the one who can make the agreements. But I have to stay here.'

'I suppose that makes sense,' Ori said. He didn't even glance at Likisi. 'We can explain it to you, and you can explain it to them . . .'

He still did not understand. Ofelia hoped he would stay this calm when he did understand it. 'I'm sorry, Ser, but it goes the other way. They explain it to me, and I explain it to you.'

'Yes, of course . . . but I meant the terms of the agreement.'

'So did they,' said Ofelia. He stared at her a long moment, his face expressionless as he worked it out.

'The . . . terms of . . . *their* agreement.'

'Yes, Ser.' She tried to sound unthreatening.

'I . . . see.' Ori looked up at the other three, who were still standing, Likisi still held by two of the People. 'I think we need to go talk about this. With all respect, Sera Falfurrias, without you. You are too . . . involved . . . to have a completely open mind.'

'Nnno.' That was Bluecloak, who had let Ofelia carry the basket this far.

'Don't be silly,' Kira said, heading for the door. No one stopped her. She grabbed the handle and pulled, but it didn't open.

'It's locked,' Ofelia said, unnecessarily. She felt a wicked glee at the look on Kira's face. Had the women she thought bad felt this way? She had seen such looks as she felt inside on others' faces. 'So is the main door. You will have to discuss it here.'

Their hands reached for pockets, for belts, and only then did they remember that they had not brought their working tools, their handcomps and shirtcoms, to a quiet dinner in the small house of an ignorant old woman who could after all do them no harm.

Power, Ofelia realized, could indeed beget wickedness; her old voice scolded her soundly for the laughter that wanted to break out as she saw their expressions shift, and shift again.

'No harm will come to you,' Ofelia said. 'But you will have to listen, and you will have to make up your mind to what is necessary.'

'Do you know what they want?' Ori asked. Practical, that one, and still calm. She hoped he would stay, later.

'They want to learn,' Ofelia said. 'It is their greatest joy.' She pushed the babies in her lap gently, and Gurgle-click-cough murmured to them. They tumbled out onto the floor, and skittered over to their abandoned creation. 'Watch them,' she said.

'Rready,' said Blueclock, and one of the People picked up the contraption and set it on a display table. The babies squeaked; Ofelia could not quite distinguish the words, but by the way the elders were listening, they were making sense. The adult picked the thing up again and put it into the schoolroom's deep sink. Bluecloak offered Ofelia an arm, and helped her up so that she could see. More urgent squeaks from the floor, and Bluecloak picked up all three babies; one scampered up its arm to the shoulder. Another reached out to Ofelia, who took it and cradled it.

When the adult turned the water on, and adjusted the

faucet, everyone could see that the babies had contrived a water-driven machine that turned geared wheels faster and faster . . . 'Zzzzt!' cried a tiny voice. 'Aaaaksss zzzzt!'

'Impossible,' breathed Likisi, but this time with no anger in his voice, only awe. 'Let me go,' he said to those holding his arms. 'I want to see . . .' They let go at once, and he walked over to the sink, peering in. 'They can't – there's not a water-driven generator for light-years in any direction . . . and yet . . . this might actually work.' He put out a finger, drew it back.

'Do you want them for friends, for nest-guardians, or as enemies?' Ofelia asked. She still didn't understand the thing the babies had built, although if they said it would make electricity, she believed them. 'If you try to stifle them – you can't do it, you can only make them angry. That's your choice.'

'But it's too fast – they're so . . . *so* smart . . .' Likisi looked around at the adults, then at the babies, then at her.

Ofelia tried not to sound impatient. 'The choice is between smart and friendly, or smart and angry. They believe that good nest-guardians – good teachers, good friends – help the young ones grow and learn . . . everything.'

'I wonder what their Varinge score would be,' Likisi said, with envy in every syllable.

'Higher than ours,' Kira said. 'We'll need larger samples, but if this group's representative, then their population mean is a good twenty points above human. And they've had these textbooks, these computer manuals . . . their development's already explosive, and with this – I'd say starflight in less than a hundred years. Without our help.'

'And aggressive in defense of nesting territory,' Ori

added. 'Aiee. It's scary.' He didn't sound that scared; he sounded eager.

Ofelia stroked the baby's knobbly back. 'Not that scary, Ser . . . here . . .' She held out the baby. They had discussed this; Ori had been the gentlest of the humans on the team, when trying to observe and interact with the People, and the People thought he should be given a chance to hold a baby. Ofelia still thought it wasn't safe, but . . . but it was hard to fear and hate anyone whose baby you had cuddled. Now Ori stared at her . . . then reached out gingerly. The baby went into his hands eagerly – a chance for something new – and licked his wrist. Then it looked back at Ofelia and squeaked. Not the same flavor – she didn't need to hear all the sounds to know that's what it meant. It focussed those remarkable eyes on Ori's face, and stretched up to lick his chin. His expression softened, and Ofelia relaxed. Kira grinned, a wide natural smile of pleasure; so did Bilong.

In that moment when everyone else relaxed, Likisi grabbed. Not the baby in Ori's arms, but the one on Bluecloak's shoulders, when Bluecloak turned to watch Ori. The baby hissed, and clawed at Likisi's wrist, but he had it by the neck, and the baby was choking.

Ofelia lunged at him, but he pushed her away easily and backed to the door.

'They have *tails*,' he snarled. 'Trained animals – smart lizards – I can't believe you're falling for this. A whole rich world, for a lot of little scaly lizards and a crazy old woman who wants to rule it? I don't think so.' The baby writhed, the stripes fading, the eyes dulling. 'Don't come closer, or I'll wring its filthy neck.' For a breathless instant no one moved. Then he pointed at Ofelia with his free hand. 'You. Crawl over here and get this door open . . . don't tell me

you don't know the lock-code. Don't stand up – *crawl*.
Or this baby's dead.'

Ofelia looked at Bluecloak, at the other humans, at
Gurgle-click-cough, and finally at Likisi and the small
creature writhing in his grasp. Slowly – her joints would
not have it any other way – she lowered herself to the
floor and started crawling toward him.

'That's better,' he said. 'It's people like you who cause
all the trouble anyway . . . they should never have taught
you to read.'

Let him talk, the new voice said, coming out of its
hiding. When he is talking, he is not listening. Or thinking.
It was hard enough to crawl; she hadn't crawled in years,
what with her knees and her hip, and now her shoulders
added to the pains.

'Faster!' Likisi said, but anyone could see that an old
woman couldn't crawl very fast at the best of times, and
this old woman was clumsier than most. She glanced up
to apologize, and saw his foot drawn back to kick, kicking
. . . and Ofelia grabbed his foot and yanked. She was not
strong enough to pull him over, but in that shift of weight
he loosened his grip on the baby, which squirmed around
and sank its small but very sharp teeth into the skin
between his thumb and fingers, at the same moment its
long sharp toes got a purchase on his arm, and raked hard.
'OW!' he yelled, reflex opening his hand; the baby dropped
away with a triumphant squeak, and four blurs past
Ofelia's head became four long knives in Likisi's body.

She crouched there for an unknowable time while others
moved around her, and Likisi's pain ended in a quick slice
of his throat. Then it was softness and warmth, and friendly
voices, someone carrying her back to her own house, her
own bed, the smell of the food she had cooked . . .

She was in her own bed, wrapped in a blanket, with the babies – all three of them – curled along her side. Bluecloak stood at the left side of the bed; the humans – Kira and Ori pale but calm, Bilong sobbing – stood at the foot of the bed, and the other People crowded behind them. She did not know how long it had been, or what else had happened; the smell of Likisi's death pinched her nose.

Gurgle-click-cough brought her a glass of cold water; she sipped it and the confusion in her mind settled back into recognizable shapes. She was safe. The babies were safe. Everyone was safe but Likisi, and he had been the only one to threaten the children.

If anyone had to die, that was the right one.

Before the armed men took alarm – long before midnight, that is – Ori had agreed to accept reality; he and Kira went back to explain what had happened (Likisi had 'gone ballistic' and threatened one of the babies and Ofelia; the creatures had naturally defended them). Bilong played the role of grieving lover almost too well; Ofelia began to wonder if she really believed all she said about Likisi, if those sobs were genuine.

By the time the advisors appeared, armed and dangerous, the apparatus had all been tidied away. Likisi's body, Ofelia supposed, still sprawled in its blood on the schoolroom floor, but she didn't have to see it. The advisors could see her bruises, and the marks on the baby's throat; they could see that Ori was well-satisfied with what had happened.

'Idiot,' one of them said, in the front room of Ofelia's house, where they came to interview the team members. Not that they had any authority to do so, Kira muttered to Ofelia, while waiting her turn. Likisi had had the civilian authority, and now it passed to her, as assistant team leader, but it was as well not to upset them. 'Idiot,' the man went on. It was the loud one. 'Old Bossyboots never did have the sense—'

'May I touch one?' Kira asked, her face gentler now as she peered at the sleeping babies. 'Yes,' Ofelia said. 'They like to be stroked here—' She demonstrated; Kira copied her, and the baby opened bright eyes, swiped Kira's hand with its tongue, and went back to sleep. 'Cute is the wrong word,' Kira said. 'But—'

'There isn't a word,' Ofelia said, 'because they're not human. They need their own words.'

'Bilong—'

'Bilong,' Ofelia said, more tartly than she meant, 'is a fool. She may or may not know anything in her own field, but in person—'

Kira grinned down at her. 'I thought a woman like you would like someone like her better . . . she's more traditional . . .'

'Go read my log notes on Linda,' Ofelia said. The baby had liked Kira; she would not have chosen her, but the baby had. So she might as well learn to like Kira herself. Kira was smarter than Rosara; maybe she could be retrained into a reasonable sort of daughter. 'And do not miss your chance when Bilong quits making such a loud noise about Likisi and notices that Ori is still here.'

Kira flushed. 'What do you mean? I'm not—'

Ofelia stopped her with a look. 'I am an old woman, but I am not stupid, or a fool. You like this Ori—'

'Well, yes, but not like that—'

'He wants to stay. You will stay. You will like him enough to become a mother. You already do; it's why you hate Bilong.' Wicked, wicked glee, to see that strong-minded woman's jaw drop as if she'd been hit with a brick. Wicked pleasure bubbling in her veins to see that woman discover that she had been seen, that her mind had been as naked to an old woman's knowledge of human nature as the old woman's body had been to her external eye.

Ofelia lay back, watching Kira through the hedge of her eyelashes. 'You will call me Sera Ofelia,' she said. 'You will help me with these babies, and the next, and you will have a click-kaw-keerrr for your own.'

'But – but—' She did not look so formidable when she sputtered like that, but she did look beautiful with the color of outrage on her cheeks.

'Good night,' Ofelia said, and shut her eyes. After awhile, she felt the mattress shift as Kira stood up, heard the whispers on the far side of the room. The babies squirmed contentedly all along her body, and she went to sleep.

The formal duties of nest-guardianship lay lightly on Ofelia; she spent the early mornings in her garden, with the babies scampering around beneath the great frilled leaves of squash vines grabbing slimerods. Later in the morning, she took them over to the center, where they joined the elders in the schoolroom. Unlike the People's own nest-guardians, she had help from other elders; they understood that she alone could not keep up with three active babies. When she needed a nap, someone was always there . . . and sometimes that someone was Kira or Ori, who had both elected to stay as her human assistants.

If it was not quite as free a life as her solitary existence, it was in other ways more satisfying. What she had least liked about community life had vanished. No one told her what to do; no one told her she didn't matter. Even the old voice finally died away, frustrated by her lack of response.

She still got a wicked thrill from speaking into the special communications link that carried her voice (she was told) instantly to the government buildings back on the world she had not thought of as home for decades. Back there, where she had been born, and lived, in the obscurity of a crowded inner city tenement, back where she had been told what she could not learn, the men who made laws listened to her. They could not even tell her to be quiet, because the link was only one way at a time. First she would give her report, and days later a batch transmission would come back for her.

She let Kira and Ori listen to it first. They felt more important, and she felt sheltered a little from the tone of the first transmissions, before they realized they had no possible way to control her. They were past panic then, enjoying each other too much, enjoying the company of the bright, endlessly curious People who came to visit.

Profile, *The Journal of Political Science.*
The human ambassador to the first nonhuman intelligence encountered in Man's inexorable advance across the stars is a short, gray-haired, barefooted old woman without a single qualification for the position . . . except that the aliens like her. Born Ofelia Damareux, in the working-class neighborhood of South Rock, Porter City, on Esclanz, Sera Ofelia Falfurrias now holds the most prestigious – and some say the most perilous – diplomatic post in the history

of mankind. What kind of government would put
an amateur – no, not even an amateur, a complete
nonentity – in this post?

To answer that question, we interviewed the Director
of Colonial Affairs. 'In my opinion,' Ser Andreys
Valpraiz said, 'it was a major blunder. My prede-
cessor, appointed by the previous administration,
lacked the decisiveness to intervene in what was,
admittedly, a confusing situation in which the designated contact had apparently become mentally
unbalanced and died following an attempt to assault
one of the native species. I inherited this mess. At
least I have ensured the proper replacement for Sera
Falfurrias, a professional with the right credentials,
with a clear understanding of the needs of both
peoples. We'll have no more of this sentimental "nest
guardian" nonsense when the next ambassador is
appointed . . . and of course Sera Falfurrias is quite
elderly . . .'

Charlotte Gathers peered at the thick silvery envelope
suspiciously. 'Silver Century Tours announces a Free
Vacation Prize Package for senior ladies.' She opened it,
to find an application for the prize drawing. She was old
enough, yes, and she had children and grandchildren. Was
she willing to take a long voyage? Yes, after that last miserable holiday week at the coast, when her daughters made
it clear just how much they resented having to pay for the
two-bedroom apartment. They were so selfish – and after
all she'd done for them! Possibilities for emigration? She
checked the 'yes' box. Maybe things would be better on
the outer worlds. She had seen something on a news show
about a planet where a little old lady was the ambassador.

For a moment she imagined herself as an ambassador to an alien race, but on the whole she didn't like odd smells and funny accents. Perhaps not an ambassador, but an ambassador's friend . . . someone to lunch with, to play cards with . . . if she could just get away to someplace exotic, and show her daughters that she didn't need them.

Charlotte Gathers did not pass the screening for nest-guardian: one look at her sour face and beady eyes, and the polite young woman told her she had won the minor prize of a week at White Spring Resort. Others made it past the receptionist to the real screening committee, and some of these emigrated to become nest-guardians, their passage paid by profits on the inventions of a very inventive People.

Slowly, the village filled again. Now people lived in more than half the cottages. Gray-and-white haired nest-guardians with striped nestlings, pale nest-guardians of the People with the slower-growing children of the humans who had moved here – Kira and Ori's children, for instance, who had learned the People's language from birth. Most mornings Ofelia woke to the sound of voices in the lane, People and human both. She had begun sleeping later, these last few years; she rarely saw sunrise these days. Gurgle-click-cough's first nesting had grown out of their bold stripes, and into the hunting pattern; they were no longer her responsibility. She had been intrigued to find that their tails and the loud stripes disappeared at the same rate. As with humans, they were least appealing in an awkward intermediate stage, when their tails were stubby stumps no longer capable of twining around things, and their stripes looked faded and dingy.

One of them hunted ideas more than game; it had helped build the first flying machine designed by the

People. Ofelia heard that all the cities on the stone coast had electricity now, and even the nomadic tribes had small computers running off batteries whose fuel was now being grown for that purpose. She didn't understand most of it; she spent more time dozing, and less time teaching.

She wasn't worried. She did sometimes wonder which version of her life Barto and Rosara would hear when they wakened from cryo thirty years hence, far away. Would they be told she'd died in transit . . . . or would they know she had stayed behind and become famous? It was a good joke either way, and while she did not, as she had once planned, die alone, she did die smiling.